CRYPTIC CITIZENS

BITPATS BOOK TWO

J LEE PORTER
ED TEJA

Nomadic Giant

Published by Nomadic Giant, LLC
nomadicgiant.com

ISBN: 978-1-949063-12-7

The cover was designed by Elizabeth Mackey
elizabethmackey.com

PUBLISHERS NOTE: This book is a work of fiction.

ACKNOWLEDGEMENTS

Many wonderful people provided their help, support, and good input during the writing and proofing of this book. Among them are Laurie Rendon, Tony Delozier, Edward Buss, Dagny Sellorin, Gisteen Porter, Lynne Gallian, Don Gallian, and Robert Phelps.

CHAPTER 1

A SIMPLE ASSASSINATION

"The propagandist's purpose is to make one set of people forget that certain other sets of people are human."

— Aldous Huxley

Waterfront
Port of Cumana
Venezuela

In the fading light of dusk, the 50-foot fishing boat, *MIS HERMANAS*, motored to a spot just offshore of Barrio El Guapo, in Cumana, Venezuela. The grizzled helmsman took the boat out of gear and let it drift toward the spottily illuminated shore.

The green-eyed man watched the young man standing on the bow as he judged the location, his practiced eye calculating the distance to shore. When he was satisfied, he tossed in the anchor, almost casually. There was a splash, and he watched the rope pay out for a moment before he turned and signaled to the Old Man at the helm, waving his hand toward the stern.

The helmsman nodded, then reversed gears, spinning the propeller backward. He hit the throttle. There was a loud roar as the fishing boat backed down on the anchor, pulling on the anchor rode and setting the hooks deep in the soft mud. The anchor rode straightened and tugged, then slowly the rearward motion stopped.

The grizzled fisherman at the helm took the boat out of gear and shut off the noisy engine and suddenly, the night became quiet.

Turning to the green-eyed man standing behind him, the fisherman snorted. "As you requested, Señor." He pointed in the direction of a shadowy building. "That's the Port Authority," he said. "The customs shed is behind it. Anchoring here in plain sight, no one is going to think we have anything to hide."

The green-eyed man knew the buildings well. He'd memorized their appearance from satellite photos, and now he scanned the coastline, quickly identifying the buildings the fisherman had pointed out. "They all look deserted."

The fisherman laughed. "You sound surprised. This is Saturday night. Those who can afford it are already drinking."

"I expected there would be a watchman."

This struck the fisherman as even funnier. "Of course, there is one, but he will probably be drinking too. When the authorities do manage to pay people, they don't pay them enough for them to want to do any work. If he is foolish enough to actually be at his station on a Saturday and not drunk, he will be inside sleeping or watching television."

The man considered that. Everything the fisherman said fit well with his own estimate of the situation. "We should go ashore right away," he said.

The fisherman nodded. "Get your men. The muchacho is lowering the boat now. He will be ready."

"Are you certain that your son knows…"

"*Mi hijo*, my son, well knows that we, he and I, are spending this beautiful moonlit night catching many fish off the coast of Trinidad. We are with friends, working silently to ensure that we do not attract the attention of their Coast Guard. Night fishing is tiring." He smiled.

The green-eyed man nodded approval, then went down through the hatch to where five more burly men, dressed in jeans and dark shirts waited for him belowdecks. "Ready?"

One of the men nodded. "Locked and loaded, Comandante."

"And our guide?"

"Nervous as shit. Just what you'd expect from a civilian."

"He'll be okay?"

The man indicated the back of the cabin where one of the soldiers held the arm of a sixth man, a thin, small man. "Enrique has him under control."

"Then it's time to move out."

Without a sound, the men came up on deck and went to where the teenaged fisherman stood in a small boat tied alongside. At his nod, the men went down a rope ladder into the boat.

The young man cast off the bowline then started the outboard. It roared to life, and he settled down, motoring straight for a narrow beach in front of the government buildings. Their chosen path kept them outside of the glare of the lights that illuminated the long dock where cargo was unloaded, or at least it had been, back when there was cargo coming into the country, back before sanctions.

Although their destination was further south, there was no good place to secure the boat there. The young man would drop them off here, then return to the boat and wait for a signal to pick them up. If they weren't back by dawn, the boat would leave without them.

The keel bumped on the sand; the two men in the bow jumped out into the shallow water. Each grabbed the gunnel closest to them and they dragged the boat partway up onto the beach.

The rest of the men, except the fisherman and the man they'd hired as their guide, climbed out and took up defensive positions. Enrique, a large man, muscled the guide out to stand unsteadily on the sand.

The green-eyed man turned to the young fisherman who was still in the boat. "Be silent while you wait for our signal," he said. As the young man nodded, two of the men grabbed the bow and pushed the boat back out into the water. The young man put the engine in reverse to take the boat into deeper water, then turned the bow seaward and headed back to the now invisible fishing boat.

As the small boat disappeared, the team stood in the darkness, silent and not moving. They waited to see if anyone had noticed their arrival. Only when the green-eyed man gave a hand signal did they move, as a single unit, heading toward the parking lot.

The lot was lit and exposed, making this the spot where they would be the most vulnerable. But it didn't really matter. The one good thing about social chaos of the kind that Venezuela was experiencing was that no one much cared what anyone else did. They focused on their own survival.

Recent and increasingly frequent desertions of soldiers from the Guardia National had demoralized the forces and left them understaffed. It was understandable. Men were deserting to find jobs that would actually pay or to scrounge food for their families. That made it hard for the loyalists to even arouse anger toward them.

The country's military, once an elite group that received special rations and treatment, had become as desperate as everyone else.

"This way," the guide said, sounding eager. An unwilling member of the crew, only in it for the money, he wanted to get his mission over with. "*Restaurante El Teide* is not far. Maybe ten minutes. On Avenida Carúpano."

The green-eyed man knew all that. The man was babbling, venting his anxiety. It wasn't a problem, and if he stayed calm for a time, that would be helpful.

They moved silently, yet briskly toward the goal, the target. This professional team didn't need pep talks; they didn't chat. Although each person had been trained by special operations of various forces and countries, they had formed into a cohesive unit. Individually, they were rogues. Under his training, they were deadly, competent mercenaries.

The green-eyed man had recruited each one himself. He selected them and then paid them well. In his experience, loyalty proved to be a commodity that could be bought. Three of his men were wanted criminals in one place or another. Two were officially considered terrorists. To him, they were simply his men. He'd worked with this team for a long time now and took comfort in having them with him.

The man at point stopped and raised his hand. They'd arrived at their destination — a nondescript bar and restaurant along a main road in Cumana. Two men stood stiffly in front of a closed door, looking alert but nervous.

Amateurs, the green-eyed man decided. No doubt they were killers, but rather than lurking in shadows, they stood where the street light put them on display. That meant you couldn't predict what they'd do, or how much fight they might put up.

The restaurant's windows were blacked out and a sign on the door said that the restaurant was closed for a private party.

As the group paused, one of the advance men scurried into the shadows. A moment later, he returned. "Other than the guards in front, the place looks deserted," he said. "The entire street seems deserted."

"They will all be inside," the guide said. "It's a political meeting."

"We only care about one of them — Carlos Herrera. You'd better be right, that he is in there."

"He will be. These are his people. They need his ideas and leadership. Every meeting they hold increases their risk of being captured, so they won't waste holding one without him."

"Good." The green-eyed man pointed to two of his men and gestured for them to move out. He saw them slip silently into the shadows only to appear moments later. Nonchalantly, they strolled across the street, each at opposite sides of the restaurant. They both moved erratically, appearing to be wobbly on their feet.

The guards standing by the front door caught sight of one of them. "Hola," the guard called out. The man continued across in an exaggerated stagger.

"*Es un borracho,*" one guard muttered sarcastically — a drunk.

The man turned toward them, as if he hadn't noticed them. Then he walked unsteadily, staggering directly at them. "*Yo quiero cerveza*," he said, telling them he wanted a beer.

"*Ya bebiste suficiente*," the guard said — you've had enough to drink.

"*El restaurante está cerrado por una fiesta privada*," the other guard said: the restaurant is closed for a private party.

"*Una fiesta?*" the pretend drunk repeated excitedly as he continued his unsteady walk towards the front door. Seeing his trajectory, one guard stepped out into the street to confront him. As he placed himself in the man's path, telling him to move on, the other advance man sipped unnoticed behind the second guard standing near the front door, his attention focused on the staged show.

As the fake drunk shouted something else, the other mercenary, the one they hadn't spotted, came from behind the guard and grabbed him in a chokehold, his arms forming a triangle around the man's neck. The hold simultaneously prevented him from calling out and cut off the flow of blood to his brain.

The other mercenary continued his pretense of being drunk and argued with the guard for the ten seconds it took for the guard being choked to go out like a light. As he slumped into unconsciousness, his attacker eased him to the ground. He stood and moved behind the remaining guard and repeated the maneuver.

Grabbing the unconscious men, the advance team dragged them to the side of the building and tied them hand and foot with plastic restraints. The moment they cleared the area in front of the door, the green-eyed man and the rest of the team crossed the street and walked to the door. The green-eyed man put his ear to the heavy door. He heard the murmur of voices.

At his signal, the men pulled out pistols. Most carried 9mm Glock 18's, a suppressed automatic version of the Austrian workhorse; a few had H&Ks equipped with silencers. The green-eyed man reached in his pocket and took out a special gun loaded with a tranquilizer dart. Although nonlethal, he found this one had a sinister quality about it. Its long, tube-like barrel made it look ominous, deadly.

His phone beeped, telling him that his two-man advance team was in position, covering the back door. Waiting a few heartbeats, he finally raised a hand. It was time to go in.

He reached for the door, opened it and stepped into the room.

Their abrupt entrance startled a group of men and women sitting around a table. They sat up straight, stopped talking, and turned to face the door.

The green-eyed man spotted Carlos Herrera at the head of the table where he'd been holding court. Herrera was the charismatic leader of the opposition party; if he'd done nothing else in his life, that alone was enough to make him a hunted man.

Herrera looked at the mercenaries and slowly stood up, to stare at them. The green-eyed man saw no fear in the man's face. Even when he pointed his weapon at him and fired, the eyes showed only acceptance… resignation, or maybe even defiance. That was impressive and something to keep in mind.

As Herrera clutched his chest and slumped down onto the floor, a woman screamed. The sharp cracks of a few gunshots mixed with the rapid onslaught of dull thuds coming from the guns with suppressors.

In the chaos, the mercenaries calmly stood their ground, calmly firing at those scrambling to escape, cutting them down. The back door burst open and the two men of the advance team came in firing. Their shots shredded the men heading for the door, making a dash for freedom.

In seconds the firefight was over, and the green-eyed man contentedly sniffed the acrid smoke that hung in the air.

"You killed them all," the guide said. His voice trembled with shock.

The green-eyed man grabbed him by the collar. It occurred to him to wonder what the man had expected would happen when an armed force assaulted a clandestine political meeting. Naivete always amused him.

"That's right. And I want you to make sure that everyone knows that's what happened."

"You want me to tell people about this? About what you've done?"

He handed the man an envelope with money in it... US dollars. "Exactly. I want you to tell everyone what you saw."

The envelope didn't hold a lot of money, but it would seem a fortune to someone living on the local economy, where inflation was over 10,000 percent in a good month. The man took it, shoving the money in his pocket without counting it. Then he glanced around and ran for his life.

With the guide disappearing into the distance, the green-eyed man watched Enrique hoist the limp form of Carlos Herrera over his shoulder and stride out of the building. "Burn the building," he told his advance team. "I want a hot fire that ensures the bodies are unrecognizable."

"And the two guards outside?" one asked.

"Leave them. We've created collateral damage to be convincing; anything the guards have to say won't change the story we want to be told. If you make a good fire, they'll be sure Herrera is among the dead."

"It will be a great fire," the man said, smiling with delight at the prospect.

As the green-eyed man and the other two mercenaries retreated into the darkness following Enrique, the two remaining men took accelerant from backpacks and began spraying the building thoroughly.

They knew their craft. They liked their work.

The green-eyed man moved quickly, yet Enrique managed to stay ahead of him, even carrying Herrera's inert body.

When he reached the shore, the green-eyed man flashed a tightly focused, high-intensity light at the fishing boat. A lazy flicker of the masthead light on the fishing boat acknowledged the signal. Seconds later they heard the roar of the outboard.

"It's done," a man said, coming out of the darkness. It was one of his arson crew. He turned, looking back, and saw the glow of a fire behind them. The keening wail of sirens started up in the distance.

Minutes later, the young man arrived, running the bow ashore. Silently, the men clambered aboard.

At the boat, the green-eyed man waited until Enrique climbed up the ladder with the unconscious form of their target tucked under his arm. At the top, he handed Herrera up to another man, then got on board. With his men safely onboard, the green-eyed man climbed up and followed the others into the wheelhouse.

The fisherman looked at him. "Ready?"

"Yes. You can get underway now, but don't seem hurried."

The man turned the ignition and the Detroit diesel engine roared to life. "We can trail the dinghy."

"Good."

"We head back to Trinidad?"

Everything had gone precisely according to his plan; that gave him several options for his next move. Going back to Trinidad was the simplest, and therefore the best. His arrangements were solid there, so he nodded. "When we reach the Boca, you will be boarded by a Trinidadian Coast Guard vessel and reproached for fishing in their waters."

"Normal shit," the man said. "They haven't any important things to do. And what do you wish me to do?"

"Do what you always do when that happens."

The fisherman shrugged. "Then, I should bribe the officer?"

"Of course." He held out a few US dollars. "Be generous, but not too generous. Too big a bribe might make him curious."

"Keep it normal," he said. "I understand."

"By the time they've finished inspecting your boat, we will be gone."

The old fisherman gave him a relieved glance. For the first time that evening, the man was certain that they wouldn't kill him and his son once they weren't needed. He'd been right to be afraid.

"You've proven yourself to be a good resource," he told the fisherman. "You and your son have done good work. We might call on you again for your services."

The man smiled, satisfied.

They had no concerns about the man talking. He knew nothing important; besides, he was a smuggler and a poacher who would have no love for the authorities. Best of all, he had no idea who the man was that they had brought on board that night — if he even knew who Herrera was.

The guide would do as he was told. The story of the evening's assault and the staged death of Herrera would spread like wildfire. Not only did the man fear this dark team of mercenaries but having been a witness to the assassination would make him a celebrity. That was his role in this scheme, to be the man who saw it all.

They hadn't needed a guide to find Herrera at all; in other respects, the mission would've gone better without him. But they had needed a witness, a local who had no interest in the outcome to shout that he had seen Herrera gunned down in cold blood.

He'd tell the world about the vicious killers who slaughtered the leaders of the opposition to the Venezuelan government. The word would be out even if the government tried to suppress it; it was more likely they'd like to promote it themselves, maybe claim that it was American, or at least capitalist forces trying to interfere with their country's internal affairs. They'd have some spin that worked for them.

As he watched the young fisherman out on the bow getting up the anchor, took in his smooth and confident movements, the green-eyed man felt certain he'd grown up working on this boat. He was at home here, in his element, just as his soldiers were in combat.

The young man was diligent. Though he'd done these tasks hundreds, maybe thousands of times, he still stayed to watch as the outgoing tide carried the boat backward, moving to the west. His careful eye noted the way the bow came around, pointing north. At the helm, the Old Man put the boat in gear, and they lurched forward.

It was a calm night with a full moon. A few minutes later, Punta Arena, the southernmost tip of the Araya Peninsula came into view.

A picture of the chart he imprinted in his mind told him they would round that point, turning east. They would pass south of the dark shape of Isla Cubagua and run under Isla Coche as they headed toward Trinidad and Tobago.

It would be a quiet run. From here on, other than the occasional foolish yacht or smuggler, they would be alone on the water. Other than monitoring their prisoner, who should stay asleep for a few hours, he had nothing to do until they reached Trinidad. By then he'd know if he'd pulled it off, he'd know if the world thought Carlos Herrera was dead.

No one would contradict him when he reported to the Old Man that he'd taken care of Herrera — eliminated him. And the news media would confirm it.

But killing the man wasn't his plan. Keeping him alive gave him an ace in the hole. He wasn't sure exactly how things would play out, but he was sure Herrera would prove useful. The green-eyed man made it a rule to take any aces dealt him without question. Once he knew more, once he saw what the other players were holding, he and Carlos Herrera would have a long talk about the possibilities. Only then would he decide what happened to him. A lot depended on the man himself, on the strength of his convictions versus the pragmatism that life in the modern world demanded. It was entirely possible he might decide that being kidnapped was the best thing that ever happened to him.

With that thought, he went to his backpack and pulled out a flask that held his last stock of Glenfarclas 1955 whiskey. He took a teasing, delicious sip. If he nursed it, these last precious drops of the fifty-year-old single malt would last him until they arrived in Trinidad. After that… well, as far as he knew, there was no more of his favorite whiskey left on the face of the planet. And he had searched.

Sometimes life was a bitch.

CHAPTER 2

TAKING SIDES

*"Time to take the shackles off. Time to end fiat slavery.
Time to end Central Banks and nation states. Time to
touch the sky."*

— *Max Keiser*

Le Tambour
41 Rue Montmartre
2e arrondissement
Paris, France

Park Dong Woo arrived at the meeting in a foul mood. The trip
hadn't started that way. He'd been optimistic, and eager to
understand some things that were going on around him. That
things had turned sour was typical.

Not that his life was terrible. Parts of it were excellent, as a
matter of fact, but all too often it seemed to simmer along, feeling
dull and annoying. As a rule, his complaint was that things never
worked out exactly right — not the way he wanted them to.

Now, for example, despite flight delays, he'd arrived in Paris in
good spirits only to find the weather oppressively gray and rainy. If
that wasn't enough, when the limo driver opened the door and he
stepped out, he put a foot squarely in a puddle. His brand-new
Wolf & Shepherd blind brogues got soaked through.

He might've dealt with such a small thing with more equanimity, but he still stung from the harangue Sherry had given him before he left home. Recently his wife had upped the intensity of her all-too-regular sermons about his many failings. This last one, which had addressed both his extensive travel and his chain-smoking, had been particularly irritating — and unfair.

Sherry knew damn well that his prestigious job with World Bank required him to travel frequently; she'd known forever that being Park Dong Woo meant he would be smoking. He'd been a heavy smoker when they met in college; he'd been a smoker for thirty-five of his fifty years and for nearly thirty of those, his wife had given him shit about the habit.

His stomach knotted up just remembering the sneer of disgust on her face.

Sometimes he regretted not listening to his mother. She'd told him that marrying an American-born woman was a bad idea. But he'd been in love.

As it turned out, his mother was right. Despite being enamored of a dashing young Korean with a bright future, Sherry remained a New England WASP through and through. She was from a 'good' family and ingrained with strong opinions and a determination that could be unsettling.

He was sure he loved her and all that, but sometimes he longed for his parent's era. There was something intelligent and attractive about a world where they would've simply arranged a marriage for him and whoever they picked as his wife would expect, and be expected, to cater to him and not bitch at him over lighting a stupid cigarette. A wife like that would make him feel good on his terms, not point out some new study that confirmed, for the umpteenth time, that he was killing himself and probably poisoning her as well.

If he'd been born in Korea it would be different, but his parents had moved from Seoul before he was born. His father took a job with South Korea's Shinhan Bank in New York.

Since he grew up in America, Sherry wouldn't buy into the idea that his Korean ancestry won him any latitude.

"Koreans smoke," he said defensively.

She laughed. "You are barely a Korean ... more of an American of Korean ancestry," she insisted. "You are more redneck than Asian."

It wasn't just Sherry's intolerant tirades that bothered him, either. The entire world was changing — it was becoming a different place, an uncomfortable place, too damn fast. Just look at how hard it was getting to find a place you could legally light up a cigarette. The whole thing fed on itself. Unmitigated change was unsettling.

On the other hand, implementing change for the good of the people was his life's work. The irony wasn't lost on him. Part of this new, uncomfortable universe was his own doing.

And Park loved his work. He enjoyed seeing the technological solutions he promoted and enabled raising standards of living and the quality of life.

As the head of the Internal Development Association at the World Bank, he acted as the liaison with governments. Currently, he was dealing with the Government of India, guiding and contributing to their Smart Cities Mission. The role suited him perfectly. He got to influence the very shape of the next generation of cities.

The official mission statement said that the program would result in an urban renewal and retrofitting program for 100 cities across the country with the goal of making them citizen-friendly and sustainable. Who could argue with something like that?

Large cities, like Mumbai, the first on the list, were bursting at the seams and barely able to provide for the people. The project would apply the latest technology to provide energy-efficient housing, high-frequency mass transportation, 24/7 water and power, and seamless internet connectivity. That meant that millions would be able to live, work, and play with maximum productivity and a minimum impact on the environment. The smart city would integrate and simplify… well, everything.

Park's job was to help define, shape, and guide the project to completion. Once Mumbai demonstrated the potential of a smart city, then they could export the same technology and ideas — apply them to other overcrowded places. Done right, their work in Mumbai would provide a template for the entire world to use.

With his double major in finance and IT, Park was perfectly suited to create the vision and define a practical structure that could make it happen.

Park enjoyed visiting India. Of course, Sherry refused to go with him. Generally, travel upset her. She preferred her routines and living in their house in Connecticut. It suited her to live alone while he commuted from Mumbai to the Liaison office in Singapore and his main office in New York.

Being honest, Park had to admit that Sherry's refusal to travel was reasonable. She had a high-profile job in nonfiction publishing with a major New York firm. Like Park, she loved her job and did it well. When the small publisher was bought up, as they all were sooner or later, by a larger company, which in turn got swept up by a conglomerate, she moved up and made a lovely salary that augmented his income. They were well off.

But that subterranean belief that she should be willing to drop everything for the sake of his, her husband's career, was bothersome and nagged at him. He hated that it was old-fashioned. All that old-world, nostalgic-for-the-past crap made him sound like an anachronism. Yet, he was hardly that. Park worked on the cutting edge; as far as he was concerned, he was a fucking pioneer, not some dinosaur.

The only explanation was his Korean DNA. Some of his attitudes about his life had to be firmly rooted there. You couldn't fight your DNA.

And now he was in Paris, smiling at the stunning face of Dione Bellamy shining across the table from him.

"It's a good idea," she said. Dione was the Managing Director of the International Monetary Fund (IMF). She was 53, three years older than Park, and still an attractive woman. A thin blonde with short silver-blonde hair, she had a delicate but sharp, almost hawk like face, and a smile that he found hard to read. He didn't mind a little Western inscrutability. It offered some irony and gave her face an edge that Park found alluring.

Now she looked up from thumbing through his proposal. She closed it and looked at him. "You've laid it out well. It's easy to see that there's something in the project for all the key players to like."

Park shook his head to clear it. Whenever they were together, he drifted into fantasies. Well, one fantasy — of having a torrid affair with her. It didn't seem impossible. After all, she was French and sophisticated; her marriage to a member of the French cabinet wouldn't be a major obstacle. At least, he didn't think it would be.

What prevented him from acting on his fantasy, making a play for her, was that she intimidated him. Even when she looked at him in a way that he thought might be seductive, her confidence made him unsure of himself and made him hesitate. Hell, he'd never even seriously flirted with her.

That made being with her bittersweet. He liked and admired her, but she was a constant reminder of his cowardice. So many of Park's dreams remained unfulfilled fantasies. After all, Park Dong Woo was not, in general, a brave man. Avoiding risk was inherent in his nature. Nothing was worse than rejection.

Part of the slim French woman's attraction was that she was also a heavy smoker. That made her a colleague, a fellow traveler, another member of the dying breed, he often joked. Her cigarette of choice, Gauloises Brunes, were smelly things, in his opinion, but that was forgivable. Sharing the habit meant they would choose a place to meet where they could indulge their shared vice. In this case, she'd made reservations at Le Tambour Café. They sat at an outside table and ordered coffees while they smoked. Somehow

Dione had managed to get an exception to the ban on smoking in public places.

Pleased to be with her again, he lit a cigarette and turned his attention to her observations. "Thank you. I worked hard to make it desirable for everyone. For it to have half a chance to succeed, everyone has to buy in."

She laughed. "Your smart city will be exactly what the Oculistica needs next. It will provide reams of big data and more."

Hearing her say the name of the group out loud surprised him, startled him for a moment. She was talking about the umbrella, global organization — one that didn't officially exist, called the Retinger Oculistica. They were both members.

The group's namesake, Józef Hieronim Retinger, was a Polish political adviser and avid globalist. He was a founder of the European Movement that led to the establishment of the European Union; he also played a role in founding the Bilderberg Group.

The Oculistica was a small, secret subset of the Bilderberg group that was dedicated to the creation of a one-world government. It worked in the background, operating through the organizations its members belonged to, such as the World Bank, IMF, various international charities, global corporations, and others who found the limitations of national sovereignty to be problematic.

Park blew out a cloud of smoke. "Dione, I'd like you to play Devil's advocate for a moment. What are the problems with it?"

She scowled and opened the folder again. "It leaves room for contractors, which is good. Governments won't like it if there is no room for kickbacks or an ability to grant prime contracts."

"That's a benefit," he said. "I want to hear the problems."

"There is the issue of using the blockchain."

"It is the best, the only viable technical solution," he said. "It pulls everything together in a giant, interlocking web of smart contracts. And it provides a perfect payment system."

She sighed. "And that raises the implication that Mumbai would be creating its own cryptocurrency." She shook her head. "You know damn well that India has a neurotic attitude toward cryptocurrency. It has them running hot and cold, embracing it one day and acting like it is immoral the next."

"Like most governments."

"With additional hysteria."

"We need to make it appear that they can regulate it."

She blew out a cloud of smoke and stubbed out her cigarette in an ashtray. "The Indian banks and taxation systems are entrenched in the current system."

Park rubbed his face. "Okay, I'll rewrite it, couch the language so it's clear that the internal tokes are pegged to the rupee. I'll add something about all external transactions being made after amounts are converted to rupees. The government can tax that easily enough."

"It's money laundering they worry about, that and the underground economy — what our Indian colleagues call the black economy."

"This new system we've designed won't allow an underground anything," Park said, puffing up his chest, "except for the occasional wine cellar, and that will need permits."

Dione didn't smile, and at first, he thought his joke had fallen flat. Then he saw she was reading, not paying attention.

"The Old Man will be the only holdout," she said. "Using technology for payments exclusively will take the focus away from his dream — The Phoenix."

Park sighed. "I know that. I just don't get it, so I don't know how to approach that."

"He is fixated on a one-world currency that the global banks control, instead of a government. Just like the Indian government, he will see this as a stepping stone to getting the world used to cryptocurrency. He wants a global fiat currency — not something on a blockchain that can't be controlled."

Park shuddered. "I see that, but..." he said as she lit another cigarette, leaning her head back in a way that let him see the lovely line of her neck. He stared, watching as she blew out a cloud of blue smoke. His mouth tasted stale.

He took a cigarette out of his own pack, tapped in on the table and lit it, filling time to gather his thoughts. The next part was tricky.

"It's true that I'll never convince him. A global fiat currency has been his dream for a long time and he's not a 'times change' sort of guy."

She nodded. "And he has the banks by the balls."

"But, just as the world changes, there are changes happening within the group. New understandings, new ideas."

Her look turned curious. "Really? Do you intend to challenge him?"

Park swallowed. "No, of course not. But there are others… there are people with new ideas." He smiled grimly. "I'm sure you've heard the rumbles."

She smiled, then rolled her eyes. "You mean him, don't you?"

Park nodded. "If anyone can implement change in the group…"

"What would make you think he suddenly cares about the monetary system or automated cities?"

"I doubt he does. But I'm sure he understands that when we implement this software, the group, and by extension, him, gains incredible power. The granular information this gives us, him, and the control that goes with it will be total. It integrates detailed tracking of every aspect of life — finance, social media, schedules, travel, correspondence in any medium… all of it."

"And if it is the group controlling things, not some global government, if the Old Man is taken down, he'd be in control."

Park nodded. "It's just speculation, of course."

"Of course."

"The ramifications are enormous. Once all the major cities are automated, that's the end of any insurrection, rebellion, or even contrary idea. We won't need Newspeak or any of that Orwellian stuff, or perhaps it's more accurate to say we will control all speech and the meaning of everything. Contrary opinions and independent thought will become as obsolete as fiat currency."

"And that undermines the power of nation-states." She grinned broadly. "I would guess that would suit him to a tee."

"I suppose it would." Then he looked into her eyes. "You like it too."

She turned in her chair. "I like that it gives the IMF direct hooks into every major financial institution. Unlike governments, the Oculistica won't have to make recommendations or ask for documentation. We just take what we want and set policy ourselves."

"That's down the road," Park said. "For now...."

"You are telling me this because you want to know what side I'm on. And it will come down to taking sides."

He sighed. It was terrible when people were so open about things like that. Park didn't like having all the cards on the table.

"I'm going to be a pawn in this battle."

"As I am. As are the others."

"The Old Man has the old guard behind him."

"And Nikolaj Romijn has his skills and his people." When she spoke of him, her smile looked like admiration, but he couldn't be sure.

Suddenly, he wondered if she was having an affair with him. The idea was upsetting. Not only did it destroy his fantasy, but it meant his words, his concerns could wind up in the man's ears as pillow talk.

"So, you think there might be a war?"

Park winced at her indelicacy. "I expect a struggle of some sort. The Phoenix would be a step back in time. The... the other side wants a new kind of control for a new world. They aren't compatible. If the Old Man wins, then I'm moving World Bank in the wrong direction, and the IMF will have to change course too. That would undermine the good work we've already done."

"Since neither of us is trying to establish a new agenda, it comes down to a simple, yet difficult problem," she said. "Who offers the most for their support, and who do you fear most?" Then she sat back. "The Old Man can make a person incredibly wealthy or ruin them in a heartbeat. And then Nikolaj has his own means of gaining cooperation."

Park swallowed hard. It was difficult to admit that a man of his sophistication found Nik, the green-eyed man, inscrutable and, as they said in the old country, totally fucking scary. "I'm not sure Nikolaj intends to offer much to anyone."

She laughed. It wasn't a pleasant laugh. "That he lets you live could be considered a win, I suppose."

"So, what do we do?"

"We go about our work and let those two alpha males butt heads. We are politicians who will adjust our arguments and align ourselves with the winner as we always do, Park."

"I'm out on a limb, though. I'm presenting my plan to the group soon. The Old Man will challenge it."

"And you want my support." She licked her lips. "I'll be happy to say it's valid and will work. But if you directly confront the Old Man and tell him The Phoenix won't rise from the ashes, you are on your own."

"I have no intention of doing that. But he will probably make the point himself."

"Perhaps. It will be an interesting meeting." A twinkle in her eyes caught his attention. It made her face come alive.

"What are you thinking?"

"Just of him," she said. "I'll be interested to see how he plays things." She licked her lips, obviously not aware of it.

"Plays things?"

"He isn't a politician and his impatience with the way things are going is clear. Sooner or later I figure he will try to kill the Old Man."

"Kill him?"

"That's what he does, right? He's our enforcer. And just now it occurred to me that I wouldn't mind that at all. That old bastard gets to me." She cocked her head. "Would that bother you?"

Something in her voice told him she was thinking of the green-eyed man in a more personal way than she suggested. Park knew he lived in a strange world in which many things were possible and perhaps it was even stranger than he'd ever imagined.

"It would depend on who replaces the Old Man," Park said reasonably. "I doubt Nikolaj would want to run the group. The politics of it…"

Again, Dione's tiny tongue flicked over her lips. "I suppose that's true, but he is changing too. And if he slaughtered that old bastard…"

Something else flickered in her eyes and suddenly he understood. The idea of watching the green-eyed man kill the old banker turned her on.

He shook his head. It seemed he didn't stand a chance with this one, so he stood and put out the last of his cigarette. "Well, I have a plane to catch. I'll see you in Seychelles in a week, I guess."

Still lost in thought, she looked at him. "Right." Then she smiled in a way that suggested her mind was far away. He was sure he knew exactly where it was.

Park left the meeting feeling an agonizing mixture of relief and shame. That he seemed to have an ally in Dione was a huge relief; she was aware of the internal struggle and she supported his proposal. And he was ashamed that once again he was leaving her without so much as making a pass at her. He should've at least tried to let her know his feelings. But those feelings, he knew, were largely lust, and that embarrassed him. Still, even if she had a thing for Nikolaj…

People said he was a successful man. By some measures that was true, but his life was filled with far too many might-have-beens. He was a prominent man who influenced major world projects, but he balked at simply asking a woman to go to bed with him.

Was it the same for everyone? Was it like that for the green-eyed man? Or was a person like that able to use his forceful personality, his brute force, to get what he desired? Did a man like that get everything he wanted?

Park couldn't know, but thinking about it gave him a sad, sinking feeling that lingered all the way back to New York.

CHAPTER 3

AN UNBEARABLE FUTURE

"Unless we change direction,
we are likely to end up where we are headed."

— Chinese proverb

A Law Office
Wichita, Kansas

The lawyer was far too skinny and, although his suit looked expensive, it didn't fit him properly; it hung on him as if he'd been sick and lost weight, but not symmetrically. The net result was that he looked frail, not prosperous and confident. That the man's name was Duke struck Joshua as ironic.

None of that boded well for having this man represent him in the upcoming battle. The opposition, his wife and her battery of lawyers was formidable. Not that it mattered; if the case went as far as going to court, he was doomed. She would hold all the cards. Government institutions were her father's playground, and he was the puppet master.

Duke wasn't fit to be David to the Goliath facing him. Joshua's only option was to be pre-emptive and move totally out of the box.

He watched the man shuffle a thick stack of papers, pushing them into a neat stack that he moved to the corner of his desk. The gesture irritated him. Joshua didn't like paperwork. More than that, it went against the grain to document everything you did. You didn't get a damn thing out of all that paperwork, and it gave outsiders leverage into your life. People like this skinny lawyer would always be in the wings, waiting to subpoena all that damn paper to use it against you, to twist innocent transactions into malevolent plots that never existed.

It wasn't merely supposition. Joshua had dealt with a bellyful of regulatory paperwork when he'd worked on Wall Street. If he had been better at paperwork, he might still be there. If he'd been more knowledgeable about the ways of the world, he would have known how to fill it out so that he didn't get his ass into trouble. But he didn't. Instead of being smart, clever, he had tried to be accurate. That got his ass into trouble.

To Jessica's father, that only proved what he'd thought all along, that Joshua Raintree was an idiot. He had expected, wanted his daughter to marry a player, a man who deserved not only his daughter, but his help. He couldn't stop his headstrong daughter from marrying him, but he begrudged Joshua both his daughter and his help.

Losing the Wall Street job hadn't been the end of things. Jessica had supported the move to Wichita and his new job. The superficial changes hadn't done anything to salvage his dreams or his marriage. The investment firm that hired him had thought poaching him from Wall Street would impress their clients. That didn't work out well. None of them seemed to be even slightly impressed… not the clients, not the investment firm, and not Joshua Raintree. Certainly not Jessica's father. And Jessica was beyond unimpressed with both her new home and her new circumstances.

He couldn't say he hadn't been warned. From the time he was little, Joshua's Chiricahua Apache mother had tried to tell him about the futility of going off to play with the suits, the whites on their terms.

"They'll use you and shut you out," she'd said. "You don't know the rules of their games and they change them as they go, anyway. They don't want you to play."

He'd dismissed those heartfelt warnings, but then he had come to dismiss most things about his mother. She had a reputation as a troublemaker. Not only a native-American activist, she was also a hippie who knew nothing about finance and Wall Street. He'd never known his father, who was some hippie she'd lived with when she was young.

Ironically, making the next major change in his life, the change Jessica wanted and insisted on, once again filled his life with paperwork… all the crap forms required to get a divorce. Life seemed to be more about paperwork (and the irony that this was supposed to be a paperless universe was not lost on him) than anything of substance.

Jessica didn't mind the paperwork at all, but of course, she wasn't doing any… the army of lawyers and paralegals her father had hired were doing it for her while she hid out in a spa somewhere in Mexico. According to court documents, she'd gone there for her nerves which had been rattled by Joshua's impossible actions.

Apparently, her rotten nerves, the problems she was having with them, were entirely his fault, as was everything else that had happened in their disastrous marriage and probably around the globe. He wasn't quite sure how her failing nerves factored into the divorce, but the mountain of paperwork she'd paid doctors to file on her behalf suggested it was a significant factor.

According to the mountain of documentation, the poor woman was barely able to function.

He blamed himself, not for faltering, but for not seeing what she really had expected of him. She had high standards, and he hadn't managed to live up to them. The price for his audacity, and failing, was a form of death, or at least a shredding of the life he'd known.

"She's demanding a healthy amount for alimony," Duke, the lawyer said.

Joshua sat still, gathering himself, staring at the man. Words had to be chosen carefully to explain to the lawyer in terms he could understand that he, Joshua, although only the client, had made an important decision. He'd seen a door at the end of the tunnel; it stood partially open and he had determined to walk through it, come what may.

The words to say all that in the current context didn't seem to come, so he took a breath, folded his hands and said: "No."

Duke sat up; his smile had gone wherever lost smiles slipped off to. "No?"

"No," Joshua said.

"No what?"

"No alimony. None."

The lawyer made a pouty face and let out a half-hearted chuckle. "Well, of course, we can negotiate the amount," he said, "but then…"

"No, we aren't going to negotiate. Not that way."

The lawyer looked at him with what Joshua guessed he intended as compassion; it stunk of pity. "There aren't many options. You don't have many."

Joshua sighed. Naturally, he had few options. According to the lawyers and accountants, there never were many options for people like him. They were to be told what their choices were by the big kids, the ones with the big bank accounts — people like Jessica's father.

They'd created a world that taught everyone how important it was to play by the rules. But that turned out to be a sucker's game. If your opponent was Jessica's father, those rules were terrible weapons that only worked against you. They locked you into their game and then the lawyers would bludgeon you with the goddamn rules until you were senseless. And penniless.

It dawned on him that there was nothing new in that revelation. That was part of what his mother had been talking about since he was tiny. That much was clear now. One day, he needed to sit her down and tell her she was right. About that, anyway.

He stretched his arms out and put his palms flat down on the desk, drew in a breath, and spoke calmly. "Duke, we aren't doing it. That isn't fucking happening."

"What isn't happening?"

"The entire farce. This rigged game. Alimony."

The lawyer's pathetic shrug, an obvious attempt to convey that they were helpless, made Joshua angry. "Unrig it."

"Well, I suppose we can ask to go to arbitration. That probably would get her less than she is asking for from the court. The problem is getting them to agree. Because you weren't married in this state and haven't been here long…"

"They won't agree and don't have to — I know that. Why would they agree to that when her dad is paying her lawyers all that fucking money to rake me over the coals? He's enjoying this."

"Well, without arbitration, the thing is, the judge will most likely give her most of what she is asking for. That's how it works."

Joshua Raintree hated the smug look on the man's face. He hated the lawyer talk, the lawyer face. He hated that most of his life he'd let morons like this tell him what his choices were. "Pick one from column A," they told him. And he had. That's what grated.

But this time it would be different. "I don't give a shit how it normally works. There is no normal here. I don't give a shit how you think things are done, Duke. I'm not paying any alimony. Not one dime."

The man held his hands apart, indicating helplessness, no doubt. "The law is… well, fuck, Josh, you know that what you want doesn't matter."

"It does this time."

The lawyer raised one eyebrow. "I don't know what you mean."

"You know I'm currently self-employed, right?"

He pointed at the documents. "It's all here. The lawyers list you leaving a nice job with the investment firm for no good reason, the fact that you gave up a decent job without notice as one of the reasons she wants the damn divorce. She found your irrational actions stressful."

"Forget their spin for a moment and listen to me. If I still worked for one of those firms, then they'd be able to look at my wages and see how overpaid I am and give most of it to her, correct?"

"Right."

"But the thing is, I work for myself now. I have private clients."

"So?"

"That makes it harder for them to tell what, if anything, I earn."

Duke nodded. "Doesn't change shit, though. Being self-employed complicates things. That's why your tax records and client list are part of the record. The court wants to be sure that they know all your income streams."

"I don't have many clients and I haven't been doing this long enough to have any tax records to show what I make."

"They base it on averaging your income. You'll have to provide ongoing statements. They have to be kept current."

"Which sucks because my gross income just caught up to what I used to get from an expense account."

"Well, there are ways they can estimate the amount you can pay."

"So that I can pay a fucking heiress more than I make?"

"Her wealth isn't relevant."

"Why not? It's supposed to be a settlement, not a robbery."

"My hands are tied. There are precedents and…"

"Then why am I paying you?"

"What?"

"If the outcome is predetermined, what do I need you for? I can fill out surrender forms myself."

"Now, now —"

"No, no. We are going to say fuck the precedents and change directions."

"I'm not certain what you mean by that."

That seemed clear enough to Joshua. "Of course, you aren't." He looked at Duke. "For just a moment, think outside the box, man."

The glassy look told him that this man had no clue what he was talking about. "What box?"

Joshua laughed. His lawyer lived, loved, hated, worked, played, and shit inside the same box without knowing he was even in one. But there was no value in pointing that out. "I mean that I believe in the Chinese proverb that says, 'Unless we change direction, we are likely to end up where we are headed,' and right now we are headed toward the edge of a cliff. I can't function, can't have a life if my wife takes every damn thing we own and gets a chunk of my income forever as well."

"It's just the way …."

"things are. I know. So, here's how we work this thing, Duke, you and me. We are going to go to their lawyers, and by we, I mean you… and you are going to say fuck that shit."

"I am?"

"You are going to tell them that we say 'fuck no' to all the standard divorce agreements. I want you to go to my witch of a wife and her arrogant asshole of a lawyer and tell them that we are going to do business differently. We are going to come to terms on a onetime buyout."

"A buyout?"

"A payoff, go away money… whatever you need to call it to make it legal and make it stick."

"She's going to want part of your income for a long time, not a cash settlement."

Joshua sat back. The lawyer didn't seem to be motivated. He wondered if he'd have more of his attention, if would have been smarter to wear a suit to the meeting instead of a tee-shirt and blue jeans. Well, fuck the guy if that mattered. He was done wearing suits.

"Tell me... will the court say she gets X percent of what I used to make even if I'm unemployed, or will they give her a percentage of what I actually make?"

"It depends, but more like a cut of what you should earn. They establish a fixed amount based on projections of your income."

"Projections... those things they use to get the weather wrong all the time?"

"Well —"

"And what happens if I have a shitty year or six?"

"Then you will have it tough."

"What if I don't make as much as I'm supposed to give her? No one is going to loan me the difference, Duke, unless you want to, of course."

"That's why it's complicated."

"Then I'm going to insist you make my suggestion... is that okay?"

The lawyer played with his tie. "Your suggestion?"

"The one I just told you. That you tell her lawyers to go fuck themselves." He tapped on the table. "Either they agree to a buyout, or I close shop and stop working. They can sue my ass until the cows come home and get nothing but legal bills. I'd rather sit in debtor's prison and rot than be her slave."

Duke smiled smugly. "Mr. Raintree, we don't have debtor's prison in this country."

"Then she can't take me to court if I don't pay the alimony?"

"Of course, she can."

"And if I refuse to pay or don't have the money I go to jail?"

"For contempt of court, not for debt."

"Right? Excuse me if I don't see a huge fucking difference, Duke. Are you saying that knowing I'm locked up for contempt would make jail nicer? And what is contemptuous about not being able to pay?"

"If your income drops through no fault of your own, then we can renegotiate the amount..."

"Great! That's what I wanted to hear. Only let's start there. I want you to tell them that I'm holding a going out of business sale. Apparently, part of her claim is that I'm a rotten businessman. We will concede the point. I'll agree to turn over my books to a forensic accountant of the bitch's choosing and he can establish a valuation of the company. Then we find a buyer, and I'll sell out. If she finds a buyer, she can have sixty percent of the proceeds. If I have to find a buyer, she gets half."

"I don't think…"

"Don't think, Duke. She wants to fuck me over, and that should do it nicely."

"Why would she accept that?"

"Because from her perspective it ruins me, Duke. Without my company, I can't follow my dreams. I can't start a new life. I'll be forced to get a mid-level job with some company, assuming her father doesn't put out the word I'm not to be hired. She won't be able to resist the prospect." Joshua put his feet up on the desk, enjoying watching the lawyer flinch.

"I can talk to them, but I don't…"

"You need to point out to them that it's the only offer on the table." Having said it, Joshua felt good for the first time in weeks. His extreme plans had sounded painful when he'd worked them out, but right at that moment, disappearing sounded wonderful. And he intended to do just that, no matter how this came out.

He needed to get away from Jessica and the reach of her family. No matter what the settlement was, her father would cast his evil eye on anything Joshua did in the future. But if he just disappeared… a sense of lightness came over him.

"I can talk to them."

"Duke, you can tell them that the specific terms are negotiable, but not the basic idea. This will be a onetime buyout. They take that deal, or they gear up for a long future of chasing a deadbeat around to try to collect. And I promise it won't be an easy chase. I'll shut down my company either way. Since she will have the house and all real property, even if they track me down, there won't be anything to get. If they find me, I'll be living in the street somewhere. I like that idea much better than the options you've talked about, or any that they might come up with."

"That's crazy."

"You want crazy? Let's up the ante. Hell, if they refuse this offer, tell them that I'll just leave."

"Leave?"

"I'll disappear. If they don't accept my plan, then I'll close the business and I'll be off the grid before she can take this to court. I can be gone in a week."

"But the divorce proceedings will go on. She'll have to go through the process of trying to find you, probably hire a detective. And she'd need to publish a statement that you'd deserted her, but eventually the court would grant the divorce."

"That's fine. I want the divorce as much as she does. But tell me, in a case like that, if I've disappeared, how will they determine the proper alimony or serve me the papers?" Seeing the lawyer racking his brain, Joshua waved a hand in dismissal. "That was a rhetorical question, counselor. I don't really care. The point is that in that scenario I won't be around. I won't be earning money for her to steal."

The lawyer waved a hand in a calming gesture, appeasing the madman, Joshua thought. Probably just wondering if mental deficiency could be used as a defense against alimony. "I'll talk to them, maybe they'll agree to the deal."

Joshua smiled. "That would be nicer for all concerned."

"What will you do? Without your business, I mean."

Joshua smiled. "I was thinking of answering one of those ads that promise an exciting career writing lyric poetry."

"Poetry?"

"Like Carl Sandburg. I can get a job as a coal-heaver in Omaha until I win my first Pulitzer Prize or become a poet laureate."

"A coal-heaver?"

"It's a person who shovels coal, Duke. It gets you in good shape. You should try it sometime. It's probably going to become an Olympic event in a few years. I know I'd be a good one, though. No slacking off for this boy." Joshua savored the momentary pleasure of the look of total confusion on Duke's face. "By the way, you don't have to worry about your fee. I've got that sucker squirreled away safe enough. But I don't know what happens after that. It remains to be seen."

The lawyer rubbed his jaw, looking impressed. "You are serious about this scorched earth strategy?"

"Absolutely," he said, although he wasn't, not entirely. The part of the business that Jessica knew about wasn't much to give up in the scheme of things. "Divorce is supposed to be about splitting up and I do want to be split from her — severed entirely. I'm going to do whatever it takes so that I never have to think about her again."

The skinny man sighed. Joshua was sure he was thinking of all the billable courtroom hours lost, all the lovely paperwork that might have been filed. "I'll see what's possible."

"I feel bad for you," Joshua said as he stood and shook the man's hand.

"For me?"

"You wound up with the wrong client in this case. Jessica has the money, the high-powered law firm, and she sure enjoys a good fight. I'm afraid it's your bad luck that you are stuck representing an impoverished pacifist who wants nothing more than to cut and run."

The puzzled look he got from the man pleased Joshua almost as much as realizing, as he left the office, that he knew almost nothing about his skinny lawyer. He didn't know if the man was married or had a family. If he had actually ever mentioned it, and it was likely that he had, Joshua had ignored it completely.

The way things were moving, the way his new strategy was forming in his head, it was delightful to think that the self-important man in the ill-fitting suit would remain, in Joshua's world, forever unimportant. It gave things a bright and shiny new perspective.

CHAPTER 4

POWER STRUGGLE

"The question is not whether we will be extremists, but what kind of extremists we will be... The nation and the world are in dire need of creative extremists."

— Martin Luther King Jr.

A Private Villa
Praslin Island
The Republic of Seychelles

They arrived through the night and early morning, coming by boat from the main island of Mahe to Praslin island, where the Old Man had his villa. Uniformed servants met each guest and escorted them to their rooms.

At eight in the morning, the servants set out an elegant brunch buffet. Then, other than the servants bringing coffee or drinks, they were left alone to talk, to wonder, to speculate about why the meeting had been called. This group was never called together unless something important was taking place or needed to happen.

Leaving them alone was a classic tactic the Old Man had used before. Somehow, knowing that didn't diminish its effectiveness.

It wasn't until two in the afternoon, the Old Man's staff gathered them together. Leading them to the veranda, they were invited to sit at a long wooden table. The table was highly polished and made of dark wood. The veranda itself had been fabricated with matte red paving stones — smooth, flat and painstakingly dry set.

From his seat, the green-eyed man had a beautiful view of the Indian Ocean shimmering in the light. Looking out to sea, a storm threatened. It blackened the horizon, intensifying the contrasts.

The inner circle, the five people sitting at the table, were all impressed by both the villa and the view, although none of them would admit it. All of them had been here before, but the effect didn't mute with time.

The green-eyed man knew that Charles Forte, the Old Man who owned the villa, didn't give a damn if his guests were impressed. No, the luxurious surroundings, the view, the privacy had been constructed for Forte's own pleasure, visible reminders of his hard-won success and therefore, his power.

None of them were truly guests, anyway. None of them had been invited for the pleasure of his or her company, and there was nothing social about the gathering. They were there to talk about important things. This was a meeting of the Retinger Oculistica, the group headed by the Old Man. And, while he was the leader, none of these were his friends.

Nikolaj agreed with the Old Man about his colleagues. These people, the power brokers he sat among, were not the kind of people he would choose to associate with either. They were office monarchs who ruled or influenced powerful organizations. Nothing about that world appealed to the green-eyed man. That factor set Nikolaj apart.

Naturally, the others mistrusted him; some even feared him. Yet they were unfailingly polite. Not that they liked him in the least, but when the going got tough they needed him.

It satisfied him that he was there because of who he was. The others, not counting the Old Man and the dark-haired woman, were part of the group due to their work — they occupied key positions in powerful organizations that wielded global influence. Park Dong Woo represented the World Bank; Dione Bellamy ran the International Monetary Fund; Osk Barstad was with Interpol.

Each of them was committed to using their organization's assets to contribute to the group's overriding goal: a one-world government.

The Old Man was a powerful person in his own right. Wealthy and connected, he'd been a mover and shaker in finance for years, mostly behind the scenes. His track record, and a wealth of leverage over politicians around the world, gave him influence over global banks and financial institutions.

The dark-haired woman, Anna Rasburn, was also there on her own right. Although she represented global corporations that were household names, she didn't come to the meetings to parrot their views. No, these powerful conglomerates came to her, asking her to consult and advise them on policy. They understood, to varying degrees, that she was connected to the global elite and were happy to pay her a retainer to keep them in the loop, to lobby for agendas she convinced them were their own.

Nikolaj Romijn, the green-eyed man, represented himself. Even a financial and political group needed to avail itself of brute power on occasion. Nikolaj had the men and experience to provide it. Most of all, he had the ruthlessness required to apply force where it would do the most good.

Looking at Anna, he smiled. She worked her clients, extracted what she wanted from them with a ruthlessness that matched his own. Insubordinate clients might be sacrificed on her altar, and they knew it.

A smaller group of four sat back from the table. This subgroup would not participate but only observe. They would listen reverently (no recordings or notes were allowed) and then report back to their masters. These were the periphery who knew about the Oculistica and curried favor by providing their support and following orders blindly.

Now everyone sat patiently as the Old Man made his entrance. Elegantly dressed, they watched as he shuffled awkwardly out of the house and toward them. They kept a respectful silence as he took his place at the head of the long table. A butler held his chair for him. When he was sitting, he began to cough. No one spoke.

When the coughing fit passed, the Old Man looked around the table, greeting each of the men and women seated there with a cool, appraising stare. The green-eyed man returned it with a studied calmness. The Old Man didn't frighten him. Few people frightened him, and with the changes going on in the world, Nikolaj found it harder to take the kind of power the Old Man wielded seriously.

Others were still intimidated. The man's eyes denied his age. Looking into those gray eyes, you saw a flickering fire of vitality that most other men never achieved.

Yet, increasingly, the Chairman looked ancient. Although his outrageously expensive Brioni Vanquish II suit had been tailored to fit him perfectly, the thin, wrinkled neck made him appear frail. His body was no longer powerful but hollow. The green-eyed man respected the power that this Old Man had held in his hands for most of his life — power he had taken. But that was fading.

There had been a time when his fierce belief in his own opinions, his unwillingness to compromise his vision, had been his strengths; now Nikolaj saw it as intransigence and weakness. The brittle, inflexible Old Man and his agenda had become trapped in a downward spiral of decay. So close to the man, the powerful Charles Forte, Nikolaj's inner jackal now smelled death.

The Old Man smiled thinly, almost as if he was trying to be friendly. "You've all come a long way to my villa, and I'll get to the point. I asked you here for a simple reason. It is time to make Phoenix happen," he said.

The pronouncement was met with a moment of silence, then Anna Rasburn touched her cheek unconsciously. "The Phoenix. Why now? The way things are going, we are getting what we need. Why bother with a one-world fiat currency? Who wants it?"

"To do what it was intended to do from the beginning," the Old Man said. "It will provide order. As to why now... because chaos is taking over the global markets. Many existing fiat currencies are becoming worthless, or at least their value is being questioned. Traditional investments are all hideously overpriced and the so-called investors are all speculators." He smiled that thin smile. "That includes the share prices of your clients. There is little real value in the market. And the craziness of this… cryptocurrency mania threatens what stability remains."

The green-eyed man took this in and sensed desperation. "This chaos isn't taking over markets. We put it there. Undermining national governments, showing their incompetence, greed, corruption… that has been the plan. Your plan. You wanted to use it to drive people to see a single world government as their salvation," he said, his accent sounding more French than the Flemish he had grown up speaking. "The more chaos there is, the easier it becomes to take control with no one noticing that they are giving up anything."

"That is true." The Old Man raised a finger. "And this is the time. Anarchy has begun to emerge, and it's time to offer the world stability. We can hold out our global vision for government and currency as a real option."

"So, we come out of hiding and announce ourselves?" Anna asked. "We've spent many years letting them think we are the invention of conspiracy theorists."

"In the beginning, we had to confront the fear people had of big banks and big government. Now that they are inured to it, now that big government is commonplace and intruding into every aspect of their lives, we need to show them that the real problem is that their national governments are still too small to be effective. A bigger entity offers more protection. Just as Europe was drawn to the advantages of the EU, we must promote the value of something truly global."

"But unlike their governments, we are unelected," another young man from outside the circle said. He was a representative of OPEC.

The Old Man scowled but answered him. "We present the solution as one put together by the world leaders. We will retain our anonymity while the world leaders promote a global currency that we control."

The green-eyed man glanced at the other faces, reading them. As usual, Anna's stern look was disapproving, but that was the way she always looked and meant nothing.

A young man sitting outside the circle looked concerned. He represented a group of international bankers and financiers that weren't mainstream banks, but small, flexible operations located in tax havens. The group worked with them often, using them to hide money, painting them as villains at times, and changing the rules constantly so that their status was always as unclear as possible.

He cleared his throat, and the Old Man nodded. "You have a concern… Go ahead."

"Sir, I'm not sure I understand. How can you make the solution apparent and still make it seem as if it comes from somewhere else?"

The Old Man coughed again. "The same way we created the Euro. A public relations campaign touts the single-market advantage and that of uniform employment rules."

"This group did that?" the young man said.

The Old Man folded his hands, nodding. "Yes, we did. From the beginning, from the first meetings in Bretton Woods, the strategy was to nudge and cajole the people — lead them toward our vision."

"But why a fiat currency and not one of the emerging cryptocurrencies?" The young man asked.

The Old Man blanched. "The advent of those damn things is one reason we need to hurry. If one gets widely accepted…"

"People are already addicted to rapid, low-cost payment systems," Dione Bellamy said. "They won't give those up to go to another fiat currency without a compelling reason."

Nikolaj smiled. Dione Bellamy was new to the group, but clearly well versed in the details of The Phoenix project. He had taken to her, deciding that the woman was brilliant. Economic data and insightful analysis flowed from her the way celebrity gossip did from other people. He found that admirable and useful.

Nikolaj also thought Dione was sexy... for an older woman, although not at all his type. Not like Osk Barstad. At the thought of the Interpol woman, he glanced over to drink in her tall Viking good looks.

She was a strong and independent woman, blue-eyed with pale blonde hair. It had been his joy to learn that this strong woman had a weakness for men who enjoyed, made an art of dominating, even punishing, strong, powerful women. Her delight at being overcome, rendered helpless, and used suited his tastes perfectly.

He indulged himself in fantasies for a time, half-listening to the discussion while picturing her bound and at his mercy, but then Dione Bellamy caught his attention again as she went on the offensive.

"Without intending any disrespect, sir, it's also reasonable to believe that countries will resist adopting The Phoenix. They will see giving control of their currency to a central authority as an assault on national sovereignty."

"Because it is," the green-eyed man said before he caught himself.

The woman stared at him for a moment before continuing. "Even if it's a good idea, well, we've seen them turn away from things that would help them before. A national currency represents tradition and has a sentimental attraction. We saw that even when the EU formed — the UK refused to give up its currency in favor of the Euro, despite realizing they were undermining the European cause. And that was long before the conflicts that led to BREXIT arose."

The Old Man nodded. "I'm certain you are correct, Ms. Bellamy. We didn't sell it hard enough with the EU."

"Sell what?" Park asked.

"Fear and uncertainty are, and always have been, our greatest allies. It was fear that drove Western governments to create the IMF and World Bank in the first place. That's why we held the Bretton Woods conference back in 1944. With fears of inflation, or perhaps even economic ruin, on everyone's minds, Harry Dexter White, representing the US Treasury Department, took command and pushed through a vision that called for the creation of the IMF and the World Bank. That broke the ice and conditioned people to the idea that sovereignty wasn't absolute. Later, those same fears made people ask how Europe could hope to compete with the United States and China. That time, we offered a different solution, that these somewhat less sovereign nations should band together and create a beacon of hope that would lead to prosperity. Change will happen, it's just a question of what changes take place. It's up to us to orchestrate it."

"It's quite a complex symphony to orchestrate," the green-eyed man said.

The Old Man chuckled. "I do like that metaphor, Nikolaj. Yes, we score it, then start the orchestra playing — we put the process in motion; after that it is only necessary to nudge it in the right direction. We must have the courage to make corrections, however. For instance, we learned soon enough that White's vision didn't go far enough. At Bretton Woods, White threw his weight behind the effort to veto a plan by John Maynard Keynes that would establish an international unit of currency, which he called the Bancor." He sighed. "Keynes saw the future. It would have been easy then."

The young man representing OPEC shrugged. "That was a long time ago — a different era."

"As the heirs of the Bilderberg Group it is up to us to correct White's error. It might be a different era, but once again the bickering monetary policies of individual states, their destructive and obsolete strategies, are not productive. A single, supranational government is what the people want and need. And our new currency, The Phoenix, will lead to that."

"We will give them what they need even if they don't know they need it." That came from Park Dong Woo, who had surprised himself by speaking his thoughts out loud.

"That is correct, Mr. Park," the Old Man said. "However, we must also help them see that they need it."

Dione shook her head. "While that's true, the world is more complex now. The digital payment systems —"

"If there must be digital payment systems, then we must provide some that use The Phoenix." He glared at Park. "The proposal you submitted to us, Mr. Park, would have people using tokens that are tied to nothing but some digital ledger. But you intend to use it for everything. That will replace the idea of money, and this is counterproductive. How can we control that? We can't discount it; we can't print more when we wish…" He held out his hands. "You see my point? Tell me how we can meet the needs of the World Bank and still accommodate The Phoenix."

Park shrugged. "We already connect the tokens used for outside transfers to rupees and dollars. I suppose that if countries adopt The Phoenix, there is no reason the tokens can't be denominated in Phoenix," Park said. "I don't really care what it's called as long as we aren't making people handle physical scrip. The rest is a banking issue."

Dione licked her lips. "We could start that way… make it a Phoenix token. As it's used by people in smart cities, it becomes a nominal currency. Any country that is doing business with smart cities, any vendors, will have to accept The Phoenix as a real currency — as the currency."

Park nodded. "It's easier to spread something than launch it, but the smart city program is a natural platform for that. Everything is new. And then, if the fiat currency of the nation is shaky, people will rely more on The Phoenix — keep their credits in Phoenix to reduce the effects of inflation."

Dione laughed. "I have no idea how we will do it yet, but the IMF can coordinate converting the tokens to a fiat currency somehow. The ledger concept would need modification and we can't use the blockchain, but it's doable. The beauty of the idea is that everyone wants smart city tech and they need us and the World Bank to get it. That would make its acceptance snowball, even without an actual global government. They'll be afraid not to use it even though we control it."

"They will preach the gospel of fear," the Old Man said. "They will spread the message that by controlling the currency we can offset the vagaries of economic uncertainty."

"Fear," Park said. "A government offers protection and safety. In this case, the fear is of uncertainty. And the governments are just going to outsource currency manipulation to a more efficient vendor."

The green-eyed man sat back and put his hands on the table. "Typically, we've relied on a combination strategy — we offer a juicy carrot and wave a big fucking stick," he said. "The threat of war and famine still serves as an effective and brutal stick, but the idea of the benign rule of an overtly paternalistic group is no longer the carrot it was in 1944."

The Old Man folded his hands on the table. "What are you saying?"

"I don't think people are big on what George H.W. Bush called 'the vision thing' anymore. They want solutions. That's why they love all this tech — it promises the moon and sometimes, literally, delivers. We need carrots attuned to the times. I bet that the youth of today see a global fiat currency as an anachronism — it's a change with no difference. They love cryptocurrencies as much because they are such a big departure, such a disruption, as because they are more useful."

"So, you think we should give up?" The Old Man didn't smile.

"No. But, if this is going to work, we need to promote The Phoenix as something new. Something disruptive in its own way.

That's why I think that doing it the way Park and Dione suggest, making it suitable for the world as it's becoming is the only way to sell it. It needs a few twists, of course. Maybe you could provide a universal basic income paid only in The Phoenix. That would get the right attention."

The Old Man shook his head and snorted. "Now you sound like some populist in favor of transfer payments."

"You know I'm not. But you damn well need to acknowledge the resurgence of populism across the world. People are asserting themselves. They see the established world as us versus them. Globalism requires a level of sophistication that is no longer in vogue and a faith in the world leadership that's virtually nonexistent."

The Old Man sat back. "That doesn't change the basic equation or the fundamental strategy. We can pressure governments, influence the people through fear, and promote our solutions as the only real ones."

"Up to a point," the green-eyed man said.

Anna waved a hand. "And pressure and influence take time. Even if you convince the leaders, governments have to pass legislation, then act on it. Except in dictatorships, that is never quick. And often these days, there is a backlash when things aren't grassroots."

The Old Man nodded. "Are you two becoming rebels within our little group?"

"Hardly," Anna said. "Call us the loyal opposition. We are insisting we see the facts clearly."

The Old Man snorted, then coughed again. "The facts, seen clearly, indicate that it is all doable. We have your companies to help pressure the governments and to convince the people." He put his hands behind his head. "With big money and global corporations behind this effort, combined with our leverage over organizations and heads of state no one will stop us." He looked around the room. "Is there anyone willing to tell me I'm wrong?"

No one spoke. The green-eyed man smiled. Asking who was willing to speak up was not the same question as asking if he was wrong. It was a clever manipulation.

"Fine, then I'll adjourn the discussion now. I'm tasking each of you to prepare a report. You will identify the steps you or your organization can take in the short and medium-term to move the world to adopt The Phoenix. Park, I want the tokens set up linked to the currency. What's that thing called again?"

"A stable coin," he said, sighing.

"Right. And so that we see all the facts clearly..." he glared at Anna, "... outline the obstacles as well."

The green-eyed man considered what would be in his report. "Action item: Kill a bunch of idiots and resistance leaders."

Then he smiled. Ending the meeting was the Old Man's way of dealing with their insubordination, their rebellion. They'd thrown down a taste of a gauntlet. His response had been to give them their homework assignments and then summarily dismissed the class. There could still be repercussions, but for the moment all was good.

As they all stood, the Old Man waved a hand at Nikolaj. "A moment of your time, please."

He sat again, waiting. When the others had left, the Old Man studied him. "Your message said that the mission in Venezuela went well. Any problem at all?"

"No problems," Nikolaj said. "I'll admit that I don't understand why you insist on keeping that miserable excuse for a president in power. Otherwise..." he shrugged.

"It's part of that chaos you cherish so much," the Old Man said, smiling thinly. "The existing president has uses; he is easily manipulated as are all vain, greedy, and foolish men. A new government would be full of excitement for their own vision."

Nikolaj thought that made a certain amount of sense. "Most of us are vain, greedy, and foolish. But he can rest easy. While killing opposition leaders won't solve his economic headaches, Herrera is done disrupting *el presidente's* sleep."

"Excellent." He tented his thin, wrinkled fingers, tapping the tip togethers. "I get the sense that you are serious in your objections to the current path we are on, aren't you?"

This was dangerous turf. "It isn't the path we are on," Nikolaj told him. "I'm fine with that."

"Then what's troubling you?"

"When I go into battle, it's important to have a good strategy. Developing one requires proper intelligence. It's foolish to fight when the enemy's new weapons make yours obsolete. The Polish Lancers attacking Hitler's tanks were less heroic than foolish."

"And your point?"

"I think the people have a new weapon and you are pretending they don't. Ignoring the new financial technology leaves useful tools on the table. Our foray into national cryptos showed that when we are involved in implementing them, we can use their existence to control the people and the government. It's easy."

The Old Man scowled. "The Tanzanian project failed."

"No, their cryptocurrency failed. There is a difference."

The Old Man raised an eyebrow. "You killed Mitch Childer for that failure."

"I killed Mitch Childer for being an ass and for putting our organization in danger. He repeatedly overstepped his authority. The fool took personal responsibility for the project but didn't put the right quality checks in place. He ignored security warnings. Ultimately, the project didn't fail so much as he failed it."

"And he paid the price." The Old Man's grin was to remind Nikolaj that he knew well that the staged terrorist execution of the former head of the IMF had been his work. "And now?"

Nikolaj knew what he wanted to hear. "Whatever you wish. We have so many opportunities. In terms of Venezuela, rather than getting into their politics, why not help them develop their cryptocurrency — the Petro?"

"It's worthless."

"Yes. As a currency. If we were to help them with it, however, as with the smart cities, it could become a useful surveillance tool — a way of getting our hands on the levers of power."

The Old Man shook his head. "It's too risky, too technologically complex."

It was easy to see that the Old Man didn't grasp the power of data. "So, what?"

"It might seem old school, but the tools we know, blackmail, bribery, appealing to the vanity of world leaders … these are all proven to be effective."

"As was pointed out, those things can be slow."

"Evolution is even slower, but reliable." The Old Man grinned. "And the occasional assassination or rogue uprising, properly timed, can act as an accelerant."

The green-eyed man nodded and gave him the only acceptable answer. "Of course."

"Are your men ready to move if we need them quickly?"

He grinned. "You mean when blackmail, bribery, and appealing to vanity fail? Yes, my men are on alert, ready to deploy wherever you need them, to do whatever is necessary."

"Excellent." He rubbed his hands together gleefully, relishing the coming battle. "Everyone needs a plan B. A coup here and there, or a hint of one is so often a useful prod."

"Yes, that is a time-honored tool."

The Old Man handed him a piece of paper. "In my old-fashion anachronistic way, I've developed reason to suspect that one of ours is dipping his hand in the till. I'd like you to investigate for me."

"Do I know him … or her?"

"Mateo Chatzi."

"I know of him." Caution was essential.

"Everything we know and suspect that he might be involved with is on that paper. I want it all verified. If it's true…"

Nikolaj stuck it in his pocket. "It will be a pleasure to learn what our colleague is up to."

"I'd appreciate it if you started with research and save the option of active interrogation as a last resort."

"Why? Do you want to watch?"

The Old Man laughed. "I just might. Actually, I was thinking that someone might have given us the tip because of a grudge."

Such things happened. "Even if the source had a motive, that doesn't mean your suspicions aren't true." The green-eyed man was glad to see the Old Man relax. "Seems I have my marching orders. I think I'll be heading back to clean my guns."

"Do that." Then the Old Man walked away.

Standing on the patio alone, Nikolaj wondered how the discussion would have gone if the man had any inkling about his private Plan B.

Not that he could be certain the Old Man didn't sense what was coming. He was no fool.

Maybe Plan B needed to become Plan A. Nikolaj could almost smell the cordite in the air. Accelerating things, stopping the waiting game might prove very interesting indeed.

CHAPTER 5

A PROGRAMMING JOB

"The future belongs to those who believe in the beauty of their dreams."

— *Eleanor Roosevelt*

Bob & Edith's Diner
539 S 23rd St
Crystal City, Arlington, VA

"You're eating that steak as if you thought it would be your last meal on earth," Claude Hoenig chuckled.

The younger man sitting across from him in the booth shrugged and pointed at the plate with his fork. "If not exactly that, it might well be one of my last American meals for a long time," he said.

The young man's name was Ritesh Samudra, and he was a programmer — one of Claude's most productive and ambitious employees. Claude didn't know him well on a personal basis, but he'd seen how well the man worked with every team he'd been on. The Indian programmers he'd hired seemed to be better at teamwork than their American counterparts. If they weren't as creative, at least they were more willing to work as a team. Ritesh was definitely a team player.

Now the young man was teasing him. "So, Ritesh, are you going to tell me why your American meals are numbered?"

He gave Claude a serious look and let out a breath. "I'm afraid it's the same reason that I asked if we could meet," the man said. He gestured at the plate again. "I honestly didn't expect to get a lunch out of it."

"When else would we have time to chat?"

The young man screwed up his nerve and spit it out. "You see, Mr. Hoenig, the thing is that my family wants me to come home."

"Home? That's Delhi, right?"

"New Delhi, the home of more huddled masses than America has ever seen."

"But it sounds like you aren't excited about doing that. Why not?"

"I will do it because it's what I must do. I gave my word to my parents that I would return after I finished college."

"That didn't happen. You finished your degree a while ago."

He grinned, conspiratorially. "With your help, I managed to stall them for a few years. That was marvelous. When you turned my internship at Hoenig Fintech into a job…"

"Which you earned."

"… I convinced them that working for you for a few years would give me experience that I couldn't get in India. But now… well, my mother thinks it is time I married. It's her dream to see me married and settled in India."

"What about your dreams? When you started here, you told me you wanted to head up my fintech staff one day."

Ritesh blushed. "That isn't our way. My parents have other dreams for me, and those are the ones that count. I've stalled them for a long time now. All of my friends from school are all getting married and starting families and so my mother is anxious."

"Why not get married here?"

Ritesh put down his fork and spread his hands apart. "That, I'm afraid, would kill my mother. She and my father have picked out a suitable bride and are planning a lavish traditional Hindu wedding. Mother would never consider having the wedding somewhere that it wouldn't inspire jealousy in all her friends and neighbors. If it isn't blocking traffic for blocks and blocks, she will be devastated."

"Now that's old school."

Ritesh shrugged. "I believe my father is already negotiating the dowry with the girl's father. They will drink gallons of tea and argue for hours. I'm sure that is giving him an incredible amount of pleasure. He loves to haggle."

"And you've never met the girl?"

Ritesh shook his head and picked up his fork. "Why? My opinion of the girl is irrelevant."

"I can't imagine that. If that's irrelevant, what is relevant?"

He chuckled. "That I'll miss all this. I truly will. But I have obligations to my family that I cannot ignore. And so, they haven't asked me to come home — I have been summoned."

"What if you marry her and come back here? I could keep your job for you."

Ritesh laughed. "And take the grandchildren to America so far from my parents? They would disown me."

Claude was aware of the strong bond of family in India. It was almost stronger than common sense. But an idea was forming. Nikolaj had talked to him about a project, a good one. It would serve a number of purposes, and just maybe he didn't have to lose Ritesh to this cultural throwback. "I hate losing a good programmer," he said.

"And I dislike leaving." Ritesh smiled. "And not just because the work and the pay are good either, although both are probably better than I'll ever see again."

Claude smiled. He knew Ritesh had gone through any number of girlfriends. "The girls?"

"And booze, which my family disapproves of almost as much. I'll miss the entire lifestyle." He sighed. "And yes, a great deal of that is because the girls here are much... freer."

Claude laughed. "I understand. And are there any good job prospects for you in India?"

He made a face. "Honestly, I've made a few inquiries and they mostly suck. I have been offered jobs, but they aren't great. My father could get me a job, but it would be a make-believe job where I did nothing. A friend who owns a software company that does facial recognition would hire me. He is trying to get a contract for a big project, but even if he gets it, the pay wouldn't be significant enough to please my father, and the job wouldn't be certain. The most likely job is to get on with one of the larger programming companies that underpay local programmers so they can underbid American companies like yours and steal American jobs."

"So, the dark secret is you want to take what I've taught you and go into business competing with me?"

He grinned. "That would be the time-honored approach. Failing that, a government job that pays well, promises the occasional bribe, and lets me turn off my brain is the best I can hope for. Only foreigners and the sons of rich men get good jobs in India and seldom do they want challenging work."

There was the opening he was looking for. "From what you've said, I think you like doing work that makes a difference in the world. Is that right?"

"Of course, I do. That's what I'd prefer. I'd like to break new ground, be able to innovate."

"What if you worked for an international organization that was making a difference, but in India?"

"That would be great."

"And, if you managed to get hired before you left the US, you wouldn't be considered a local hire, so the organization could justify paying you a higher salary, even though the work would be in your home country."

Ritesh chewed a French fry thoughtfully. "My parents would like that. It would be much more prestigious and justify the money they spent putting me through college here." He stared at Claude. "Why are you helping me like this?"

"Because I like you and, to put all my cards on the table, there might be a way you would be helping me. We might be able to work together even with you in India on a project that's a lot bigger, more vital than anything you've done. It would incorporate infrastructural work with the financial tech you've been doing."

"That is something I'd enjoy."

"One hitch… the job I'm thinking of would be in Mumbai. Since your parents live in Delhi, would they insist that you be there?"

He laughed. "New Delhi. And no, being in the same city won't be an issue. In fact, I would prefer to find work in another city if I could. My parents want me to have a good job and would be content that I was in my home country. For my purposes, I'd rather be out from under their constant watchful eye. Ideally, I'd be far enough away from them that I could get away with making periodic visits home to let my mother pamper me and to parade the grandchildren in front of them. Mumbai would be perfect It's a two-hour flight — and longer by train."

"Then perhaps we can help each other."

He eyed Claude carefully. "Is this job legal?"

Claude grinned. "Perfectly. And completely aboveboard. It's even prestigious."

"I was afraid it might be something on the dark web."

"No, this would be plain old programming I'm afraid, but on a challenging project. If I can get you in. I can't promise anything today, but I have a meeting with some people coming up next week about the project I have in mind to put you into. I think they'll be glad to have you. Get me an updated copy of your resume right away and I'll see if I can swing it. They'll appreciate a high-level hire who doesn't need a lot of paperwork for visas and work permits."

Ritesh let out a breath. "That would solve a lot of problems for me. I'd never forget a favor like that."

"Will your parents let you stay and keep working for me until we sort this out?"

He grinned. "To obtain a high-paying, prestigious job in India? Absolutely. My father would be delighted. He'd use the possibility of me having a very good job at home to demand a larger dowry from my future wife's parents."

"What if you don't like the girl?"

Ritesh shrugged. "Then she will bear my children and I will otherwise ignore her."

"You're good with that?"

He smiled. "I have to be, and so does she." He glanced up at the menu displayed over the counter.

"Then I'll do what I can."

Ritesh smacked his lips. "They have great fudge sundaes here."

"Knock yourself out, my friend."

As the young man ordered his dessert, Claude Hoenig thought through everything Nikolaj had told him about the project. It was exciting, and things were coming together nicely. Having Ritesh on board, adding his naïve enthusiasm to the project as well as his ability to work in the Indian culture, they moved a step closer to having the team they needed.

"Your friend's company... he is doing work in facial recognition?"

"Yes."

"Send me some information on his company. Maybe we can help him out too."

"Excellent," Ritesh said as the waitress put the sundae in front of him and he dug in.

Claude watched him eat. It was likely that the big project the facial recognition company wanted in on was the same one. How many could there be? And here was a chance to get another tendril into that pie. Helping make the project happen would let him learn more about what exactly was going on.

He needed more details on where this project was leading. Beyond the fact that millions of dollars would be involved, why was a group like the Oculistica concerned about the specific technologies used to make it happen? That was the thing that bugged him. From the outside, this project's political overtones weren't in line with anything the Oculistica cared about. So, he'd dig deeper and find out why Nikolaj cared about it.

When he knew a little more, then he and Turner could have a chat. There was much Claude still didn't understand, and Charlie was in a far better position to put all the pieces together. If this project threatened the US in any way, they needed to know quickly.

CHAPTER 6

BUYING FREEDOM

*"Happiness lies in the joy of achievement
and the thrill of creative effort."*

— *Franklin D. Roosevelt*

**A mobile home parked in a lot
Between Hard Rock Stadium & FL-826
Miami Gardens, Florida, USA**

Tricia Campbell fidgeted uncomfortably in a cheap leather chair that sat in front of the metal desk and stared at the man who had started her in this business. She was focused. She needed to understand exactly what he was asking of her.

"You want me to help a client cheat the government by lying to the IRS?"

"Not cheat the government, simply find a way to reduce the tax burden," Carney said.

"Find a loophole."

"Exactly. I want you to use your knowledge to help him. You are a tax lawyer and know the ropes, the ins and outs. This guy wants us to relocate him; he wants a brand spanking new citizenship with a passport to go with it, from a country that is … kinder to the rich. That's no sweat and it's perfectly legal, but in the meantime …"

"His income is taxable in the US."

"And that doesn't make him happy. He wants to be from somewhere else, so he doesn't have to pay so much."

"I can take a look at his finances and see what's possible, but do you realize that as long as he is a US citizen, even with a new citizenship, even if he lives in this new country, he has to pay US taxes?"

"Sure. That's why, once he's settled, he'll give up his US citizenship."

"He can do that, but I doubt he'll be very happy when he finds out that he has to pay an exorbitant exit tax."

"What?"

"It's something we can thank the Clinton administration for. If he renounces his citizenship, which is the only way he can stop paying taxes on worldwide income, he has to pay a shitload of tax up front."

"Shit. How does that work?"

"These days, renouncing his citizenship means he'll have to pay capital gains on the market value of all his assets, less some confusingly calculated deductibles."

Carney smirked. "Well, we need to fix that. You see the problem, right?"

"Sure, I do. He won't like hearing he has to buy his freedom. The whole point of that exit tax is to keep people from taking their money out of the country and then escaping taxes."

"Then that's your first job, Tricia. This is the kind of thing we talked about; part of bringing you on board is to help the clients we are relocating deal with tax issues. Sounds like this is the big one — the elephant in the room."

"Let's be clear, Carney. We talked about helping him avoid taxes. He wants to evade them."

He shrugged. "Fine. You're the expert. Call it what you like."

"It isn't what I call it. Tax avoidance is a time-honored tradition. Tax evasion is illegal."

"And lucrative. And profitable."

The man's smile grated, but she knew he couldn't help giving her his salesman's face. It might be the only face he had any more, not that he dealt with his clients face to face very often. He ran his operation out of this shabby beached mobile home to keep costs down, and if he had to meet with clients, he'd do it at one of the nicer hotel bars or restaurants.

It was a nice bit of camouflage. Only the consultants who worked there, people like Tricia entered the actual office of ONE FOOT ABROAD: Relocation Consultants. The company web page had a picture of a high-rise that Carney had downloaded from a developer's brochure.

She sighed. "It had better be lucrative, given the risks involved."

"You afraid?"

She laughed. "A little." She didn't want to admit that the idea intrigued her. It was something she had accepted the inevitability of without looking at it closely.

"So, you minimize the risks — do your legal magic. Just find creative ways to alter their tax liability and relocate their assets in a way that maintains their privacy."

She composed herself. It was always hard to explain tax law to people who weren't even accountants. There was nothing intuitive about any of it. "I've worked through some of those problems with my first clients and found things we could do. I've given the issue some serious thought and done some research on options."

Carney nodded.

The truth was that it was exciting. Thinking of ways around the problems, circumventing the laws instead of using them, gave her a thrill. Unlike simply finding legal ways to avoid taxes, trying to work out dodgy but effective ways to help clients get out of them, all together, was fun.

It would be good money, too. Ever since getting out of school and working in tax law, she'd found that helping people understand their rights and showing them how to follow the law was boring and confining. Working for the tax firm had made her feel old and stodgy and that sucked.

The few times she'd helped clients play a little fast and loose was more the thing to get her blood going. Then she met Carney.

Carney ran a company that ostensibly helped people who relocated to other countries. Originally it did just that. Agents would help cut through the red tape, walk newly minted expats through the minefields of buying property in other, strange new worlds, and getting their kids enrolled in private schools.

Tricia met Carney when she was thinking about buying a timeshare in St. Croix. His previous, now bankrupt company had acted as the sales agent. They'd talked.

In the end, she and her husband realized they didn't take enough vacations to merit buying a timeshare, but for some reason, she'd stayed in touch with Carney. A year later, he called to ask her to consult with some of his clients.

"Real estate?" she asked.

"No. I bought a relocation company. I'm dragging it out of bankruptcy. My clients are relocating to other countries and I need help with the legal issues — getting them residency and citizenship in other countries."

She'd laughed then. "What do I know about that?"

"What's to know? It's legal shit and you're a hotshot lawyer, right?"

"I specialized in tax law. It's a different universe."

He ignored her objections. "They overlap. You are a smart kid and there is lots of tax stuff involved." He was right about that part. "We use local immigration law firms in other countries and hand off the paperwork to them. Mostly I want our in-house lawyer to help ease our clients' troubled minds. You will make them realize we are looking out for them. And I'd need you to get up to speed on what documents they need so we get everything to the lawyers in the destination country."

It sounded strange, but it was both interesting and, she expected, doable. Out of curiosity, she used her free time from her tax law job, to test the waters.

To her amazement, she liked the work and naturally, the workload escalated. As she learned the ropes of this undiscovered (for her) world, it opened her eyes to a new universe of fascinating and complex legal issues. She spent days resolving conflicts between the laws of the country of origin and the destination. Some of the discrepancies were hilarious and some treacherous. Every case was unique.

The clients were interesting too. Some worked for companies and were being transferred abroad. Those tended to be routine. The individuals choosing to leave the country were a different breed. In general, she found them dynamic, but some were paranoid and some downright weird. But they were all wealthy and willing to use their resources to get what they wanted.

She found there was a growing demand for people who could assist these paranoid, rich, and weird characters. By simply pandering to them, she quickly grew her business. Her name was passed from one to another, and now she was enjoying herself immensely.

Soon, over the protests of both her boss and her husband, Tom, she quit her job with the tax law firm. She went all-in with helping both her own clients and the ones Carney sent her. He viewed her as an extension of his business and was happy with her keeping 80 percent of the fee they charged.

Tom couldn't understand why she'd made the change. Not at all. "You are leaving a good job with a respectable firm," he said as if that said all there was to say on the matter.

"It's a boring, repetitive, mind-fucking job," she told him. "This gives me a chance to interact with a broad range of people, the laws of multiple countries, and the clients are people who are doing things."

"It's speculative. The clients are as flakey as that Carney character. It could all fall apart," he said.

Hearing his litany of complaints made her realize that Tom was as boring as her job. He wasn't the kind of man she could tell that she'd overstepped the rules many times. Hell, that was the best part, working on the edge of things. She moved from being a lawyer, which had become tedious for her, to working as a fixer — never knowing what might need fixing. Sometimes fixing things required that she walk a tightrope without a net. Although it could be dizzying, it also made her feel alive.

She tried to explain it all to Tom but didn't get or like her new work. He didn't see its value or how it could be stimulating. Excitement and fun weren't high on his list of values. "It's all so uncertain," he said. "There's no consistency."

"Exactly," she said.

"International law is in flux and even countries come and go. Tax law will be there forever."

When he said that, she realized that his certainty was precisely what she was glad to leave behind. The very uncertainty of relocation work, the way the work had to flow, adapt to the realities of the world, appealed to her.

The difference in their attitudes put an enormous strain on their relationship. Although she was working out of Tom's townhouse, she realized that once she took her business to the level she wanted it, built a steady, sustainable business for herself, she'd end things. That would be the smart time to move out and dump him.

Not yet, though. Doing the job properly meant learning a lot of new things and developing an ability to be flexible about how things were done. Tom was right that the regulations could change midstream in a project. Sometimes a little money in the right hands made the process clearer and paperwork go faster. Cash crossing a palm could even give her early warning of changes that might affect a client.

At first, she told herself she was simply taking advantage of loopholes in the rules. For instance, in some countries, it was legal to hire immigration officials to fill out paperwork. A small overpayment ensured the paperwork was also approved quickly. After a time, she exulted in the thrill of bending and even breaking stupid, pointless restrictions.

Eventually, Tricia began to accept that the weird and thrilling experience of handing an envelope of money over to a minister or judge in return for information or a ruling actually excited her.

"I'm bribing people," she thought, somewhat giddy at the idea. "Government officials." That was something criminals did, yet she didn't feel like a criminal.

Over time, she winnowed the morass of regulations and rules down to what was actually required for each stage of expatriation, from simply getting residency, to obtaining full citizenship in another place. That last part was essential.

As long as they remained US citizens, expatriates were stuck paying income taxes. That encouraged people to abandon their citizenship, even though the US State Department charged an individual more than two thousand dollars to do so. In 2016 over 5000 people gave up their US citizenship — a twenty-six percent increase over the previous year.

Her fee was nothing in comparison to a lifetime of taxes.

Her latest client, Mr. Jeffries, was a particular challenge. He had significant assets, and many of them were income producers. The fly in the ointment was IRC 877 — the expatriation rule. Under a complex set of conditions, if your net worth was two million or more, for instance, the government took the market value of everything you owned and calculated your gain or loss as if it was sold that year. Then you were taxed on that.

If she wanted to make her mark on this business, she needed to find ways to help her lovely rich bastards, her clients, take their assets with them and not pay an exit tax.

She'd burned the midnight oil and found a solution.

When she presented her discoveries, her new client didn't seem particularly thrilled with her idea. "So, lady lawyer, you think me buying some fucking art will solve my problem?" Jeffries asked.

He was sneering in the way of a boy who had been told he had to eat his zucchini. "I don't even like art. I don't know shit about art."

Tricia smiled at the wrinkled face, knowing her smile was insincere, almost painful. She wished she could like him. But she didn't and she couldn't afford to pick and choose clients. Most of the really rich ones she'd encountered had turned out to be unpleasant; several were real assholes. But she accepted that. When you were a hired gun, you couldn't expect the highest bidder to be a sweetheart.

"You don't have to like art. You aren't even going to keep it."

"Then what the fuck..."

"I just need you to buy it. Actually, I have an expert who will select the pieces for you. You just write the check."

"Buying this crap helps me get out of taxes?"

"Yes. Or you can just pay capital gains tax on everything you own. Your choice."

"And how does buying overpriced art help me do that?"

"Losses offset your gains."

He cringed. "Losses are as bad as taxes."

"Not if they are temporary. In the tax year before you renounce your citizenship, you obtain residency in a country such as Panama or Ecuador. Those countries allow you to import household goods duty-free. We ship your art collection along with your household goods, but it is stolen in transit."

"Stolen."

"By us. Then it is resold. We can even have it pre-sold before you ship it."

"At a loss."

"Yes, but that gives you money that they don't know about outside the country. It doesn't raise red flags like wiring money, and it isn't as risky as trying to take it in bearer bonds or cash without declaring them."

"Shit. Won't they figure out that the stuff wasn't actually stolen?"

"No. We can find… agreeable shippers who have arrangements with customs in the destination country. You'll have documents saying that US customs agrees that you shipped this valuable art and another saying it never arrived."

"It stinks. It's sloppy."

"It's cumbersome but a pretty damn bulletproof way to do what you want."

He scowled. "You could give me up."

"And get charged with felonies besides losing my license to practice law? That doesn't work out well for me either."

"I didn't realize…"

"Well, please do understand that if I advise you to do anything that isn't entirely on the up and up, I'm putting my neck on the chopping block. You could easily plead that you just followed my advice and worse case you'd get some penalties tacked onto the tax bill. I stand to lose a lot more."

That was language Jeffries understood. "Fine, then."

"I'll be leaving for Ecuador next week to set up your new citizenship."

"You have to go?"

"I need to get the assistance of some government officials and that requires a face-to-face meeting and some thick envelopes."

Jeffries nodded. He understood bribery. "My assistant will wire you the money."

"I'll have my art expert contact him directly, it that suits you."

"That's perfect. I don't need to be involved." He made a sour face. "I don't want to be involved."

When Jeffries left, she let out a long breath and let herself enjoy a sense of relief. He was right. Her plan was shaky. She was sure it would work, but ultimately, what she needed and wanted was a partner who knew everything about international banking — the rules, the loopholes. She needed someone who could help her explore financial options.

The question was where to find the right person, one with the knowledge, who thought creatively and didn't mind blasting through a few hard-nosed regulations. But her program was coming together. Sooner or later… she hoped it would be sooner.

Then she turned her attention back to the present, which meant Ecuador. Fortunately, the residency programs there were fairly straightforward and didn't require much in the way of special efforts on her part. It was a matter of collecting the right documents and sending them to the attorney there and then making Jeffries jump through the hoops.

In the meantime, Tricia Campbell had some exciting firsts ahead of her. She was about to launch her new career and make her first trip to Ecuador.

Tom wouldn't like the idea of her going to Ecuador any more than he liked much of anything else she was up to.

A tingle rippled through her at the knowledge that she was going to be breaking the law. Several laws. Fuck what Tom thought. This was exciting shit.

CHAPTER 7

RACE DAY

*"There is nothing — absolutely nothing —
half so much worth doing as simply messing about in
boats."*

— Kenneth Grahame, The Wind in the Willows

Offshore, circumnavigating
Grenada, west Indies

Water hissed against the hull of FINAL OFFER, a sleek Farr 395 40-foot racing sailboat, as she flew past Fort Judy. She had all her sails full and was moving at well over 14 knots. At the helm, Anna Rasburn spread her feet apart for balance and concentrated on her course, automatically calculating the set of the current.

The choice of this tricky and dangerous course was deliberate. It meant she'd be running close to shore, threading the narrow passage between the rocks close to the shoreline and the porpoises — the name given to a set of almost invisible rocks just a short distance offshore.

Running so close to the rocks was a gamble, but it would put FINAL OFFER on track for a straight shot to Prickly Point, where she could round Point Saline at speed before shifting to a slower tack to run the final leg close-hauled back to Grand Anse — the beach where the resorts were. That was the finish line, where the race around Grenada — the Spice Island of the west Indies — would be decided.

"Keep that sheet tight, Jock," she shouted at the foredeck monkey on the bow. It was his job to meticulously adjust the lines that controlled the huge spinnaker, the sail that channeled the steady pressure of the trade winds into forces that propelled the sleek boat to the west.

Drenched in spray, the young man was tethered with a rope around his waist that let him use both hands to control the nylon that billowed out ahead of the boat. He turned and smiled, giving her a thumbs up.

The subtle nuances of managing a boat on the Caribbean Sea meant nothing to Jock. She'd hired him away from the crew of the 100ft supermaxi WILD OATS XI where he'd done the same job on the Sydney to Hobart race. That was serious racing on treacherous seas. The man had skills. The fact that he was easy to look at didn't hurt one damn bit.

Her other crew member was a woman named Phillipa. A slender blonde in her twenties and a good sailor, she worked from the cockpit with Anna, handling sheets for the mainsails while Jock was forward.

When they tacked, all three of them had their hands full. Anna glanced over her shoulder and saw her competitor swinging further out to sea, gambling on stronger wind and more room to maneuver.

If DINGO's navigator got it right, they might have an advantage; that far out, she could make the turn with a gentle tack that would let her carry more speed around the final point.

Both strategies were sound, and Anna had to assume the captain and crew of DINGO knew their Ker 11.3 as well as she understood the signals that FINAL OFFER gave her. Over time and a lot of races, she knew her boat.

DINGO hailed out of Trinidad and had won her fair share of races too, including this race the year before, but this was the first time Anna and FINAL OFFER had competed head-to-head with them.

She licked her lips in anticipation of the key turn. This one would be close and hard-fought to the end — just the way she liked them.

The two sailboats were well matched. Jason Ker had designed his 11.3-meter yacht to fight with the Farr in the 40-foot racing class. Naturally, in the light air of the first leg, the two of them had walked away from the other eight boats in their class.

They'd separated from the fleet well before David Point, where they'd turned east to round the northern coast. On the run down the Eastern coast of the island, in the shadow of DINGO, choosing to stand further out to sea even on that tack, was the only other boat she saw.

Now they were hurtling through the water, running before the wind. It was time to think about the turn. Both she and DINGO were on a starboard tack that set them up to make the turn at Prickly and then the one at Point Saline, near the airport.

The first turn was a minor adjustment. The final turn would determine who won the race. If she could keep ahead of DINGO to the point, she could force them wide. They'd have to head out to keep FINAL OFFER's sails from blocking their wind. Then they'd have to stay out, giving them a longer run to the line, or they'd have to drop behind her and hope to pass her on the windward side.

The two boats rounded Prickly Point neck and neck. Both crews sheeted in their mainsails to extract the maximum speed. Now Anna could taste victory. If she held her line, she'd have the advantage. Still, it was a white-knuckled run.

"Prepare to come about," she shouted at the crew. It was a tricky maneuver. Jock would have to drop the spinnaker and collapse it into its bag while she and Phillipa brought in the main and the inner jib. Timing was everything.

Suddenly, before she gave the command, Jock dropped the spinnaker and pounced on it to get the air out. He pointed toward shore. "Williwaw," he shouted.

Without looking, Anna turned the helm, pointing FINAL OFFER's bow in toward shore, and Phillipa let out the boom just as the blast of air hit them. Williwaws were sudden, violent rushes of air that came from onshore, usually where there were hills or mountains. If the sails were tight, the force could knock a boat down.

Her heart in her mouth, Anna felt FINAL OFFER righting on her keel. She glanced at the coastline. There were rocks off the point, but...

"Helm alee," she shouted as she spun the wheel, turning the bow north, toward the island's shoreline. The current was pulling them Westward and they might just scrape by.

Phillipa swore as she sheeted in the boom, pulling the sail. Jock untied himself and slithered back to the cockpit to grab the jib sheet and pull it in.

The boat shivered, and then the sails gathered wind again and she heeled hard over, her rail going under and foam rushing back toward the cockpit. FINAL OFFER lurched forward, and Anna heard the comforting hiss of water passing along the hull. Now they skimmed the coastline.

Anna gritted her teeth and let her eyes dart from the sails (watching the red tell tails on the leech), to the compass, and the depth finder... and then back again. She forced herself to breathe as they passed through the area where her knowledge of the rocks wasn't intimate. Then, with the airport appearing on their beam, they shot out away from the shallows into bluer, deeper, safer water.

"All right!" Jock shouted and pointing behind them. "That fucking nails it."

Anna looked back and saw DINGO chasing them… she'd fallen back. "That williwaw blew out their spinnaker," Jock said. "They didn't see the signs soon enough."

"Wow," Phillipa said.

Chuckling like a madman, Jock ducked down into the galley. A moment later he popped back up, holding three brown Caribe beers. "We don't have a lot of sailing left to do now," he said, handing them around. Then, clutching his bottle by the neck, he went forward to sit on the deck with his feet hanging off the windward side. Phillipa tightened the sheet to compensate for the ballast his weight provided, and the boat gained even more speed.

"Sheet her in a bit more, then go up there and join Jock," Anna told her. "Great job, guys."

A few minutes later, FINAL OFFER crossed the line two boat lengths ahead of DINGO. She was first in her class, first in the fleet. Anna smiled and pumped her fist in the air.

The yacht club would be going wild that night — this was Grenada, after all. No matter who won, there was always a hell of a celebration. That suited her mood. The world she lived and worked in was an uptight universe of type A assholes out for what they could get — people just like her. As Jock dropped FINAL OFFER's anchor, and she heard it splash into the clear water, Anna looked forward to unwinding with some serious partying.

CHAPTER 8

BRIEFING TURNER

"Everyone sees what you appear to be,
few experience what you really are."

— *Niccolò Machiavelli, The Prince*

Bob & Edith's Diner
Crystal City, Arlington, VA
USA

Charlie Turner was the ultimate morning person. He had to be. Here it was, only fifteen minutes before five in the morning when Claude Hoenig came in for his breakfast and the man was sitting in a booth drinking coffee.

Claude often had breakfast at Bob & Edith's Diner, the retro café on South Twenty-third street. He thought he ate early, but Turner looked settled in, like he'd been there for a while. He was waiting for Claude.

Bowing to the inevitable, Claude sighed and slipped into the booth across from him. "Am I that predictable?"

"Hey, I work for the CIA," Charlie said. "It's my job to predict what people will do and where they will be."

Claude shook his head. "So, you are not only claiming to be good at being sneaky, but saying that I'm a person of interest?"

There were few people in the place. The one waitress, a cheerful middle-aged blonde named Helen, dealt with everyone well enough. She had a watchful eye that monitored the state of coffee cups and plates with a professional skill. And she wasn't the only one. Claude noted the way Charlie scanned the few patrons, memorizing details, watching for cues, anything that might hint of danger.

A lifetime of spy work made that an automatic reflex, and this was Charlie relaxed, at ease. Claude knew it because he'd been trained that way too. It was actually a good reminder. Since he'd left the agency and turned his attention to financial technology, playing with computers, he'd gotten lax.

It was good to see Charlie and be reminded not to be careless.

"Of course, you are a person of interest, Claude. You are ex-CIA. That means we care what you do and where you go. We'll always care."

He knew they did care, on some level. When Claude left the agency to start Hoenig Fintech, a financial software company, he and Turner had stayed in touch, meeting for lunch now and then. When Claude's company began playing on the international scene, when he came into contact with the globalists of the Oculistica, Claude felt an obligation to keep his old comrade current, to feed him information about the group's activities. In return, Turner and the agency could be counted on to provide help and information of their own.

Becoming a global player in finance, moving from the world of spies and spy craft and into being part of the evolving information world didn't mean that Claude's allegiance to his country was in any way diminished. He saw it simply as a change from being part of the team, to representing the 'right' side on a freelance basis. And he used new tools for the same hunt.

One reason he left the agency was that he thought they were woefully behind the technology curve, at least in some areas. Going independent let him chase the world he saw emerging. But morally, ethically, and politically, he was still connected to the agency and what it represented. The major difference now was that he knew that what was good for the US wasn't always good for the world.

Once in a while, that produced conflicts that he needed to deal with.

Yes, Charlie's agency would always care, but not so much out of concern for his wellbeing, but out of concern for an asset that might be useful.

"I'm touched, Charlie. Now tell me ... what do you need?"

"Can't an old friend look you up without it being a big deal?"

"Sure, but he never does."

"Touché. I've been neglectful."

"So, this little not-so-accidental meeting is about business. What have I done to deserve this attention?"

"Well, the business isn't exactly you or what you've done."

"You already know everything about Tanzania and what happened there."

"Old business," he said, waving a hand. "Today we are more into current events. For instance, we heard that you are involved in building a magically smart city over in some fucking place."

Claude picked up the menu and buried his face in it. He always ate the same breakfast but hiding behind the menu gave him time to think while the other guy couldn't see his face. Charlie Turner read faces like some people read books. After a minute, he put the menu down. "That's right. We are putting a magical city up in the sky; building it of moonbeams and rainbows."

"Is that so? I heard it was squarely on the ground — someplace called Mumbai."

"Yeah. That's just the first one, though. It's functioning as a test bed funded by the Indian government. There's a bunch of cities scheduled for updating."

"And you are updating them to the point that they do magic, like tracking the citizenry?"

"The World Bank hired my company to guide the evolution of some of the tech. Mostly it's finance, but we have to work with the other groups. They want it all designed as standard units so that it can be replicated for other cities around the world."

"Your buddy Park Dong Woo expects to use high tech in cities to solve the problems of hunger and peace in our time," Charlie said. "Some shit like that."

"Canada is doing the same thing. Google is involved in a big project there."

Charlie nodded. "I know. We share tech with them. It's a friendly universe."

"Bullshit."

Turner grunted. "Okay, we twisted their arms until they agreed to pretend to share."

Helen came to the table and poured Claude a cup of coffee, then topped up Charlie's cup. "If you are ready to order... I already put in Claude's order."

Charlie gave her a smug grin. "Is my amigo here that predictable?"

"No, sometimes he gets wild and crazy and comes in on Wednesdays instead of Tuesdays."

"A real rogue. Well, bring me whatever his usual is." Charlie grinned. "I hate making those kinds of decisions."

"A real dynamo," she laughed. "With such a sharp and effective decision-making strategy, you must be a business tycoon."

"No," he leaned on the table. "Actually, I get paid to kill people for the government."

She laughed. "You and about sixty percent of the idiots who come in here. The rest are retired special ops people."

"Hey, this close to Washington, you take the customers you get."

"With all the spies and jackals sitting in this place drinking coffee and eating pie, there can't be much spying or killing getting done in the real world." She looked around. "My tax dollars at work, right?"

Charlie scowled. "Even spooks have to eat. And having them here should give you a warm, safe feeling."

She snorted. "Only when they tip."

"I think she likes you," Claude said as she left.

"I'm not sure, but that would show good taste. Now, about your current employer…"

"You want to know about The World Bank? Why, anything you need to know is right there online, Charlie. I'm surprised at you. Wikipedia is your friend."

"I'm thinking more of a few people that you know damn well are behind this operation and not official members of the visible organization. The people who are promoting the smart city thing."

"The Retinger Oculistica," Claude said. "Same folks as Tanzania."

"Except for the unfortunate head of the IMF."

"Yeah. Well, you have to assume that the new lady is part of things. All I know is that they are an elite group of power-hungry and influential folk. They do a good job of pretending they don't exist and believe no one else knows."

"And how are they doing these days? Are they all cozy and happy?"

So, this was what the meeting was about. Inside scoop on a nonexistent organization. "I've heard rumblings of a little dissension between the ones that see lots of potential in emerging technology and those that aren't so keen on it."

"Like the tech used to make those magically smart cities magically smart?"

"Not so much the smart city as the financial systems underpinning them. Part of what makes the cities so efficient…"

"Assuming they turn out to be efficient…"

"Yeah. Well, it depends on them being cashless and having a payment system that is based on blockchain, so it can't be hacked easily and is cheap and fast. Things have to happen instantly. Once you get that, once the money is just data and you have the means for handling it, then contracts, deals, control systems, everything gets put on the blockchain, or a blockchain anyway."

"Is the rift serious?"

Claude grinned. "You probably know more than I do. I'm not sure what is going on, except that there is opposition to getting rid of currencies that central banks create by fiat. If this scheme works, if it gets wide acceptance, it will do that in spades. So, I can understand why the folk at The World Bank are nervous that their efforts might be squashed. And they know there is resistance. Suddenly, a corporation that was supposed to supply a light-rail system for the city is hesitating, wondering if they should do it at all. That fits with the rumors that forces within the group would like to see the project definition a lot less technical."

"Is it a fight?"

"Not at the moment, but the key players, the few I've met, aren't the type to play a low-stakes game. If they butt heads too squarely, there will be some trouble. The fallout for the previous head of the IMF was pretty serious."

"Getting beheaded is definitely serious. But we can use dissension."

"Could you? Seems they are running every damn thing. It wouldn't surprise me to find that you work for them too and don't even know it."

"You always did have a view of world politics that managed to be cynical and naïve at the same time, Claude."

"That was one reason I got out of the racket," he said. "Too often, for my tastes, the work we did turned out to be based on both of those attitudes. I joined up to do good things; despite all the push to be expedient, I never managed to accept that doing bad things accomplished that."

"And although you know your country does the same nasty stuff everyone else does, and although you work for the Oculistica…"

"I remain a patriot." He shrugged. "Contradictions abound. And my poor conscience is soothed because I work for the World Bank, not those thugs."

Turner smiled. "The World Bank. A smug and self-righteous group of bastards that are in the pocket of the Oculistica, just as most of the major banks are."

"Like I said, for all I know, so is the CIA."

"Not yet, anyway. But we do have some hooks into them. Some of the things they are doing are useful."

"How is it useful?"

"You know we fund new technology, right?"

Claude laughed. "The CIA offered me startup money, so yeah."

"Well, one of the little strings attached to the rather significant funding we provide is giving us a key to the back door so we can slip in and out without leaving footprints."

"Slip in and collect data?"

"Sure, collect data, but also tweak algorithms, or even bring down a system if that's necessary."

"I assumed all that. The folks with the tinfoil hats do get a number of things right."

Turner smiled. "Yes, they do."

"Let me get this straight... the CIA is concerned that the internal struggle of a possibly fictitious deep state group might impede its secret mission to infiltrate the global smart city projects. If the wrong side wins, the group might even abort those dream projects altogether."

"Oh my, and to think the director always thought you were the slow kid in class. Wait until he hears about this."

"It does sound odd to think of a joint project of the CIA and the Oculistica."

"It would be if they knew it was a joint project. Leave out that tiny bit of information and it makes perfect sense. At least as much as the ones we've done with other bad guys, like the Contras in Nicaragua."

"The ultimate covert operation. You let the bad guys implement tech that tracks everything and everyone, so you don't have to do it."

"That's the high-concept version."

"Why are you telling me this?"

"I didn't tell you anything. You told me."

Claude laughed. "Maybe I did. What was the point of having me tell you this?"

"I simply wanted you to know, if you didn't already, that there might be fireworks. We are fond of having one of our own on the inside."

"And, naturally, you have a particular plan for what I should do if the fireworks start."

"Naturally. We wouldn't let an old comrade thrash in the wind, not knowing which way to turn. In general, we tend to be pro-technology and against regressive globalism."

"Nice turn of phrase. What does it mean?"

"You know damn well what it means, old friend… that you are going to be asked, or forced, to take sides in a power struggle."

"I've stayed neutral so far."

"The stakes are increasing. We've heard rumors too, and we don't like what we hear. If the old guard wins, there is going to be a major banking conflict. If the new guard starts edging toward cryptocurrency payment systems… well, we think we have a finger in the pie already. If nothing else, it's an even playing field."

"The new guard tested the waters in Tanzania, and it didn't go well."

"They think they learned a lesson there. So did we. It was a wakeup call."

"To join the crypto wars."

Turner shrugged. "The point being that if the big guns go to war, they won't do it alone. They will be actively lining up troops. You will be in the middle of that struggle, and your actions will speak volumes."

"I'm all about actions, if I know what actions are needed."

"That will become clear, I'm sure. In the meantime, we need you to entrench yourself as deeply as possible in any of the financial tech projects. When you are asked, and you will be, to take on more responsibility, take it. Make yourself indispensable."

"My best guess is that they will want me to work as a vendor to the World Bank and government projects."

"Perfect."

"That's going to require more resources than a small company like mine can come up with."

"Your beneficent Uncle Sam will provide. If you need to hire people, travel, get equipment … he will accommodate you."

Claude grinned. "And I submit an invoice through the usual channels for my expenses? Do I get a contract?"

"Yeah, just like Ollie north did. No, asshole, you call me, tell me what you need, and I hand you the cash in a darkened parking lot, like in the movies."

Claude knew that in reality he'd be paid through bogus invoices for work and equipment outsourced to his company — work that didn't ever happen. "Just like old times. And you think this mastermind group won't notice where this money comes from?"

That earned him a grin. "Sure, they'll know. They understand that no one ever completely leaves the CIA. They've already factored that into whatever evaluation they've made of you, and it seems like they haven't seen that as a problem so far. Maybe they'll think you are playing both sides. For all they know, it's all a con and you are kicking back money to me."

As Helen brought their breakfast and put it in front of them, Turner looked up at her smiling face. "Not that I'm complaining, but how is it you are so cheerful this early in the morning?"

"My shift ends in an hour, darling. That's how. This is my Friday and I'm going home to my boyfriend for two days."

"Ah," Turner said. "Sweet love."

"Well, hot sex, at least," she said.

They watched her leave. "So," Claude said, "you want me to enter the fray, throwing my everything behind whatever this globalist new guard wants to do."

"And let us know who is on which side."

"I'm sure you know more about the overall group than I do."

Turner laughed. "Maybe. You know we always wonder if we really know what we think we know. Independent confirmation requires that I not give you any clues. Besides, we are hoping you can make the pro-technology crowd the winners."

"So, I back Park's project and promote the smart city idea even when it meets resistance."

"Basically. See what you can do to make sure they win."

"Then I need you to share some information."

"On?"

"Nikolaj Romijn."

Turner put down his fork. "That slippery bastard... I've wondered which side he would take."

"Word is that he is lining up with the pro technology camp. He wants to meet, and if I have to deal with him, I want to know more about him."

Turner nodded. "Okay. It'll take a couple of days."

Claude had been sure Charlie would come through. "So, if I have to do more for this effort, you will pay for it?"

"The American taxpayers will. They are good at that."

They ate in silence while Claude mulled over the idea that effectively he was going to be working for his old employer again. At least this time he was doing work he liked.

When they finished, Turner stared at him. "Any last questions, concerns?"

"Tons, but not many you'll answer."

"It's so nice working with a pro," Turner said. "You understand the need to know crap and that you'll have to wing it."

As Claude got a refill for his coffee, Helen brought Turner the check.

"What makes you think I'm the one with the money?" he asked.

"I've been a waitress for ten years, darling. I know."

"You did say you'd pay expenses," Claude pointed out.

Turner faked a groan and took money out of his wallet and handed it to her. "Keep the change."

"Oh, I will," she said.

"I'll be in touch," Turner told Claude.

"I know. It goes with the territory."

As Turner got into his car and drove away, Claude sipped the cooling, somewhat bitter coffee and considered his situation. Working with the CIA would complicate things; on the other hand, being involved with them would mean he would have the funds to expand his business. The complications weren't worth too much thought. It all seemed inevitable anyway. His work would entangle him this Oculistica group and that meant either joining them or making sure the CIA knew where he stood. He couldn't see a less complicated path.

Working at the cutting edge of financial tech naturally meant being involved with global banking. That automatically got you, and your software, swept up in some dark intrigues. The international and supranational organizations, whether they were well-known ones, like the IMF or World Bank, or ghost groups like the Oculistica and CIA had conflicting goals. There was no way to avoid them, so it was best to accept that you needed to work with them and deal with it.

When he finished his coffee, Claude walked outside the diner and breathed in the cool morning air. The sun was just breaking through and the air was still fresh. That wouldn't last. The commuter traffic, now just starting to fill the roads, would fix that.

He turned toward his car, his eyes automatically scanning the area for all the things a spy was trained to scan for. At the edge of the parking lot, at the exit, a man sat leaning back against the metal upright post that held a yield sign, a jar in his lap and a sign, handwritten on cardboard, propped up against him.

"War vet. Please help."

Nothing about the man raised his hackles, and beggars were becoming an all-too-common sight even here in the suburbs. Claude walked over and stared down at the man. He looked fit. When he returned the look, his eyes were clear. He wasn't a drunk.

"Where?" Claude asked.

"Based in Kandahar," he said. "Fucking Afghanistan."

"How many tours?"

"Three in that sandbox, one in some other hole."

"When did you get out?"

"Six months ago."

"Where's home?"

The man coughed, then spit. "I've got no fucking idea, buddy."

Claude nodded. He fished out a ten-dollar bill and handed it to him. The man took it and stuffed it in his shirt pocket, nodding.

"Wish I could do more."

"Don't we all?" the man said.

There wasn't much left to say, so Claude walked to his car. People served in different ways and they suffered differently too.

CHAPTER 9

PARALLEL COMPANIES

"A time comes when you need to stop waiting for the man you want to become and start being the man you want to be."

— *Bruce Springsteen*

Wichita, Kansas
USA

Joshua Raintree had been evolving the idea of his grand escape for a couple of years. It had been clear that marrying Jessica was a mistake from the moment he stepped into the Wall Street job her father arranged for him. The job and marriage were both cages he didn't see until he was squarely inside them.

He wasn't free, but he could dream.

Even back then, he had taken notice of a change in his industry that interested him. It was the emergence of Bitcoin that intrigued him. No, actually it was the technology of the blockchain, the digital technology that used a distributed ledger to make all cryptocurrencies possible and free from the control of banks. The idea of that, the freedom and security it provided for financial transactions, the possibility that it could turn the entire financial payment system on its head, intrigued him. Bitcoin was merely one incarnation, one cryptocurrency. There were many, each with its own strengths and weaknesses, but they shared the promise of amazing possibilities for the future.

Unfortunately, to the people in his firm, to most of his colleagues, the entire world of cryptocurrency was considered nothing but a scam — a tool for laundering money or making dark web transactions.

He first heard about it while sitting in the breakroom talking to a guy he'd met and gotten to like named Kenny. Kenny worked in IT. He was a blockchain enthusiast in love with the technology. He wasn't one of the first on the bandwagon, but Kenny had bought some Bitcoin at less than a thousand dollars, just for the experience of doing it. Then he'd moved into so-called 'altcoins,' wanting to explore what made each a little different.

"I have no idea," he said when Joshua asked him how much he'd invested. "It's scattered all over the place. I run a few nodes myself and I do some mining — that's just to do it, to understand it better." Even though Joshua was just beginning to understand that nodes were the computers that made the blockchain possible and that mining was a term for being part of the process that verified transactions taking place on the blockchain, the technology that made that happen, how you did those things, was still over his head.

What he did know was that Kenny was in love with what he called the 'elegance' of the blockchain. He didn't care that much about making money.

Back then there were few cryptocurrency exchanges, and the ones that did exist were sketchy as hell. After much searching, and with help from Kenny, Joshua found someone to sell him a thousand dollars' worth of Bitcoin.

Knowing it was there, that he'd reduced fiat currency to a code printed on a paper wallet, gave him the sense that he possessed a precious secret. He had something of value that no one else in the entire world could access. That simple epiphany ignited his imagination and soon he was studying everything available on the subject, watching videos, reading about it, and visualizing the future it could create.

As the technology evolved, and his secret stash of coins grew, he realized that his crypto had a special benefit — no one knew he had it, not a bank, not the government, no one. He recorded the small amounts that he squirreled as cryptocurrency as a business expense. With no record of his investments there was no capital gains tax or any other monitoring, unless and until he converted it to dollars again. That appealed to him.

Just as Joshua suffered with the dullness of the work he did, the routine IT work a financial investment company required him to do bored a genius like Kenny. One day he announced he was moving on.

"Where to?"

"Freelance stuff at the moment. I'm moving to Panama next week to work with some people writing code for ID systems they make that involve sophisticated biometrics. There are some interesting challenges in that shit. Not like here."

After Joshua lost his job on Wall Street and he and Jessica made the ignominious move to Wichita, he stayed in intermittent contact with Kenny, but the man stayed on the move and his messages, increasingly infrequent, came from Singapore, India, and Chile.

Joshua felt a twinge of jealousy.

Still, he had his life to lead, and once he started work at the new firm, he tried to settle down and be a good investment advisor. He knew he could do the work, but his heart wasn't into the company's investment philosophies. They fed their clients a steady diet of blue-chip stocks and gilt-edged Treasury certificates. From his perspective, they could just give clients a printout and say: "Buy these. You can't go wrong."

The managers he worked for didn't appreciate his lack of enthusiasm for the tried and true. When he complained, they made a strong point that he was not, under any circumstances, to put clients into 'risky' positions, like penny stocks, or shudder, that dreadful evil, cryptocurrency.

Thus, Joshua's time there was doomed to be short-lived. So, for the few months the job lasted, he kept up with the latest changes in blockchain and the various cryptocurrencies. As the technology evolved and became more widely accepted, he decided it was time to launch his own business.

In the beginning, he found clients that weren't much different from those at the firm he'd left. When a few among them indicated that, for the right return, they were open to taking more risks, he put his knowledge of the new financial technology to work. Soon, for the handful of clients that he got along well with, the ones who were serious about gambling on higher risk investments, he was trading in cryptocurrency on a regular basis.

"Using a blockchain, distributed ledger technology reduces the risk and exposure," Joshua told them. "Smart contracts mean that whatever we agree on will happen or your money is kept safe."

"How?" was the most common question.

"Every transaction takes place using distributed ledgers, which makes it harder for… other people… to track your trades, to know what you've invested in, much less what you paid or what you got when you sold. They can't figure out much more than knowing you bought some cryptocurrency. After that, it's impossible to track. We move it into a wallet and someone who knows their shit can see if there is any coin in the wallet, but they can't know who owns it. Once you move the bulk of your assets into crypto, we can push and shove it around without anyone knowing."

For the right clients, the argument had a lot of appeal. Sensing a shift in the attitudes of the government and the encroachment of new government regulations, he didn't broadcast this service.

Over time, his financial services split almost naturally into conventional and those involving crypto. The crypto-based clients were concerned about their privacy as much as they were making money, so other than what was recorded on the blockchain, he didn't keep records at all. Nothing for an agency, or, as it turned out, his wife's lawyers to find.

That business, along with his own investments, became the core of what Joshua Raintree now called his parallel company.

Off the books, for himself and his clients, Joshua was investing in coins themselves, and also initial coin offerings (ICOs), trading lesser-known digital currencies the way some people did fiat currencies, and even buying into companies that were creating the new wave of technology... buying tokens they issued in lieu of stock shares and paying for them with Bitcoin or Ethereum. The unregulated nature of it all made him feel alive. It was the Wild west all over again, and he managed to recapture the way he had felt when he first got into finance. Trading without a net. It was invigorating.

This ghost company he ran parallel to the official, licensed investment firm.

The division seemed natural. It was difficult, if not impossible, to meet the IRS reporting demands for crypto transactions. The incentive for himself and his clients was to skip doing it altogether. And now, facing a divorce, when he told his lawyer he'd sell the company, he was only talking about the visible business. He meant the one that managed his clients of record, his most conservative, conventional clients. The parallel ghost company and its smart contracts that he'd built gradually weren't visible.

For that company there was no paperwork.

That, too, suited Josh. He hated paperwork and found it delicious, almost sinfully so, to have a lack of paperwork be the foundation for his metamorphosis.

Things went according to plan. The so-smart lawyers Jessica's father had hired brought in three accountants in a virtuoso display of bookkeeping overkill. For days they combed through his paltry and intentionally sloppy records, learning everything about that business and his personal accounts.

Knowing that a hungry dog can root forever, he'd deliberately left them a couple of things to find. When they gleefully uncovered some stock certificates he hadn't mentioned and a bearer bond in a safe-deposit box, he acknowledged that they had caught him out.

Dizzy with their victory, they reported a company value slightly less than he'd estimated. A local financial management company — the very firm he'd worked for briefly — was delighted to buy the business for the full amount. Forty percent of that gave Joshua a small amount of cash. It was plenty to cover his expenses and his imminent departure.

Jessica's father was delighted.

After they signed the divorce papers, Joshua felt a veritable rush of relief. He was free.

"What will you do now?" Jessica asked him when they met at her lawyer's office to sign the final papers. He could tell that she sniffed the presence of undiscovered money, but she had no idea where to look for it.

"I'll travel," he said. "Spread my wings and fly."

"Where?" The idea made her scowl. He wasn't sure if it was the idea of an unplanned trip, or that he was going to indulge himself.

"Why would I tell you? Your father would probably buy the country just to make sure they didn't let me in."

"Don't be cruel."

"Me?" He laughed. "I'll tell you — I don't really know. I'll probably head to South America to start with. I've been to Europe, but not to South America. And living is cheaper there. You didn't leave me with much, so cheap is important."

"You didn't deserve any breaks from me," she said, her voice trembling.

Joshua looked at her and, at that moment, caught a glimpse of the woman he'd fallen in love with, the woman she'd been before they'd inflicted so much pain on each other. He wondered if she was as relieved as he was to call it a day.

"I probably didn't," he said. The reaction he saw on her face gave him a flash of pleasure. It had been a long time since either of them let their defenses down, and now he saw that admitting he might be wrong had caught her off guard. "You have a valid point. We haven't exactly treated each other with kindness for some time, and for my part, I'm sorry about that." He was sorry, and for some reason, it seemed important that she know it.

"Money," she said. "It came between us."

"More than that." For the first time, he saw their life with clarity. Their love, which he thought intense and powerful, had probably been more passion than real love. They'd both felt the heady attraction of being intimately involved with someone who came from a background that was completely different from anything they'd ever known. But that was the allure of novelty, and over time it evolved to dismay. They learned that each presented them with things they couldn't understand or deal with. What had been affection finally blossomed into near hatred.

"I wonder sometimes..." he said.

"Me too."

"Why did we ever get married?"

"It's what people do when they are drawn to each other," she said. "Even if the reasons are screwed up and they shouldn't be attracted to each other."

"But, from the beginning, we knew that we each wanted such different things from life. I was always confounded by your desire for nice, upmarket things."

She snorted. "You can't understand wanting nice things?"

"When we had them, it didn't make things right."

"You didn't understand my world, and so you threw it all away," she said.

"Not deliberately."

"It seemed that way."

"I couldn't be what you or your father wanted me to be."

"You didn't try."

"I did. But I was never going to be a corporate star, and I had no interest in politics."

"You could've done well."

"We always knew those differences existed. It seems obvious that your happiness was my misery and my happiness would disappoint you."

"Hardly obvious. Stupid, perhaps."

"Deep down, I think you knew too. But it wasn't until I screwed up the Wall Street gig that it came out in the open."

She watched his face. "I knew that you never liked my friends, but you are rather brilliant in your way and I thought you'd prove them wrong. I always thought you deliberately messed up to get fired."

"You did?" He laughed. "No. It was simply that I hated what I did. It was nothing meaningful, and I was aching to be free, but if I did something deliberate, it wasn't conscious. I'll admit that I was glad when it ended. I just couldn't keep doing that."

"Others did it. Our friends …"

"Your friends. If you'll remember, I never liked them. That always was your world, Jess. It never sat well with me. The games, the rules… I could feel it closing me in."

She shook her head, standing there with her hands on her hips, looking indecently gorgeous. "You never liked rules or anything that made you feel trapped, including commitment."

Maybe he was just being greedy, or perhaps it was that he'd never have her again that made him speak so plainly. He looked at the slim, dark woman and knew she was gone from his life. He tried to recall the last time he'd made love to her. If he could remember that moment, he wanted to recall her face, remember seeing her face with passion on it.

"That's why I couldn't agree to interminable alimony. Better to take what I can pull together and hit the road."

"I can't see you spending your life as a bum," she said.

"A hobo," Josh said. "Not a bum."

"There's a difference?"

"Hobos travel to work. And I'll work. Not with some soulless company. I'll find something... maybe even restart the business I had here. But I'll do in a new place where the game is different."

"Looking for what?" she asked, smiling. "It's the same game."

"No, I'd make it something different this time. Something with more joy in it."

"You want your freedom that badly. You were willing to risk everything, to give up what you'd worked for, for this uncertain future of yours?"

That she was accepting his story, understood that he was telling her the truth, pleased him. "I'd do it again in a heartbeat, Jess. There is wisdom in uncertainty — life."

"That's the part that baffles me — suddenly you don't care about your security. How many times do you think you can start over, Josh? You're already forty-five. At some point, even you have to think about building for the future and stop gambling."

"Do I? I don't know that I agree that's worth the effort. The future is a pretty uncertain place, Jess. Chasing after the things I might need in a world that could be far different from what we imagine... I find it hard to get behind that. So much could fall apart. Deferred gratification won't necessarily pay off in this volatile world."

"So, you will revert to being the grasshopper you were just out of college? Live for this season?"

Joshua licked his lips. "You found it sexy once."

"When I thought you'd outgrow it."

Joshua held up the divorce decree. "So now we see that despite both of us making this a painful deal to reach... despite us throwing lawyers at each other instead of talking, I have to admit that this is probably the right solution."

"You're happy with the settlement?"

Joshua savored her surprise. "Actually, I'm happy just to have things settled. You get the house and your car and the cash from half my business. I have the rest of the cash and a car to sell. Who knows whether it's an equitable arrangement? Honestly, I don't give a shit. I'm happy that we can walk our own paths — away from each other. By the way, this conversation has been the best one we've had in ages. Maybe the most honest discussion ever."

She sighed. "I suppose we needed the distance in order to have it."

Joshua was certain he still needed a lot more distance from her world, and time, lots of time. "I suppose we did." He held out a hand. "Now that we agree on our differences, rather than be your hated ex, I'd rather be an old boyfriend you sometimes think of fondly."

She laughed. "And let you off the hook for all the pain you caused me?"

"Exactly."

She took the hand and shook it. "Okay then. Daddy still wonders what I saw in you… sometimes I do too."

"It's a fair question, what we saw in each other, although you were an alluring package, Jess. You still are and that's my one regret."

"What do you mean?"

"Not getting to fuck you anymore."

Her smiled showed that his comment pleased her. "When do you leave?"

"That depends ... do you want to buy my car?"

"What?"

"I'm leaving as soon as I sell it. The title to the car is the last, rather tenuous link I have to this world. The money I get for it will buy me a plane ticket… somewhere. And it feels great not knowing where that will be yet."

"I don't want your car, Josh. I don't need it. What about all your other stuff? What will you do with it?"

He grinned. "Give it all away. Goodwill and Salvation Army have these great big trucks and they will send one by so that my life can disappear into the abyss that is the cargo hold. If there is anything you want, get over and grab it before it all disappears."

She shook her head. "There's nothing I can think of." She gave him a curious look. "You are really doing it. This wasn't just a game."

"I am."

Saying it, the truth of it all rippled through him. Suddenly Joshua Raintree was heading out into the great unknown. Traveling without a net. His mother, the flakey, hippie, Apache woman, would probably be proud of him.

He hadn't seen his mother in a number of years. They increasingly had found it difficult to talk, to find common ground. But at that moment he wanted to call her and tell her what he'd learned, that he understood. He couldn't though — he had no clue where she was. The last time they talked, she mentioned she was moving again.

"Where?" he asked. "Why?"

"I'm going wherever I'm meant to be," she said. "I am going because I'm meant to be there."

He found that logic hard to argue with. Impossible, actually. And even harder to understand.

But that was Mom. It felt odd to miss her. And somehow, recently she'd begun to make more sense. Or the universe had shifted slightly.

CHAPTER 10

AFTER HOURS

"Demands for solidarity can quickly turn into demands for groupthink, making it difficult to express nuance."

— *Roxane Gay, American writer and professor*

At anchor
Outside of St. George's Inner Harbor
Grenada, west Indies

It was near midnight when Anna and Jock got back to the boat from the celebration at the yacht club. It had been a mixture of tedious, self-congratulatory speeches and partying with a bunch of rowdy sailors. They were tired and happy. She had the trophy for winning their class tucked under her arm and too much good food and booze in her belly.

Riding out to where they'd anchored FINAL OFFER, Jock had made sure his body brushed against hers, feeling warm and arousing. The emotional high from running the race, winning it, the celebration, and the prospect of spending the night with Jock, who had proven himself an expert lover, had her dizzy with anticipation. Then, as she climbed up out of the dinghy, Jock ran his hand over her ass, as if she hadn't gotten the message that was in a mood to please her. Any thought of sleep was hours away.

Climbing over the lifelines, in the dim glow from her masthead light, she saw a dark form in her cockpit. In that instant she knew, somehow, who sat in the dark, waiting. As Jock came on board, he saw him too. "We've got company," he said, bristling protectively.

She handed him the trophy they'd won. "It's okay, Jock. I need to take care of some important business. Take this below and find a safe place for it. Take a shower and wait for me."

Jock gave her a puzzled look. "Business? Now? Here?"

"Never mind," she said, making her tone sharp. "You go below decks and wait for me. Shut the hatch."

Jock scowled, hesitating for a moment, as if he hoped she'd change her mind. Finally, he shrugged and waved the trophy. He walked past the man sitting in the cockpit, turning the hatch and then went down the ladder. The hatch scraped as he reached up to close it behind him.

Anna sighed, then sat on the cushions at the helm — behind the wheel. She opened a small compartment, taking out a bottle of Glenfiddich and two glasses. She poured the drinks, put the bottle away, and handed one to the man.

Letting herself down into a seat facing him, she sighed. "You have shitty timing. I'll assume that whatever this is about couldn't wait."

"Maybe it could have," the man said, his familiar voice deep. "You know I can get fucking impatient. It eats at me."

She knew his impatience all too well, and his words touched something deep in her. "Since you are here screwing up my night, you might as well tell me what's eating at you."

"The Old Man."

"Is getting older and angrier."

"We need to talk about him. About his plans."

Sitting in the dark, she could barely make out the man's face, but she knew those green eyes by heart and could picture the way they burned into people when he wanted something.

If she could see them in this dim light, she knew she'd see them fixed on her. He knew her well; he knew his magic worked on her.

Because they still worked together, there were times she worried that he knew her far too well. He knew how to manipulate her, knew what buttons to push. Yet, it also meant that he didn't bother to resort to cheap tricks. They weren't necessary. He knew how much they were alike and counted on the fact that they were pragmatists.

Whatever they'd had together once was long past, and the present conversation wasn't even about them.

"Do we really need to do that? Why talk about the old bastard?" she asked. "Why waste time talking about him? I try not to even think about him."

Having said her piece, she took a sip of the Scotch and held it on her tongue, savoring it. The quiet, being on her own turf and feeling the gentle motion of the sea under the hull, gave her some control of the pace of the conversation… if she could decide how to use it to her advantage. Nik's presence here meant that he needed something. He rarely needed something from anyone, so if she could figure out what it was, that might give her a bit of leverage.

It was best to have some leverage in dealing with Nikolaj. Even Anna considered him to be a dangerous man, but from her perspective, that was more because he could be unpredictable than due to his ruthlessness. In general, she was useful to him, and that protected her. Still, despite their past, despite their previous relationship, if he was preparing for a conflict that involved her, then she needed to find all the levers she could.

"So, tell me what concerns you. I know you aren't happy about the Old Man's plans to convince the world to seek salvation through The Phoenix fiat currency… has something changed?"

He laughed. "What's changed is that I'm tired of pretending I give a shit about the Old Man's doomed plans," he said. "I'm done with that." He hesitated and missed his moment. The way the world has gone squashed any chance he had to implement The Phoenix. Now it is just an anachronism. Even if it still had any potential, implementing it would take forever and wouldn't be certain." He smiled. "Just as you told him at the meeting."

"He does have the banks, the traditional finance people, and governments on his side. That's a lot to offset once it is in motion. If anyone can pull it off...."

"Did you know he had me assassinate the opposition leader in Venezuela?"

She laughed. "No. I heard on the news that he went missing and that there were stories he was killed... I'm not surprised though. To the Old Man, a country in distress is a potential resource — something to be plundered."

"He was worried that Herrera might stage a successful coup."

"That's a reasonable concern. The way things are going, almost a certainty. And of course, he asked you to solve that little problem. But if you are through pretending his agenda matters, why did you do it?"

"That's got little or nothing to do with The Phoenix. He asked me to take care of it and it was no big deal."

"Okay, play that game for the moment. But if that's all there is to it, what's the problem? You didn't come here for a drink."

"The problem is him shitting on my plan."

"Your plan? I didn't know you had one."

"I'm going all in on the smart cities as the future."

She laughed. "Won't all that surveillance make it harder for you to run your little missions? I know that the advent of biometric data for identification has slowed you a bit."

"Slowed me?" He laughed. "Not at all. We've just had to improvise and learn new ways. That's always the case."

"So how do smart cities help you?"

"They don't directly, but they will have consequences that are going to create new opportunities for me and you."

The Scotch suddenly tasted better. Anna let herself feel a moment of satisfaction. Nikolaj was admitting he needed her for support and was selling his program to her. "Tell me more."

"The way I see things, all this global organization and power consolidation stuff the Old Man is fixated on, the one-world fiat currency, is complete bullshit. And never mind a global government. The reality is that with the tech that is emerging daily, the nation-states are being pushed to collapse. The rich, the large corporations, are tired of paying for services they don't want or use. They are tired of supporting welfare states."

"That's old news."

"The advent of smart cities, as they realize their true potential, will break the national governments completely. They will have the ability to offer the corporations, the rich, what they want from governments, without the overhead. They will be willing to band together, giving up sovereignty... just as countries joining the EU are doing."

"Which is what the Old Man says will get them to accept global government."

"But this will be a movement to downsize. The reason the nations are failing is that they are too big and trying to be all things to their growing populations. The smart cities won't have a place for people who aren't productive, who can't afford the price of entry."

"But the cities are within the sovereignty of nation-states."

"They don't have to be. And that's where this is heading."

"Independent cities?" Anna grinned. "Like Ancient Greece?"

Nikolaj consider the idea. "I suppose, somewhat like that. And each would offer its own version of freedom, or at least protection, at a fixed cost."

"How can a city offer protection? It can't raise an army."

"There's no need for armies in an information-based world. Everything of real value is moving into the digital world. You can't invade that; you can only hack it and governments are woefully inadequate at providing that kind of protection."

"But if there are physical enemies, maybe gangs who want to loot?"

"A small group like mine is far more effective for those things. If you look at the wars that are still being fought, the trend is already toward fewer soldiers, more drones and technical weapons. And even there, they'd do better if they sent in even fewer, better trained specialists."

Anna laughed. "The economies of scale for war are failing?"

"What do your clients really want from a government? A safe haven. And increasingly The Physical aspect is simply a place to put servers, not office buildings. And what if there are entities that offer that service but don't tax residents… a straight fee-based service? You park your treasures here and we will protect them. If they get complete protection and the freedom to operate as they wish, are your clients going to care if the provider is called a government or a service organization?"

"Not really."

"That's the future. Things are going to explode. It won't be pretty."

"And you want in on the ground floor."

He smiled. "I do. We can offer our services to the service providers."

"Our services? What do they need from us?"

"When there is no government, companies will want to outsource protection from aggression from outsiders; they'll need sophisticated technology to maintain order inside their locales."

"The smart city tech …."

"And we tap into the data. We stay on top of the changes."

"That's ambitious."

"Not any more than the original plan of a one-world government with a single currency. That model is clumsy, awkward. With ours we co-opt everything. We hire the best techs and make over the world in a free-market model. We will have people begging us to let them join in creating and using our systems and we can ensure we have complete control of all the large-scale projects. Your clients can access portals that will let them know what people want as soon as they want it; we will know what pleases and upsets them, and what they intend to do about it, and where and with whom. This is the new espionage — complete oversight, instant information; this is the new road to total political power."

"Ambitious," she said again, "but possible."

"We have a window of opportunity."

"And you want to crawl through it and take control."

"And you aren't ambitious? Since when?"

Sometimes she worried that he knew her too well. "A step like that... going around the Old Man could be dangerous," she said, calmly. "Mitch Childer broke ground going down that path and failed. Even though he had permission, his failure cost him his life."

"That's why rule number one is 'don't fail'."

"It isn't just the Old Man's disapproval to worry about. My clients would not appreciate being directly involved with any serious tampering with global payment systems, for instance. And it sounds like you intend to do a lot of tampering."

The green-eyed man laughed. "Fucking with global systems is what your clients do best. They compromise cybersecurity to get the data they use to create targeted ad campaigns; your corporations help governments hack elections; hell, we've stolen money for the war chest from the SWIFT system and blamed it on the BRICS countries ... what haven't we taken a shot at? And now, I see an opportunity to seize the reins, to take charge of all of it. This is a historical moment, and governments and your clients are all fumbling it. They are missing the key point. Technology is changing too fast for them to understand it even when it's their own tech."

"How does that help us?"

"Until now, we've always used the Hegelian Dialect: Problem-Reaction-Solution."

"We have?"

"Sure, it's almost a cliché... we create the problem and then, when things get crazy, we provide the solution — our solution."

"So, what changes?"

"Now we move aggressively. We insert ourselves into the changes, the solutions we offer. That lets us own the somewhat less-than-brave new world that is emerging. We can be running everything ourselves, not directing the actions of the ones who think they are power brokers. We can be the power directly."

His passion amused and surprised her. "What do you need from me? Most of my clients are already pretty much on board with the idea of rigging the game. They'll work with the IMF and World Bank even though they know we own those groups, but there are limits. They already get bad press for being global companies that screw national governments out of taxes. This would be blatant."

"For the time being, all we need is their influence. I want the big corporations to assure the World Bank and IMF that they'll sponsor our programs even if the banks oppose them. We might ask them toss in a few dollars here and there to make the smart cities happen."

She tipped her head and pictured what he was asking. "I can promise that they'll go for that much if it gives them some influence on what that involves."

"For Mumbai, getting things rolling, I need you get me the public support from some of your clients and some specific participation."

"What industries?"

"Start with smartphone networks and the phone manufacturers," Nikolaj said. "Can you bring them on board?"

The idea made her chuckle. "That's a piece of cake. Telecomm companies are dead easy. Whoever becomes the key provider can bundle proprietary technology into the program. Then, when other countries and cities implement a cloned program, they'll own the market. What else?"

He nodded in the dark. "Mass transit is a problem for Mumbai. The project's success hinges on effective mass transportation, and I understand the Old Man is pressuring your light-rail manufacturer to pull out of the project. I want them to stick with it."

She winced. "That was a hard sell to begin with... they were asked to do it for cost and all they get is good publicity."

"And an exclusive for the next cities, this time at a profit."

She smiled. "The current CEO might need to step aside to ensure they don't fold."

"We need to make sure they are committed."

She heard the steel of determination in his voice. "Are you telling me to play hardball?" She was teasing him. Of course, that was exactly what he was demanding.

He licked his lips. "I want you to put their nuts in a lemon squeezer and make them do exactly what we want. If things get rough, I don't want them to have the option of backing out."

That was exactly what she expected and had been hoping to hear. It fit well with her own plans, and Nikolaj was a formidable ally. "I can arrange that."

"Soon," he said.

She considered it. That gave her a number of opportunities to make bank in the stock market. She finished her drink. "The Old Man will be furious."

Nikolaj nodded again. "You ensure we have a major player in mass transit; get a light-rail system in place and leave the Old Man to me."

She smiled and refilled their glasses. "Then it's outright war."

"Soon it will be. For now, it's more of a covert operation."

"It had to come to that, eventually." The Old Man and Nikolaj had been crossing swords more often lately. She wondered if the Old Man was losing his grip. He was definitely locked into his old-school plan, and everyone saw that Nikolaj was more in tune with the times. "Fighting with him will still be risky. He has the banks..."

"I'm not going to fight him on his turf. I'm not a politician. But I'll make sure that his allies have scraps to fight over when I've taken him out. That will keep them busy. They'll fight each other to replace him."

"I'm looking forward to seeing what that looks like." She touched her chin, wondering if Nikolaj was intending lethal force. "We will need the banks."

"We will make them want to be on our side. A lot of the younger members haven't been happy working in the Old Man's shadow."

"Okay," she laughed. "No more details."

Imagining what she needed to do to carry out her part of the scheme made her blood grow hot. A tremble of excitement ran through her at the very idea of breaking the Old Man's grip.

It was times like this, Anna thought, that she lived for; these moments made life delicious. Just like courting danger to shoot the rocks to round the island first — a total rush. Nicky's new game promised to be far more thrilling than running the narrows in the race.

Whatever went down was going to be serious shit, and when it hit the fan, the adrenaline surge was going to be orgasmic. She'd be there in the middle of it. "Okay, I'll get your fucking train donor. Let me know what else you need."

He raised his glass and looked into her eyes. Even in the darkness, it seemed that he could see into them. "You love this," he said.

Anna realized she'd been holding her breath. She let it out and felt her tension melting. "I've been waiting for it a long time."

He raised his glass. "To old times."

Seeing him like this, thinking of the old days, the more dangerous times that had accompanied her rise to her current position was sexually exciting. Nikolaj knew her too well.

"While you are here, I want to talk to you about Mateo Chatzi."

"The contractor? Beyond the fact that he's a thief? The Old Man wanted me to check him out. He thinks the guy is stealing."

"That would be his biggest worry. My problem with him is that he sits on the boards of directors of several corporations. I've learned he is selling off large amounts of stock in those companies — my clients' stock."

"Cashing in?"

"It doesn't seem to be some big scam. There isn't any significant insider information. I did some checking, and he doesn't have any large debts coming due, and there's no reason to think any of those stocks will drop. My clients are nervous. They think he might know something they don't."

Nikolaj chuckled. "The Old Man has had him working on some renovation projects in Greece. Of course, he's been skimming, and maybe he knows the Old Man is onto him. He might be trying to go underground."

"Is whatever he is screwing the Old Man out of big enough he couldn't talk his way out it?"

"Probably not. That's troubling."

"If he disappeared, that would unsettle things for my clients. It could trigger investigations looking for insider trading schemes. That alone would trash their stock."

"I'll look into it. You're right about Mateo — he's nothing but an old-style crook. He has no loyalty to the Oculistica; he works for the Old Man. So maybe this is good. If he and the Old Man have a side project going …."

She laughed. "Catching them pulling something on their own would suit you to a tee."

Nikolaj leaned back. "Me, Anna? I'm just a former mercenary who manages the enforcement arm for our group."

Listening to him talk, her brain floated in memories of him. "That expensive suit doesn't hide that you are a brute."

He smiled. "I can remember a time when you didn't seem to mind me being a brute or wielding a firm hand."

She hoped he couldn't see how she trembled slightly as she refilled their glasses. "No, I didn't. I was young and inexperienced."

"And now?"

"You took care of the lack of experience. You indulged yourself with me."

"And we both found it exhilarating."

She couldn't deny it. "That was a different time, and we were different people."

"And now, as a powerful woman in your own right, you can assert your uncompromising nature and dominate that young man below decks."

His take on her situation amused her. They were dueling, as they always did, but there was an odd comfort in having Nikolaj as her opponent. "Oh, is that what I'm doing?"

Nikolaj took a long sip of his drink. "Seems so. One thing that I think you learned from me was that you preferred being the one in charge. You found that delicious. That girl in Madrid ...."

"Never mind about her."

He grinned. "Making your stud wait patiently for you is part of it. What good is power if you don't exercise it? You know you can make him want you like he's never wanted the young girls on the beach."

"You are a little too clever at times, Nicky," she said, then chiding herself for falling back on a pet name. "But you are right. The woman I am now enjoys having men doing her bidding. It is satisfying to have a young stud wanting to please me. Of course, men like that tend to be arrogant and headstrong — they require the proper training, they need to learn their place, which is patiently awaiting my instructions. The most desirable of them can find that difficult. It is a challenge."

He stood and drained his glass. It was his way of ending the talk. "Fine, Anna. That's your business."

"I've heard that Osk rather enjoys your crude attentions."

"She does seem to." He didn't sound surprised that she knew, but then, for both of them information was their lifeblood. "She enjoys a variety of 'experiences.' Just this evening, I left her ashore in a rather compromised and painful situation that will make her glad to see me return. When I get back, she will beg me to do some things I suggested earlier, things she was reluctant to enjoy." He looked into the darkness. "So, if you are sure that you understand your part in the drama that is about to unfold …."

"Oh, I do, Nicky."

"It is going to get dangerous quickly."

She laughed. "We both know that you wouldn't bother with any of this if you didn't think it would get dangerous."

That stopped him for a moment, then his smile flickered. "Then, I will leave you."

Anna heard a small outboard starting up and smiled at the classic scene playing out. Nikolaj was no romantic, but he loved intrigue.

Standing up so that his men could see him and emptying his glass would be the signal for them to sweep in from the darkness and pick him up. Their timing had to be impeccable. Nikolaj was fanatical about timing.

She raised her glass. "I think we have a good understanding of our roles… as vague as the goal might be."

"We know that verbal agreements on the dynamics of our organization are always subject to interpretation," he said. "It has to be that way. I'll let you know when I learn what Mateo might be up to."

"Seeing as you are in bed with Interpol," she teased.

"Fucking the Viking bitch is a matter of sheer pleasure," he said. "However, she can be useful for business in a number of ways. I have much better resources for intelligence."

A hard-bottomed rubber Zodiac came alongside at the boarding ladder and Nikolaj walked over to it. The two men sat forward and aft, clutching FINAL OFFER's railing as he climbed down.

"Enjoy your young man," he said. The engine roared, and they sped off into the darkness.

As the dinghy's wake slapped against the hull and the yacht rocked, she heard a sound. Turning, she saw Jock standing in the shadows of the hatchway, looking at her. He was naked, and in the dim glow of the masthead light, she found the sight of his aroused body delicious. "I intend to do just that, Nicky," she whispered.

She let herself think about the dangerous waters Nikolaj was steering them into. It would be a high-stakes and dangerous game that promised to keep her excited for a time.

Jock was a lovely toy and she would indeed enjoy him. But for the moment, she wanted to sit in the dark with her drink and evaluate the situation. The task was formidable. Doing what Nikolaj wanted meant finding the inevitable weaknesses, the chinks in the armor of her targets and exploiting them ruthlessly.

The prospect was just as heady and exciting as having sex with Jock, having him please her. She looked at him, allowing herself to admire his body.

"Go below and wait for me," she told him. With a nod, he disappeared down the hatch. Anna hesitated, wanting to savor the glow of anticipation of the things that now built up like black clouds on the horizon. Sailing was good; sailing in a squall, pushing the rigging to the limit made life good. And Nikolaj was definitely stirring up some kind of storm.

This had been a good night and was going to get even better. She'd been sad that she had to leave her boat on Monday and return to work, but now... she knew the weeks ahead were going to be challenging, but it was the kind of challenge she lived for.

CHAPTER II

SEAT MATES

"If you don't know where you are going,
any road will get you there."

— Lewis Carroll, *Alice in Wonderland*

Fort Lauderdale-Hollywood International Airport
Broward County, Florida USA

For reasons that are uncertain, although that must have something to do with its location (north of South America and near to Miami), Fort Lauderdale serves as a major hub for frequent low-cost flights from the US to Central and South America.

When he arrived at the airport Joshua Raintree was thinking that this area, whether you liked it or not (and he couldn't tell if he did, given that all he saw was the airport) offered the charm of being able to say: "You can get there from here." It wasn't anywhere he'd go otherwise.

For his first trip outside the United States, he was cautiously testing the validity and value of his new passport. Every time it was examined and handed back to him, it seemed like a major victory — and a relief. Things were going well. So far, he had successfully relocated his existence, presumably along with his luggage, in an awkward stepwise fashion from Wichita, Kansas's Eisenhower airport, to Atlanta, Georgia. Then he'd gone on to Fort Lauderdale — all in less than five hours.

Now he was having an overpriced celebratory drink in a sports bar near the gate where his flight would depart for Quito, Ecuador.

And after that?

Nothing came to mind. Past the departure time listed on his boarding pass, he had no particular timeline. He'd deliberately refrained from making plans and had little idea what would happen once he got on that plane. There was nothing but the irresistible desire to follow his bliss and see where that led him. He wanted to embrace a sense of total aimlessness, wallow in purposelessness.

And yet, he had glimmers of vague intentions. Visiting Colombia held an allure, but exactly when he might point his nose in that direction was an open question. There was a deliciousness in not knowing. For the first time, his life was his own and it felt — magical.

"Why didn't I do this years ago?"

He had asked himself that simple and obvious question several times on this trip. With each step toward the unknown, with each flight that carried him away from the old and toward the new, he felt less visible, less trapped.

Nothing had actually changed, of course, but emotionally he was on a high.

He watched the other passengers coming and going and let himself wonder about them idly. They were a wonderfully eclectic group: well-dressed men and women of all sorts with wheeled carryon bags buying water and snacks for their next flight, sometimes grabbing up a magazine or book. Others in shorts and polo shirts or tee-shirts and backpackers in jeans huddled where there were electrical outlets, competing for electricity to recharge phones and laptops while making calls and watching movies. Rabbis and priests mixed with turbaned Sikhs. He even saw a saffron-robed monk, a short man with a shaved head and an odd smile.

They were all beautiful today. It was glorious.

Wanting to be comfortable, Josh himself had chosen to wear jeans and a tee-shirt but topped it with a sport coat. He had a small carryon that held his laptop and had checked one bag. Besides the clothes he wore, every material thing he owned was in that checked bag. The heady and delicious thought of that made him feel free as he'd never felt before. He was self-contained; nothing pulled him backward and the direction he had decided to call forward was still vague and undefined.

Beyond staying in Ecuador for a time, and then visiting Colombia, he had no plans at all. Along the way there would be things he needed, things he wished he had brought, but that was fine. He'd enjoy making do, finding what was available wherever he found himself.

To celebrate his escape, Joshua had splurged on a first-class ticket; when the call came, he was among the first to show his ticket and claim his window seat in the first row.

His pulse raced. Now the adventure truly began. At the moment the jet's wheels left the ground, that was the instant he'd really be abandoning his old life and starting fresh.

As he settled into his comfortable seat, a lovely redhead stopped to put a bag in the overhead compartment above him. Then she smiled at him. "Hello," she said as she slipped into the seat next to him.

As she fumbled with her seatbelt, he looked her over. It was a chance to evaluate her without staring rudely. His guess was that she was in her late twenties or early thirties. As she smoothed her skirt, he took in the lines of her nice figure. When she snapped the belt securely around her and turned to look at him, smiling, he saw sparkling green eyes and caught a whiff of delicate, intoxicating perfume.

Suddenly the four-hour flight to Quito showed additional promise beyond getting him out of the country.

"Welcome to the first row," he said, chuckling. "It's the best seat in the house. I'm Joshua Raintree."

"Tricia Campbell," she said.

A flight attendant offered them a drink. Joshua was pleased when she ordered a Scotch, as he did. She was friendly and not uptight. Another good sign.

"Are you a businesswoman?" he guessed.

"Actually, yes. I'm a lawyer. Mostly I work as an independent consultant."

"Consulting on…?"

"Expatriation," she said simply. "I help people move abroad. You?"

"I'm moving abroad," he laughed. "But I don't have a consultant. I'm a wayward, although reasonably successful, financial advisor, who recently refocused his career on easing the pain of the too-visibly rich."

"Ah."

"Ah?" He smiled and waited.

"Your choice of words: 'Too-visibly.' Being rich is no crime."

"And yet, trying to hang onto wealth often attracts unwanted attention from both official and even less savory quarters. Avoiding that attention skirts certain gray areas of the law, as you know, counselor."

"Does it now?"

He smiled at her evasive reply as the flight attendant handed them their drinks with a napkin. "You tell me."

She smiled back, acknowledging the unsaid. "Perhaps we are in similar lines of work; we just offer alternative solutions."

He frowned. "Does that mean we are competitors? I'd hate to think that we couldn't be friends."

"Not competitors. My services help corporate executives assigned to overseas posts."

"They need a lawyer for that?"

She laughed. "There are other clients who move themselves. And they just might do it to reduce their visibility."

"To the tax authorities."

She raised an eyebrow. "Among others, savory and less so."

That she echoed his words pleased him. "So, our customer base overlaps."

"I suspect we offer similar, yet quite different outcomes to specific segments of the market."

"The market of the too-visibly rich."

She raised her glass. "Exactly."

"And how does that work? How do we offer different outcomes?"

"You perform financial handwaving to make your client's wealth less visible, less official — nontaxable."

"And you?"

"I relocate them to places where the taxes are less onerous, or even nonexistent."

"So do I, it's just that my clients don't have to move."

She laughed. "I suppose that's true. My clients tend to not want to have to worry about the bookkeeping tripping them up. Relocating is a way of breaking free of you home country's tax regime."

Except for the focus on taxes, that was exactly what Joshua was doing, except that he hadn't found a specific destination. "How about the exit tax?"

She frowned. "That is always a challenge."

"Not for my clients," he said, thinking it sounded more boastful than he'd intended.

She cocked her head. "What then? Clever accounting and application of various tax loopholes are the only tools that I'm aware of," she said. "If you know of other things, or have some idea..."

She was trying to find out if he knew something she didn't. That was nice, even flattering. "If my clients want to relocate, they can take their wealth with them easily enough."

Tricia started to say something, then stopped.

"What?"

She scowled. "Did you see the story on the news last night about them arresting someone who was carrying cash on a flight out of the country?"

He nodded. "I did. Seems the woman was treasurer for some political group and was carrying twenty-five thousand dollars. From what I heard, it wasn't the money they objected to, but that she didn't declare it."

"There have been cases where people declared money and it was still confiscated. The government's powers keep expanding and aren't always logical or fair."

He shook his head. "It's stupid, anyway. I don't see why you should have to tell them how much money you have with you."

She gave him a thin smile. "Because it's the law and says you have to on the form?"

"Forms," he snorted.

"The problem is that there are forms and then there are forms. For instance, when you sign a form saying you won't hold an event coordinator liable if you get hurt bungee jumping or whatever — those are worthless. They are intended to keep you from suing. In reality, a person can always sue — the disclaimer has no legal power. But they fool people. Other forms, however, are significant and filling them our falsely constitutes lying under oath."

He shrugged and looked out through the scratched plastic window. An empty baggage cart skittered away toward the terminal like a startled centipede as the plane began backing away from the ramp. They were moving. His adventure was truly beginning.

"Well, I'm going to be out of all that now."

Talking with Tricia, he'd ignored the background chatter of the captain and flight attendants welcoming them aboard. Now he heard the familiar messages, this time repeated in Spanish. It was a pleasant reminder that he was not only heading away from his old life but finally leaving the country, going where people spoke another language. He was going to a new and different world.

Remarkably, he realized that this was the same excitement he'd felt when he first learned about cryptocurrency. The information had opened a door to a rabbit hole. He stepped through and into a world that redefined money. It was an actual thrill, and the world he knew offered damn few of those.

Now he glanced at Tricia again, taking in her smooth skin, small nose. It wasn't a gorgeous profile, but certainly one he wouldn't mind seeing beside him in bed.

He realized that she looked nervous, and it dawned on him why. She'd been probing with her questions.

"Don't worry," he told her. "I don't think anyone in Ecuador will care how much money you are carrying. If there was going to be a problem..." he tipped his head, "... it would've been with TSA."

She let out a breath. "How did you know?"

"The way you turned the conversation to that subject... and the concern I heard in your voice."

"It isn't cash," she said. "I didn't even realize, until I saw on the news, that a cashier's check was still a problem."

"The authorities consider it money all right," Joshua said. "And now, because they've created so many incentives for people to get money into other places, the government has grown concerned about capital flight. It upsets the apple cart that people are voting with their dollars, and voting for other places, taking their money out of the country." He tapped the form. "Those declarations are intended to discourage people and make it more difficult to leave with your own money." He grinned. "It's a strategy that worked for a little while. But they aren't keeping up with the changes."

"What do you mean?"

"Honestly, if you'd wanted, it's easy enough to fly to Ecuador, open an account and wire the money there. No harm, no foul."

"That's... in your terminology, too visible."

Joshua gave her an amused smile. "I see." He rubbed his chin. "I mean no offense, but are you under the impression that your cashier's check is untraceable?" The look on her face was delicious. Also, it told him that he and this lovely lady seemed to share much more than adjoining seats.

"I was hoping it threw up fewer red flags," she said.

"Not really," he said. "Not with the government paranoid about capital flight."

Her gaze was cool, level, calculating. He liked that careful appraisal. "Do you have a better idea?"

He nodded. "I do. Emerging technology conflicts with the old concepts about money. The rigidity of thinking about currency, money, has created a paradox," he said. "Probably more than one."

He took out a thumb drive and held it up. "On one hand, a government could argue that this drive represents currency. Yet it isn't money at all. It's simply data. But that data is exchangeable for goods and services, and so, in that sense, it is money. Yet, I can honestly put on the form that I'm not carrying money or any bearer bonds or anything like that."

"How?"

"Cryptocurrency," he said. "This is a digital wallet, yet the money doesn't exist in any physical space. Or rather it exists anywhere and everywhere, so my wealth doesn't move... it is simply wherever I am, wherever I need it."

Tricia made a little cluck with her tongue. "And how would I transfer money using that ... cryptocurrency?"

"You'd exchange your cash for Bitcoin, or some other crypto, and store it in a wallet. But the wallet isn't physical, it's just data and you carry that data with you."

"But if someone steals that drive you are up shit creek."

"Not really. Certainly not to the degree you are if someone steals your cashier's check. I have multiple copies of the data on that drive—as many as I need. If it's lost or stolen, I can use a private code to recreate the wallet later."

"But can't the thief access your money?"

He shook his head. "Not without my private keys."

She shook her head. "That sounds remarkable."

"It is." He enjoyed watching her face as she considered the possibilities. Her palpable excitement was, well, exciting, and the look in her eyes struck him as damn erotic.

"What's your schedule like in Ecuador?"

That stopped him. "My schedule? I don't have one."

"No meetings?"

He laughed. "I'm running away from home."

"Really? How does that work for business?"

He grinned. "I'm becoming one of those digital nomads you read about."

"Then I'm jealous. How long have you been doing that?"

He looked at his watch. "Around 83 hours now. It's going great so far. I think it's going to work out well."

"Wow, all that time — you must like it."

He ignored the sarcasm. "I definitely do. I totally control my schedule. My meetings are largely online; most of my clients are referrals, so I don't need to meet them physically."

"And why are you going Ecuador?"

"To see it. It's just the first stop on the grand tour. Later, I'll probably head to Medellin, Colombia for a while."

"Why?"

"From what I understand, it's got modern conveniences, lower prices than Ecuador, and great weather. But I thought that I'd check out a couple of other places on the way, get a feel for more of the planet, as it were."

"As it were."

"Ecuador has always intrigued me… I've read about life in the Andes."

"Do you plan to be there a while?"

He bit his lip, thinking. "As long as things are interesting." He let the last word hang in the air, wanting her to know he was interested in her.

But her mind was racing. "I wondered if you would be willing to spend some time teaching me about this new tech. Show me how I might use some of what you know? For a consulting fee, of course."

Or other considerations, he thought. "I might."

"Where are you staying in Quito?"

"Wherever I can find a room, I guess. I haven't booked anything."

"You are flying to a new country with no hotel reservation?"

As he nodded, he saw that his newly found sense of adventure appealed to her. "It's an adventure," he said. Her reaction amused him. But saying it out loud made it sound adventurous, so he decided not to admit that he simply hadn't thought of making a reservation. He'd only thought as far as booking this flight. After that, everything was unplanned, vague.

It even struck him as odd that he hadn't booked a room, but now it meant he could pursue interesting opportunities, like this lovely lady.

Happily, he was certain that his attraction to her was evolving from more than his sense of adventure. She was breaking out of her own life, just as he was. She was going in a different direction, coming from an entirely different place. But now their paths had crossed. Everything that was happening gave him reason to hope that this delightful lady might be receptive to having an affair with him. That would be a grand way to begin his adventure, his new life.

"I'm staying at the JW Marriott in downtown Quito."

That she volunteered that information pleased him. It suggested he was right, so he smiled. "Impressive."

His teasing made her blush. "Well, I know little about Quito, but I was told it's convenient for the meetings I have scheduled."

"And probably very upmarket."

"As it has to be. My trip is about getting my clients resident visas and passports. That requires dealing with government ministers and lawyers. They'll expect me to put on a show. They wouldn't be impressed if I was staying in a hostel. That's the reality of representing rich people in my line of work."

"How much of a show?"

She wrinkled her nose. "I'm not sure what you mean."

"Will it keep you busy all day and night?"

"Not really. I have a few key meetings — a few lunches, and a few of the bigger ones for dinner and drinks."

"And, after you cash the check you forgot to declare, you use the cash to negotiate for some items, see if you can curry a little extra favor for your clients?"

She looked embarrassed. "It's a money-driven world."

"And that side of it is the more interesting part, isn't it? Finding out exactly what can be bought and paid for is intriguing." Like buying your own divorce.

"It is," she admitted, and he sensed a kinship was forming.

"And it's exciting because it's a walk on a wilder side."

"Like the song."

"Walking on the wild side takes many forms," he said softly, putting his hand on hers. He heard her suck in a breath, but she left her hand where it was.

The flight attendant came with their meal and they ordered refills of their drinks. When they finished and ordered another drink, he took her hand again.

"Tricia, I can probably help you figure out some new angles to accomplish what I think you are after. The financial stuff. To be effective, I'll need more information because the strategies need to be client specific."

"I appreciate that, Joshua, but I'm afraid I can't tell you the person's name or much about them. Confidentiality and all that."

"No problem. The person's identity doesn't matter, just their financial situation. What I need is a rundown of the situation and what he wants you to accomplish. I need to know his significant holdings, approximate amounts of cash, and what he's willing to liquidate. Then I can determine what is possible."

"For a fee."

"I've been known to work for room and board," he said. When she didn't react, he smiled happily.

The rest of the flight disappeared as they huddled in conversation. They stayed together as they passed through the perfunctory examinations of customs and immigration.

Then, with their bags on a cart, and with no discussion about what would happen next, they found the shuttle that the hotel had booked for her. Unconcerned to find there were two passengers instead of one, the driver chatted amiably during the twenty-three-mile drive into Quito from the airport.

They heard almost nothing the driver said. The moment they settled into the seat, he slipped an arm around her and she leaned against him. Her red hair was soft and fragrant and her body warm and arousing. She seemed as content as he to let things flow as they headed for her hotel, leaving unsaid that he'd be sharing the room, at least for a time.

Knowing so little about her heightened the erotic quality of the encounter. She was a delightful mystery, and he forced himself to not ask questions about her. He didn't want to know if she was married, where she went to school. None of that mattered.

Joshua had broken free so he could enjoy the moment, live in the present. This encounter was one to savor for what it was. Putting more weight on it than that might destroy its beauty.

And it was beautiful.

CHAPTER 12

A ROCK AND A HARD PLACE

"The trouble with the rat race is that even if you win,
you're still a rat."

— Lily Tomlin

Crystal City, VA
USA

In all the years he'd been going to the Methodist Church that sat right near Juan Garcia Park, and it had been more than thirty of them now, Claude Hoenig had always admired the pastor, Dr. Michaels. Although the good doctor was never a riveting speaker, Claude found comfort, reassurance in his simplistic take on Biblical principles.

He often thought it would be nice to live in the world that Dr. Michaels talked about and believed in. It wasn't much like the world he knew.

When he was at home, and not overwhelmed with work, he and Dolores, his wife, never missed a Sunday service. When he wasn't around, she went alone. She always went.

It amazed him to realize that in all those years he had never heard the man repeat himself. Even when the subject was the same, he found a new, simple and direct, take on his text. Revisiting a topic, he would dig deeper, or get his flock to think at a tangent. There was a skill to doing that, and he admired the work that must take.

That admiration caused him to listen respectfully, even when he disagreed with the pastor, felt certain the man was too much an idealist. Such hard work and consistency deserved his full attention. It was exactly like being lectured by the CIA director in the old days, he thought.

But today he found his mind drifting so much that it was a good thing there wasn't a pop quiz after the sermon. He couldn't for the life of him even remember what the subject was. Instead of focusing on the sermon, his mind had been elsewhere.

Normally he saw speculation as a useless exercise. Even today he thought it was, yet he couldn't help but wonder why the green-eyed man wanted to meet later today. Claude seldom dealt with him directly — the group never discussed what the man did, at least not with him. That was why he was interested in finding out what Turner could tell him about the man.

He'd know soon enough — Turner promised to get him the report on the man after church — in time for his meeting.

When the service ended, he went through the ritual of shaking the pastor's hand, thanking him for the sermon (taking a few cues from the comments Dolores made) and then stepped out into the humid, sunlit day.

Glancing across the street, he saw Turner standing by a nondescript Ford Taurus, dressed in a suit and looking as if he'd attended the service himself. Excusing himself, Claude left Dolores talking with the head of the Women's Guild about some charity event and crossed the street. As he approached Turner, his friend smiled and held out a thin manila folder.

"You could've come inside," Claude said. "I'm told sinners are always welcome."

"Can't manage that," he said, shaking his head. "Not anymore."

Turner's wife had been what Claude always called 'a serious Christian,' the kind of person who put religion above everything else. She and Turner had been the backbone of their church, a Presbyterian assembly that met not that far away from this church.

When she was diagnosed with inoperable brain cancer, she and Charlie turned to the church. They held vigils and prayed. Her end was slow and painful, and Charlie saw her pain, her suffering as a rebuke, a refutation of all he believed.

Once he'd put her in the ground, Turner refused to return to the church, and he severed his relationship with all the church members.

He rededicated himself to the CIA. There were stories of agents that he disciplined for saying, "God bless you."

Wanting to help, Claude had asked about his loss of faith.

"If God let that woman die... then nothing about that way of thinking makes any sense," Charlie said, sounding bitter. "But the work we do... that still makes sense. Cause and effect, action and reaction... that's what I believe in now."

There wasn't much a person could say about that. As a friend, he accepted it but couldn't help feeling sad when he saw Turner bury himself in work, taking on any job, regardless of the danger. Probably because he was so focused, he became a star and moved up the ranks.

He glanced back at the church. Not a soul was paying any attention to two men in suits talking by a dusty sedan across the street from a church. He opened the file and scanned it. "Any highlights?"

"One," Turner said. "And it means you need to watch your back. This guy is a stone killer. If that isn't enough, some of the people reporting to him, if the stories are true, make him look like a boy scout."

"That's just 'a scout' these days," Claude said as he flipped through the pages. "They let girls in now."

"I doubt anything would make him look like a girl... scout or not."

"Just want you politically correct in case the recording of our conversation gets released under the Freedom of Information Act."

Turner grinned at the tired old CIA joke. The thing was, Turner was right. Solid Turner was always right. This was the dossier of one scary motherfucker.

"Does this help you?"

Claude grinned. "It's always nice to know something about your dining companion. He and I are having lunch today."

"Reading that would give me indigestion," Turner said.

"He puts on a smooth, elegant show. I don't even think it's camouflage, just that he's a dandy. And I've worked with him before and know that he's sharp as a razor."

"And this lunch?"

"He asked to meet. He must want something from me."

"And you'll provide it."

Claude shrugged. "If I'm going to survive, I need to be on his good side, be important to him. He's becoming a significant player. So, if there is a war ...."

Turner snorted. "Becoming a significant player? That asshole has been the power behind several thrones that we know of. And that isn't a metaphor in his case. Recently, he's done nothing but gain strength and consolidate power. At the rate he's going, he'll soon own several small countries."

"How can one man be that big?"

"He's working with some of Europe's major crime bosses. Not bad for a kid from rural Belgium."

"From what I understand, he is working for the crime bosses, not with them."

"But he is doing their heavy lifting. Providing protection and muscle. So, who is the real power there?"

"That's a valid point. And you think he sees himself in a larger role?"

"Do you remember Mad Mike Hoare?"

Claude did. "The mercenary? Thomas Michael Hoare? The one who tried to overthrow the president of Seychelles back in ...."

"In 1981. He led fifty-three mercs into the country and got into a firefight at the airport there. Hijacked an Air India jet to escape. They had quite a little crowd of nasty people. They called themselves Ye Ancient Order of Froth Blowers (AOFB)."

"Sounds like a pub group."

"It should. They stole it from an English social club in the 1920s. Anyway, a young Nikolaj Romijn was studying political and military science in England when he met Mad Mike. Mike was there on a book tour."

"Proving that crime pays."

"Or, at least, that audacity pays. Anyway, those two apparently hit it off. Mad Mike became something of a mentor to our young killer. A year later, Nikolaj joined the Foreign Legion. By then it was a shadow of what it was in its heyday and he was disappointed, probably due to a lack of rape and pillage. After a tour in Chad, fighting insurgents as part of a European mission, he got bored."

"Well-trained and bored. Dangerous combo."

"Exactly. He turned his hand to applying his military training to more profitable and adrenaline-pumping work. At the time, he was a Captain. Apparently, he was the sort of man who inspired loyalty in his men, because when he left, he took his entire squad with him."

"They all deserted?"

"Depends on who you talk to. I got the impression that the Foreign Legion was happy for most of them to disappear, so they called it a mutually agreeable departure."

"He went freelance."

Turner nodded. "His early clients were some nasty people, some of the worst. He and his guys left a trail of blood that no one really wanted to follow. That money and an appreciation for tech from the beginning let him become a rather shadowy figure. As a result, we don't have much definitive on him since then." Turner laughed. "Matter of fact, I couldn't even prove in court that your guy is actually the man in this dossier. It's all tenuous."

"But you are sure."

Turner nodded again. "I know damn well that he's directed a number of operations and I'm fairly sure that he personally took part in several high-profile clandestine hits." He snorted. "The truth is that our side has used him as an outside contractor too."

"What?"

Turner looked embarrassed. "The needs of the moment — pragmatic patriotism. You know how that is."

Claude did. It was one of the seamier aspects of the agency's work.

"In terms of recent events, we know he provided muscle to help a man named Mateo Chatzi with what they quaintly call business expansion efforts." He smiled at Claude's puzzled look. "Chatzi is a Greek contractor with lots of political connections. We think that the Oculistica helped him out in return for him using his businesses to launder money. To make sure he was successful, your man helped convince a few competitors to accept early retirement."

"Sounds like a sweet arrangement."

Turner scowled. "Although Chatzi seems to have fallen off the radar all of a sudden. We don't know if that was his idea, or if he was disappeared over some dispute."

"It's a volatile business relationship, I'd imagine." Claude smiled and held up the folder. "I assume there is a price for your providing me with all this?"

Turner nodded. "Just keeping us up to date. If you hear anything about what happened to Chatzi or anything you think we might like to know, that would be lovely."

"I'll send you a summary of my meeting."

"Do it with the encrypted email. I reactivated your key."

"That was kind of you, not to mention thinking ahead."

"It was the least I can do for an old friend."

"Of course, once the project you are working on is in place, we'd appreciate learning that information about it flowed freely. We have our sources, but they are limited in scope and detail."

"Of course, in return, you will continue supplying assistance and information." The irony was delicious. Now Claude found himself an unsanctioned, off-the-books asset of the CIA.

"Not to mention money," Turner said. He nodded toward the church. "Now, I think Dolores is looking for you."

She was. As Turner got in the Taurus and drove away, Claude went back to the church, chatted a bit with other people, then he drove Dolores home.

"I have a meeting," he told her.

"Of course, you do," she said. "Even on the Lord's day."

"A colleague is only in town today," he said. "I didn't choose to meet on Sunday."

"A technicality," she said sternly. "You've always been lax that way. And you didn't just chat about Bible subjects with that Charlie Turner."

Dolores had made it abundantly clear that she didn't excuse Charlie from turning away from God just because his wife died.

"I have to make sacrifices to do good work," he said.

"Not by works of righteousness which we have done, but according to his mercy he saved us," Dolores said smugly. "Titus 3:5."

"Right," Claude said. Then he shut up, as he should have when she'd started in about Charlie. Dolores could be stuffy at times and, in his opinion, altogether too certain of the truth of her beliefs. A little uncertainty would have been appreciated.

After he dropped Dolores at home, Claude drove to Bob & Edith's Diner. During the drive, he turned over a single question that plagued him —what did this man want from him? It had to have something to do with the rift in the Oculistica. Otherwise, they had little to talk about.

Under normal circumstances, getting a backgrounder on someone dangerous that you were dealing with made you feel more confident. This time it hadn't done the trick. He'd always imagined that the green-eyed man was not someone to cross and now the information Turner had given him confirmed that the man was, as Turner said, plain scary.

He thought about the time he'd worked with the man in Tanzania. He'd come across as civilized and elegant — a man with extensive resources and a taste for expensive things. That is, until Mitch Childer, head of the IMF, had been beheaded. It wasn't hard to see whose hand had been behind that.

Claude had heard there was discord, that that the green-eyed man was standing up to the Old Man. For Nikolaj to allow any conflict to be known suggested there was an active struggle to take over. That changed the analysis, and the dossier reinforced his concerns. The man was totally ruthless and had no particular allegiance except to himself.

So far, Claude had found himself aligning himself with the green-eyed man. In the past, it had been simply a matter of them being somewhat alike, practical men who came to similar conclusions for their own reasons. Of there was a power struggle, he'd inevitably be asked to take a side openly.

Claude had no bone in that fight. Choosing the lesser of two evils held no appeal. If you were forced to pick a side in a struggle of Titans, it was smart to side with the most likely winner. The green-eyed man was, in Claude Hoenig's estimation, that person. He represented the first of a new breed that was quickly rising to the top of the food chain.

He was a ruthless killer with no conscience. There was nothing new in that, but unlike the brutes of the past who were manipulated by politicians, he was no fool and under no one's thumb. He knew how (and was happy) to leverage the emerging technologies as weapons — tools of control. Unlike the politicians that had been running things, he had no political agenda to encumber him. He could work with anyone and use anything, and his goal was control itself.

How the great public saw him, how they wanted to vote, what they wanted to call their form of government, none of that mattered. Not to the green-eyed man. Sovereignty, whether personal or national, was irrelevant to him. If he was in control, whatever illusions others had, they were welcome to them.

The idea of control with no philosophical underpinning, no ethics or morality, frightened Claude Hoenig as much as anything. He'd grown up a religious man and a patriot, steeped in the superiority of a moral country that protected freedom and was ethical. Years of spying had shattered the illusion that any country would remain morally superior, but he'd managed to retain his belief in a higher power.

But that was his personal god. Here and now, for the sake of the world, of his country, of his family, he couldn't ignore the rising power of the green-eyed man. Now the part of him that was pragmatic, a realist, caused him to join forces with this man, and now he'd have to see it through. Being on what he knew would be the winning side gave him the chance to look for opportunities and gain leverage. If he did it well, then he could provide some direction, some moral imperative to it all.

It was Nikolaj who had decided they should meet at Bob & Edith's Diner in Crystal City. "It's my favorite place in this part of the world," he said. "And I owe it to you."

Despite his affinity for elegance, it seemed that the man had discovered an odd love of American food. Claude had brought him there when they'd worked together before. The first time, it had been an experiment and a way to show him that he didn't feel a need to impress him. It had worked. The man had loved the restaurant.

When they finished their chicken fried steak and mashed potatoes, the green-eyed man wiped his mouth with a napkin. The genteel, almost delicate gesture charmed Hoenig, and he wanted to smile.

He resisted. It was best to play some cards close to the vest and not let others see your naked reaction or even notice that you were paying attention to details.

The green-eyed man put down the napkin and turned to business. "Park talked to you about the Colombian software company, I believe?"

"He did."

"And you bought it?"

"Lock, stock, and barrel." With CIA money behind him, it hadn't been a problem. Park had identified the tech this company was developing as essential to the Mumbai project. The small startup company, based in Medellin, Colombia was working on various aspects of associative learning – artificial intelligence systems that could find patterns in rapidly changing data. "They ran out of money for more development. I made myself their White Knight."

"Things are accelerating, and I need you to get them up to speed quickly," he said. "As fast as possible."

"I'm on it. My people are reviewing the status of their projects and some existing products they were about to release. We are looking at the way they fit into the smart city projects."

"Well, it needs to happen fast." The green-eyed man looked toward the counter, thinking.

"What's the rush?" Claude let his mind run through the various projects on his plate.

"Is there a specific timeline?"

Nikolaj shrugged. "No real timeline – just as soon as you can make it happen. The challenge is that the Old Man is trying to strong-arm the banks and corporations into backing off the project entirely. He's suggesting they are going to run afoul of some laws the Indian government passed to preclude dealing with fiat-to-crypto currency exchanges."

"How is that relevant?"

"It isn't, except in his head. You see, he intends to scuttle the project. He wants to convince the nervous Nellies that the government will declare the tokens used within the system a de facto crypto. With almost every government waxing hot and cold on whether it is great, but only if regulated, or it's inherently bad, or inherently good, it isn't hard to sow confusion. Never mind that, in this case, the people can't exchange the tokens for anything but city services or Rupees."

"I can push," Claude assured him, "but we need to take enough time to make sure we do this right. We can't afford problems like the ones we had in Tanzania."

The memory stung. It still carried the sense of lost friends and shattered ideals. Things had changed in Tanzania — that was when the crypto Claude had helped implement, a state-regulated digital currency, had failed spectacularly. Instead of carrying things forward, making the financial world more stable and faster, the crypto shrugged. Everything had collapsed.

"Yes, I agree." Nikolaj looked out the window. "The Old Man is putting us between a rock and a ... what is it you say?"

"a hard place?"

"Exactly. We need to get the project moving faster than we thought, faster than we'd like to. Every day we delay, every setback is fuel for his rants. We can overcome them, but he can make it even harder to achieve our goals. We need to backtrack and sell the backers on things they already know are true. They fear the Old Man and need lots of reassurance, and probably substantial bribes. So, we have to be cautious more quickly." He smiled. "That is possible, yes?"

Claude nodded. "Yes, of course, it is. It's just more difficult."

"No one said taking over the world would be easy."

He smiled, but Claude doubted he was joking. "Park is having trouble motivating the programmers in India," Claude said. "It's important that we keep them in the loop."

"Why not fire them and use your own people?"

"Politics." Claude sipped his coffee. "The Indian government has dug in its heels and insisted that much of the tech be developed locally, by Indian-owned businesses. They want the benefit of doing that work."

"Damn."

"I can break out the tricky part of the code and have them subcontract it to our Colombian company. Once I do that it will be easier to push it forward."

"So, Park can't control the Indian programmers?"

"It's difficult, but I'm going to talk to him about hiring one of my programmers, an Indian who needs to return home. He's done good work and could lead the project."

"Don't ask. Tell him to do it."

"That might help on another front. The software company, another Indian contractor, that is developing the facial-recognition software, is behind schedule. It turns out that the founder is old school chums with my programmer. I'm hoping he'll be able to dig his heels into the guy."

"That depends on relationships far more than I'd like."

"I'm not sure why they are behind schedule and I was going to head there and learn more, but if Ritesh, my programmer, is in place, maybe he can get it moving faster. Meantime, I'll go to Colombia right away. I'll need to hire more people and ensure they have the tools they need."

The green-eyed man nodded. "Yes. That is the thing to do." Claude found it curious how easy it was at that moment to see this man as nothing more than another hard-faced businessman involved in a business venture.

No one looking at Nikolaj would guess that he was a killer — a leader of killers.

Of course, most leaders ordered killings sooner or later and so did most patriots. Turner and Claude had both been there, in a situation that required ordering or executing assassinations. But encountering it in the private sector was unsettling.

Somehow it was easy to justify murdering people, rationalize it away when you did it to protect your country. But the green-eyed man was a mercenary who killed for money and power.

That was the difference between them, but Claude began to think it was a murky and self-righteous distinction. At the end of the day, their actions, the results were the same. It made Claude uneasy to think they might actually be more alike than he wanted to believe.

Now the green-eyed man looked at him. "Considering the time pressure we are facing, and the Old Man's absurd objections, what if you bought the facial-recognition software company? Perhaps, if you ran it …."

Claude swallowed. He couldn't appear to have unlimited finances. "We'd have to buy out the owner. The World Bank can't get into the software business, at least openly, and I'm going to have to invest more in Colombia as it is."

The green-eyed man simply nodded. "I had my people set up a dummy company to fund whatever you need. From the outside, it will look like a group of investors established an incubator for funding technological development. I'll send you the details. You'll be the president of it and have access to the money."

Claude considered it. "We can buy part of it if we need to. Owners of startups are often greedy."

"So, invest in the company to get them going. Buy more than half so we have control and see if they perform. If not, we will take over."

Hoenig thought for a moment. Courting a small company like that should be easy. Even though they had a contract with The World Bank, they'd be cash strapped. "I have to look. The Indian government will insist that over half is in Indian hands, but if the front company has an Indian arm ...."

"Good thinking."

"I'm sure the founder will be delighted to part with a chunk of the company to have money for development. If I lavish praise on the founder and make him CEO, I can make him think he's on his way to becoming the next Bill Gates."

"Consider buying the guy a new car for being cooperative. If he won't play along, then I expect you to break his balls."

Claude caught the cold undercurrent. It wasn't a joke. "Do you want to know the details?"

The green-eyed man smiled. "I know your reputation and trust that you will carry out my instructions just as well as you used to follow the directives of the CIA. You understand the goal and I don't give a shit how you accomplish it."

The level gaze told Claude he was being confronted. The man was putting all the cards on the table. Oddly, he found dealing with a man who should be his enemy an exciting proposition. As he said, they both wanted results. "Then send me the paperwork on your incubator, and I'll get to work."

Nikolaj held out a hand. "Excellent. Since I have my own fires to fight, I'll leave now and let you get to your work."

"I guess I do have a plane or two to catch."

As they shook, the green-eyed man said, "I like working with you, Hoenig. Unlike the politicians, you get shit done. You are like me in that way. Results are what matter."

The words, intended as flattery, sent a small chill through Claude. "I suppose so."

"I want you to coordinate closely with Park. I'll let him know that you and I are of a like mind. He can turn over the hands-on software project management to you and focus on his other tasks. We need him keeping the banks in line. Keep him in the loop, but as far as decision making goes, you and your various crews have a free hand. Just make this fucking project happen."

"I will," he said.

And he would. Nik's plan put him in a perfect situation. He would be knowledgeable about the smart city project, which didn't seem to be any sort of threat to American security. It was a testbed, a way of finding out if the technology would work citywide; they'd learn if they could truly create an internet of all things and if people would use it, accept it. If people didn't accept it, after all, it was rather pointless.

The work would keep him and his company at the forefront of everything going on that was truly significant. It would make him rich. Beyond that, owning the to-go firms for smart city tech, as well as fintech would give him insights into any global shifts of power.

All along the way, they'd collect data … tons of data. By providing technology to countries, giving it to them, they'd have access to so much that would otherwise be considered part of vital national intelligence and kept secret from everyone.

He could feed that data to Turner. Then the good guys would have it and be able to use it to predict and prevent terrorist attacks. With data from major cities, they could identify criminal behavior as it developed. With predictive algorithms, they could prevent crimes and ensure a safe and functional environment for everyone.

How could that possibly threaten anyone?

CHAPTER 13

ON THE DOCKS

"In a closed society where everybody's guilty, the only crime is getting caught. In a world of thieves, the only final sin is stupidity."

— *Hunter S. Thompson*

Improvised Dock
Near Lavrion, Greece
Attiki Peninsula

The slim German put down the bag of cement he was carrying, carefully stacking it on the one under it. He stepped back, noting that the bags below were at odd angles. He wiped the sweat from his forehead, realizing that the sloppiness annoyed him. The other workers didn't seem to care, but he did. It wasn't that much harder to align the sacks, and the results looked better.

But that sloppiness was predictable. The other men had no interest in doing more than the minimum required. He understood, even though he didn't approve of the attitude. These men had no interest in neatness. They were day laborers, mostly Arabs who were immigrants from Algeria, Lebanon, Syria, and Yemen, mixed in with a scattering of Greeks and others.

To a man, they were underpaid. Their wages were kept totally off the books and their very existence unrecorded. The bosses didn't care about them and they didn't want any EU bureaucrats who might snoop through their records caring about them either.

While the men were thankful to get any sort of work, they resented the situation. It seemed that they were being taken advantage of. The work was hard, and the conditions would make a safety inspector blanch.

The German said nothing about the sloppiness, the cavalier attitudes toward the work. No one cared what he thought. Even the burly and foul-mouthed Spanish foreman, Jose, didn't seem to care if things were stacked neatly. No, the boss's attention was on making sure that the materials that Franz and the other men unloaded wound up going on separate stacks.

Franz noted that there was some pattern to the way they directed the men to load some of the materials on pallets sitting well away from the bulk of the cargo. Normally, to be efficient, it would be a matter of piling things on one pallet and then the next. Or come code might link a particular pallet to a specific job site. Then, after the customs officials cleared it, a local trucking company would reload it onto trucks that would haul it to construction sites. A single stack made more sense.

But then he'd seen a lot that was curious. A little research determined that the ship was owned by a company that barely existed. That company was owned, in turn, by an agricultural company, that was owned, in part, by a Greek shipping magnate, named George Kallimasias.

None of that was a surprise to anyone, and scarcely a secret. Kallimasias was one of the major players in global shipping; he was described in official documents as owner, consultant or managing director of Commercial S.A. and Fairport Shipping—two large shipping companies.

Kallimasias and his enterprises, whatever they might be into, weren't of any particular interest to Franz or the man who had sent him. They didn't care what sorts of deals the shipping company was involved in. Who they bribed or what rules were broken didn't matter. No, Franz had inserted himself so that he could observe what happened once the cargo was delivered. He was there to see first-hand what happened to the cargo he was being paid to unload.

The first useful bit of information he'd uncovered was that he recognized some of the muscle. The crewmen were unarmed, but armed men were on board and under the direction of Jose. One of the men was a lieutenant of Mateo's, and that was significant.

Now, as they unloaded the cargo, Jose directed a straightforward percentage of each item into a separate location. His first thought was that these contained drugs, but he dismissed it immediately. The bags were identical — the separation was simply a numerical thing … Jose was setting aside a percentage of the materials. But for what … and for who?

Possibly all he'd discover was simple theft. After all, despite the economic troubles Greece was having, Lavrion was in the midst of a building boom. New boutique hotels and cafes were cropping up everywhere. Most likely the materials would be sold to someone building a house, or perhaps Jose had a project of his own going. Even here in Greece, it was easy to make a tidy profit on the construction of cheap apartments when your materials were free.

If so, Mateo was off the hook, and it was simply that the lieutenant was getting paid off.

"Are you on break or some shit, Franz?" Jose shouted at him in broken German. The grammar made his orders almost unintelligible at times, but the effort he put into trying to speak to Franz in his own language was worth a smile.

"No, I'm not on a break." He answered the man in fluent Spanish. It was a petty thing, showing his command of Spanish. That was vanity taking the stage, and not smart. Showing that he was multilingual made his cover of being a dock laborer a little sketchier, given that his accent was Castilian and flawless. Still, he couldn't resist letting the arrogant foreman know that he wasn't an idiot. Before Jose could think of something to say, Franz turned and walked up the gangway to get another bag.

Above him, sitting on the metal railing, a crewman in a greasy tee shirt and jeans smoked a cigarette and looked bored. In a larger port, the materials they were offloading would be palletized and a forklift would do the hard work. In one of the major ports, they'd roll everything on and off in containers.

But this port was a backwater and never intended for serious cargo. It didn't have the infrastructure to handle containers, so it had to be done this way. Oddly, the actual terminal wasn't far away, yet here they were, where the small freighter had tied up alongside the quay.

The crew put out the gangway. The laborers, most of them, including Franz. temporary help hired on the docks unloaded the cargo. They did it the old-fashioned way, muscling it one bag at a time out of the hold, down the gangway and to the stacks that awaited the next truck.

He understood that, too. It was actually efficient and covert at the same time. The amount the men got paid was almost inconsequential, but no one would complain. And, of course, no one would talk. Most of the workers were illegal aliens or people who couldn't get or didn't want regular work. Whenever a ship came in, the men would queue up, trying to get hired. Joining that throng had been easy.

With the high unemployment in Greece, there were always more willing workers than were needed, and Franz had been lucky to get the job. Jose had seemed suspicious of him from the start, but he was strong and young, and at the end of the day that was what he wanted and needed. Besides, the old adage says: "Keep your friends close and your enemies closer." It was a wise thing to do to keep the men you doubted right in front of you.

At the bottom of the ladder, he encountered a man sitting on the stack of bags. Franz's arrival startled him, and he jumped up and gave Franz an embarrassed smile. He'd been taking a break out of sight of the foreman.

"Break is over," Franz said in English. "Not that you took one, of course."

The man gave him a guilty smile, then shrugged, turned, and grabbed a bag of cement. "To work then." He tossed it to Franz, then hoisted another one onto his own shoulder, settling it comfortably. Franz shouldered his and the two of them headed to the ladder again.

As they went down the gangway, Franz nodded in the direction of the pile of materials that stood alone. "I wonder about the extras."

The man looked over. "Extras?" Apparently, he'd never paid any attention. None of his business.

"All that material we put aside. Do you ever wonder where those are going?"

"No. It doesn't pay to wonder," the other man said. "It isn't even healthy to wonder about such things."

Franz gave him a smile. "You're right. It's none of our business."

As they carried the bags to the main stack, an ancient green Mercedes panel truck pulled up, kicking up the brown dust. Two men got out of the truck and opened the side door. They went to the stack that had been set aside and began hurriedly loading the cement into the van.

Jose and another man wandered over to the van. Franz recognized the second man; he hadn't heard his name, but he served as Jose's flunky. As he watched, Jose said something, but the men with the van ignored him. Jose swore loudly at them in Greek, and finally one turned around. Jose handed him a clipboard. "I have to count the fucking bags as you load them and you have to sign for what you take," he said.

The men scratched their heads a bit and finally managed to sign the paper. "Just like real business," Franz muttered to himself. The man with him shot him a look. "It's either a convincing act or these thieves don't trust each other."

The man looked frightened. "Please, κύριος," the man said, using the Greek word for 'mister.' "Don't fuck things up. I need this work. I have a family."

"That must be hard."

The man shifted the cement bag drooping over his shoulder, then dropped it on top of the one Franz had put on the stack. "I couldn't leave them behind, so it is what it is."

Franz understood. Curiosity was a luxury an illegal immigrant couldn't afford. He'd be well aware that, given the nature of the people who ran the operation, snooping could be deadly. Franz knew that too, but he was being well paid to snoop.

His little subterfuge was getting results quickly. He'd already learned the first piece of what he wanted to know… that the rumors of Mateo's people skimming on projects were true. Now he needed to find out where the materials went and who was behind them.

While it wasn't clear that Mateo knew what was happening, Franz did now know that it was his crew doing the stealing. The information on the clipboard might give him a chance to discover who was the beneficiary of the theft. He'd come here to learn the truth, and it seemed unlikely he'd learn any more working on the docks. Now he wanted to get a look at that clipboard. At the very least, it might give him the answers to a few of the questions the boss would have.

He had an idea of how to accomplish that feat, but it wouldn't do to have any witnesses. He turned to the other man. "You better go back to work. Or, better yet, go smoke another cigarette out of sight somewhere."

"And you?"

"Me? I don't exist. I think perhaps it would be best for you to let Jose catch you fucking off this time. That way he'll know what you are nervous about and not ask too many questions."

The man's face brightened. "Good idea."

"And we never talked, right?"

"Never," the man said. "I never even saw anyone who looks like you." His eyes were thankful as he scampered back up the gangway.

Franz turned his attention to the green Mercedes. Jose was talking to the men; they'd closed up the van and were smoking cigarettes. Staying close to walls, he moved closer as Jose took a page from the clipboard and handed it to his flunky. "Put it with the others," he said. The man nodded and headed toward a shack that Jose used as a makeshift office.

Franz moved silently, circling behind the shed. The flunky dawdled, killing time, and Franz got there first. As the man stepped into the shed, he swung the door closed behind him; Franz ducked through before it shut and stood behind him. Unaware of his presence, the man carefully put the page in an inbox, slipping it under a small fragment of a concrete block that served as a paperweight.

Franz saw the man's shoulders tense as he began to turn around. As the flunky noticed him for the first time, Franz moved toward him, grabbing the man's jaw in one hand and cupping the back of his head. One arm pulled, and the other pushed, twisting his head violently.

Franz heard the expected snap of his neck and saw his eyes grow wide before he slumped onto the floor, a limp and silent corpse.

Stepping over the body, Franz went through the papers. They proved to be detailed records of the shipments — manifests that contained everything he needed to know about the operation.

At the top of the page was the name of the customer: Σπίτι του χρυσού.

He stared at it, trying to remember his Greek. It was something like "House of Gold." There was also a name he didn't know and an address. Franz took out his cellphone and snapped pictures of all the pages. He wasn't sure what all the information meant, but the boss would know. The green-eyed man always managed to figure out what was going on. He'd work out if Mateo was cheating, or if his men were.

Franz didn't really care. All he cared about was pleasing his boss. Nikolaj would be glad to have copies of actual documentation, maybe pay him a bonus. That was what mattered.

When he was done, Franz restacked the papers as he'd found them and put the piece of crumbling concrete back on top of them.

Opening the door a crack, he peeked out. From the doorway, he could see the men unloading the boat. None of them were looking in the direction of the shack. You never looked in the boss's direction unless you wanted trouble, and none of them wanted any trouble at all.

Franz picked up the dead man and hoisted him over his shoulder just as he had the bags of cement. Stepping through the door, he walked along the dock, away from the activity, until he came to a crumbling concrete wall. There'd been a warehouse here once. The paperweight probably came from that wall.

He dropped the man on the ground and gathered up bits of rock and concrete, stuffing them in the man's pockets. He removed the man's shoelaces and tied them around his ankles so that his jeans would act as a bag, and then undid the man's belt and filled his pants with sand. When he couldn't shove any more in, he redid the belt, pulling it tight.

Grabbing the man by his arms, he dragged him to the edge of the dock. He glanced around, seeing if anyone was looking. The pier was empty. He pushed the body off the edge and watched it plunge into the brackish water a few feet below.

His entry made a small, quiet splash that interested no one but a few fish, who flickered in, hoping for a treat. Well, this would be a nice treat for them, the hungry fish. The man wasn't useful for anything else now.

"Eat hearty," he said.

With his work finished, he turned away, walking away from the ship and following the dusty road into town.

Tomorrow he'd send in his photos and make a video report. In a day or so, maybe a bit longer, he'd be given a new assignment. He had no idea where it would be, and that pleased him.

Like the green-eyed man, Franz didn't believe in being in a fixed location for long. It made you vulnerable. The thought that they shared that one thing made him smile.

He was happiest when there was lots of work and he was going wherever they sent him; nice places and not so nice places paid the same. And it was the work he liked.

Franz enjoyed the variety, the uncertainty of his life. Being sent to different places and asked to kill different kinds of people meant that he was always facing new challenges. It was a rush.

Confronting new dangers made a man's blood hot. Although he'd never show it on his face, his blood was boiling now, and it felt good.

He wanted to savor the feeling… the arousal of several hungers and then the process of satisfying them. That was the reward for a job well done.

First, he'd have a long, hot shower and then a leisurely meal at a tavérna. He'd seen a couple of promising places nearby, places where he could eat and would be likely to find a woman to spend the night with him. Yes, he definitely wanted a woman for the entire night, and it was best, less complicated if she was a professional. He had plenty of money and was willing to pay top dollar for what he wanted… and she would earn her money.

As Franz walked through the cobblestone streets, heading for the small, inconspicuous room he'd rented, it occurred to him that he was a fortunate man. After all, in this insane and chaotic world, how many people truly liked their jobs and life?

CHAPTER 14

SINGAPORE CONNECTION

"Government, even in its best state, is but a necessary evil; in its worst state, an intolerable one."

— *Thomas Paine*

The World Bank Liaison Office
10 Shenton Way
MAS Building #15-08
Singapore, 079117

The office that the World Bank provided Park Dong Woo for the meeting was as modern as the idea of working in Singapore suggested. The tiny and prosperous city-state served as financial headquarters for many major companies from around the world. As such, it made perfect sense for the head of the Internal Development Association at the World Bank to have a presence there, even though the home office was in New York.

Despite its importance, the office wasn't located in the convention centers of power. This was deliberate, as it made it a perfect location for meetings like the one he'd arranged. There was little chance of accidental encounters with political or business reporters.

Not that the meeting would be secret. As a public figure, little Park did could be totally secret; trying to be secretive just piqued the interest of the media. Holding a meeting in Singapore to discuss operations was entirely business as usual… completely normal.

Normal… as usual these days, Park sat at the table and immediately found himself craving a cigarette. It seemed a travesty that he couldn't smoke in his own office.

He dropped the resume on his polished walnut desktop and looked at his visitors. Nikolaj waited patiently, Claude Hoenig, seated in a high-tech office chair across from him less so.

"I have to admit that this guy sounds perfect for the job," Park said. "That he's an Indian national certainly simplifies a lot of things."

Claude nodded. "I thought it might. It will make it easier for him to lead a team… they might resent an outsider, and he won't need a visa."

"I like it. The government likes us hiring Indians for their projects, so it's good politically." Park looked up. "And you are vouching for him, Claude? We need to be sure about this."

"Within reason. Working for me, Ritesh proved himself to be reliable, trustworthy, and a capable programmer. He isn't the most creative guy on the block, but you don't need that from him. He is a bit arrogant but will want to show his stuff and prove himself to you. For the rest… we can hire geniuses by the bucketful."

"So, he'll fit in?"

"If you keep in mind that he is what I refer to as a corrupt idealist, then you can be assured that he will move mountains for you."

The green-eyed man laughed. "Okay, that's a new Americanism on me. What the hell do you mean by a corrupt idealist?"

Claude folded his hands. "That's a person who will do everything he can to make something happen when he is convinced that he is working for the good of the many, while managing to ignore the fact that he is being paid handsomely for his work while his countrymen suffer in poverty."

"In other words, your typical non-governmental organization type," Park Dong Woo said.

Claude winced. "I suppose so. I expect that Ritesh would fit right in working for one of those NGOs, except they don't pay enough."

"Fortunately, we can, if he is up to the task."

"And he is. He's rather impressed with titles, so you can use that as well. And he'll follow you. With your double finance and IT degrees, not to mention your title, he'll look up to you and leave the visionary crap in your hands. He'll love being associated with a project like this and never ask a single question. Give him a fancy title and he'll be a real worker bee."

The green-eyed man snorted and made a face. "Why would such a smart guy be so pliable? Why wouldn't he care what the goal was? I mean, his name will be on the project too. It's going to be part of his resume." Both Park and Hoenig looked at him. He smiled and held up his hands. "I'm not questioning your judgment; I'm asking an honest question. I don't understand."

"He's a product of his time and place," Park said.

Claude smiled. "Right. He sees himself as part of an elite that is destined, even obligated to make the world a better place — but he hasn't any clear idea of what that means, at least beyond a better life for him and his family. As I said, he's no visionary. He needs someone to point the way."

"And yet you want him to lead the group?"

"Under supervision. He'll lead them to execute the tasks we assign him."

"Is he good enough?"

"Ritesh did brilliantly in school and while working for me. He also caught America's celebrity fever. We can use that."

"How?"

"Being in charge, even at a lower level, will appeal to him. He'll get to lord it over his friends and prove to his family that he is successful."

The green-eyed man laughed and shook his head. "That's one of your greatest exports, Hoenig, this concept of celebrity. It manages to elevate people in their own minds, validating them while eliminating the need for actual accomplishment."

Claude Hoenig winced. "True, up to a point." He didn't appreciate painting things in such stark terms. "Some celebrities do deserve their fame. And the point is that Ritesh sees himself as part of great things. He wants to be a mover and shaker who will change the world, which is exactly what this project is about. And the situation serves his personal needs. His family insists that he move back to India. The opportunities for doing great and noble things and earning big money are more limited. He dreads becoming a local hire, a low-paid cubicle drone. Without this job, that fate seems inevitable. His parents have arranged his marriage — his life."

"Making him a man caught between two worlds," Park said.

"And as good a programmer as you need for the project. He is creative enough to implement functional tech without thinking too much about its implications."

The green-eyed man pursed his lips. "And how soon can he be available?"

"As soon as we give the word."

Park chuckled. "If we decide today, my human resources people can get started on the paperwork. What do you think might be a good title for him?"

"It's your project," Claude said.

"Then how about Smart City Program Integration Chief?"

Claude laughed. "What does that mean?"

"I'll be damned if I know, but it covers a lot of bases."

"Nice," the green-eyed man said. "I just hope you guys are keeping this relatively quiet… not the Smart City Program, of course, but our involvement in it."

"We keep your entire existence quiet," Claude said. "So, not that it matters, but who are you concerned that we keep this from?"

"The Old Man," Park said. "He has his own plan, and he doesn't like this one at all."

Claude sighed. "Tell me, are we doing an end-run around the Oculistica? That wouldn't end well."

Park shook his head. "Not at all. This project has been in the works for some time. It's a matter of public record. We've written press releases on it. What we are keeping to ourselves is that members of the group..." he nodded at the green-eyed man, "... are promoting it and attracting corporate partners."

Claude shook his head. "Since I'm not officially a member of the group..."

"Just a useful colleague," the green-eyed man said.

Park frowned. "Forgetting the Oculistica's goals for the moment, and despite the Old Man's resistance, I have a job to do." He nodded toward the green-eyed man. "If I can have a little assistance and still have the World Bank and its official partners bask in the glory of its success, then I am happy."

"Some of that glory would come to you," Claude said.

"Yes. That's as it should be."

Claude smiled. "The fact that we work together," he said to the green-eyed man, "is why I suggested having Park's people hire Ritesh directly rather than involving my company directly in the India operations. If they hire him, he'll be on their payroll, but under our influence. That shouldn't raise any flags."

"Excellent."

Park nodded. "A perfect combination. Couldn't be better."

Claude picked up his briefcase and held up some papers. "There's an additional benefit to you working with Ritesh. He has some buddies in India, old school chums, that have a startup software company. My people are checking them out as possible vendors for the project. Of course, that's another place where the 'corrupt' part of corrupt idealist really comes into play. Ritesh can use his influence to help us get them on board and control them. If he gets them the contract, that will give him status with his old chums... and they, in turn, are connected, politically and through family and business. We get entrenched quickly. That means that, from the outside, this will appear to be pretty much as if it is an Indian government venture being executed for them by The World Bank."

The green-eyed man stood up. "Then we are agreed. Do we have what we need to proceed?"

Park paused. "For now."

"Good. Once we have momentum, even if our association with the project is suspected or sniffed out, by then we will be unstoppable. The benefits of the project will be so compelling that no one will care what they've given up or that the Old Man has his nose... what is it Americans say: 'out of its joint'?"

"Close enough." Claude looked at the green-eyed man. He alternately saw him as some sort of a cross between a philosopher and a thug — he managed to embody both. Claude had seldom known anyone who could bridge that gap.

Even though he came from the world of espionage himself, despite years spent with the CIA and knowing both stone killers and the moralists who killed out of conviction, he had never known anyone who had a foot so solidly planted in both worlds.

There was a compelling philosophical idea behind everything the green-eyed man did, and yet his execution went beyond ruthless. He could be thoughtful, strategic as well as tactical, yet the man would, and had, killed without any thought at all.

In some ways, he saw the man as a modern equivalent of a ronin — the masterless and dangerous samurai who, in the turmoil of ancient Japan, fought for the highest bidder. And yet, Nikolaj did have a master, or at least a cause. For many years, he had worked with and for the Retinger Oculistica and supported their cause.

In this complex world, that had put the mercenary and Hoenig, the ex-CIA agent and American patriot, on the same path, working together. Now he wondered what would happen if their causes diverged.

For the moment, Claude's own momentum put them in synch, opposing the will of the Old Man. This was a minor collision, and a small test of wills, but the possibility it could escalate was there.

The downside of relying on a great ally was that they could be an even greater enemy. Both Nikolaj Romijn and the Old Man were powerful and dangerous. A smart person wouldn't get caught between them. It was better to pick a side, and Claude's money was on the warrior, rather than the banker/politician. Even if the Old Man had ruled with an iron fist for a long time, the world was changing fast. Ironically, the warrior was adapting to the technological changes while it didn't seem the Old Man was keeping up.

Claude's own allegiance to the Oculistica was pragmatic. One thing that drove him out of the CIA was the idea that the leaders of his own country were straying from its ideals and no longer took the moral high ground. They no longer focused on the rule of law and protecting the people — things a younger Claude had been ready and willing to die for.

In its current form, the bloated government bureaucracy had taken on a life of its own and it placed protecting that new life on a higher plane than the lives of its people. It stole their freedoms to protect its own integrity. It was willing to sacrifice them to preserve a national government that was increasingly no different than any other government. The things he loved had been sacrificed for survival.

Claude Hoenig had played his own role in that shift. It had taken some time to learn that his own country was simply another player in the struggle for power; it had taken longer to decide that it was no better or worse than other governments. The Oculistica was likely not much different either, but initially, he'd seen the vision of a single, unified government as an admirable thing. Or a vision that could be admirable, if the world government had the right values and some sharp teeth.

That wouldn't stop atrocities, but it would prevent global wars and reduce the growing threat of extreme nationalism. It wouldn't save the world, but it would make it safer and more stable.

Although he was less certain now, on balance he still felt he was doing good. While Claude hated that he couldn't explain all that to Charlie Turner, because he was doing what he thought was right, he didn't think he was betraying the man's trust — or his country. He didn't think anything the Oculistica was doing threatened the US. It might seduce the people into handing over control, but that was what democracy was all about, right? If the will of the people favored a new umbrella government, then that would be an evolutionary step upward.

He was sure the Oculistica would win by stealth. They packaged things to get the world to hand power over freely. Some countries would inevitably resist, and Claude knew that when they did, Nikolaj Romijn was the might that would be applied — discreetly, selectively, at just the right points to take down the opposition or pave the way for the offered solutions. But that was no different from what he had done for his own country; taking out a few targets in order to avoid global wars was a fair exchange in his book.

Claude had worked with the man long enough now to know that he was focused and if you were on his team, a reliable ally. Still, when he took a step back, Claude Hoenig was intimidated by him. From his point of view, the proper technical term for a man like that, a man as ruthless and smart as Nikolaj Romijn, was 'fucking spooky.'

"So, we will make this happen. You need to call Ritesh to make the offer. He knows I forwarded his resume, but he shouldn't know that I was involved in the decision. He already knows that my company is involved in aspects of the project, and that's more than enough."

"Marvelous." Park put the resume in a small, black-wire basket that sat on the window ledge. "I'll call him today and fly him out here for an interview immediately." He grinned. "I assume his boss will give him enough time off to do that?"

Claude nodded. "I'm pretty sure that can be arranged."

"Another step," the green-eyed man said. He picked up his small leather-bound notebook and slipped it into his jacket pocket. "Now, I'm afraid I have some business to attend to."

Claude grinned at him. "You know, I could've sworn I saw Osk Barstad in the hotel this morning. At least, I thought it was her." He knew he had seen her. The question was whether the green-eyed man would admit to it. He did.

"Yes. She came with me to discuss some Interpol business. She is following up on a person of interest."

"Who?"

"Do you recall that Tanzanian woman who helped your old chum Wyatt Osgood escape from jail over there?"

"Rashmi Patel," Claude said.

"That's the one."

"From what I heard she was just someone who got swept up in his escape. I didn't think she was actively helping him."

"Nevertheless, she was involved. Now Interpol has reason to think she came to Singapore and there is no indication she has left. That's why, when she heard I was taking my jet here, Ms. Barstad asked to fly out with me so that she could follow up on that lead."

"I thought the charges against her had been dropped. Wyatt's too."

The green-eyed man nodded. "True. There isn't an active warrant for her arrest. But that doesn't mean she isn't still a person of interest to us."

"That episode is over," Claude said.

"Is it? In my opinion, finding out what she knows could be extremely useful. I doubt we completely understand that failure in Tanzania, and we certainly would like to learn who arranged the logistics of that little escape. How was it managed? All we know is that it was well coordinated, with the precision of a military operation. So far, we haven't identified anyone within the Tanzanian government who was in a position to do that."

That made sense. "So, you want to know who cared enough to go to such lengths to spring a couple of programmers?"

"Exactly."

"And you think she is here?"

"There are no hard leads yet. Interpol got some hits from facial recognition systems at the airport — Singapore is more advanced in that regard than some countries. Now Barstad is checking into those a little more closely, using feeds from other camera systems. Fortunately, Singapore is well equipped with digital surveillance. If she stayed anywhere in the city, we will find her."

Claude was tempted to ask if they had any hits on Wyatt Osgood. Wyatt had worked for him in what now seemed another life; he and Wyatt had once been friends, and possibly still were. And although Wyatt had crossed swords with the Oculistica, he hadn't done a thing to Claude... not directly. Perhaps they were friends who found themselves on opposite sides in a war.

No, they weren't opposite sides, just different sides. A war like this, where power was sought in the cyber world, would have many nuanced sides. Some of them would be declared and others would be undeclared causes being fought for. Wyatt had opposed the specific implementation of the project in Tanzania, not the fact of its existence. He'd been upset by the potential for the loss of freedom. But freedom and privacy were becoming the main casualties in the struggle to implement technological solutions to the world's challenges.

The Oculistica itself epitomized that very struggle. It was a group warring within itself. Not many of its members liked each other, but they shared a vision or at least parts of it. It was complex, curious, and at times, awkward.

And it was a small universe. If Rashmi was involved in things, Wyatt might be as well. They had escaped together. If Wyatt really had risked his life to stop the project in Tanzania, Claude didn't even want to think of his reaction to the goals underpinning this new interest in India's smart cities.

He wondered what he would he say to Wyatt if he were to run into him one day.

He understood what Wyatt, the idealist, hated about those projects, and he doubted that the man cared much one way or another about the existence of the Oculistica. He would oppose a one-world government in principle. To the Oculistica, Wyatt was a declared enemy. They left him alone only because they thought that with him on the run, they'd rendered him insignificant.

In Claude's opinion, that estimate might be optimistic. The thought made him wonder if he'd be willing to stand idly by if they targeted his old friend.

He had no idea at all.

CHAPTER 15

LEFT FOR DEAD

"The fear of death follows from the fear of life.
A man who lives fully is prepared to die at any time."

— *Mark Twain*

Quito, Ecuador
Medellin, Colombia
Hispania, Colombia

It had been a pleasant interlude in Quito. Joshua and Tricia wallowed in the mad and passionate novelty of an affair. They both had pent-up emotions that the trip freed them from.

While she was at her meetings, he wandered the city, going up Pichincha Volcano to lookout Cruz Loma on the *teleferico*, the cable car, eating world-famous ceviche at Jimmy's — a food vendor in the Mercado Central, and just letting himself fall into the new and different rhythms of the city.

When they were together, Tricia told him about her work and the changes she was making in her life. She told him how she was thrilled to be breaking new ground, finding out what it meant to be free of the constraints of her previous work and her marriage, and her conceptions about what life ought to mean.

In return, he told her about his world and its changes. He talked about his divorce and the way he'd found that segment of his work that he truly enjoyed and, in the process, found himself.

Along the way, he explained the thing that he'd found so many people never understood — that money was a fiction. A useful one, certainly, but more an idea than something concrete.

"Money is essentially trust," he said. "It's implemented in some form or another, usually tangible, like in precious metals or currency, but also less tangible forms, such as ledger entries for a bank account. But people forget that those numbers have no intrinsic value and their 'money' is only real as long as everyone agrees it is. Each form has advantages and disadvantages. Gold and silver can be protected but have to be stored and are less liquid. The less tangible forms are more elusive, which makes them better for transporting, and also for secrecy and privacy."

"I want to understand," she said.

"How much do you want to understand?"

She smiled. "Enough to make plans. Enough to use the information." Then, in detail, she explained the formidable challenge her client faced.

"So, the tax lawyer wants to become an anarchist," he laughed, teasing her. "You are challenging the government's right to tax them."

"I suppose I am," she said, relishing the idea as much as she did their affair. She'd gotten swept up in it, accepting it as part of her new life, as the way the new Tricia acted.

"Then you need to rethink having clients store their wealth in government-controlled creations," he said. "When you use their systems, it's hard for them not to know what you are doing. And, thinking long term, you should advise them not to put wealth in fiat currency in the first place. They need to learn to do business on the blockchain. The government can't monitor payments made with cryptocurrency; unless they use a centralized exchange, no one will know what their income or assets are."

"To do that, I need your help," she said.

"Yes, you do."

"And what a team we would make. I can come up with clients who need both our services."

The idea appealed to them both, and they began to talk about the possibilities of working together, considering all sorts of wonderful options.

But then, too soon, their time in Quito was over. Tricia had to leave. "I have to return to Florida," she said. "I've made some arrangements and need to work with my clients getting them new passports."

"When?"

She scowled. "I've been stalling. I should go tomorrow."

He nodded. "Then I'll head out to Colombia as I'd intended," he said.

"I wish …."

"I'll miss you, Tricia, but Florida holds no appeal for me. I made promises to myself that I intend to keep. Besides, you need to shed your husband, get closure on what you are leaving. Between that and doing your work, you wouldn't have time for me. And I wouldn't have your full attention."

"That makes me sad."

"You should rejoice. We are creating something new — each of us separately and as this team you imagine. You do need to go back — alone. Cut those old ties cleanly and start building your new life from the ground up. Break free of your marriage and focus on finding those 'special needs' clients that you need me to help with. I'll be developing financial options we can offer them that will expatriate their money. When you have a serious one, a big fish that needs what we can do together, maybe we can meet somewhere. We can plot and plan and screw our brains out."

Hearing his enthusiasm, Tricia could almost taste the future, the bittersweet flavor of what he was proposing. They would separate yet work on that future together, complementing each other's skills, energy, and passion.

Although part of her wanted to stay in Quito and continue the affair, she knew it would end, and sooner rather than later. Joshua was restless and neither of them wanted a relationship that dictated their lives. Now, having emerged from oppressive lives, they were both eager to step even further into the unknown.

This way, there would be the prospect of other marvelous times together. And now she was sure that she would find and enjoy the company of other exciting men as well. This sweet taste of freedom had proven addictive. In fact, as they were about to separate, she saw that one of the things that excited her about Joshua the most was knowing that although he cared for her, he wanted them both to be free.

"That sounds perfect," she said, knowing that perfect didn't mean easy. "I'll miss you... miss making love to you, but we need to move forward."

He began to unbutton her blouse. "And we still have tonight."

The next morning, as they dressed, he saw tension in her body. "You look worried," he said.

"Not worried, just thinking about being home again."

"What's the concern? Are you worried about your husband?"

"I'm worried about me. I'm not good at pretending and I can't imagine that I'll ever want to let my husband touch me again." She caught him studying her face, and she laughed. "Don't worry, I'm not suddenly in love with you. I hope we get together again soon, and that when we do, we wind up in bed, but what I'm thinking about... It's more that this affair, that having had sex with you, made me realize the wonderful possibilities."

"Then it's definitely time to make your move," he said. "Tell him as soon as you get home. Move out and get on with your life."

"I'll think about that on the flight back," she said. "I'll seriously think about it."

With much left unsaid, and so much unknown, they were about to follow their separate paths — paths that were now, somehow, intimately connected.

Joshua suffered the tug of mixed emotions too. Being rational, trying to look at things, his life, objectively, he was sure that a large degree of the attraction and excitement came from the remarkably spontaneous way their affair evolved. From the moment they met on the plane it had unfolded as if it was meant to happen.

He'd enjoyed her company, and the sex had been wonderful, but now it was time to move forward. And his next move hadn't changed. This had been a delightful side trip, but now he was back on his way to the city of Medellin. Nothing had changed about his desire to see it.

The next morning, he made his travel arrangements online and found an Avianca flight that went to Medellin via Bogota, avoiding the tourist center of Cartagena. Happily, it left not long after Tricia's flight back to Fort Lauderdale. So, after a breakfast from room service, they went together to the airport where he saw her off. They promised to stay in touch, then he went to his departure gate.

Once again, he felt that his trip, his adventure, his new life, was just beginning.

As if the remarkable adventure in Quito hadn't already made his trip a success, Joshua found Medellin to be everything he'd hoped for. He took to the city immediately. He took a room at the Hotel Laureles Loft in the Laureles neighborhood area and found it was an area of pleasant tree-lined streets and not much traffic.

The hotel was simple, especially compared to the lavish room at the JW Marriott he'd shared with Tricia in Quito, but he liked it. The charming staff provided a simple breakfast and coffee and answered questions, but otherwise left him alone. There was a grocery store down the street that also sold liquor and nice restaurants within easy walking distance, including one that offered Cuban cuisine.

It was a wonderful base for his explorations of the city.

In general, he found Medellin clean, as cities go. It was modern, with good infrastructure and friendly people. The costs of living were moderate. Overall, he decided it would be a good place, a cheerful place to live and a suitable base for his new operation.

Before committing himself, however, he decided to scout some outlying areas. The guidebooks talked about the picturesque rural areas, with coffee plantations and greenery. It was worth a day or two to find out if they might not be even better. A city held more promise, but there was something intriguing about being in a more rustic environment, and he was in no rush to decide.

Still, he felt that, unless he saw something spectacular, he'd return and set up his base in the city.

The places he wanted to see were some distance from the city and he saw several companies that had excursions, but Joshua wanted to move at his own pace. When a taxi driver approached him near the store, he spent some time talking to him.

"The coffee plantations," the man said. "You must see them."

They agreed on a hundred dollars for a day excursion to a place called Jardin. "You will like Jardin," the driver told him. "It's a beautiful little place. It's a long drive, about three hours each way. We can stop in Hispania for a break, have a coffee. That's an even nicer town in my mind."

That sounded like the kind of casual day Joshua wanted. The driver seemed friendly and spoke decent English, which would help. He gave the man his cell number, and they agreed that the driver would pick him up at his hotel early the next morning. As he was traveling light, he decided to check out of the hotel. He wanted to have the option of staying out in the country if he liked it.

As this was the slow season, the clerk told him he'd keep his room for him in case he came back.

It was still dark when Joshua stepped outside. A few minutes later a car pulled up. A big man got out and looked at him — it wasn't the man he'd made the deal with.

"Who are you?"

"I drive you," he said, stumbling over the words. He opened the trunk, scooped up Joshua's bag and tossed it in. Then he opened the back door. "You get in."

"You aren't the man I spoke to," Joshua said. He felt uneasy; had a sense of things being wrong.

"Manuel sick," he said.

"Why didn't he call?"

The man shook his head. "We go. See Jardin, Hispania."

Joshua considered calling it off. Last-minute changes were not a good omen and made him feel uneasy. On the other hand, this man had gotten here before daylight and was expecting to earn a day's pay, and he seemed to know the details of the arrangement. It would be strange since they couldn't really communicate.

"We go," the man said again.

He tried to think of the Spanish words he needed to tell the man he'd changed his mind. It just didn't seem like fun anymore, and maybe he could just give the man a few dollars for his trouble and send him away. Once things started going wrong, when the intention turned to shit right away, they seldom seemed to improve.

"*Muchas personas en el camino ya*," the man said. Joshua stumbled over his fast speech. He worked out that the man was talking about lots of people on the road. He was worried about traffic. "*Necesitamos ir ahora.*" He wanted to leave now.

Joshua balked. Even if he paid for the tour and didn't go, hell, the man would probably prefer that. But the man was impatient, swinging the door and Joshua's bag was in the trunk. Deciding not to upset the man more, Joshua got in the car.

His actions made him angry with himself. Being meek was stupid. He hated that his instinct was to try to please people. Most of the time that didn't work out well, anyway.

But he had a lifetime of hesitation to overcome. Working as a financial advisor had taught him to go along with clients, most of whom were powerful and didn't appreciate some glorified clerk, as they saw him, trying to stand up to them. As a result, trying to please people had become second nature. Now, even though he was turning his life around, changing it to put the emphasis on what he wanted, he wasn't totally there. He'd let the fact that his bag was in the trunk and the driver's irritable attitude make the decision for him.

That was wrong, and he needed to learn to be harder, more insistent on having things done his way. Good Lord, he was paying the bills, after all. He was the employer. He just needed to make that feeling real.

Tired from berating himself, he leaned his head against the window and stared out at the dark scenery. The car roared out of town on the Autopista, the freeway, then turned onto the main, and apparently only highway—a two-lane road called Remolino-Hispania. Medellin sits in a valley and the road to Hispania twisted and turned as they traveled through the Andes. The driver had been right about traffic. Even this early there was a fair amount of it and periodically it backed up.

The driver, displeased by the progress, was muttering under his breath.

"*Tranquilo*," Joshua told him—relax.

"This day is long. More time than we agreed."

Again, Joshua felt uneasy. The man was changing more rules. "I agreed to pay for a day trip." He pointed at the traffic. "From what you said, this isn't unusual. *Es normal?*"

"Normal," the man said. "But…"

Joshua knew this racket; he wanted Joshua to offer more money. "Look, we have a deal. But if this is too hard on you, then we can go to Hispania and have lunch and go back. Forget the extra hour to Jardin."

The man sulked and said nothing. That was fine. At least the muttering had stopped. Of more concern was that he began texting on his phone. Not that they were moving fast, but it was unnerving.

When the driver stopped at a roadside food place, Joshua was happy to get out and stretch his legs. "I need to make a call," the driver said, holding up his phone. Obviously, something more important than food was on his mind.

Joshua took a seat at the counter in the open-air restaurant, looking at the grill that served as a kitchen. It was a popular place, possibly the only one for miles. The coffee was good, and the food was fresh, if bland.

After he ate, Joshua walked back to the car. The driver was standing there looking annoyed. "*Listo*? Ready?"

They got in the car; the driver turned the key and impatiently put the car in gear. They lurched out into traffic cutting off a motorbike.

Joshua started to say something but decided it wasn't worth it.

Half an hour later, the driver pulled off. It was another roadside stop, but this one had no restaurant, and it was empty. There was a small store that looked closed and a gas station that was definitely closed, probably permanently. The car pulled between buildings and Joshua felt his stomach tighten.

"Out," the driver said.

Joshua leaned forward. The man was texting again. "Why? Where are we?"

Suddenly his door was yanked open. A burly man grabbed him by the arm in a cruel grip that made his biceps ache. He pulled back, but the man was dragging him out of the car. "What the fuck!" he shouted, struggling.

He clung to the door, to the car, but the man peeled his fingers away and pinned him in a crushing bear hug that squeezed the air out of his lungs. Another man stepped forward, saying something to the driver in Spanish.

The driver popped the trunk, then got out and went around to get Joshua's bag while the new man started patting Joshua down, roughly yanking his wallet out of his jacket pocket and tossing it on the hood of the car. Then he removed his passport and a money clip. All it held was the hundred dollars he'd promised the driver and about ninety thousand Colombian pesos — a little over thirty dollars.

The face the driver made told him that he'd expected to find a lot more. He rifled through the wallet impatiently, removing the cards and studying them. "No ATM cards?" he said, sounding surprised as well as angry.

His heart pounded knowing that he had no idea what they wanted, other than money. He obviously was turning into a huge disappointment as a robbery victim. There could be consequences.

"No. Only credit cards," he said. He had no idea what to say to make them leave him alone, how to convince them that he didn't have anything they wanted. Even if he had known, he could barely squeak out a reply. The man holding him was still slowly crushing the life out of him. He could smell the stink of the man's sweat.

The driver was rummaging through Joshua's bag. "Laptop," he said, throwing Joshua's clothes on the ground. "*Nada mas.*" Nothing more.

"Money," the man next to him demanded and, without waiting for Joshua to answer, smashed his face with a huge, rock-hard fist.

The man holding him said something Joshua didn't understand, then they threw him to the ground. One man put a knee on his head, grinding his face into the dirt and gravel; the other began ripping his clothes off him.

Growing frustrated with trying to tear his jeans with his hands, the man pulled out a knife. It was sharp, and the blade tore his jeans into ribbons. The man worked fast, not worrying about the blade slashing Joshua's skin. He felt the warm rush of his own blood on his skin before his attacker managed to find a special pocket Joshua had sewn into them. Inside that pocket were his crypto wallets... looking much like memory sticks. The man stuck them in his pocket.

The man kneeling on his head lifted his knee, grabbed Joshua's shoulders and turned him so the man with the knife could continue cutting away what was left of his clothing. There was nothing for them to find.

When he was naked, all three of his attackers argued about something, then they began kicking him. He was shrieking — he could hear himself crying out with the pain. Then he saw a blur of motion as a foot, encased in a heavy boot, caught him squarely in the face.

Then he lost consciousness.

CHAPTER 16

A NEW CLIENT

"I am a citizen of the world."

— *Diogenes the Cynic*

JW Marriott Hotel
Avenida Orellana 1172
y Avenida Amazonas
Quito, Ecuador

"You did it!"

Tricia Campbell sat back in the seat in the lobby bar at her hotel and gave herself permission to feel proud. She let out the tension she'd been holding in, dissolving it into a long, slow breath, then sipped her pisco sour.

She'd just returned from the airport. The job was done. Her newly resettled client had his residency and loved the villa she'd found for him in Esmeraldas, on the northern part of the Western coast. She'd been sure it was a good choice for him. It was a beach town, but also home to both an international seaport and a small airport. What the city might lack, if anything, was only about six hours away, by car, in Quito. That would keep him from feeling trapped there. That was always a concern with people who'd been active in the business world.

It was early afternoon, and the bar was empty. It was quiet. Television screens showed the World Cup games going on, but the sound was down.

A heavy-set man in a suit came walking toward her. He looked Hispanic and not much like a businessman. The way he carried himself reminded her of an old boyfriend who'd been a mixed martial artist. Most of the time he didn't want people to know he was one, and he moved the same way — more catlike than he wanted to appear, and unable to move with the clumsy gait of someone untrained.

His attempt to mask it made her wonder if he worked for the hotel, maybe in security. She watched him glance around the room before walking to her table.

"Ms. Campbell?"

She looked him over and nodded.

"My name is Jose Defamo. May I have a moment of your time?"

"Do I know you?"

"No, you don't. But I know who you are. More importantly, I know what you do."

Curiosity overcame her. It was a little unsettling to be recognized anywhere, much less in a hotel bar in Ecuador. Her job wasn't one that made her visible. "Really? How is that?"

"Raul Jordan mentioned you to me."

Jordan worked for Maria Fernanda Espinosa, Ecuador's current Minister of Foreign Affairs. He'd been the one she'd paid to shepherd her client's paperwork through the bureaucratic tangle. This Mr. Defamo might not look like a businessman, but he was connected with the right people. He wasn't someone she wanted to ignore.

She held out a hand. "Please, have a seat."

He pulled out a chair and sat. "May I buy you a drink?"

She cocked her head. "Why?" Although she thought him good looking in a feral way, she doubted this was a come on.

"As a thank you for speaking to me," he said.

She smiled. "All right."

He signaled the waiter, who reluctantly pulled himself away from the silent soccer match. "Another of whatever she is drinking, and I'll have a lemonade," Jose Defamo said.

Another oddity. He wasn't drinking. She didn't mean to stare at him, but he smiled and said: "I'm in training. Alcohol isn't a help."

"A help? I suppose that depends on what you are training for."

He nodded. "True. I tend to get fixated on fitness and booze doesn't help that any."

"No. But it can make you forget that you are out of shape."

He laughed; he had an oddly pleasant laugh. It took a moment for her to realize that what she heard under the laughter was confidence. Jose Defamo who was sure of who he was — he could laugh at himself easily. That made him both charming and dangerous.

"What can I do for you, Mr. Defamo? What is it that I do that is of interest to you?"

"Not to me. To my employer."

"Your employer?"

"Who must be, for the moment, nameless."

"I see," she said. Even as she said that, she realized that she didn't see at all. This was moving into new territory, being approached by dangerous men who worked for others, people who must be nameless. "Actually, I don't see at all. You will need to enlighten me. I can't do much for nameless people."

"I understand," he said, then he sipped his lemonade.

"Is that good?" she asked. "The lemonade?"

He smiled. "It's horrible. I think it is a punishment for not ordering alcohol, or perhaps the logic is that a customer would realize that it requires alcohol to improve the flavor."

"Marketing," she laughed. "It's everywhere." She tasted her own drink and was thankful for the alcoholic hit. "But you were saying?"

"My employer requires a … lifestyle change. He is in a situation that makes it prudent for him to relocate, but for reasons I can't go into, that change cannot be public."

"So, a normal residency somewhere is out of the question."

"Any paperwork with his name on it would complicate things for him."

"Ah." The picture was starting to unfold. "So even though he needs new government identification, the new government needs to be in the dark about his identity." She wrinkled her nose. "That's a challenge."

"One that I am hoping you are up to."

"I've just started doing this relocation business."

"Yet at least one client has a new identity."

That he knew that much unsettled her. "You seem to have discovered that quite easily. So, whatever I did for him… I doubt that is what your employer wants."

Defamo smiled. "No. Bribing officials to change a name is easy enough, but it is both transparent and insecure. Furthermore, my employer has a need that makes the challenge even more daunting. His new identity must be able to withstand biometric analysis."

"Yes, I know that identity cards are linked to all sorts of physiological data that can ensure the person is who he or she claims to be — fingerprints, facial recognition, height, weight, eye color …."

"And more shit all the time. My boss needs to be able to pass from country to country without some computer popping up with his original identity being detected. And beyond that, he also has substantial assets that he wants to bring with him to his new life."

She let out a long breath. "Whew. I appreciate you coming to me, but I'm afraid that is out of my league," she said. "I've never done anything like that."

"And yet, my research indicates that you are the best person in the world for making this happen. Maybe the only person who can find the cracks a person can hide in to avoid surveillance. I know you've been exploring the options, making inquiries in areas no one else is. You've managed to help some clients elude the US exit taxes. That alone is impressive, although not relevant in this case."

She sat back. It bothered her that this man knew so much. He was right though. She'd been researching exactly those things. Not that she'd solved the problems… it was still early days. But she had decided that the best, most effective course for getting her clients relocated involved getting them a new identity — one that managed to let some pass through the web of biometric data.

The woman that Defamo had referred to had been a test case. She had the money to buy a citizenship in St. Kitts; Tricia had greased some palms and got it issued under a new name. But the biometrics were tied to her old passport. Her new identity was a fake, and if she traveled outside the Caribbean, she would be spotted.

"My research is incomplete," she said.

"Understood," he said. "I'm asking you to complete it. For a substantial fee, of course."

"What is your timetable?"

"As soon as possible. The situation is … fluid. If things go badly, he can remain out of harm's way for a time, but sooner or later … he would be pleased if things could happen rather quickly."

She ran through her options. When she'd talked to Joshua last, right after he arrived in Medellin, he'd mentioned some ideas he was going to pursue about being invisible while preserving assets. She hadn't talked to him since and needed an update. "I can start working on it."

"Good. My employer would like to ensure that you are able to concentrate on this project. He'll want reports on progress in case he has to pursue other options."

"So, you want to hire me now?"

"As his relocation attorney."

She smiled. "I'm not cheap."

Jose Defamo returned the smile. "And my employer is not poor." He handed her a slip of paper. "Would this be enough to begin the research in earnest?"

It was a big chunk of change. "I think it would."

"How would you like to be paid? We'd prefer to avoid writing a check."

She reached in her bag and pulled out a piece of paper. Joshua had told her she needed to be prepared to answer this question. And so, she was.

"You need to be as invisible as your clients," he'd said. "How can they trust your digital, ephemeral solution if they don't see you using it?"

Now it both surprised and pleased her to see his prediction coming true this quickly. She pushed the paper across to Defamo. He picked it up and stared at it. "That is the public key for an account," she told him. "It will accept the payment in Monero... that's a cryptocurrency."

Jose Defamo scowled. "I don't know shit about that." Then he smiled. "But that's for the financial guys to sort out," he said. She could tell he was pleased. "Is this like Bitcoin? I've heard of that."

"Monero is even harder to trace than Bitcoin, which is saying a lot."

He shrugged. "Whatever."

"Once the deposit is made..." she said, emphasizing her point, "how do I make my reports?"

"The phone number below the figure, which you might not have noticed, is a burner phone that I will have with me. If you have any breakthroughs or questions, call me immediately, any time, night or day. If I don't hear from you often enough, or if the boss gets anxious, I'll call you. I have your number."

"In more ways than one," she thought.

"Then, if we agree, if we have a deal, you start work as soon as this Monero stuff is in your account." He grinned. "Now, I'll pay the bar tab and let you get back to work."

"I'm done for the day," she said. "Although, I'll probably go to my room and start making a few phone calls."

"The minister's flunky said you were someone who got shit done," Defamo said approvingly. "The boss likes people like that and tends to pay bonuses to people who show him they are motivated."

"Then tell him he can warm up that bonus machine," she said.

As Defamo paid the bill and left, Tricia felt good… more than good. She was elated. Her dream was coming together, and in a much bigger way than she'd ever imagined. All of a sudden, she was dealing at the highest levels, playing with big money.

The work wouldn't be easy. She didn't con herself about that. From the sound of things, Jose's boss had to be a wanted criminal. She'd have to scramble to meet all of his needs, but that's what it was all about — learning to do the things that a client needed.

If she could accomplish this — shit she'd be able to write her own ticket. The money for this job was just the beginning, which was a good thing, since she'd be investing a lot of it in making contacts, pulling things together. She'd have to create an entire apparatus to accommodate a variety of clients.

She thought about a fancy hotel in Bangkok. She'd seen a show about it on the Internet. The video travel blogger SindiLux had done a wonderful video of it. It looked like a wonderful place to have an adventure. If she could please this client, her chance to spend time there looked closer than ever.

Joshua had explained how her Monero wallet worked and that it took a little time for the money to show up in it. He'd even transferred some money from his own wallet into hers so she could see how it worked. Now she was interested to see it working when someone she didn't know transferred money into it. A lot of money. Enough to make her feel like she was playing with the big kids.

Of course, that also meant the stakes were high. With people who had trained fighters working as messengers, people who could insist on remaining nameless, you knew the stakes were very high.

If you failed, they'd want a lot more than a simple refund. And there was the question of the identity of the person that the unnamed client was hiding from. If someone with resources like this was afraid, then she was definitely playing with fire.

And it felt fucking good.

A tingle of excitement rippled through her that was almost sexual. Hell, it probably was sexual. After all this time, Tricia Campbell was a consultant, working for the rich and invisible. She was touching an inner circle of sorts. And, best of all, they had started coming to her.

Now that was a success she could savor.

CHAPTER 17

A MEXICAN VACATION

*"True independence and freedom can only exist in
doing what's right."*

— *Brigham Young*

Acapulco, Mexico

The airport limo dropped Meghana and her parents off right at the large, ornate front door of the resort. Standing in the hot sun, blinking her long eyelashes behind her sunglasses, Meghana Singh was already wishing she'd stayed home.

She let out a sigh, certain this would be a long, dull vacation. As the bellman put their baggage on a cart and eagerly rolled it into the lobby, she straightened her sunglasses and followed her parents inside, hoping there would be some young people around.

The bellman was old and ugly, and the resort reminded her of the expensive retirement home where Babu had moved when the Old Man was starting his long path to death. She hated that place. Of course, she saw that it was perfect for caregivers and the inmates (as she called them), but boring for visitors — and bleak.

On this hot afternoon in Mexico, the sand-colored walls, the Indian/Mexican décor made her think the style should be called 'early rustic boredom.' And the ugly, old bellman belonged there.

"What am I going to do for fun at this place?" she asked her father, waving her hand around in an encompassing gesture.

Aditya Singh let out an exasperated sigh. "My lovely girl, this is an elegant beach resort. It has swimming pools and beaches." He nodded toward the concierge desk. "They can give you more information on all sorts of activities."

"Although it is the low season," her mother said. Meghana knew that was a dig at her father. With all his money, he did stupid things to save money. Her mother, a Korean, didn't just let things lie, the way Indian women did. She often wondered if her father regretted not marrying the Sindhi woman his family had arranged for him.

She knew that it had been an uncharacteristic act of defiance. "How did that work out?" she wanted to ask.

"We are going to our room now," Aditya Singh said. "Why don't you check out your room and then take a look around, maybe read a book by the pool."

She snorted. Read a book? Were they serious? She was twenty, a college student, and a virgin. They expected her to be a good girl, and if a place like this was dull under any circumstances, it offered nothing for a good girl.

When they were ensconced in their rooms, hers adjoining that of her parents, she had to admit the room was nice. But it was too big. Having a big, empty room, even a nice one, reminded her that she was there basically alone, rather than with her best friend in Paris.

After taking a shower and putting on fresh clothes, she went back to the lobby. Off to the side was the Aztec Bar. She wondered idly if Aztecs drank alcohol. Corn liquor maybe?

Although it wasn't likely that anyone in the bar would have a clue, the question bouncing in her head was enough of an excuse to check it out.

Other than a few symbols on the wall that she assumed were Aztec (and how would she know? Mumbai university didn't have a lot in the way of Aztec studies) it looked like the only other bars she'd ever been in. They were all hotel/resort bars. She and her friends didn't drink.

She got out her phone to take a photo to send to her best friend, Watika. "Having a shitty time, wish you were here," she wrote before realizing she had no internet. Well, there was an internet connection, but she had forgotten to get the password from the front desk.

Another dismal failure, she thought, totally aware that it was a little thing and she was being petty. But she still stung from the disappointment of being in Mexico instead of Paris. Meghana's parents had insisted she come with them. Even though Watika's father had told her Dad right out, in plain Hindi that she was welcome to join his family on their vacation, Meghana's father wasn't having that.

The reasons he gave were all bullshit, but he had made up his mind.

The bartender, whom she'd been aware of as only a silent presence in the corner, looked at her quizzically.

She returned the favor, and pronounced him a definite improvement over the bellman... He was younger, cuter, but his face was wrong — it told her that he was not someone she was remotely interested in getting to know.

He moved toward her making her worry that he would try to make conversation with her, maybe flirt with her. "A coke with ice, please," she said.

That stopped him. He nodded. It was a trick she'd learned from Daddy. When a servant of any kind showed interest in what he was doing or just him, he gave them something to do. "It reminds them of why they are there, and it isn't to become my pal," he told her.

In some things, Daddy was wise.

When he delivered the drink, the man silently slipped back into the shadows where he could see anyone come in.

She picked up the glass and held it high. "To me," she said. "To getting through the next ten days without going out of my mind."

"Only ten days to learn about this beautiful country?"

The man who'd come up behind her made the day seem a little better. He was Mexican, she guessed, who spoke perfect English with a fascinating accent. She guessed he was about thirty... old enough to be interesting without being an old fart. He dressed in white linen pants and shirt, with wraparound Ray-Ban sunglasses that masked his face.

"How do you keep that outfit from getting sweat-stained in thirty seconds?" she asked.

He smiled. "I spend my time in air-conditioned rooms, like this one."

He was being clever and charming, but she hadn't worked through her disappointment yet, and saw him as a perfect target for her mood. "So, are you a professional drunk, or still an amateur? Or maybe another bartender?"

"I could be any of those. Actually, I arrange tours for the resort."

"Tours of air-conditioned rooms?"

"I don't go on the tours. I just set them up, right from my little desk in the corner of the lobby."

She remembered it then. It wasn't much. "And send the suckers out to get melted."

"They want the experience. That doesn't make them suckers, just people who like things you don't."

"Okay."

"And what kind of tour might appeal to Ms. Singh?"

She looked at him in surprise, and he grinned. "The hotel gives me information on guests so that I can be proactive. You might not think to ask."

That made sense. "Do you have a tour of a kimchi plant?"

"The Korean dish? Not so you'd notice. Sorry."

"Well, that's the level of my mother's cultural interests. If it isn't food, and Korean food at that, you can forget it."

As she digested the idea that this man had her family's personal information, she realized that at some point he'd sat down on the barstool next to hers. He had an elbow on the bar and faced her.

She finished her coke. "Would you happen to have any tours that include shopping in Paris?"

"Afraid not. Souvenir shops are conveniently located but we have about zero Paris designers."

"Too bad. I was supposed to be in Paris in two weeks, but I'm here instead."

"Couldn't go to Paris for some reason?"

"I could go, but I wouldn't be allowed to spend much of anything. Being there with no shopping money would be worse than not going. And embarrassing."

"I see. So, Daddy has money problems?"

"Yes, but it isn't that he doesn't have money. I just don't get to spend it."

"Is he cheap?"

She chuckled. "Yes, but he says it's because the tax people are watching him closely and would spot large credit card purchases. He's told them he doesn't have much... he bought gold. This family trip strained the budget, which is the amount Daddy can get away with spending and not attract attention. But I don't even know if he'll take any tours."

It surprised her that the words tumbled out, telling this stranger the story, laced with the venom of her disappointment. But she couldn't even tell Watika the truth. She trusted her friend — up to a point. But her father's brother worked for the tax people and she might feel obligated to spill the beans.

And this man was so easy to talk to. He flirted, but nicely. He was subtle about it, made his words flattering.

"Well, to cheer you up, you must have a margarita," he said. "I'll pay the tab so that your Daddy doesn't get upset with your spendthrift ways."

She'd heard of margaritas. They sound exotic and wicked. "I don't drink," she told him automatically.

"But coming to Mexico and not drinking a margarita is like going to Paris and not shopping for clothes."

"It is?"

"You wouldn't insult our traditions, would you?"

She looked around. They were in the middle of the room. The bartender was there. What could it hurt to taste one? "I'll try it but if I don't like it...."

"You don't have to finish it."

The bartender made the drinks and put them in front of them. She picked up her glass and licked the salt from the rim, then tentatively sipped it. The taste was like nothing she'd ever had. "It's good."

"You sound surprised."

"No, it's just..." the second sip was just as cool and refreshing. "Tell me about your tour business," she said.

"It's the hotel's business, not mine," he said. "I just use a list of contacts I've developed to put together tours. I know people who can provide boats, cars, busses, even planes, at a variety of prices. What I do is simply package those things appropriately."

Her new mentor signaled the bartender. "Two more of these wonderful margaritas."

That was when she realized she'd finished the first one. She barely remembered sipping it. The bartender poured two glasses and gave them to the man who turned and handed her one.

"To Mexico," she said.

"To tequila," he said.

He began telling her about a nearby fishing village. "It has old-world charm flowing out its doors and windows," he said. "I could take you there for a lovely lunch. You could see how the people really live."

It sounded nice, very pleasant, but his words were fuzzy; the room suddenly felt odd and Meghana got dizzy. She remembered being told that alcohol could do that, and she tensed. It would be all over for her if her parents found out she'd been drinking. She'd have to put off whatever trip the man was talking about and take a nap. She wanted to sleep it off before she met her parents for dinner.

"You don't look so good," the bartender said.

"I feel odd," she said. Her eyes weren't focusing properly, but she did notice that the man slid an envelope across the bar to the bartender. "That should cover the drinks," he said. "I'd better get this one to her room before she passes out."

"Right."

He helped her to her feet. It wasn't proper to let a strange man touch her that way, but what could she do? She couldn't seem to stand up straight, much less walk. He put an arm around her, and she leaned on him gratefully as he led her out of the bar.

It wasn't until much later that it dawned on her that he had taken her through a different door. Instead of going into the lobby, he'd taken her outside, into a parking lot. As they stood there, a van pulled up in front of them.

She clung to the white shirt as someone slid open the side door. She was getting limp as hands grabbed her and stretched her out on the floor. As the door slid shut, she heard the man's voice. "Yes, I gave her enough to keep her calm until you get there. I'll call the parents in an hour."

CHAPTER 18

CARMEN

"Acceptance of what has happened is the first step to overcoming the consequences of any misfortune."

— *William James*

Hispania, Colombia

Through a rent in the fog of pain, Joshua Raintree slowly became aware that he was being moved. Something had jostled him, and the movement sent new tendrils of pain running through his body, waking him from his stupor. With a fair amount of struggle, he managed to open his eyes. He was bouncing along, cradled somehow, and looking up at a man's face. Then he realized the man was carrying him in his arms.

He groaned, and the man looked down at him. Even though the face was rather blurry, he thought he saw concern in the brown eyes. The man said something to him. The voice was deep, and it resonated in his own body painfully.

Under the circumstances, Joshua's Spanish wasn't up to understanding what was said, assuming he was speaking Spanish, but it sounded reassuring. His brain made a token effort to process the sounds, then gave it up as futile.

"You have a kind face," he told the man.

Then he passed out.

Moments later, or maybe it was weeks, he became aware of someone poking his chest. A stocky woman with a frown wrinkling her forehead and nose was pushing something against his chest. The pain from that touch was enough to make him cry out, but somehow, he couldn't. Something about her was reassuring. She made him think of someone's mother — maybe even his. If you gave the woman high Apache cheekbones, she'd fit the part perfectly. He made a note: he wanted to find out who she was so she could play the part of his mother when they made the movie of Joshua's life.

"*Tiene muchas heridas,*" the woman said.

Joshua didn't understand a word of that, although he was pretty sure she was talking about him, and with great authority. It sounded serious.

It seemed odd to be unable to move and have to lie there with people poking you and talking about you. And in Spanish, no less. Somehow it was flattering, even if the part of his brain that understood a smattering of Spanish seemed to be on vacation.

He let his eyes, the only body part that didn't seem to hurt when he tried to move it, wander around the room, taking it in, trying to understand where he was now that he wasn't lying on the side of a small highway in rural Colombia. A small room. There was a crucifix on the wall and a tacky picture of Jesus.

A younger woman stood at the foot of the bed, listening attentively as the older one, the one poking him, spoke to her. She seemed to be giving the younger woman instructions. She nodded, indicating she understood. It was good that someone did.

He was glad it was her — she was gorgeous.

He faded out again, waking to find the younger woman washing him. That touch hurt too, but it also felt good. He decided he could get used to being touched by her.

When life passes in fits of wakefulness, time loses meaning. For what seemed an eternity, he drifted in and out. Each time he was conscious, he learned something. The woman was almost always there, and he heard the man, the possessor of that vague, kind face, call her Carmen. Inside his head he said her name to himself — Carmen.

The man's name was Arturo, and when Joshua heard her say it, the sounds flowed from her lips like honey.

But then he was prejudiced. She was caring for him, saving him. If Arturo had a kind face, hers was angelic. Her sparkling brown eyes and quick smile were framed by black hair. When it came to her figure, he decided he would rate her as curvaceous. She had lovely breasts that he tried not to fixate on when she worked over him.

She was a diligent caregiver. It seemed that he had only to open his eyes, and she was there, offering him juice or water. She fed him, bathed him.

He wondered what her husband thought of her washing another man's body. Of course, in his condition, he wasn't much of a man. The bastards had kicked him in the testicles hard enough that they were swollen and sore, like the rest of him. That reduced the problem of embarrassing incidents when she was touching him.

Periodically, the older woman, who seemed to be a doctor, or at least she served as one in his case, came in to check on him. She showed Carmen how to change his bandages. She listened to his heart. She looked at him wisely and explained that: "*Muchos órganos están magullados.*" He got that she was talking about his organs, but at least it didn't sound ominous, and she gave him a smile that went nicely with that interpretation.

The periods of wakefulness grew longer, the pain subsided, and his strength returned. His right arm was in a cast. His torso was bandaged tightly.

He tried to talk to Carmen, but his Spanish was still foggy and her shy attempts to speak English ineffective. He was able to tell her his name and let her know that he knew hers.

One day she brought a priest to see him. The sight of the man in his cassock and collar startled Joshua. That made the priest laugh. "I'm here as a translator," he said.

"Can you translate whatever the doctor said about me? Am I going to survive?"

"According to Carmen, the doctor says you had bruising of your body and organs. Your arm was broken along with a number of ribs."

"That sounds about right — it's how I feel."

"The good news is that she is quite sure you will live."

The priest looked to be in his mid-thirties, and he had short brown hair. He looked athletic for a priest. He spoke with a slight accent, but his English was clear.

"Live? Is that what I'm doing? For a time, I wondered if Dante was right and I'd fallen into some sort of purgatory where I was condemned to lie and suffer for my sins."

The priest's eyes twinkled. "Perhaps there is some of that too. We all do have to suffer. You just seem to have gotten an overdose." He nodded to Carmen, who stood by the door. "But the presence of angels should make you realize you aren't in purgatory at all."

"Point taken. But how did I get here? I remember the man carrying me, but…"

"As I understand it, Arturo was walking along the road and found you. It seems you were robbed of… literally everything. Even your clothes."

"So …." Joshua's brain was befuddled, and he couldn't think of anything witty to say. "I guess so." Where the fuck was Oscar Wilde when you needed him? He was finally talking English to someone, and it seemed a wonderful time to exercise a quick wit. Nothing else seemed to move easily. The bits he could find that didn't hurt were stiff or in a cast.

"With Doctor Martinez's supervision, Carmen will nurse you back to health. After that … I hate to bring this up, but will you want to make a police report about the incident?"

The priest chose his words carefully and the way he said it, made it clear that he thought reporting it to the police was a bad idea.

"You asked, but you don't seem to favor me reporting this."

That produced a smile. "Not really."

"So, why not?"

"This is rural Colombia, *amigo mio*. A police report accomplishes little out here. Maybe in Medellin…"

"You believe that doing the paperwork wouldn't do anything at all?"

"Mostly it would make work for the *policia*." He frowned. "Extra work tends to make them extremely irritable and unpleasant."

That suited Josh, but he had no clue how things worked here. He needed more local knowledge. "What if the police don't even know that I'm here? How about that?"

"Your discovery is already known and even the *policia* listen to gossip. Eventually, they will feel obligated to check on you, even if it's just in case your government makes inquiries about your health and wellbeing."

"Fat chance of that happening."

"Well, if you choose to report the crime, I'm afraid that there is little chance that they will catch the men. Even if you could identify them, they are likely no longer around. There really is little point in stirring things up."

Joshua grinned. "Maybe it's better this way. They didn't get much."

"No? They took everything you had, no?"

"There wasn't that much to take. I think the reason they beat me is that they expected I'd be carrying more money." As he talked, it came back to him. "It was when they discovered I didn't have an ATM card that they got really upset."

The priest nodded. "That sounds about right. They see a rich gringo and their expectations become very high and then they are passionate in their disappointment."

"That's an interesting way to put it. As far as my things go, they are welcome to what there was. The only sad thing is that they've stolen my access to my funds. Without online access, I can't even get money wired to a local bank and without my identification, I couldn't even get the money out of the bank, anyway." Joshua grinned. "Not having identification is another good reason not to file a report."

"So, you don't wish to see the police?" Relief relaxed his face.

"No. They needn't bother making a trip here either. Could you tell them for me that I appreciate their concern, but my Spanish is *muy* horrible and that I just tripped and fell?"

He approved. "I can do that. The jefe will be delighted to hear this news. A gringo tripping and falling, hurting himself doesn't require any reports at all."

The man clasped his hands behind his back and rocked on his heels. "As far as the rest goes…" then he paused, leaving Joshua to wonder what he meant by 'the rest.'

"Carmen and her brother will take care of you, and as you regain your strength, perhaps God will help you find a way to reclaim your identity papers and such. The consulate in Medellin could help with that, I suppose."

He didn't seem convinced that the consul would be of much use, but suddenly the priest's words registered. "That would be nice." He answered automatically. It was the right answer, but he was paying attention to what he said. His fogged brain was wrapping itself around the idea that Arturo was Carmen's brother. The friendly guy wasn't her husband or boyfriend. Despite his current condition, he was pretty sure that was the best news he'd heard since, well, ever since he learned he wasn't going to die.

The priest smiled at him, watching. He wondered if the Jesuits taught mind reading. It wouldn't surprise him, given the thin, knowing smile on the priest's face. He decided to change the subject and force his mind away from Carmen — the angel of the supple body and soft, yet strong hands. He trembled slightly. "By the way, Father, would you mind telling me where I am? I know I'm in Colombia. I'm clear on that much. Beyond that, I have no idea where this is."

The priest laughed again. "My apologies. Of course. You are in the town of Hispania. Arturo runs a hardware store here. And Carmen keeps house for him." The priest took Joshua's hand. "Are you a Catholic?"

"No."

"No one is perfect," he sighed. "If you require any spiritual guidance, or just want to hear some English, feel free to send for Father Bowman." He pointed to his chest. "That's me."

Then Father Bowman smiled and left, Joshua realized that he rather liked the man. He might be a priest, but he was a good guy and knew the ropes.

The room felt empty. Joshua looked out the open window. Dark clouds had gathered on a mountaintop, making the light grayish. He thought about this odd situation, how although he'd spent some time in Hispania now, he didn't know how long he'd been there. And however long that was, he'd never even gotten his first look at the place.

Those factors sort of defeated the point of travel.

He pictured going to one of the online travel sites to comment on Hispania. "While it's a beautiful drive, I can't recommend being transported by highwaymen." He laughed and then had to suppress a cry of pain. The damn ribs were taking their time to heal. The pain, the darkening sky made the room seem dark and dismal.

Then Carmen swept in with his lunch tray and suddenly the room was full and bright.

As light and airy as his sick room had been, when Carmen started taking Joshua out for walks, he felt a load had been lifted from his shoulders. There was something freeing about being mobile, being outside. Finally, he was able to see the town.

And he loved it.

It was a small place, with stores and houses clustered around a beautiful park. A kiosk in the center of the park sold coffee and when he was finally able to walk that far, she took him there. They'd sit and drink coffee in the sunshine while he regained his strength.

And they talked, communicating in simple, ungrammatical sentences that made him feel like a child. Yet, he knew that children absorbed their language skills, they acquired them through this trial-and-error process.

Curious townspeople stopped by, wanting to meet this strange gringo. They wanted to stare into his odd gringo face, shake his hand, and speak to him, or more importantly, hear him talk. They were interested, friendly, and largely kind, even solicitous. A few muttered sympathetic things about los bandidos. They indicated that were unhappy about what had happened to him and were embarrassed because it reflected badly on their area.

Slowly he recovered his strength and made friends.

One day he saw a young man, a teenager, working on a laptop computer that Josh knew all too well. He pointed. "Do you know the boy with the computer?" he asked Carmen.

"That is my cousin, Miguel," she said.

"Will you introduce us?" he asked.

She went and talked to the young man, then led him, laptop under his arm, to their table. The men shook hands. "*Mucho gusto,*" Joshua said: glad to meet you.

The boy nodded and sat down. Joshua's Spanish, while not grammatical, was improving rapidly. Total immersion, living in the language, was doing that for him. Now he was able to learn that Miguel Arturo Rodriguez cracked pirated games and sold them to the other kids. The kid was a hustler and Joshua admired him.

"That's a very nice laptop," he said.

A flicker of apprehension came into the boy's eyes. "A man sold it to me recently."

"Really?"

He could see that the situation was dawning on Miguel. The kid was sharp. "I don't know the man. People know that I understand the devices. They bring me electronics they don't need or don't want. I fix them for resale."

Joshua smiled. The kid was a specialized fence. "I don't care about the man or how you got the computer."

The boy relaxed. "Was this yours?"

His honesty gave Joshua pause. "It was. Now it's yours, it seems."

"If it was taken..."

"What I do care about are some other things. Was anything else with it?"

"Anything else?"

"*Otra cosas*," other things.

The boy shrugged. "Nothing good."

"Some memory sticks?"

The kid's eyes flashed. "Yes, but they were damaged. I couldn't read what was on them."

Joshua felt hope swelling up. If they were still around... "Do you still have them?"

"No one uses them. I threw them away."

Joshua's heart sank again. It had to be his encrypted memory stick and his hardware wallet. "Damn."

"I might be able to get them back for you." The boy grinned. "The garbage is not taken out often."

Josh nodded. "Those aren't damaged. They are encrypted and don't read like normal memory sticks. If you could find them, if you were to bring them to me, I'd be grateful."

"Grateful?"

"If you were to find them and bring them to me, and loan me your laptop, I'd be grateful enough to order you a new laptop. Uno mas, ..." he struggled for the words, then relapsed into English. "One much better than this one. We can even get one configured for gaming if you like."

"Verdad?"

"Verdad. I'd be delighted to." And he would. With those in his hands, Joshua could regain his financial world, access to money, clients, everything.

When push came to shove, and with the prospect of a new computer in the offing, finding the "damaged" memory sticks didn't take long.

Carmen helped Joshua back to the house above Arturo's store and by the time they'd settled into chairs, Miguel was back, holding out the thumb drives, clearly hoping they were the odd, but desirable treasure. They were.

Borrowing Miguel's current laptop, the one stolen in the robbery, Joshua went online. In the process, he noted that the node he'd been running for Monero, his favorite anonymous crypto, was gone.

"My node…"

Miguel grimaced. "I reformatted the disk. What was it for?"

"I was processing crypto transactions. That was part of the network."

"Sorry. I didn't…"

"It's only an inconvenience. I'll rebuild it. It isn't that difficult." In fact, he had everything he needed on the encrypted memory stick to get it up and running again — once he had a new computer. He would download the software and set it up again. Most everything he'd had on his computer could be restored with the right keys and seeds and passwords. And they were all on the encrypted memory stick.

"This node… is that mining cryptocurrency?"

"Not exactly. But I've done some of that."

"I have a lot of computers," Miguel said. His voice was hopeful.

"Mining only really makes sense in a few cases," Joshua said.

"Would you teach me?"

Joshua looked at him with wonder. It had been a long time since he'd met someone so eager to learn. And he was sincere. It was refreshing.

"Sure. We can create a crude sort of server out of whatever computers you can get running." He laughed. "You can even add in this one. But first, we need to move ahead on getting the new computers."

He logged into a site he used to buy computer equipment. Luckily, he remembered his password, which meant he could access his profile. His credit card information was there. Then, in consultation with Miguel, he ordered two high-end laptops, with Miguel's having more video RAM and a faster graphics processor.

"Can I borrow this for a while... just until the new ones arrive?" he asked. "I need to check my cryptocurrency and my emails. My clients will be worried about my long silence.

Miguel nodded. "I have others, not so good, but..."

Josh grinned. "Well, I don't need much performance. Take this one and bring me one of the others that isn't as good." The kid's smile told him they had a deal.

"Can you show me this cryptocurrency?" Miguel asked. Eagerness made his face glow. "I've read about it."

"There isn't much to see," he said. "But you can watch me access my wallet."

So, with Miguel sitting next to him while Carmen made lunch, Joshua checked his wallet. It was intact. He let out a sigh of relief. As he'd told Tricia, it was safer than a cashier's check. It was nice to be right.

"Those numbers represent the amount I have of the coins," he told Miguel.

"But you can spend this as you could regular money?"

"I can spend this more readily. I'll show you later."

He went to a currency exchange and checked prices. They'd stayed stable while he was out of touch. That was good. His clients wouldn't have been panicking.

"If you need to work, I can get the other computer," Miguel said. When he left, Joshua checked his email, deleting the hundreds of SPAM emails, as well as the "where are you?" notes from anxious clients.

He wrote a generic email and sent it to each of his clients. It simply said that he'd been injured and out of touch, but that all was fine now. Details, answers to specific questions, would come later.

An email from the delicious Tricia Campbell, however, required an answer. She had thought of an angle that would let her project jump way ahead. She'd thought it through as far as she could. Now she needed technical help.

He sat back, considering her idea. It struck him as ambitious, but shit, she was presenting him with an elegant and insightful challenge. What a thing to try! He had no idea if, when you got down to the nitty-gritty, her idea would work. None at all. The specific knowledge to make it happen was well out of Joshua's area of expertise. Yet he was sure he knew the perfect person for her to bounce the idea off of.

"Sorry for being slow to respond, but I'm dealing with some chaos here at the moment," he wrote back. "You need to contact Kenny Lu." He included Kenny's complete contact information, which was still happily stored in the cloud. "Tell him that I think this is the perfect gig for him, considering."

When he hit send, Joshua was feeling a lot better about so many things. He'd been at the bottom of a dark well — helpless, both physically and financially. Now he was climbing out. He'd found his spirit and the desire to get back in the game.

Arturo came up from the store and Carmen served them a lunch of rice and beans. When Arturo went to reopen the shop, Miguel returned to swap laptops. He gave Joshua a battered Dell that was definitely past its mandatory retirement age. For his immediate purposes, it would be fine.

Yes, things were looking up.

Despite the language gap, he found talking to Miguel easy. Of course, many of the words they shared were neither English nor Spanish, but the language of geeks — they spoke of RAM and processes, cryptocurrency and hashing, blockchain and private keys.

Joshua felt that he had found a base and a comrade. Maybe even a home. And, looking at the way Carmen watched them working, seeing the soft curves of her body, the warm, welcoming eyes, the lovely breasts, he began to hope he might find even more.

A small success that leads toward recovery can be a heady thing. He allowed himself a smile.

Despite everything, Joshua was back in the game.

CHAPTER 19

A LIQUIDITY PROBLEM

*"Occasionally words must serve to veil the facts. But
let this happen in such a way that no one become aware of
it; or, if it should be noticed, excuses must be at hand to be
produced immediately."*

— *Niccolò Machiavelli, Instructions to diplomat
Raffaello Girolami*

**L&T Technology Center
Mumbai, Maharashtra, India**

"Your brother-in-law is here to see you, sir. He doesn't have an
appointment, but he said it was important. Family business."

Park Dong Woo looked up at the young Indian woman, saw the
questioning look on her face. She was from the secretarial pool and
worked as his secretary whenever he was in the office in India.

He was sure that she was something of a plant who reported on
him to some minister of the Indian government, but that would be
true regardless of how carefully he screened people, and he didn't
have time and energy to worry about it. He wasn't even sure if he
cared what they knew about his activities, anyway. Most of what
happened in this office was routine. The work he did here was
intended to execute the project exactly as it had been agreed upon.

Secrets just made life difficult.

Aditya Singh's visit came as quite a surprise. His sister had said
they were going on vacation in Mexico — the entire family. Now

there was some urgent family business. Aditya wouldn't come unannounced unless it was a big deal and urgent. "I didn't expect him," he said. "Send him right in."

When she ushered the man in, Park didn't think he'd ever seen Aditya looking so stressed. Whatever had him reaching out this afternoon was a serious matter. Without asking, Park got up and poured him a whiskey... a double. When he handed it to him, the man took a grateful swallow. "What's wrong? Tell me. Is it my sister?"

Aditya shook his head. "It's Meghana. She's been kidnapped. We were in Mexico ...."

"Kidnapped! What do the police say?"

Aditya shook his head again. "We didn't contact the police. The kidnappers said they'd sell her into slavery if we contacted the police."

"What do they want?"

Aditya snorted. "What do you think? They demand money. Lots of money." He was on the edge of tears, the brink of despair. "I need your help, Park. Some fucking Mexican cartel has our little girl. They sent us back here to arrange payment for her return."

"My sister is here?"

"At home, crying her eyes out."

"You know I don't have a lot of money, but of course I will help." His head spun, and he thought of Osk Barstad. "I have private connections with Interpol..."

Aditya held up a hand. "They will return her to us. They said they won't hurt her, but I need help with the money — getting it to them."

Park resisted asking how much they were asking, how it happened... the details didn't matter now. "Can't you just wire them the money?"

Aditya let out a long sigh. "They want cash. And if I convert my holdings... Park, I'll go to jail." His grin was painful.

"For what? Paying a ransom isn't a crime."

"Not for that. I was so fucking clever. I've been squirreling away my reserves into gold. You know what the government thinks of that. It's a crime. So, I never declared the gold or the income I used to buy it. The tax people smell something, but my accountants are the best."

"And you pay regular bribes."

"That too." He shrugged. "Bribes are a cost of doing business, but they only work up to a point. Normally that means that the tax people won't dig too deep, but now I need to come up with a lot of money quickly and I have a liquidity problem. I don't have the ability to borrow enough, so I will need to sell gold. But I can't let that become public. I can sell it privately, which will be fast if I take less than the market price, but even when I have the money, I can't use a bank to make the transfer." Then he stopped, his face pasty white. "Of course, I will if I have to — Meghana's life depends on me. But if you can help…."

Park knew Aditya as a confident man. In fact, Park's private opinion of him was that he was overconfident and overly proud. He only suffered him out of love for his sister. But he didn't actually dislike the man, and he had been a good father to Park's niece. And she needed his help.

"Of course, I'll help," he said softly. "What do you need me to do?"

"Find a way to transfer the money secretly."

"I don't know how to do that."

"Park, you transfer money all the time. I'm sure some of those transfers have to be kept hidden. And you know bankers who have international connections. I know nothing about international transfers. When I pay for things abroad in business, I write a damn check."

Now Park had to ask. "How to do it depends on the amount. How much are we talking about?"

"Two hundred and fifty thousand US dollars."

Certainly, that was more than enough for the tax authorities to go after. With that much paid out easily, they'd smell more. "And you can get access to your gold easily?"

The man winced, picturing it. "Yes."

Park grinned. It was probably hidden in the house somewhere under the floor. Aditya was clever in some ways, but in others, not so much. Now he thought through the logistics of the problem as he walked back to his desk. Gold could be sold easily enough, especially since Aditya was willing to take a loss.

"Given that this needs to happen quickly, I think you'll have to use cryptocurrency."

"Bitcoin?"

Park shrugged. "Some crypto. Most of the ways I know of to transfer that much discretely are cumbersome and slow — and easily traced back to you."

"And you can help me make a crypto transfer? I don't even know what that means."

"I think I know of a way to make it happen. Actually, I don't know how to do it, but I can bring in someone who can do it for us, discreetly."

Aditya sank his face in his hands. "Whatever you need to do. But it has to be quick."

"I can't be directly involved," Park said. "I can only make the introduction.

His brother-in-law nodded. "I understand. If you can help me make the right connection, I will be grateful, as will your sister."

Park cringed at the pointed mention of his little sister. Bringing her into it at this point seemed gratuitous and ungrateful, as if he wasn't already doing everything he could to help.

He picked up his phone and made a call. When he hung up the phone, he scribbled an address on a piece of paper and handed it to Aditya. "You need to meet a man named Ritesh at this address in thirty minutes."

Aditya stared at the address. "Why here? Isn't this an industrial park?"

"It's best if this meeting is not in my office. This is his office."

"Of course," he said, getting up, still looking dazed.

After Aditya left the room, Park considered the situation. It struck him as odd that a Mexican cartel would target a mid-level Indian businessman. They were always after targets, of course, but what alerted them to Aditya? What made them certain he could raise that much money in such a short period? Crooks this sophisticated would know that even rich men had liquidity issues.

Given that, it wasn't too much of a stretch to imagine that Aditya Singh wasn't the actual target. The intrigue swirling around him, the politics playing out within the Oculistica, and the politics of working with the Indian government made it easy to imagine that this was a setup to ensnare him. Perhaps someone wanted to involve him in illegal or at least off-the-books financial dealings that could be held over his head later.

Anyone would understand helping out your niece, but if the means used weren't legal, his position could be compromised.

It took little effort to list a number of people who might like having leverage over someone in his position. He just had to hope that bringing in Ritesh would give him a buffer — isolate him from whatever irregular activities they might need to use. For all he knew, the Old Man had hatched this plot to ensure Park sided with him as the tensions with Nikolaj heated up. It didn't seem likely that Nikolaj doubted the strength of his hand.

And it could just as easily be about the smart city project. Ministers were always trying to promote the companies of relatives as vendors or hint that someone they knew would be perfect for some plum position.

He put all that out of his mind. Meghana was his family and needed what little help he could provide. If it came back to bite him, that was what it was.

Thinking of Nikolaj made him consider another possibility. The man liked action and might be convinced to execute a targeted rescue. He had no doubt the man could find Meghana faster than anyone else. That, however, was problematic. If that worked, if the green-eyed man freed Meghana, it would obligate him to the man to an extent he'd like to avoid. Just being his ally was stressful enough. And, if it failed, his sister would never forgive him. He'd save that as a last resort.

Aditya Singh didn't like Ritesh Samudra from the moment they met. He sighed and let that go. In his experience, you couldn't afford to do business only with people you liked, or you'd never get anything done. Often as not, the people you liked weren't the best choices for doing the dirty work. No, you worked with the ones who knew how to accomplish things, especially in the gray areas entirely foreign to you. Later, when you no longer needed them, you could bathe and get their stink off you.

Money, and how to make it, were things he knew. He totally missed the irony that banking and finance were things he hired underlings to do for him. The technology of transactions summoned up a mystic realm far removed from his experience.

To give the devil his due, this Ritesh grasped the situation long before he finished explaining it. From the flicker in his eyes, Aditya saw that this upstart little boy thought he was in control. Regretfully, for the moment he was.

"Can you help me?" Aditya asked. "Will you?" was what he meant, but he'd never show such helplessness. "I need to know now. I'm expecting a call from them in a few minutes to check on my progress."

Ritesh smiled thinly. "There are ways." He held up a finger. "First of all, when they call, ask them if they will take payment in Bitcoin," Ritesh said casually.

"Park mentioned that. Why?"

"Because it will make things much easier for us. Using cryptocurrency will let the government watchdogs sleep peacefully while we do what we must do."

He'd heard of it, of course, but didn't know much about it. The government frowned on it. "How does it do that?"

"It is digital money, not cash."

He knew that much. "But I don't have any."

"I know people who can convert your gold to Bitcoin easily enough. It will cost a sum to ensure it is done secretly, but it is doable. Once you have the Bitcoin, then we can transfer the money to the cartel directly, instantly. No bank needs to be involved."

"And the cartel will accept digital money?"

"You have to ask, but they should be delighted to. It spends nicely, and their IT person would be able to arrange it."

"The cartel has an IT person?"

"Everyone does, if they are doing business globally."

Aditya sighed with relief. This sounded exactly like the salvation Aditya Singh needed, which was good since his phone was ringing. He didn't have time left to get more details.

"Daddy!" Meghana was on the phone.

"Baby girl, are you all right?"

"I'm okay. They haven't hurt me but… I'm scared."

"It will be fine, darling girl."

"She has a right to be scared." The voice was hard. "Unless you are doing what you were told, she should be very scared."

Aditya firmed his voice as he did when negotiating. "Of course, I am doing exactly what you said. I'm taking care of it right this moment. Don't hurt her."

"As long as you are making the payment you don't need to worry. The girl is a spoiled brat, but we have no desire to hurt her."

"To make that happen faster, I have a question... can I pay you in Bitcoin?"

Silence greeted his answer. "Cryptocurrency? Why?"

"I assume that neither of us wants this transaction monitored." He looked at Ritesh, who nodded. "A wire transfer can be traced. A cash withdrawal would be noticed, and I would have to hand-carry cash to you. A withdrawal of this amount will alert the authorities immediately, and they might confiscate it while they investigate. We can't risk that. With Bitcoin, I can send it to you today. We can end this."

There was a pause. "I need to check. Perhaps that's possible," the man said.

"Please. It will let us resolve this quickly."

"I'll call back in an hour."

When the man hung up, Ritesh smiled. "They'll find out how to do it. It's easy enough and they'll find it irresistible."

"And you can arrange to convert the gold to this Bitcoin?"

"We can change it as soon as you have the gold."

"I can take wherever you say. How long will this payment method take?"

Ritesh picked up his phone. "I have things set up already. As soon as we have the Bitcoin, we can make the transfer. The time varies, but within a few minutes they will have confirmation."

Despite his concerns for Meghana, part of Aditya's brain was wondering why he hadn't investigated this Bitcoin sooner. Everything was still vague, but he could see that it offered chances to cut out the bastards who ran the banks as well as the vultures in the government.

Now, because of his ignorance, he'd be paying through the nose to have this despicable programmer do something that was apparently rather simple. Something his own people should have brought to his attention.

He sucked in a breath and steeled himself to the inevitable. This man would screw him on the price of the gold and probably for the transactions as well. That was his own fault. He shouldn't be in this position.

Once Meghana was safely home, he'd put his people to work. Better yet, he'd fire the fools and find people to teach him all there was to know about this Bitcoin shit.

The next time the man called, he simply said: "Monero. The boss says you can pay in Monero, but not Bitcoin."

"What the fuck is Montero?" Aditya demanded.

Ritesh smiled. "Monero. It's another cryptocurrency. Tell him that we are fine with using it," Ritesh told him. "Monero works even better."

Aditya was sure his sigh of relief was audible. "Yes, we can do that."

The man snorted. "Of course, you can. I'll send the address. Make the transfer by eight in the morning my time."

"I'll do it before then."

"Then, as a reward for your cooperation, your precious girl will be in a first-class seat on the flight leaving here at eleven o'clock — untouched. Otherwise, she'll be starting on a rather different kind of trip."

Ritesh's nod reassured him. "You'll have it later today."

"Good."

Then, before he thought to demand to hear his sweet Meghana's voice again, the connection went dead.

A text message with the address soon followed. "What is this?"

"The address of his wallet," Ritesh said.

Aditya looked at it and sighed. "This jumble of numbers and letters is where you will send my gold?"

Ritesh laughed. "If it makes you feel better, think of it this way. All I will send him is a string of ones and zeros."

That didn't help Aditya's mood at all. Only the thought that his daughter would be coming back to him, his baby girl, eased the pain.

CHAPTER 20

CRYPTO CITIZENSHIP

*"Government means always coercion and compulsion
and is by necessity the opposite of liberty."*

— *Ludwig von Mises*
Human Action: A Treatise on Economics

We Hotel Aeropuerto
Nte 33 165
Col. Moctezuma 2a Sección
15530 Ciudad de México, CDMX
Mexico

The airport hotel turned out to be perfect for the time she had and well-suited for her purpose. It was efficient and had the amenities required. But the location was the best part. Tricia Campbell landed in Mexico City, went through the formalities of immigration and customs, and then rolled her suitcase out to catch the shuttle.

Within ten minutes, she was checking in, and a few minutes later she was drawing a hot bath while checking her email.

The room was a bargain in terms of convenience for the price and not just convenient for her. Later that evening, Kenny Lu, the man Joshua had recommended to her for her project, was flying in from Bangkok. He had a two-hour layover before catching a flight to Peru, and they'd intended to use it productively. They could have a nice dinner and talk about her proposition.

She'd learned that Kenny traveled continuously — always on the road. He worked remotely and at customer sites for a company that specialized in machines that provided biometric ID. They weren't the biggest player in the market and their customers were smaller countries with small budgets who needed to meet international standards or risk having their citizens go through rigorous immigration procedures when they arrived in the EU or USA… or Mexico, for that matter.

When she discovered exactly what Kenny did, suddenly it seemed as if meeting the demands of her potential new client was going to be possible. But when Joshua had gone silent for a time, she'd worried. Had he changed his mind? Had something happened to him? They were, she knew, quite different questions.

She told herself not to worry, reminded herself that tech wasn't always the only solution. There were other options, but everything else seemed more dangerous and trickier. And finding a solution didn't stop her from worrying about Joshua. How could he just disappear?

Forcing herself, she focused her attention on other possible solutions. The fact that they were dangerous wasn't a game changer for her. The timid Tricia had been swept up in the excitement of flitting from country to country, dealing with the low-profile rich and… breaking the law. She couldn't deny that she loved it.

As she worked with clients, giving them the results they wanted, her name was passed along in a network that she hadn't even known existed before. She was a resource, and it was heady stuff. It was what she'd wanted. And it wasn't just the work, but the entire new life she'd embarked on. The affair with Joshua had told her that she was right about how empty her marriage was and that she had choices.

She still hadn't confronted her husband; Tom seemed blissfully unaware that she was changing. Well, blissful was the wrong term, but the only part that seemed to have him unsettled was her globe-hopping ways, the constant trips and meetings... all the things that she found enticing.

From her perspective, that she was meeting interesting, sexy men, who were attracted to the glamorous woman she was becoming, was a bonus.

And, on top of it all, the work itself was intoxicating. She mapped out paths for people, broke ground. And that was the real value of the project she had in mind to tackle with Kenny; if they could make it work in some form, it would be a giant step forward. She already had several strategies — systems in place to make things happen—but they were mostly one-off solutions.

From a business point of view, that wasn't effective. She wanted a standardized, tested approach to the biggest problem that her biggest clients faced. Even an expensive solution, if it worked consistently, was better. She could easily pass along the costs to her growing client base.

When she was ready, she went down to the hotel bar to wait. Kenny's flight was due in at six, and they'd share a drink before having dinner.

She sat at the bar and before she'd been there ten minutes a charming man with an Italian accent hit on her. It was a soft approach, an offer to buy her a drink... just the opening move. He was good looking, and she was unhappy about having to send him on his way, so she tossed out an option. "I have to meet someone for dinner," she told him.

He sighed. "My bad luck."

She smiled. "I don't expect it to be a late meeting, however."

"Perhaps I will come by here later, then. If you are not busy ...."

"If I am here when you come by, I might be interested in that drink."

He smiled, eyes flickering enticingly. "Then I will make the effort to find out."

"It would be a possibility."

His name, he said, was Calderon. On a whim, she told him her name was Natasha. "Natasha Goldman," she told him, as she shook his hand, enjoying the strength he radiated. Lying about her name pleased her as much as the rest of the situation.

She'd always liked the name Natasha, thought of it as a darker, more mysterious name than Tricia. Her own name sounded far too wholesome to suit him; it wasn't at all the right name for a woman who did the kind of business she did and certainly was not right for the woman she felt she was when arranging to meet a strange man in a new country.

An electric tingle of excitement ran through her. The combination of the possibility of a tryst with a handsome man, in a country she was just passing through, was a deadly, seductive combination and she loved it.

"I should be alone when my business associate arrives," she told him.

"Then I can buy you a drink to be sipping when he arrives," Calderon said.

The idea appealed to her, so he ordered her a vodka martini, then smiled. "Later tonight," he said and left.

The encounter made the entire stopover seem even better.

When Kenny arrived a few moments later, she was glad that he was there for business. He wasn't at all interesting to her as a man, but as a potential business asset, he was impressive. He had a lanky, off-center body and an oddly lopsided face graced with a constant smile. She liked him immediately.

"Joshua told me I'd be glad to meet you," he said as they went in the restaurant and a waiter seated them.

They ordered drinks, and she thought about the uncertainty she'd heard in his voice. "You must have an idea what I'm proposing," she told him. "I mean, even if he didn't give you details …." She knew Joshua had said nothing.

"You want to be able to create valid biometric ID," he said, shrugging. "That's what the machines I'm working on do, so what else could it be?"

Kenny consulted for a company that made the equipment countries used to process requests for biometric ID. The old ID was out, and everyone was switching over, so the timing was perfect. Because this was all about security, the software was all very proprietary, very well guarded, and impossible to access. For anyone but Kenny, that is.

"Joshua said you might be willing, and were certainly able, to make that happen."

He nodded. "It is possible," he said. "But it depends ..."

"On what I'm doing with it. Of course."

"See, I helped develop the software. It was just a couple of us in a garage set up with lots of computers and tons of junk food. I was working by the hour for some guy with deep pockets. I got the impression he didn't think much of us — the ones who do the coding. At that point, I wasn't even sure we'd get paid."

"But you did?"

He laughed. "As it turned out, we did. I even got a bonus. Once it was up and running, the guy created a real company and called it Data Certainty. He called the machine IDPOSITIVE. He was the president and chief salesman. He was good at that, apparently. Once he got customers, he needed someone to fly around to do installations, then make sure the machines were working properly and to train locals in the procedures. He called me. It sounded like fun and here I am."

"So, the machine sold."

He laughed. "Like pancakes, at least for a specialized market like that. They have trouble keeping up with demand." He scowled. "Hear what I said? Pancakes. That's a funny saying. Who sells pancakes anymore?"

"IHOP?"

"Right."

"Your deal sounds pretty sweet."

"He pays me okay, but I think he's a bastard and it's gotten boring."

"So, you are interested in working with me?"

"Joshua gave you a good recommendation."

"He thought you'd be interested in working with us to create what he's called crypto citizens."

"Wow!" Kenny laughed. "He finally caught the bug big time then."

"And wants to use it. We want to help people go off the grid without having to worry all the time. We want them to have real identities that they can prove."

"Okay, then. Let's talk about the machine I work on and see if what I'm doing fits in. What I think would be interesting, and useful to you, is the reason it sold. There are other machines that make biometric ID, but they are super expensive. This is a low-end model, as such things go, but it works well. The main customers are smaller countries that can't afford the top-of-the-line gear but still need to comply with international regulations if they don't want their citizens on the no-fly lists, or having to go through all sorts of extras checks at immigration."

"Smart marketing."

"Very, but one reason I've soured on it a bit is the same reason it might work perfectly for you. See, a new investor came along with more money. He asked me to add in a new feature." He grinned. "It was a simple thing, easy to do. I checked around and found that this new investor was actually a CIA front company that specializes in giving a helping hand to high-tech startups that work in areas that affect security."

"That would be most areas, these days."

"Right. For them to invest, all we had to do was add a little code. This code gives the CIA access to the machines without the owner of it having a clue. That means they can monitor identities and gives them the ability to stick in some identity information and create biometric IDs for whoever they want."

Tricia began to smile. "And you have access too?"

Kenny paused for a moment before smiling and nodding. "I wasn't sure how I'd use it, but I added a few little modifications of my own that I neglected to put in the documentation for the code. I thought of these undocumented features as a method of investing in the future. My future."

"That sounds perfect."

"In some ways it is. You still need a valid identity of some kind. There has to be a real person living in the country you are making the ID for. The protocol checks and the application being processed are cross-linked to birth certificates and other existing identification. You can't just crank out a passport in any old name. But, if I have a real name and birth certificate, I can replace all the other data. If the real person applied for a passport, that would set off all sorts of flags. As far as I can tell, the CIA uses this for short-term ops. Yours would need longer lifespans and no surprises. They'd need to withstand careful scrutiny."

"But, if I have the identities you need, then we are good?"

He raised his eyebrows. "You can get that information about real people?"

"I have the complete identification files for people who are recently deceased."

He shook his head. "That's a problem. The system cross checks death certificates. If the person is dead, that record will pop up and the data will bounce. It will be rejected."

She smiled. "The person who sold me the identities was able to prevent their deaths from being recorded. What I propose is that we make the dead live on with new faces and small alterations of the data. New death certificates will be created in the names of the clients assuming the new identity. That allows us to create a narrative: Mr. X visits Chile and dies. Mr. Y, a Chilean who looks remarkably like Mr. X, leaves the country."

"Bait and switch," Kenny laughed.

"Sort of. But not exactly. More replaced or substituted than switched."

"Are you comfortable that these identities are real? Fakes won't work. If we put a bogus name into the system, it could raise a flag and that could trigger a complete audit."

"They are guaranteed authentic. I've purchased them from a reputable, but entirely corruptible source." She slid a letter-size manila envelope across the table. "Don't take my word for it. Here is one set I took out at random that you can use to make a test. There is everything on the recently deceased and the photos and physical description of the new occupant of that history."

"That works."

"If you need anything else, let me know; if I have everything you need, if this flies, get me a passport, ID card, and driver's license in the new name. The old address is fine. That can be changed later. I didn't include the current name of the client. You shouldn't need that. It will only appear on a death certificate."

Kenny nodded. "That's perfect. I appreciate a little distance from the client and any real data. Do the photos need any work?" He smiled at her puzzled expression. "Every country has different specs for those forms of ID."

"No. They are the size required for Ecuador."

"Ecuador? Is that the only country we will be dealing with here?"

"Ecuador and Guatemala, to start with."

"Both are dead easy."

"Later on, we can look at other countries you have… connections to and see which might be suitable for my clients. There are a number of factors involved in picking a country."

"I leave that part to you," he said. "I don't need to know about that." He fingered the envelope. "The less I know.…"

"Once we have the new ID, the client can open a bank account and get legitimate ones."

He nodded. "The substitution won't be cheap." He took out a notebook and wrote down a figure, then tore off the page and pushed it over to her.

She glanced at it. It was higher than she'd hoped, but doable. "Is it a lot of work?"

He chuckled. "Not so much, but I've gotten greedy. Have you seen the price of pizza and beer lately?"

She laughed and pointed to the steak he was eating. "Fair enough. Haven't we all gotten greedy? Look, there is real money in this. If you do it right, you'll be able to charge a bundle and there will be a steady stream of work. I expect demand to be pretty constant. We do this well, if we prove to be a good team by combining our resources, we will pick and choose our clients. With my contacts and the other services I offer clients, we will be able to extract maximum value."

Kenny sipped his wine. "Well, I think we have the basis for a beautiful friendship."

"So, you will let me know if you can do it?"

"Oh, I can do it. Here's what we can do... I'm heading to Peru now." He glanced at his digital watch. "In fact, I have to get to the gate soon." He looked up. "How many names are we starting with?"

"One, to prove it works. Client number one."

He nodded. "I'll review this stuff and if everything I need is there, I'll access the system in Ecuador. I should go there and do it locally. The system will process the request for a replacement ID, and it will be sent out within days. Have you got an address in Ecuador?"

"The name and address of the law firm we are using are in the packet. You can get to it that fast?"

"If your information is good, there's no reason it shouldn't go straight to the machines that make the passport and cedula... the citizen ID card."

"Then I'll plan to hang around toward the end of the week in Quito," she said, forcing herself not to show her excitement. Having it happening quickly made her pulse race.

"I take cash," he said. "On delivery."

She slid him an envelope. "Here is a deposit. Maybe once we establish a working relationship, we can do it in Monero," she said.

He laughed and took back the piece of paper he'd written his price on. He opened a small notebook, looked up something, then wrote an email address. Then he put it on top of the envelope and pushed them both back to her. "Send an email to that address and I'll send you my Monero wallet public key," he said. "Transfer the money there. I'm not thrilled carrying cash around."

"I'll send half tonight," she said. "When I get the documents from the lawyer, I'll send the other half."

Kenny nodded, put his notebook back in his pocket, then stood and picked up the envelope with the client and identify information. "Then thanks for dinner, which was good. I look forward to doing a number of these."

"I'm looking forward to it too," she said. It was all she could do to keep from bubbling over. It was coming together. She didn't know Kenny, but his confidence, his calm assurance made her certain this would work.

After he left, she ordered coffee. After coffee and perhaps a dessert, she'd go back to the hotel bar and find out if the attractive Calderon was as reliable as he was charming. If she was lucky, he'd also be just a little dangerous. Danger, she was learning, was an addictive substance, found in all sorts of interesting places.

The thought put a smile on her face. The life she was creating got better all the time. Who would've thought that, at heart, Tricia wanted a life like this?

CHAPTER 21

CATCHING THE TRAIN

*"Any form of coercion and control requires
justification —
and most of them are completely unjustifiable."*

— *Noam Chomsky*

Bellagio Shanghai Hotel
No. 1 Zhapu Rd.
Hongkou Dist
Shanghai, China

Anna Rasburn stepped into the elevator of the Bellagio Shanghai wearing a simple silk black sheath dress and high heels. Anyone seeing her would think she was a businesswoman or a wealthy woman in Shanghai on holiday. Inside the elevator, a slim Chinese woman dressed in a business suit waited, holding a tablet computer.

She tapped it and looked up. "Ms. Rasburn," the woman said by way of greeting.

Anna nodded and stepped to the back of the car. Her bodyguard, Roger, followed her in. The man wore an expensive suit and could pass for a business colleague or even her husband.

Wordlessly, the Chinese woman handed Roger a passkey; he took it and waved it in front of the sensor before pressing a button for one of the floors.

"How is it going?" Anna asked. "Is he engaged with them?"

"Everything is as you wished," the woman said, handing over the tablet. "It is playing out as you requested." She smiled. "The girls you provided certainly know their work well."

Anna glanced at the screen and saw a video of a Chinese man in his late thirties in bed with two tall blondes. "It's a live stream," the Chinese woman said.

"Excellent, Ms. Yaong." She stared at the tablet. "I find it curious that Chinese men seem to have a fondness for Russian girls," Anna said. "I wonder why that is?" She glanced at Ms. Yaong. "Asian women are so beautiful."

The woman shrugged. "Variety, I suppose. They are blonde and tall. And, in this case, they seduced him."

The three people on the screen were on the bed, naked. The man knelt while two girls stretched on the bed — one performing oral sex on the other while the man watched and ran his hands over their bodies, from time to time muttering instructions to them in English.

Anna looked at the woman. "So, this is Mr. Chan, your boss."

"It is." There was no emotion in her voice.

"You are also recording all of it?"

"Of course. As you instructed."

Anna stared at her, sizing her up. After a moment, she handed the computer back. "How long have you worked for Mr. Chan?"

"Three years now."

"As his personal assistant?"

"Yes."

Anna already knew that, just as she knew that the woman was looking for a way out of her job. That had been why it had been possible to hire her for these tasks. She was being paid a fair amount of money, but Anna was pleased with her work.

"How will you play this situation?" Anna asked her.

The woman looked surprised. "What do you mean?"

"The money I'm paying you will allow you to walk away from your job, from him. But when this is done, you will also have some personal leverage over him. That could be useful to us both."

The woman was intrigued. "How?"

Anna pointed to the tablet. "You are planning to keep a copy of the video, aren't you?"

"I...."

"Don't worry. I don't care. You might find a good use for it."

"You think I should blackmail him?"

"You would have that option. I wouldn't want you to actually expose him, but the threat of doing so would keep him in line. And if you were to keep your position that might be useful for me and profitable for you."

"You want me to stay with him?"

"I want you to consider about all the possibilities, examine your options. You are a smart woman. Your Mr. Chan is about to be promoted. It will be very sudden, and a surprise to all. If you stay and have the video, you can negotiate with him and improve your situation."

"You said you could find me another place. Mr. Chan disgusts me."

Anna cocked her head. "I can and if that's what you want, I will. But consider that most people wind up being disgusting, Ms. Yaong. If you are really going to insist on having a new job, I will keep my promise. I simply wondered if you would consider the option of staying on. I'd be willing to pay you well to act as my eyes and ears."

"I really don't wish to." Then her eyes flickered. "I know someone who would love to do that, however. His previous assistant would love to come back under these changed circumstances, especially if she had this video in her hands. She'd make his life hell."

"A vindictive woman might use them to keep him in line."

"Have you ever worked for a banker?"

"No, but I have a degree in finance."

Anna nodded. "Then send me the information on this woman, and later we can talk about your new position."

Whether Ms. Yaong stayed put or moved to a new place, the woman would be in Anna's debt, but the woman was probably right to move on now. Chan didn't have much of a future. He'd do what he was told, but eventually, that would frustrate the stockholders and they'd replace him. Ms. Yaong, however, was just beginning to demonstrate her potential usefulness.

In terms of her alliance with Nikolaj and moving things toward his new goals, his biggest blind spot was the finance people — the old guard. Having this bright young woman embedded with one of the major banks or even the IMF would help Anna help him a great deal.

But now they needed to deal with Mr. Chan. She would have to interrupt his games with the Russian whores and explain his brave new world to him.

When the elevator stopped, the three stepped out onto the plush carpet of the hallway. There were three suites on this floor. The woman pointed to a door.

"You two wait here," Anna said.

"Ma'am," Roger said, catching her eye.

"I won't need a bodyguard in there, Roger. Mr. Chan is not a threat. You keep Ms. Yaong company and see that no one interrupts my meeting."

The bodyguard nodded and handed her the passkey. Anna went to the door, swiped it, and stepped into the living room of the plush suite. She walked toward the bedroom door and opened it, letting it bang against the stops. "Well hello," she said.

Startled, the naked man on the bed the man turned to look at the intruder. He shouted something in Chinese that sounded like a curse, then he switched to English. "What the fuck? How dare you barge in here?"

He looked around as if someone might explain what was going on. Beside him, the girls kept on with what they'd been doing, with the one on her back moaning.

The man held part of the bedcovers in front of his body in an attempt at modesty. He seemed surprised that the women ignored Anna's intrusion.

"Mr. Chan, how are you?" Anna swept into the room and took a seat in a velvet-covered chair that faced the bed. "I'm Anna Rasburn. We've met before, but in a boardroom, not a bedroom." His tense expression pleased her. "Perhaps you remember me. I consulted with your company a few years ago."

"But what the hell...."

"I apologize for interrupting your celebration, but I have some tragic news and a question."

"Tragic news?"

"I'm afraid the CEO of your company is about to die in a horrific accident."

"About to die? What are you saying?"

"I'm saying that in a little while you'll get a call from your firm's PR person. She will be desperate for a statement from you. You see, the news will be out that someone discovered the lifeless body of your boss. The poor man is, or soon will be, dead through some horrific accident."

"What happened?"

"I don't know the details. I'll read them in the news, like everyone else. What matters is that, as the vice president in charge of worldwide sales and the former CFO, that makes you the de facto CEO. Naturally, the markets, your stockholders, will need reassurance that despite this tragedy, there is still a firm hand on the tiller." She looked at the girls. "Or, in this case, a firm hand on the tits."

"He will be dead? What the hell is going on?"

"This is our version of a field promotion, Mr. Chan. Your boss didn't want to cooperate, move with progress. He was doing the bidding of the global bankers. That was a bad decision. But you are made of sterner stuff. Therefore, temporarily at least, you will be put in his place. In a few days, the board will hold an emergency meeting and confirm you in that position — assuming we can come to an understanding and that you seem to be upholding your end of it."

"What are you talking about?" he sputtered.

"We are talking about your future," Mr. Chan. "I suppose you know that the about-to-be-late chairman intended to turn down a proposal to participate in the Mumbai Smart City program."

"Yes. I remember something about it. We were doing it for goodwill and PR. It wasn't a big thing."

"Ah, but it was a big thing. Perhaps not to him, but to us, it is very big. And now I want to know how you feel about that project. Are you for it?"

"I... Liang is really dead?"

She glanced at her wristwatch. "Not yet. But soon enough. Let's save some time and save you the angst of having to decide something so important to your future. Mr. Chan, you are wholeheartedly in favor of this project. In fact, you think your company should be playing an even larger role than it originally committed to. That is how you feel, Mr. Chan. And as CEO, you will make that happen. Your company will provide the light-rail system, including the engineering, at cost. It will be the best system you've ever produced."

Suddenly the man took stock of the situation. He looked at the naked women, who were stretching languorously on the bed. "These women work for you."

"Yes, they do. I'm the proud owner of the finest escort service in Shanghai."

He let the bedding fall and stood there naked. "So, this is your big lever?" he demanded. "If I don't do what you want, you intend to tell the world that a businessman was caught fucking some hookers? That's not news. Telling the world won't hurt my career at all."

She laughed. "No, exposing your adventures in some small-time illicit sex won't do that at all, although your wife and family might feel differently. On the other hand, there is the small matter of prostitution being illegal in China."

He looked at the women. "I didn't pay these women. I didn't even know they were hookers." He sneered. "My lawyers can get any charges dismissed easily enough."

"Perhaps you didn't know they were professionals, but it would come down to your word against theirs. However, for our purposes that doesn't matter — the ladies' little deception was only to get your attention." She smiled. "And I seem to have it. You haven't called anyone to throw me out."

"What makes you think I will play your game?"

"Because of something I know about the transaction you hired these ladies to celebrate."

"Business?"

"While I'm sure that your board will applaud today's sale of a rather large-scale system to Malaysia Rail, it might not be beneficial for you if they learned how you got it. A few hookers are nothing, but the deposits you made to a certain bank account in Luxembourg, deposits that are linked to a government minister, are potentially career threatening."

The man's face changed. There was no way she could speak about that without having proof… he was hemmed in. His moment of defiance passed, and his bravado evaporated. "What do you want?"

"Exactly what I told you."

He shook his head. "That's it? You want us to reinstate our involvement in that stupid little project?"

"Yes. Specifically, I want you to authorize a budget to make that light rail you are building for Mumbai first rate and I'll expect you to deliver it on time." She smiled at him. "That's all for now. After that we just want you to be a good little CEO and enjoy your bonuses. From time to time we might contact you about other matters. When we do, if you do what you are told you can have a long and prosperous career."

A sneer came to his lips. "I could tell the world that someone arranged this so-called accident you tell me is going to happen. An investigation into his death might uncover that you had Liang killed. He was a friend of mine."

"But Mr. Chan, that wouldn't be a good idea at all. Yes, they might discover he was killed, but unfortunately, any honest and transparent investigation would uncover horrifying facts. They would find that an assassin was hired and that the payment to the person who arranged the accident came from your account. And, while you might not know it, there is evidence that your friend was intending to fire you. He'd already talked to some board members about replacing you and bringing in fresh talent."

"What?"

"So, you see, drawing attention to the possibility that the CEO's death wasn't an accident wouldn't be clever of you at all. It certainly doesn't hurt me. I have no connection to it whatsoever."

It was true that Anna couldn't be tied to the death. Although she felt certain it was being handled by Franz, working under the direction of Nikolaj, even that was an assumption.

As Chan sank back in despair, leaning against the headboard, oblivious to the two naked women in bed with him, sitting on either side of him, running their hands over him, she knew he'd accepted what she said. Finally, his eyes focused. "You want me to approve the project as the temporary CEO."

"Yes."

"And then the board will confirm me as CEO?"

"Correct."

"You can guarantee that?"

"Guarantee is an odd word, but I assure you that nothing has been left to chance, Mr. Chan. Nothing. I've even had the details of the project, the extent of your firm's future involvement in it, and the terms, sent to your private email account. This is what you will give your people, without modification."

"But I'll need to review the proposal."

"There is no need for you to go to that trouble, Mr. Chan. Besides, we do not want any mistakes about the level of involvement you favor creeping into the proposal, now do we?"

"No," he said, tonelessly.

Anna stood. "You will sign the proposal and forward it to your people. With that settled, I will leave you to your celebration. That phone call is coming soon. After you deal with the tragedy of your boss's untimely demise, feel free to return to fucking your brains out."

A cell phone on the nightstand sounded. He stared at it. "I should send the girls away."

"Oh, they should stay the night as contracted, Mr. Chan. These ladies work for my escort service and also will monitor your conversation for me. They are both fluent Mandarin speakers. By the way, we do appreciate your business. Enjoy yourself with them and consider it my treat. I'm paying them a considerable amount, so indulge yourself. Call it pussy for cooperation. But first, you'd better take that call. I'm afraid it is going to be bad news."

He grabbed the phone and listened. His eyes widened, then he began speaking Chinese at a frantic pace. But then, to Anna's ear, Chinese always sounded frantic.

She nodded at the girls, got up and walked out.

When the door of the suite closed behind her, she smiled at Ms. Yaong and handed back the passkey. "Did you hear all of it?"

"Yes. And it was recorded. It will be sent with the video."

"You've done good work here, Ms. Yaong. If I could convince you to stay on the job for just a month, if you were watching things long enough for me to be certain he does as he is told, I'll be glad to pay you a bonus. Bring back the other woman to do the day-to-day work if you like. Tell Mr. Chan it's my wish for him to have two assistants for the time being. In return, I'll see to it that your next job is much more than being someone's assistant."

Pleasure crossed her face. "Can I openly wield the stick you've created for yourself?"

"That too. Let him know you work for me… and that he works for you. He won't be in his job long, but while he is, you can use your position to indulge yourself."

Ms. Yaong gave her an amused smile. "I would be delighted to do that, Ms. Rasburn. Thank you."

Anna turned and nodded at Roger; he took an envelope from his coat pocket and held it out to Ms. Yaong. "In the meantime, here is your fee for the work you've done," Anna said. As the woman hesitated, Anna gave her a look. "You requested to be paid in cash on completion, I believe. That's your money."

Her nervous gaze flickered up to the corners of the hallway. "But.…"

Roger put the envelope in her hand. "The cameras on this floor are all disabled," he said.

She let out a breath, then took the envelope and bowed. "Of course." Then her phone rang.

"I imagine that is Mr. Chan," Anna said. "He most likely will need your help writing a statement."

She nodded. "He does need help with such things. Is there anything special he should say?" The woman was enjoying the prospect of dictating to her boss for a change.

"There is a statement in the envelope with your money," Anna said. "He isn't to alter it."

Ms. Yaong grinned and nodded. As she stepped aside to take the call, Anna headed to the elevator with Roger behind her.

As the door closed, he took out another passkey out of his pocket. "Your room?" he asked. "Or would you like to go to the bar for a nightcap?"

She touched his arm and moved close to him, putting her face against his chest. "To my room and my bed," she said. "After you fuck me, then you can bring me a nightcap."

"Yes, Ma'am," he said.

Anna only used a bodyguard when she was in big cities. It was a hassle having a shadow. Since she felt the need for one in Shanghai, given all the time she had to spend with him, it would damn well be a man and a hot man at that. For the money she paid, she wanted to enjoy some benefits of having a bodyguard that had nothing to do with feeling safe.

She'd brought Roger with her from her New York office. Unlike some men she hired, he wasn't actually an eager lover. Some of them came onto her, but Roger never did. He was married and her intelligence about him was that he didn't play around. But he did what he was asked to do without question. Given the amount of money she paid him to do her bidding, she was sure he'd do his best to please her.

She let her hip rub against his crotch and felt a positive response. She savored it. She wanted to celebrate her little victory and that gave her reason to suspect that Roger's best was going to be rather good.

CHAPTER 22

PAYMENT PROCESSING OPTIONS

"What is the value of security if freedoms within it are subject to the government's unchecked will? What freedoms are we defending if, in the name of freedom the government can take them away because of a person's appearance or nationality? Who will decide — and under what standards — whose freedom stays and whose freedom goes?"

— Andrew Napolitano, A Nation of Sheep

A Large, Well-Guarded Hacienda Outside Mexico City

Don Pedro studied the man reporting to him, watching closely to see all that his body language might tell him.

The man, Hector Lopez, had worked for him for many years now. He was a known quantity — loyal and unimaginative. He was a little man with an accountant's squint and the cheap suit of an underling. He would never be more than that, but his reports were as trustworthy as it was possible to expect. Even so, there were times when you needed to see the person. Their body told you the things the person wasn't sure of, even the things he didn't wish to mention.

Taking in the way Hector stood, seeing that he was relaxed and at ease, Don Pedro was reassured. His loyal minion harbored no doubts about the validity of what he was saying, which was: "The payment was made instantly."

"Then this... arrangement, this technology works for our friends in Cartagena? They are happy using this digital money?"

"Absolutely. They were delighted to be paid in crypto, in Monero. In fact, their IT woman asked me why it had taken us so long to learn the new ways. Of course, considering how easily, painlessly it went, she would say that."

"They get their money faster, I suppose," he told the man.

"There is so much more to it than that. If we send them physical dollars, those dollars must be laundered, and that costs them. Handling cash creates many additional overhead costs and problems — they have to provide security for the cash, and of course, pay bribes to bankers or launderers. And there is always the chance of all of this being traced back to them. When we make payments in Monero, there is none of that. The ledger entries are completely anonymous."

"Like a secret bank account?" Don Pedro asked.

"Even better than that. No one needs to open an account or show identification. They create a paper wallet and we send money to it."

"And why are you expressing all this concern for our supplier's wellbeing?"

"Because it helps us too. Our people in the US and Canada would be pleased not to have to deal with sending cash to us. Smuggling dollars here from the US and then on to Colombia is not only expensive, but it has many risks."

Don Pedro sat back in his overstuffed chair and wondered why, with all the money at his disposal, it didn't seem he could find a doctor who could stop the never-ending pain in his hip. At fifty-five, he was way too young to feel like a damn cripple.

Lately, his infernal wife had been after him to stop eating potatoes. She said it would help, but that had to be bullshit. Potatoes? She'd read it somewhere.

But then his wife was against him eating wheat and dairy too. Next thing she'd be after him to stop drinking. That was a laugh. What kind of cartel boss didn't drink?

A man who tried to be fair, Don Pedro had to admit that the woman took her own advice, and it seemed to work well for her. Even at forty-five, she had the fashion-model look that had attracted him to her in the first place. But shit, no more fucking potatoes? What kind of life was that?

"What exactly are you proposing?" he asked Hector.

"That we convert our float account, the one that we feed with money from the payments of distributors in the US and Europe, into Monero. If you permit us to use cryptocurrency in our dealings with them, they can send it to us instantly and almost for free — the same as the way we got paid the ransom and as we paid Cartagena. We want to store more of the float, the money used for large purchases, in Monero."

Just to take the man out of his comfort zone, Don Pedro snarled. "And where do we keep this Monero shit? From what you people tell me, it isn't really anything I can touch. You expect me to buy something that I can't hold in my hand? That makes me nervous."

"It's a record, no different than an IOU, or a bank deposit. You can't touch those, yet the figures themselves are reassuring. In this case, the money is even safer. The ledger these entries are kept in, the blockchain, can't be hacked and there is no way to trace it to you. It is data that we store in a digital wallet."

"A fucking wallet? Not even in a safe?"

The man sighed. "Sir, remember this is a digital currency. The wallet is digital too — numbers printed on paper if you like. It is safer than *dinero* in a safe. Our businesses will flow better, profits will be higher, and there won't be any nasty bank accounts that report to the government."

"But it isn't fucking money."

Hector sighed. "If that is true, then ask yourself why the people in Colombia are so eager to get paid with it? It's very much real money in the important sense that you can buy things with it. While it's true that not everyone will accept it, even some governments will take payment in crypto."

Don Pedro sat back to consider what the man was saying. Or to appear to consider his words.

The truth was that he knew more about cryptocurrency than he let on. When the Indian businessman had offered to pay in Bitcoin and his IT man had assured him that this stuff was a good idea, even better than cash, he'd started reading, exploring. He had heard about it before, of course, but he knew little about it.

After some quick studying, he'd been delighted to test it and the ransom payment was a perfect opportunity. Coming in the way it did made it basically free money, after all. The transaction had gone smoothly. He'd loved the fact that it didn't involve banks, which cut down on bribes, and it was instantaneous. There was a lot to like about this shit.

He didn't like his people to know that he had such an intellectual curiosity. They might think he was getting soft.

Keeping that secret had served him well. It meant he could sit back and evaluate what he was being told, often getting more advanced ideas than he could come up with on his own. That gave him the best of both worlds and the added advantage of being able to tell when one of his people tried to shit him.

Whenever possible, he liked to be seen as the crude, unschooled but diabolically clever Don. Like in the movies. That way his actual knowledge caught them off guard. Like those Colombian bastards. They looked down on Mexicans.

This time, however, they were playing it straight. He thought it might be because the IT guys were talking directly to each other and it wasn't the macho bosses posturing like banty roosters.

"You are telling me that you think this a good way for us to do our banking?"

"Not only is it a great payment system, but we don't have to worry about currency fluctuations. In the time we held the crypto that the Indian paid us, its value, in dollar terms, nearly doubled. Effectively, we got the next shipment from the Colombians for half price."

"But it could've gone down, too."

"Yes, but it retains its intrinsic value."

"I like things that double in value," Don Pedro said as if he'd just thought of it. "What would you say about putting all our reserves in Monero?"

"All?"

"Not just the float. If it's good for part of our wealth, why not all of it?"

"You want to change over to crypto completely?"

"Mostly. Not totally. But for a large number of things. Some of the crackdowns and the sanctions that are going on … the money we have in banks can be frozen. It isn't safe. But this can't, right?"

"No way."

"The fucking US Federales are always freezing this or that account. We usually get it back, but for a time we lose access to our money. And that is a pain. From what you are telling me, they can't touch this stuff."

"They can't, but you want all the cash in crypto?" Hector was perspiring.

"You said it was safer than in a safe. Sounds fucking good to me."

Watching the man was amusing enough to make him forget the pain in his hip. The little man was learning that it was one thing to suggest a strategy and quite another altogether to have Don Pedro to go all-in on his idea. "Well, yes, but…"

He knew that it went against every instinct the man had to put everything in one pot. "Unless you were lying, I think that's what we should do with every fucking peso and dollar we have. Convert everything that isn't needed for bribes, local payoffs, and whores and other normal operating expenses."

"I can, but…."

Don Pedro smiled. "I like the idea. How marvelous that I can snap my fingers and send money anywhere without any bank or government knowing. With that kind of liquidity available to us, we can negotiate better deals." He was going to say more but stopped himself. The way the accountant's face lit up when he heard Don Pedro talk about liquidity told him he was saying too much.

"I suppose we can do that."

"If I say we can, then you better damn well know we can do it, *chico*."

He let the level of menace in his voice rise to a satisfactory level before smiling. "Let me know when it's done. Better yet, send the IT guy to me when it's done. I'll want him to explain it all once more." Then he winked. "Not that I'll understand a word of his gibberish."

When the man nodded weakly and left, Don Pedro got out a cigar and lit it. His wife wouldn't be back from the city until the next day. She had a keen sense of smell, that woman. But if he got the chica he was screwing out of the house in time for the maid to air out the house and wash the sheets and his clothes, his wife would never know he smoked in the house.

In his own damn house.

Although this cryptocurrency stuff showed promise, it heralded a new age. Keeping up was getting harder. Staying on top, harder yet. He did it because that's who he was. That's what kept him the Don.

And he liked this crypto shit. It was perfect for him. But other things... There were things about the old way of doing things that he missed. Mostly he missed the time when a Don was the boss in his own home.

It was nice to hear that the value of the crypto had doubled. Doubling the value of a ransom you'd already collected had a lot going for it. And that didn't count the Euros he'd been paid for kidnapping the girl in the first place. Why they'd wanted that girl grabbed was a mystery, but they'd paid him well.

They'd wanted him to ask for a ransom and said he could keep it. They didn't seem to care whether it was actually paid, and that was odd. There were strange forces at work. But then they were fucking gringos. Their brains worked differently than the superior Latin brain. They'd even thought he was too dumb to know that they were CIA. How hard would it be to guess?

The girl had been a cute one. *Muy bonita.* And fresh. If the deal had gone differently, if the father hadn't paid the ransom, he might've enjoyed her.

He put aside the thoughts of how he might teach a girl like that to please him before sending her to work in one of his whore houses. Money was good too, and Don Pedro had been in on both ends of a deal. And he'd promised not to hurt the girl if they paid the ransom. It was a substantial one, and the father paid, so Don Pedro kept the bargain. In that sense, when it came to business, he was a man of honor.

Most of the time, at least.

234 // CRYPTO CITIZENS

CHAPTER 23

NEW BUSINESS

"Reality exists as an objective absolute — facts are facts, independent of man's feelings, wishes, hopes or fears."

— *Ayn Rand, "Introducing Objectivism," The Objectivist Newsletter, Aug. 1962, 35*

Panaderia y Cafeteria D'Mario
Hispania, Colombia

Once they started working together, it didn't take long for Joshua to see Miguel as someone with amazing potential. He devoured anything digital.

Before Joshua came along, the kid had already been making money hacking pirated video games for people. Colombians loved the games as much as other people, but most couldn't afford to play them. Even the poor could afford to pay Miguel a small amount to get them playing.

Miguel was fascinated by what Joshua did. He had a knack for evaluating the relative values of things — the core of trading. All the charting that Joshua did wasn't his cup of tea, but he quickly learned to read the news and estimate its impact on the price of various cryptos.

Joshua gave Miguel a small stake which he put into several wallets. Soon he was making money doing trades. That success, his natural aptitude for trading and his ability to learn quickly, delighted Joshua.

The kid had initiative, too. He was a hustler in the best sense of the word. Within days of seeing how money was made online and how Joshua invested for people, he convinced a number of local people to pool their resources and let him invest it for them. It wasn't a lot of money, but with Joshua keeping a watchful eye and offering the occasional tip, he built a portfolio of lesser-known cryptocurrencies, such as Monero, Dash, and Litecoin.

And he was having fun.

Meantime, Joshua was back to work doing the same thing on a larger scale.

When he saw Miguel scrounging up old computers and interconnecting them, he learned that the boy had read about mining crypto. "I want to run a Monero node to see it work," he said. "And, if I can get enough computer power, we can start mining crypto."

As time went on, Joshua turned over some of his routine work to Miguel and spent more of his time working for Tricia's growing client base. These people had large amounts of cash, and the need to invest it privately, discreetly, and, if possible, keeping the transactions untraceable.

That put Joshua on his own massive learning curve, finding new ways to meet their needs. It was time spent profitably.

And now Tricia had one specific client she wanted him to focus on. His name was Juan Torres, and he was a General in the Venezuelan Army. "Somehow, he has amassed a large amount of money," she told Josh. "It's in a bank in the Cayman Islands."

"And we don't ask how he got more money than a General earns in a lifetime?"

"We don't want to know," she agreed.

They were talking over a secure phone link that used an encryption scheme Miguel had found and modified to make it their own. That made it more secure.

"Now my client wants to disappear," Tricia said. "He sees the writing on the wall."

"That must be rough. Those people are resourceful if they can write on the walls when there isn't any paint left in the country. It's a total failed state."

"And oddly, failed states often produce new wealthy people … it's all very mysterious," she laughed. "But it's good business for us. He has friends and, as a good general should, he wants to lead by example."

"Where are we with him?"

"I've got Kenny doing his ID. That will be ready tomorrow. But I need to make his hidden money disappear completely. Then I want it to reappear in an account in Estonia. He wants to be certain that the money is waiting for him before he disappears."

"Estonia?"

She chuckled. "This general has developed a taste for capitalism. It seems he has already established his e-residency using his new name."

"Electronic residency is good. That simplifies things, but I'll need access to those Cayman bank accounts. Is he ready to turn it over to me?"

"Not you, silly. But he's happy to turn it over to Freedom Investments, LLC."

"And that is?"

"That is you and me. I created a company. Generals like official-sounding things with tons of documentation." She laughed. "But I made Miguel an officer in the company. He is the CEO, actually. I registered the company in Panama."

"Miguel?"

"Why not? I like him and it's handy to have a Spanish speaker as part of it all, so he's now our CEO."

Joshua shook his head at the way Tricia was enjoying her new life. He was delighted for her. "And what am I in the Tricia Campbell master plan?"

"In the master plan? Ah, well, in that incredibly secret document, you are my colleague and occasional lover — when our paths cross."

The words made Joshua grin. In his new world, Tricia was the only kind of partner he could imagine working with. She took initiative. As she learned her trade, her confidence had grown, but she was a straight shooter. "In terms of the new business you are the co-owner, with me, and also an employee."

"Fair enough."

"I'll send you the account information and you can get the money."

"Send me the company documents and I'll open a new account in that company name that this general of yours, and other clients for that matter, can use to deposit payments." He laughed again. "Better yet, I'll have Miguel open it, him being the CEO and all. Might as well be official. It might be handy later."

"Will you put that in the Caymans?"

"No, I'll tuck it away in another small bank on another small island in the Caribbean. The Caymans are a money laundering cliché. Maybe Anguilla. I know a banker in Anguilla who is long on promises and who has a gambling debt. He'll be glad to do a few favors to ensure we have some extra levels of privacy."

"This general is a priority. Can we get this done right away?"

"Is he in danger?"

"Yes, but more to the point, he is a test case for this kind of relocation. I have a much bigger client waiting in the wings, who is pushing me. He wants his new identity tomorrow, but he is also cautious, and his minion wants to see proof of our concept before he gives us the go ahead and turns over his accounts. They want to see that it works."

Joshua laughed. "He wants another sucker to try it out first."

"Exactly."

"That's smart, if bruising to our fragile egos."

"Your fucking ego, Joshua, is fortunately made of stainless steel. And this new guy, it's fair to say, doesn't care about our feelings. He cares about himself and no one else. That's why I am dealing with a rather nasty looking intermediary."

"He does know that his intermediary can't babysit his money once we get our hands on it, doesn't he?"

"He does. He's pretty sophisticated. He knows a lot about the way we work; he's clear on the fact that the only way his money can pop up elsewhere and be accessible to him in his new incarnation is if he lets go of it in the here and now. I don't think he's worried about that. As his flunky said, they know where I live. He is more interested in ensuring that our efforts don't leave a trail. I suspect that his life might be in danger and not from a mere government."

"Is organized crime after him?"

"Maybe, although I'm guessing he is involved in organized crime at a management level himself."

"It would be nice to know who might be trying to track his money."

"Does it matter?"

"Once we start, no one can stop or track the hand waving Miguel and I do, so in that sense, no. But it would be nice to know what to be on the alert for. That would give us a better idea of what tracks we needed to cover. If we can't find out, then I'll just be extra careful. After all, if we help him, his enemies become our enemies... until they need to disappear, of course. Just keep in mind that if he is scared of someone, and he is bad news, we could get slapped down by the people looking for him."

He waited out the silence as Tricia thought it through. "Can you cover our involvement in his disappearance?"

"Up to a point. Digitally, sure. But if they catch the guy and torture him, all bets are off."

"Okay. I'll see if I can't get a few hints of who might object to the rebirth of our client. Now that I've convinced him we can handle this with utmost discretion, I don't want to spook him."

"You might tell him that the more we know about who might be chasing the money, the better job we can do hiding it all. Governments, for instance, have different resources than pissed off corporations."

"That's good."

"Then pass along anything you do learn."

"Of course."

"As soon as you send me all the information, including copies of the general's new identity, I'll set up an account in that name." He paused. "Tell him he'll be banking with Change Bank in Estonia. I'll put his money, less our fee, into it. I'll convert everything into a cryptocurrency for the transfer, but Change will make it available to him as a multi-currency wallet and an ATM card. He can access his ill-gotten wealth in Euros or dollars if he, foolishly, prefers."

"You are a zealot," she laughed.

"A pragmatist," he said. "I love this shit."

"I've already encrypted a file containing the access information for the Cayman bank and all the details on his new identity. One question: why convert the money to crypto and then back to some form of cash again?"

"To make it a double-blind transfer," Joshua said. "Buying crypto makes the money untraceable. Then we deposit the funds in an account created for a new person, which gives him money he can spend. Figuring out what and where we sent the money would require tracking both the money and the identity — I don't think either is possible."

"If all goes well, we will have all the business we can handle."

"Two of your previous clients still have me managing their money," he said. "We are doing well for them too, my CEO and me. The management fees make for a nice additional cash flow."

"Aren't you sitting pretty then?" she laughed.

"You aren't doing so bad yourself. Have you ditched that husband yet?"

She sighed. "I haven't gotten around to doing it officially. He knows it's all over though. But you are right; I need to cut the cord. The marriage is nothing but a distraction."

"Still."

"You're right."

When they rang off, Joshua was left with a good feeling. He wanted to connect with Tricia again, be with her. Maybe they could meet up in Quito. He had fond memories of her, of the great sex they'd had. He liked her, enjoyed being with her. It would be a treat.

Of course, he had Carmen now. She was so different from Tricia. Uncomplicated and old world, in many ways, she seemed to thrive on being his woman, taking care of him in and out of bed, and doing what it took to make him happy. He was getting spoiled — he loved it, too.

He wasn't sure where that would lead. Everything seemed new and in flux. Look at the work he did. Every day there was a new opportunity or threat, sometimes both, to his cryptocurrency world. He couldn't imagine what his work would entail six months from now. What coins would be the ones he liked? What exchanges worked best for him? What banks would be best? What countries would support or crack down on traders like him?

The tone on his phone alerted him to a call from a number he didn't know. That was curious and unusual, not to mention unsettling. He didn't give the number out casually. Tricia and Miguel were the only ones who called this number. He didn't want to answer. It had to be someone misdialing. But what if it wasn't?

He needed to know who it was. Holding his breath, he answered and heard a woman's lilting voice. It sounded oddly familiar, although it wasn't anyone he knew. How could that be?

"Joshua Raintree?"

"Yes."

"My name is Boone and I've heard good things about you."

The announcement made his hackles rise. "Who have you heard about me from?"

"Kenny Lu," she said. "You've also interacted with some people in my group."

"Your group?"

"The Bitpats," she said.

"I've never heard of you."

She laughed. "I'm delighted to hear that. You see, we are a close-knit crowd of what some people call digital nomads. Kenny is one of us."

That sent up more alarms. If Kenny was talking out of school, there could be trouble. Being compromised now would undo everything. "And what good things have you heard about me?"

She chuckled. "All manner of them. I understand you are a proponent of individual liberty."

That was a vague enough accusation. "I can admit to that," he said. "Even to a stranger."

"I understand that you and your friend Tricia Campbell are doing important work together. It could be more important than you know. I'd like to talk with you about taking that up a notch."

"What? And why?" How did she know about Tricia or him, or that they were working together? Now he was on edge.

She laughed again, a pleasant laugh. "Those are things we don't want to chat about this way. Even secure, encrypted phones can be, and are, hacked, in my experience."

"Yet you called me," he said.

"To introduce myself and arrange a meeting. I'd like to meet you and talk face-to-face."

"Are you local?"

"To you in Colombia? No. I'm in Singapore at the moment, but I can be in Medellin tomorrow. If you'd be willing to meet with me there, it wouldn't take long to determine if the two of us should do more than chat."

"More than chat?" Repeating her questions made him feel like an idiot, but she'd caught him totally unprepared.

"From what Kenny tells us, we should be working together, helping each other."

Joshua's mind raced. Whatever Kenny was, he wasn't a rat. This had to be big, and it had to be right. "Send me your flight information when you have it. I'll meet your plane."

"Let's do better than that."

"Better?"

"I dislike airport meetings. This is Monday. How about this? On Wednesday evening, by six, I'll be in the poolside bar of the InterContinental Hotel in Medellin. It's not right downtown, it's at Calle 16 in Variante Las Palmas. Could you meet me there?"

"I'm sure I could."

She laughed. "Okay then, I'll ask it correctly. Will you meet me there?"

"That sounds intriguing," he said.

"Intriguing enough for you to show up?"

He laughed. "I suppose so."

Excellent," she said. "I think we will have a lot to talk about."

"In that case, I'll get myself a room at the hotel," he said. "If it's that important, we don't want to be rushed. If what we have to discuss is as big as you are suggesting, then we should take as long as needed."

"I like your style, Joshua Raintree," she said, sounding delighted.

Whoever this Boone was, he needed to find out what her angle was. He'd pump Kenny for information, of course, but no matter what he said or how nice she sounded, he needed to find out who Boone was. She had managed to get inside his business far too easily and without him even aware he was being checked out. Clearly, he had some security problems to deal with besides Kenny. She could help him find them.

"I'll see you there," she said. "I've warned Kenny to expect your call." With that enigmatic comment, she was gone.

"Miguel," he called. "Is there a reliable taxi driver in this town?"

Miguel poked his head in. "Reliable for what?"

"Showing up on time and driving as if he doesn't have a death wish."

"To go where?"

"Medellin. I need to meet someone."

"When?"

"Wednesday evening at the InterContinental Hotel."

He grinned. "Medellin? While you are there, it would be good to look at getting another server," he said. "We could use it for additional mining."

"Good thinking. But I'll be rather busy, so maybe you might want to go along? I could send you to buy what we need."

Miguel brightened. "Medellin? Of course. That's a good idea. With your terrible Spanish, you will need me, or they will rob you blind."

"We will be there a couple of days, so Carmen should go too. She'll enjoy staying at the hotel, I expect."

Miguel smiled. "Oh yes, she will. El InterContinental es muy elegante. I'll arrange for a real car to take us early that morning," he said. "No taxi."

"And your cousin will drive."

Miguel smiled. "Everyone in town is my cousin, so si."

As Miguel left to arrange things, Joshua's thoughts returned to this Boone — the woman who knew far too much about him. It was impossible to know how, or even who she was, but she was flying halfway around the world to meet him. That was a good sign. She didn't mind holding the meeting on his turf, more or less. His guess was that when they met, things would either get interesting or extremely complicated. On second thought, based on his experience, those two were not mutually exclusive. Certainly, meeting Tricia had enriched his life both those ways.

And then he had another thought — a nice one. The hotel was on the far side of the city. On their way through they could make a stop. Carmen would need some nicer clothes for that hotel. While they were there, he would buy her a skimpy bikini. She'd look good in one.

CHAPTER 24

THE DISLOYAL OPPOSITION

*"Hope, in reality, is the worst of all evils
because it prolongs the torments of man."*

— *Friedrich Nietzsche*

Marina
San Diego, CA

A sense of excitement was palpable from the moment he walked
into the marina. People were hustling about in the sunny October
San Diego morning, hauling boating gear, coolers, duffle bags, and
pushing hand trucks loaded with provisions. Others were on boats,
checking the rigging for the fourteenth time, greasing things that
were supposed to run free and bolting down things that needed to
stay in place.

Floating on the anticipation that bubbled up around him, the
green-eyed man slipped unobtrusively through the bustling crowd
and toward the sailboats moored snug in their slips.

"Man, this is going to be so fucking good," a young man
shouted as he walked by drinking a beer.

"That storm out by Hawaii means we'll have some fucking good
wind," a young woman walking in the other direction agreed.

Although he didn't share it, Nikolaj understood their enthusiasm, their jubilant mood. The annual Baja Ha-Ha Rally was about to start.

The comically named event was a 750-mile rally, from San Diego to Cabo San Lucas, for boats over 27-feet long. Today was preparation. Tomorrow was the Skipper's Meeting and Kick-Off Party. The race began the next morning. This was his chance to catch Anna.

He made his way to the slip where FINAL OFFER was berthed and saw her slim figure, coiling lines near the mast. He shook his head, thinking how odd it was that whenever he saw her, he was taken with her athletic build, her svelte sexiness as if he'd never seen her before. When he thought of her, it was always as a colleague — a ruthless and dangerous associate who, fortunately, usually had reason to side with him.

Once, when younger, they'd shared a bed, but that could never last. They were too independent, too driven. But one thing they shared, one common interest that kept them working together, was that neither of them wanted to be the person in charge. The trappings of power quickly became a constraint. And while it was important for people to understand you wielded power, neither of them cared to be a figurehead. Those people were tools.

He walked to the boat and stood there, hands in his pockets, looking for all the world like a tourist as he watched her. Her competence amazed him. He admired competence and valued it as the rare commodity it was.

"Nik," she said. She stood with her arms resting on the sail, which was neatly flaked on the boom.

"Got a few minutes?" he asked.

"Just a few. The race —"

He waved a hand. "I know. Sorry. My timing always sucks."

"Come on board." She glanced at his feet. "You dressed right, at least," she said.

He had worn boat shoes for the occasion. "I didn't want to piss you off. You're a bad woman to piss off."

"And you need something." It wasn't a question.

"Dione and Park are in town. We're staying at the Sheraton."

"Suspiciously convenient."

"We need to meet. It concerns you."

"I have a lot to do."

"This is important. And you can finish your day here. Just come by this evening. We can have dinner in the room and talk."

She wrinkled her nose. It made her look oddly like a girl, rather than a woman. "Okay. I can get everything done by seven and meet you at eight."

"Good. The Penthouse. I'll leave a keycard for you at the desk."

"This isn't going to make me miss the race is it?"

"I don't think so. It shouldn't. Just a heads up."

"You brought Osk?"

He grinned. "I did."

"Then you'll be able to amuse yourself until then."

"I have plenty of amusements besides that Interpol woman. And she works too, you know."

"Look, if you are going to interrupt my race preparations, I get to taunt you."

"I thought this was just a cruiser rally, for fun."

She made a sour face. "I race to win, Nicky."

"You do everything to win, Anna. That's why we get along."

"Then get your landlubber ass off my boat and let me finish my work."

"Aye, Captain."

With a mock salute, Nikolaj stepped back on the pier and headed back to where he'd left the rental car. He knew that Anna had been teasing him, but the woman knew him too well. He had plans for the time until the meeting and the thought of Osk the way he'd left her, tied to his bed, whimpering, put a spring in his step.

When Anna arrived at the hotel, she found Park, Dione, and Osk were already there. She gave each a cordial hello, took a drink, and turned to Nikolaj. "Okay, we are all here. It's time to explain why I am eating from room service in your hotel and not at the marina bar."

Dione Bellamy smiled at her. "It's not a big deal. We are just being asked to change our fundamental strategy. Nikolaj has discovered the future and wants to lead us there."

"Putting aside your sarcasm," he said, "basically, you are right. We are changing directions."

"I thought you saw the Oculistica as the future," Park said.

Nikolaj paused. "I do. But it is clear that we've been spinning our wheels. To get to the goal we've all pursued, we need to refocus our efforts."

Park shook his head. "Please be clear. Refocused on what?"

"On the future... a practical future. We have arrived at a tipping point and I intend for us to sway the result."

Anna smiled. "You've come up with something the Old Man hates."

"Not exactly. It's more that all of us, with our own agendas, have helped push the Oculistica in a new direction. I suddenly saw what that was. Until now I've never had a particular vision."

"Other than power," Anna said.

Nikolaj nodded. "I have been part of the group for all this time because it seemed to be the future. But things change. The advent of information technology, financial technology ... your specialties, have made the means that the old guard chose and refuse to relinquish, increasingly obsolete."

"The Old Man has resisted it, for certain," Dione said. "He didn't even like the existing digital payment systems, and it's clear how much they've done for us."

"And he has tried to slow the smart city project," Park added. "When he thought it was just a bureaucratic construct, he didn't mind. Now he is panicked that it will render his Phoenix project completely pointless."

"It does," Dione said. "I've told him that it is already."

"Which caused him to try to sabotage your efforts, blackmail sponsors into dropping out. I had to have Anna lean on some of her clients to keep them on board. Explain his fears, Dione."

She scowled. "It's the digital money combined with distributed ledgers. If cryptocurrency succeeds in any form, that's the end of the power the banks have over people. Business doesn't need bank accounts. They'll be reduced to dealing with loans. If smart contracts become the norm, then the legal profession takes a hit. All those are part of the power this group was formed to exploit. So, he panics."

Park nodded. "I know that he's been convinced the tokens we use for payment processing in the smart city project, especially if factored in with the idea of a universal basic income paid in tokens, will undermine his Phoenix plan entirely." He scowled. "There is no way he can accept the idea of a world without money as he understands it."

"This is the new power," Dione said. There was a glimmer in her eyes.

Nikolaj nodded. "And it isn't a future he and his cronies want or can understand. They've always valued information, but mostly as a way to get more cash. This is alien to them. He intends to muster his forces and stop it."

"He can't," Dione said. "It's far too late."

"But he can make us lose our relevance," Nikolaj said. "We can't afford to become irrelevant."

Anna noted the way Nikolaj's eyes darted over their faces, closely monitoring their reactions. That he'd invited them to this meeting didn't mean he trusted any of them.

Park took a big swallow of his cola and put the glass down. "This puts us in a squeeze."

"Worse, Park. Because you've been doing your job, he will view you as a clear and present danger."

"What?"

"You backed Herrera to take over in Venezuela, correct?"

"The entire global community did."

"And the Old Man had me take him out."

The room grew quiet, and Park turned pale. "But we, the Oculistica, were financing his coup through the international organizations."

"I know, Park. Everyone knows that the World Bank wanted regime change in Venezuela. The Old Man wasn't ready for it to happen yet and without Herrera it would be postponed."

Nikolaj poured a drink and walked to the window. "I called you here to tell you that you are at war. Whether you want to be doesn't matter. To a certain extent, it doesn't even matter who you would prefer to back — the Old Man has determined that you and I are his enemies. Anyone who is promoting the technology driving the information age is an enemy."

"You can't stop progress," Dione said. "I told him that."

Park came back inside, wafting the smell of cigarettes and looking calmer. "Everyone tells him that."

"From his point of view, if you were his ally, you'd be putting your energy into helping him convince governments to increase their regulation of it and slow it. Tax the crap out of tech companies to make innovation less profitable."

"Is that what he wants?" Dione asked.

Anna suddenly laughed. "It is. It makes sense now."

"What?"

"The unusual amount of time he's spent in India. I wondered what drew him there."

"What's India got to do with him stopping the projects?" Park asked.

"Some of their political posturing about cryptocurrency and insistence on fiat currency is tied to the Old Man. I'm sure of it. He can make life easy or hard for a lot of politicians there and they prefer it easier, even if the decisions they have to take a stand on are stupid."

Dione looked at Osk. "You are closer to him than most. Do you think this is accurate?"

Her lips twisted into a sour look. "No one is close to that man. I can tell you that he had me assign people to watch all of you." She laughed. "It didn't take a genius to figure out that the Old Man would hire a private agent to watch me — and he did. I had him arrested in the Madrid airport. It turned out that this private investigator was actually smuggling drugs."

Nikolaj laughed. "A short career."

Park trembled. "So, what do we do? About the Old Man, I mean. He scares me."

The green-eyed man refilled his glass from the wet bar and then faced them. "That depends on what you want. Park, I want to prove you correct."

"Me?"

"Your proposal about smart cities, your support for regime change in Venezuela are both important, and we can still make those, and several other things happen."

Dione tapped Park's arm and smiled. "Congratulations. You picked the right side, it seems."

Park had the look of a weatherman who was being swept up by a tornado he had predicted but somehow never believed in. He was catching his breath.

"We need detail," Anna said. "Otherwise this is just rah for our side that's no different than the Old Man's spiel."

Nikolaj smiled. "Then settle down and let me tell you what we are going to do and how we are going to do it."

Dione went to the bar and grabbed the bottle. "I truly want to hear this, but I'm going to need more than one refill to keep my equilibrium."

Anna realized they were about to learn what was really going on. For the first time since she'd met the man, Nikolaj Romijn was showing his true ambition. It had to happen sooner or later, and now she had a front-row seat.

The question was what the price of admission would turn out to be.

Reaching over to grab the bottle from Dione, she refilled her glass, then handed it back. She looked up and the green-eyed man began.

"For many years the Oculistica has worked with traditional allies, such as global bankers, to achieve common goals. They've even been part of our group. Together they fought for world stability. They believed that in a stable world, free markets would flourish, and everyone would prosper."

"And that didn't work out well," Dione said.

"No, it didn't go as planned. Obtaining those things, in that era, demanded big government. Hopes of stability hinged on military might — large well-equipped armies. This was the heritage when our group formed. The danger was another global war. The armies were needed, but also expensive, and countervailing power struggles made them a hindrance to prosperity. But things have changed since then."

"Armies are still necessary," Park said. "The threat of retaliation is still a deterrent to some upstart causing trouble, confiscating goods."

"Wars are fought differently now. Terrorists are the big danger, not an invasion. Today's armies use drone strikes, cyber warfare, dozens of tactics that don't require the huge military-industrial complex. We don't send hundreds or thousands of men to battle anymore. A small strike force, one that is backed by technology, does it all. And when there is no army, a handful of people with suicide bombs works."

"So how does that affect us?" Dione asked.

"The original intent, to create a one-world government, is fundamentally a political and philosophical goal, not a practical necessity for us. In fact, it is a luxury we cannot afford. A look at the European Union shows just how unified and clumsy such a construct would be, even if we implemented it."

Dione lifted her glass. "And yet, the tribal warfare that nation-states wage on each other is still troubling. Trade wars, actual wars… the charter of this group was intended to eliminate that."

"I'm not saying the problem has gone away, just that the time for the old solutions has passed. And others are seeing it already. There have been numerous efforts to create independent sovereignties."

"Libertarians and tax dodgers," Park snorted.

"And yet, despite your derogatory and reflexive response, perhaps they are the wave of the future. Ask yourself: why is that idea attractive to anyone? Because independent and productive people are sick of working and paying increasing taxes in return for less. Increasingly tax money isn't spent on the arguably good causes it is taxed for, but to pay for the government itself."

"Because the government acts in its own interest," Anna said. "Just as a company would."

"And a new sovereign nation that doesn't do that is refreshing. But when it is built by idealists, it runs into problems. But we, my friends, are in a unique position to create something truly new… actually, it is being created anyway. But we can accelerate it."

"What is that?"

"Countries that have a government that isn't really a government, but a service provider."

"How the hell?" Park started.

"Imagine a country that allowed anyone to live and do business within its borders if they were willing to pay an annual fee to operate there. Think of it as a private club. They pay dues to belong and the club protects their privacy, but it doesn't care what they do or how they do it. They wouldn't be regulated or taxed, and the annual service fee would get them protection from external threats and internal strife. They would have access to a judicial system that did little but adjudicate disputes."

Park looked stressed out. "Without a tax base, who builds roads or bridges?"

"Whoever needs them," Nikolaj said. "It's the same for schools, churches, libraries… Already major corporations are setting up the right kind of training to get future employees with the qualifications they need."

"Nik, you've become an anarchist," Anna laughed.

"I'm nothing but a pragmatist," he said. "Because I've never been political, I could see the immense failure communism represented, and now I've realized that the time of government in general is done. It's washed up. I have people and groups coming to me, wanting me to provide them with protection. Ironically, it is their own governments they need protection from. In some way, they are being threatened. Another example is that Dione's bankers make millions by hiding their clients' money. Again, who are they fearful will take it? Their own governments. It seems only reasonable that there is a market for a place they can live and do business that is inherently safe. One where they don't need those protections."

"Complete peace of mind, for only a few dollars more," Anna said, grinning broadly.

"Exactly."

Dione was scowling. "Obviously, I'm hearing this for the first time, but there are so many difficulties with this plan…" she said. "I don't even know where to begin." After a moment, she smiled. "Of course, there are many problems with the existing system, which is why we've been working so fucking hard to change it."

"Exactly. So, if we are going to change the world, which has always been our goal, let's change it to something new and efficient, rather than the same thing, but bigger."

"And you have specific ideas as to how and where we can do this?" Anna asked.

"More than ideas," Nikolaj said. "It's going to happen. It's already starting, and I called this meeting to get you to work with me on it."

"The Old Man ...."

"If your do your part, I will protect you from him."

"But doing what?" Park asked. "What is our part?"

"In your case, Park, I need you doing exactly what you've been doing — keep working to make your smart city project viable... and transferrable."

"Transferrable?"

"I'm going to want you to implement it in Venezuela. A smart city built from the ground up."

"Venezuela? They don't even have food and medicine. How will you...?"

"Don't worry about the viability of it, just work with me, Park. Assume those issues are taken care of and the new government is exactly the kind I've talked about, not the kind they have now or anyone else has either."

"Herrera," Anna said, making his name into a hiss.

"I heard he was dead," Dione said.

Nikolaj nodded. "He was supposed to be, but I might have forgotten to kill him."

"He is working with you?"

"I am only the catalyst. He is a patriot who is creating a new, innovative government that will accommodate our shared vision. But that will require your help. I want his government officially recognized and banks providing financial assistance for the country's recovery. I, and some other new allies, will provide the rest.

Dione looked uneasy, but she nodded. "I'm on board. I can make the bankers think it is business as usual. But if I need to take sides within our own group, I need to know that the others are with you."

The green-eyed man smiled. "No need to concern yourself. Shortly, there will only be one side."

The room grew quiet.

After a moment, Park stood and walked to the balcony.

"I'll take that as agreement," the green-eyed man said.

"You are audacious, I'll give you that."

"And this is just the start, Park," he said. "The Old Man and his buddies thought they were going to be rulers of the globe, but they were fighting the very thing that will enable us to do exactly that. They had no idea what was going to be possible."

CHAPTER 25

HIGH-END SERVICE

"Everything that is really great and inspiring
is created by the individual who can labor in freedom."

~ *Albert Einstein*

The Bahia Grand Panama
Panama City, Panama

Tricia Campbell sat back, swirled the drink in her glass, and let herself reflect on everything that was happening. There was a great deal happening in her life. A hell of a lot. Most of it was good. All of it was exciting.

And she was learning, constantly. She'd never considered traveling to Panama. Not that she had anything against the country, but it had never been on her radar. To her, it had always been the place where they dug the big canal. As it turned out, it was a marvelous place for someone like her to do business.

Her suite in the elegant Bahia Grand Panama was wonderful — luxurious and damn convenient. Flights came and left from everywhere, and the hotel was perfectly situated fifteen minutes from Panama International Airport, ten minutes from the financial district, five minutes from Commercial District, and, if a client had a tourist bent, they were twenty-five minutes from the Panama Canal.

Her executive suite on the twentieth floor offered a stunning view of the Gulf of Panama. Idly, she wondered about getting a condo in the area, a place that would be a base/office location. She didn't really need one yet, and she did have a nice apartment in Quito.

Turning her attention from the view and her own appraisal of the place, she looked over at the gray-haired man who sat in her sitting room sipping a tall whiskey. The man looked nothing like a businessman; he made her think of someone who'd spent many years working at hard labor, maybe as a longshoreman. She thought a man like that should be retired, sitting on a beach somewhere, wearing a Hawaiian shirt and baggy shorts, drinking margaritas and ogling girls in bikinis.

But he wasn't. He was here, in her suite on business. He was sitting there telling her that he needed her services.

She could check his story, learn more about him, but there was no advantage in going to all that trouble. When it came to it, who he was didn't matter in the least. Not to her. What did matter was that he wanted her services, and he'd already sent a large deposit, in Monero, to a wallet Joshua had set up for her. She'd seen the irreversible transaction show up on her laptop. Joshua had seen it too and sent a message confirming it.

Joshua was a careful man, and she appreciated that about him almost as much as some other, more intimate things about him.

One other thing that was different about this client was that he had a bodyguard... Jose Defamo. Defamo had made the initial inquiries about her services. He'd been forthright and calm and was more than a little intimidating. Now he was standing in the hallway outside her door, undoubtedly giving anyone who looked his way a feeling that they should go another direction. It was the only look she'd ever seen on his face — an intimidating indifference that made you feel he could tolerate you, be cordial, or kill you without changing his demeanor at all.

Jose's presence outside her door gave this deal making a heightened air, a sense that the stakes were a little higher than simply getting a new client relocated, moved into a new, secret life. The atmosphere was a little more electric, a bit further out there.

That undercurrent of tension made her blood pound. It was as if life was washing through her letting her feel its power. Although this particular client struck her as an entirely unattractive and undesirable man under any circumstances, the situation turned her on.

It was a revelation. After years of being a dull tax drone, Tricia found that she had become a bit of an adrenaline junky. She liked this new persona... a lot. A whole hell of a lot.

"So, you can give me what I want?" the man asked. His voice was raspy, a smoker's voice.

"I can get you what you need — a rock-solid identity," Tricia said.

"Bullshit," he said. "Buying an identity is always gonna be bogus. You might get me some good paper, but that ain't fucking holding up if Interpol, let's say, were to take a close look."

She shook her head. "I'm not talking about simply supplying you with papers that have a new name on them. I'd provide a completely new identity — a real one, made to order."

"That's what you'd say. You want a sale."

"Three of our clients have used our new identities to travel. The ID we created got them through some of the most stringent screening in the world."

Mateo Chatzi, the client, laughed. "I hope you don't mean New York. I could take a fucking poodle through immigration there using a tag that said he was the president of France. That only takes balls, not good biometric ID."

She nodded. It seemed incredible to her, but what she'd learned in the last year told her that his statement was a small exaggeration, but not entirely wrong. She had been amazed at how easy it could be to get through screening if you had ice water in your veins. "Not New York," she told him. "We feel that Singapore is a more worthy test," Tricia said. "They are good at spotting fake IDs."

"They are," he agreed. "Tell me about the tests."

"We got an Arab whom you might have heard of, a man with a price on his head, in and out of Tel Aviv, with no problems."

Chatzi smiled, looking almost pleased. "Now you are talking. Getting through Israeli security takes more than bribes."

"Even elsewhere, bribes just attract attention," she agreed. Then she smiled at her own words. A year ago, she'd never been outside the US except on vacations to Canada and Mexico, now she was conversant with all aspects of the immigration processes in numerous countries. Over time, she had become far more conversant with the ins and outs than the sovereign governments of those countries would appreciate.

She experimented with the pluses and minuses of many options for getting people into places undetected, but that required involving outside help — Coyotes or Snakeheads, the people smugglers. A better option was when her clients were detected by authorities, but as another person. There were numerous options for that too, but still they forced her to rely on people she didn't know, either buying clients forged or stolen documents, or bribing officials. Those were all risky options, and not suitable for clients who wanted a new identity.

But now, working with Kenny, she'd eliminated all that overhead, and, more importantly, the chances for a screwup. "I can give you real documents," she said. "I can create an identity for you that will stand up to any scrutiny. Any at all. I'll hand you an entire new life that you can step right into."

"How?" he asked.

She shook her head. "Do I ask you where you get the money to pay my fee? No, I do not. Do I even ask what you do for a living? No. I don't. And I don't want to know who it is that you want to hide from, who might want to track you down. None of that is my business. This is my business. If you doubted my ability, you wouldn't be here. You definitely would not have paid me an advance, so stop fucking around."

Mateo Chatzi sat in his chair looking stone face for a time, then smiled. "I like you," he said. "You have guts."

"And I have, or can get you, the documents you want, the new identity."

"I need to move fast," he said.

"You won't get to pick your new name."

He scowled and twisted his mouth as if something tasted bad. "Why the fuck not? For what I'm paying I should get anything I want."

"Because someone else chose the name around seventy-five years ago. If you are in a rush, then I can give you a choice between two identities that are possible right now. If you insist on picking a name, you'll have to wait for a time. Maybe forever."

"What would I be waiting for?"

She grinned. "The grim reaper. We need a person in the right country, who is the right age, and who has the right name to die. If you have time, you are welcome to wait. It's your choice."

He sighed. "So, what are these choices?"

She took two three-by-five cards out and put them on the table between them. "Matino Closino. He was an Italian who moved to Chile when he was twelve. He had been living in Concepcion."

Mateo raised his head. "And now?"

"He isn't living anywhere at the moment and won't be unless you choose his name. If you don't choose him, then tomorrow his death certificate will be issued by the government. If you pick him, then we can get you a driver's license, cedula, passport, and a bank account within days." She licked her lips. "Since we have a body, we can have a death certificate issued in your name, if you like."

He nodded. "The other one?"

"Antonio Claude, from Quito, Ecuador. He has never had a passport and lived in Quito all his life."

"That's a lower profile," Mateo said approvingly. "But I was hoping to live in rural Guatemala. I've heard good things about San Antonio Palopó."

Tricia smiled. "That is pretty straightforward. With either identity I can get you residency there. Once we have the new identity, my people will run a very straight-up application. Nothing to attract attention. That gives you another layer of protection."

He poked at the card marked Antonio. "I like this guy. He has no record, I take it?"

"Clean as they come. We ran a police check. He was, and will be, a very quiet man. Never married and had no family still living. He worked for a business equipment company as a sales rep, right in Quito."

"How fast could you set me up as this guy?"

She nodded. "I get you the documents within a week. With those, you fly in and get a tourist visa. I'll make an appointment for you... for Antonio... with an immigration lawyer I use there. We can provide the police clearance from Ecuador, the background checks, bank statements... everything you need."

"Bank statements?"

"I'll set up a bank account for you in Antigua and give you the routing number and account info. Once you deposit a nice chunk of cash in it, the government knows you, the new you, won't be a drain on the system. That ensures your residency application goes through. A little grease will make it even faster."

Mateo sat back. "Sounds good. I never mind paying for grease."

The plan would go like clockwork. Tricia knew it was good. "I'm glad you approve."

Mateo stood. "I'd invite you up to my penthouse suite ... to celebrate." He scowled. "But I guess you have work to do." He looked her over. "And although you are sexy as hell, mixing business with other pleasure is for idiots."

"No offense taken," she said, relieved not to have to deal with that.

"Truth is, I prefer professionals for every aspect of my life," Mateo said, winking. "It guarantees a certain level of satisfaction."

"I imagine that's true," she said.

For her part, she found it interesting that she found being involved in intrigue sexually arousing. Basically, she'd discovered that getting away with something, breaking the rules was hot. For the first time in her life she understood why other kids in school, rich kids, had shoplifted from stores. It wasn't the item, but the thrill.

But Mateo had the right attitude. Even though the idea might be lovely, she didn't want to screw clients in any sense. Having her on and off affair with Joshua and working with him was pushing the envelope.

There were other options, however. On most evenings, the hotel bar attracted plenty of hot guys. It was likely that most of them were business people passing through, as she was. That meant she didn't have to worry about emotional complications.

"So how do I contact you when things are ready so that you, Antonio, can go visit Guatemala?"

"Call Jose on the same number as before," he said. "He takes care of all that shit for me. He'll arrange to pick up the documents and get them to me. Once I have the residency and I'm there, living under this new name, you get the balance of your rather expensive fee."

"As we agreed. I happen to think my expensive fee is reasonable for what you are going to get… what's a brand-new life worth?"

He grinned. "There is that."

"Where will you stay until then?"

He smiled wryly. "Better for us both if you don't have any fucking idea where I am."

She raised an eyebrow. "Why would I give up a client?"

He grinned. "Not saying you would. But there are people who might ask around, looking for me, who might pay even more than I'm paying you to learn my location. Or, worse, they might press for answers in a forceful manner, if you know what I mean. It's much better you don't know a fucking thing."

She held out a hand, and they shook. "You're right. There's no reason I would need to know that. I was just making stupid chit-chat."

He nodded. "It happens. But it's those little slips that get us fucked."

"Us?"

"The people who wander around in the margins, live in the shadows. Regardless of the reasons we are there, we have to be more careful than the tourists."

"Agreed." It gave her a rush that he included her in his strange, dangerous world. It was true, too. She felt it more all the time. Every day, every step she took, every client she helped disappear took her deeper into this shadow world.

Once she'd helped clients do whatever was legal to avoid taxes. Now she helped clients avoid detection, and that meant breaking laws. The change was profound.

Tricia Campbell had found herself.

When Chatzi started toward the door, she followed him. As expected, Jose stood calmly alert, facing the door. The way his eyes seemed to track every movement was creepy, but also intoxicating. He was strong, powerful, and her client's flunky.

In her short time in business, she'd had clients that she would describe as nasty and ruthless, but none of them held a candle to these two. She was glad to be working for them and not against them.

When she closed the door behind Mateo and went back into her suite, her eyes flickered over the wonderful view — a view only the elite could afford.

Tricia Campbell was among the elite. The heady thought made her dizzy, as if she were intoxicated. And she was, but with success. Success on the dark side of the universe.

Then she went to the coffee table to refill her drink from the barely touched bottle.

Mateo Chatzi's words echoed in her head, making her realize that, if she was truly one of this mysterious group, ethereal people, then she needed to make provisions for a time when she might need to disappear too. If the authorities suspected her game, if they worked out that she was undermining their global surveillance, she was in trouble.

When she got back to Ecuador, she would immediately get on the task of getting herself a new identity. She didn't need to use it until it was necessary.

She decided to get one for Joshua as well. Kenny probably had several. He knew the game he was playing.

As she finished her drink, she thought it might be time for her to call Joshua and Kenny Lu. They needed to know that the new client, their first for their high-end service, was on board. They'd need to know the correct new name and make certain things were going smoothly on their end.

Reaching for the phone, she hesitated. There was no reason to rush, and she felt she deserved to savor the moment. It was still afternoon which gave her plenty of time to order a good meal from room service. After she ate, she would take a long, hot bath and enjoy a drink as she soaked. Then, relaxed, it would be time to indulge herself however she wished.

Later, when things would be getting going for the evening, she'd go down to the bar. There, beaming with success and confidence, she would look around the room, drink it all in and see what was on offer in the way of attractive and available men.

It was a wonderful, erotic thought. Of course, with the money she was making, if the pickings were unaccountably slim, she still had options. The concierge would be delighted to arrange things for her if she decided to follow Mateo's lead and treat herself to a professional. There was something appealing about engaging a young stud whose business, whose entire goal, was her pleasure.

The idea gave her a tingle. Having a young man at her beck and call, indulging her every whim, was an incredible rush. But there was plenty of time. First, she'd check out what was available for free.

But some other night … The prospect of such a scrumptious, wicked indulgence, the idea that she had the ability to do that any time she wished, made her tremble.

CHAPTER 26

A SHIP ADRIFT

"What do you want to be a sailor for? There are greater storms in politics than you will ever find at sea. Piracy, broadsides, blood on the decks. You will find them all in politics."

— *David Lloyd George, Former Prime Minister of the UK*

The Border between the Arabian Sea and the Indian Ocean Somewhere halfway between Addu Atoll, Maldives and Ras Hafun, Somalia

Charles Bishop was tired; his eyes were sore from hours spent sailing under the hard, tropical sun. He had been single-handing his 30-foot sloop ALBATROSS across the Indian Ocean for two days now and hadn't made nearly the progress he'd expected.

This time of the year, the prevailing winds were supposed to be southeasterly, exactly the push he needed to get from Colombo, Sri Lanka to Mombasa, Kenya. Yet here he was, struggling to keep from heading northeast, drifting up into the Arabian Sea.

Before he'd gone to sleep that night, he'd doused the sails and put out a sea anchor, but it seemed that during the night some freak current took him well north of where he wanted to be.

At this rate, pretty soon he'd have to break down and turn on the diesel. He'd need to start motoring, or he'd wind up in Yemen. Already, according to his GPS, he had gotten way too close to the

Arabian Sea. On his chart, the border between the Indian Ocean and the Arabian Sea was defined by a line that ran from Addu Atoll in the Maldives to Ras Hafun, Somalia.

It was an arbitrary demarcation, as most of them were, but just seeing the name of the country, Somalia, made him shiver. It conjured up stories of modern pirates as vicious as those in the Malacca Strait, north of Indonesia... another place he'd be passing through.

Those weren't good places for an unarmed man alone on a sailboat. Of course, sailing around the world took a person to a lot of places that weren't safe, and ultimately you just faced up to that. The honest truth was that if something happened to him on his circumnavigation, he might just become another mystery disappearance — not as famous as Amelia Earhart, but just as lost. No one back home had the money to pay the kind of ransom pirates demanded; there was no one who knew his schedule. He didn't have anyone waiting for him. No one would bother to file a missing person's report if he was snatched from his boat.

Mostly, he liked it that way, but at times like this, he wondered if his chase after independence didn't veer off into foolishness from time to time. Well, you couldn't change things midstream.

A dot appeared on the horizon dead ahead, making his blood race. Whatever was out there was big enough to be a boat. Could it be pirates? He switched on his radar and began plotting the object.

After a few minutes, he realized that whatever it was, it was drifting, dead in the water and just moving with the wind and current. As a result, his boat was steadily closing on it.

While it wasn't unheard of for pirates to lie low and let their boats drift, watching for prey, that tactic made more sense at night. He had heard of them drifting in the dark with their lights off, tracking the running lights on a victim's boat until they were close enough to strike.

At least that's what he'd been told by the Coast Guard when he checked out and happened to mention that he intended to sail around the world. The young Coast Guard officer wanted him to know that such things happened. He was earnest and young.

Or perhaps the punk was putting him on, trying to scare him. Even if it was true, he was in bright sunlight and soon enough he'd be able to see what was really going on. According to the radar, the two boats were alone out there.

He got out his binoculars and scanned the horizon, looking for smaller boats the radar might miss. Sometimes, he'd been told, pirates would leave their mothership and attack in high-speed rigid inflatable dinghies.

Not today, though. His binoculars were high powered — an expensive and welcome gift from his daughter, the financial wizard. All they showed him was endless miles of achingly flat, hard, blue water.

With no other viable options, (what the hell could he do about it now if it was pirates? He couldn't outrun them) and more than a little curiosity, he held his course, heading for the stationary boat. All the time, he continued anxiously scanning the surrounding ocean with binoculars and radar.

The light wind made his progress slow. It took several hours before he could make out the shape of a 120-foot yacht lying still in the water.

Out to the east, a storm had begun pushing swells toward the African shore, and as Charles dropped his sails, both boats rocked. He couldn't see any sign of life on the lavishly appointed ship.

He called out over a bullhorn, trying to raise the crew — anyone. There was no answer, just the lapping of the waves against the hull. He sighed, turned on his engine, and motored close.

Coming alongside, he saw two men lying on the deck in awkward, unnatural poses. Worse, they lay in pools of blood.

His own pulse pounded as he pulled up behind the yacht and took the boat out of gear. It was still moving forward as he walked out to the bow where he secured a mooring line to the bow cleat. Holding the other end in his hand, he jumped to the yacht's teak swim platform. He quickly tied the line off to the stern of the larger boat, then let out some line. When he was sure ALBATROSS was trailing comfortably, he climbed the ladder to the deck and walked forward.

The fiberglass walls of the boat were riddled with what he guessed to be bullet holes. What else could they be? As he climbed to the bridge, he found three more crew, two men and a woman, lying in their own blood. These had guns of their own clutched tightly in dead hands. Apparently, there had been quite a shootout, but the crew, if that's what they were, had been on the losing end.

Charles had done a tour of duty in Iraq and he'd seen plenty of dead people before, but these were all civilians. Somehow these violent deaths seemed different on a yacht — more sinister.

A quick search of the boat turned up more bodies in the cabins and the galley. Starting to feel nauseated, he tried not to touch anything as he made his way back to the bridge, intending to radio the authorities.

Someone had anticipated him. When he stepped onto the bridge, he saw that the radio and navigation equipment, all the electronics, had been smashed. As thorough as the attackers had been, it seemed likely the engines were trashed too. Apparently, the idea was that if anyone managed to survive the assault, they would be stranded. Him stumbling across the ship so soon after the attack (and the bodies weren't yet putrefying) was pure accident. They were off the shipping lanes.

Charles made his way back to ALBATROSS. He reeled in the mooring line and stepped onto the bow and made his way to his own bridge. He knew that he wasn't within range of anyone on shore with his VHF radio and he didn't have a ham radio, but he could try to contact a passing ship.

He switched the VHF radio on and switched to the International distress channel, channel 16. He listened to the static for a minute before pressing the transmit button.

"Mayday, mayday, mayday," he said. "Sailing vessel Albatross, seven degrees north, fifty-nine-point-seven east." He paused and looked at the name on the stern before continuing. "Vessel in distress, I repeat, there is a vessel in distress.... Motor vessel Phoenix. There are multiple fatalities... over."

As he expected, he got no response. He repeated his message and waited. Nothing.

While he listened for a response, he evaluated the situation. Everyone on board was dead. The ship seemed sound and in no danger of sinking, so there wasn't a rush to do anything. And he was probably as safe here, at the scene of the crime, as he was anywhere. The pirates had surely already gotten everything they wanted.

He reached into the cabin and pulled out his Emergency Position Indicating Radio Beacon (EPIRB) and switched it on. This was an emergency distress beacon that would begin transmitting a coded message on the 406 MHz distress frequency via satellite and earth stations to the nearest rescue coordination center. Undoubtedly, the stricken yacht had one of its own, but it had probably either been removed or disabled. His own would work fine. Now all he had to do, all he could do, was wait.

When rescuers finally arrived, they'd take over. He imagined the officious attitudes of whatever Coast Guard came and found him astern the disabled yacht. They'd take his statement and shoo him away like an annoying fly. He'd never find out what had happened on board.

Essentially, that was fine with Charles. Circumnavigating was his way of living lightly on the world, not getting too attached to anything but his boat. He'd go on his way and never give a thought to why someone killed all these people. He'd never wonder if there were any others who'd been taken. And that's what he thought had happened.

He couldn't help but think that this looked like a professional job. The attack had to have been fast and deadly. A team had boarded the ship with a purpose and left no survivors.

It was interesting. The nature of it made him doubt that any details would make it to the news. It was all rather curious, intriguing. And he knew that this was his one chance to learn something about the dead or the attackers.

One thing he wondered about was who owned the yacht, this PHOENIX. It was a fancy, expensive boat... not huge as luxury yachts went, but pretty elegant, and it was custom built. Charles knew yachts, and this was no production model. That meant its owners had shelled out a pretty penny. Who could afford a boat like that?

He went back aboard the yacht and went to what appeared to be the Captain's cabin, rummaging through the desk. In a well-marked folder, he found the ship's papers, noting that they listed the owner as a Gibraltar Corporation — also named PHOENIX. That was useless information. It would be a shell company.

"Fucking paranoid bastards," he muttered, laughing.

Surrounded by so much luxury, Charles decided to turn his attention to satisfying more basic matters. The dead people no longer needed their provisions, and his boat was running low.

He went down the ladder to the galley and found a walk-in cooler. That was promising. Picking up a carry bag that was sitting on a counter, he went inside. It had two parts: the inner section, for frozen food, held some lovely steaks that went into his bag. In the outer section, he collected some potatoes, onions, and broccoli. With his bag full, he left.

On his way out, he saw a wet bar, well-stocked with expensive booze. It seemed only right that whoever owned this boat would give him some compensation for finding it, so he tucked several bottles of a lovely single malt Scotch under his arm, thinking they'd be lovely additions to the galley on ALBATROSS.

Back on board his own boat, with nothing particular to do but wait, Charles opened one of the bottles and fixed himself a stiff drink. It tasted much better than the rum he'd been relying on. Getting out his grill, he attached it to the lifelines, hooked up the gas bottle. He put the steaks in his freezer, but left one out to defrost, thinking of making a marinade of soy sauces and garlic and vinegar.

His mouth watering, he returned to the yacht with the empty carry bag to get some ice and more booze. The wet bar was liberally stocked.

Back on ALBATROSS, he fixed a fresh drink, put away his provisions, then set the steak to marinating.

An hour later he was happily watching the steak turn brown next to a potato wrapped in tinfoil, as he sipped a cool drink.

If anyone had asked him what he was doing, if someone came by and found him tied to a yacht with all those dead people on board, he would tell them he was waiting. Waiting to be rescued.

If anyone wondered why he was calmly making his lunch right next to the carnage on the next boat, he'd point out that he had done everything he could. Now, he was left to wait without knowing how long he'd be waiting.

Long ago, Charles had learned that there was plain waiting and there was pleasant waiting. When he had a choice, he preferred to wait in comfort. The ill fate of those aboard was tragic, but they no longer needed the booze and food, and adding them to his stores would do a little to make this interruption in his trip more pleasant.

Sipping the fine booze and smelling his lunch cooking, a contented Charles decided that if the authorities were too slow, if they made him wait there too long, he'd make a few more trips back to the yacht. It would be foolish to waste an opportunity to find out if there were more things that the dead no longer needed and that a sailor alone in a big ocean could make good use of.

CHAPTER 27

MEDELLIN MEETING

"The desire of gold is not for gold.
It is for the means of freedom."

— *Ralph Waldo Emerson*

InterContinental Hotel
Medellin, Colombia

Boone, in her incarnation as Sindi, knew her hotels well. She'd seen all sorts, and the InterContinental Hotel was everything she expected it to be. Her suite was elegant, with a view of the city of Medellin. It had a sitting room, with a small office and a balcony, and a lovely bedroom.

Anchara wouldn't think much of it, she thought. The girl had developed a taste for the fancy beach resorts and some of the truly elegant hotels they'd been in recently, in places like Bangkok and Mexico, and Tanzania.

But then Anchara was in Singapore, sulking because Boone hadn't brought her on this trip.

When she checked in, she'd found a message waiting for her. Joshua had called to let her know that he was on his way to the hotel along with two other people. She booked them rooms on a floor below hers. As she'd asked for the meeting, she didn't expect them to pay for their rooms or food.

Before she went to her room, she left a message asking them to check-in, freshen up, and meet her for a drink at the restaurant/bar out by the swimming pool.

She changed into a bikini and went down. Reflexively, she found herself checking out the place for camera angles that would give her blog viewers an idea of what the place was like. But she wasn't videoing on this trip. This was another kind of business. Today she was in a fancy hotel as Boone.

It seemed odd. Boone in a hotel like this, without Anchara.

She turned her attention to some of the young people clustered around the pool. She enjoyed seeing the half-naked sunbathers stretched out on lounge chairs.

She found a table on the grass behind the pool that offered shade and a clear view. A lovely brown waitress took her order for a sandwich, a bottle of Jameson's, and a bucket of ice. "I like to have well-balanced meals," she told the girl, who smiled.

Boone was looking forward to meeting Joshua Raintree and getting a sense of who he was. He'd come with a great recommendation and the work he was doing with Tricia, from what Kenny reported, was innovative. An alliance with those two could prove useful for all of them.

She spotted them as they came out of the lobby area in swimsuits. Joshua was tall and good looking. The woman with him, a Colombian she guessed, was attractive… not a glamorous woman, just one with honest good looks.

The young man with them was wearing swim trunks. She watched the way his face lit up when he saw the pool. He headed straight for it. Joshua glanced around and spotted her. She smiled and nodded.

As the young man hit the water with a splash, making an awkward dive that managed to land him in the vicinity of two attractive girls, Joshua and the woman reached her table. "You are Joshua? I took the liberty of ordering for us," Boone said.

"Nice, reliable choice," Joshua said, seeing the whiskey. "Yes, I'm Joshua, and this is Carmen. It seems our loyal sidekick, Miguel, got sidetracked."

"Young women and a pool must be irresistible."

As they sat, Carmen looked at the booze. "Could I get some iced tea?" she asked in Spanish.

"You can have whatever you like, lovely lady," Boone told her, speaking Spanish. "If you are hungry, order yourself some food. I've already eaten."

"We stopped for lunch on the way," Joshua said. "Thank you for getting us such lovely rooms."

"I've never seen such a place in my life," Carmen said.

"They don't have anything like this is Hispania," Joshua said. "And she's only been to Medellin a few times in her life."

"Then enjoy it while you are here," Boone said. She let herself imagine showing Carmen all sorts of new things, then she touched Carmen's hand. "Joshua and I need to discuss business for a time. You are welcome to stay and listen, but if you'd prefer, there are massages available right over by the pool. There are also pedicures and manicures that you might enjoy. And even the pool itself, which Miguel seems to find enjoyable."

"Miguel appreciates the fact that the girls are nearly naked," Carmen said. Then she smiled. "Those other things sound very nice, but they are all very expensive."

Boone shook her head. "Not today. For you, who are my guests, they are free. It's my treat. You put the charge on your room and please add a generous tip."

Carmen looked dubious. "I can do this?"

Joshua pointed to the passcard for the room. "Just show them this."

Carmen stood up. "Then I will go and at least see what they offer."

"Anything you want, Carmen," Boone said.

Carmen looked embarrassed. "This is incredible."

"Thanks for that," Joshua said as Carmen went off to explore. Boone couldn't help but admire her nice ass as the Colombiana walked away to learn about the joys a five-star hotel and an unlimited budget could afford.

Boone turned her attention back to Joshua, pouring him a stiff drink before she refilled her own glass. "I'm making an obvious and shabby attempt to buy affection from the outset," she said.

"It's working well," he laughed. "Telling me rather gives it away, however."

"If I'm right, then it will be fine because I think we can do some amazing things together."

"And what sorts of things are we going to do together?"

"Augment what you and Tricia are doing already."

"I'm curious how it is you know, or think you know what we are doing."

"You cater to people who want to disappear. Some are rich who want to avoid taxes. Some are villains who need invisibility, having pissed off the wrong people."

"For the sake of argument, let's say you are right."

"I am."

"Obviously, you are well connected, what do we offer that you don't have?"

"We could use some help in re-identifying some of our people."

"Re-identifying?"

"They've got identities that are no longer as useful as I'd like, so I'd like to get them new ones. They aren't trying to disappear, just shed one for another — what Tricia does for her clients."

"Then you should talk to her."

"Oh, I most certainly will be doing that, but we had some thoughts for your end of things as well."

"My end?"

"Moving money."

"Ah."

"I understand that you do that well and that you can manage money well too. I'm interested in opening an account with you."

"That's easy enough, depending on the kind of account and the source of the money."

"And I want to propose an idea that you can use when you need to cloak the fact that a client needs to relocate funds from the US abroad permanently without paying the exit tax."

"That's the sticky wicket. Tricia has schemes, and some are a bit clumsy."

"One we can offer, can make happen, is the ever-popular failed-investment strategy."

"You have to know that those words, failed investment, shouldn't ever be uttered together."

"Except when it is useful."

"And how is it useful… for her clients?"

"On his own, not through you, the client invests in a company that we set up in some country known for shaky deals. The company buys crypto through a new exchange, but the exchange abruptly folds, and the client loses his money. Naturally, he takes a tax loss."

"Bad things happen all the time."

"The local government investigates and declares it was Ukrainian or north Korean cybercrooks and there is no recourse."

Joshua laughed. "Only the company doesn't lose the money."

"They simply send it to a new wallet set up for the new identity."

Joshua considered it. "That should work. And I like that we are totally disconnected. There is no way anyone can connect the failed investment to Tricia or me. Or you."

"Exactly. Scheme number two is that the client gives us a password or two to his company computers. In this case, our genuine north Korean hackers inject ransomware and freeze them. The client calls the FBI. They check and verify what's going on, including that the client paid the ransom. Only our hackers, being unethical SOBs, drain the company accounts before unfreezing the computers. Your client, now penniless, decides to sell his company at a loss and move to another country."

"I like it," Joshua said. "And the ransom demanded is paid in Bitcoin?"

"Monero. And the business accounts are all converted to Monero on an exchange, but it's a bogus account owned by our north Korean devils, who immediately transfer the money to a wallet and close the account."

"A nasty lot."

"Yes, they are."

"And you, your people do all that?"

"For a commission and costs. The money comes to you. The client gets a new identity courtesy of Tricia and you filter money back to the client via a bank account in their new name, in their new country, or in an offshore account."

"Some of each," Joshua said. "We keep the amounts we transfer variable and use a variety of banks. I like adding to the confusion. Even if the powers that be do manage to track what I'm doing, I do my best to make sure they have to work hard to get any information they can use."

"So far you are doing a fine job."

Joshua nodded toward the pool. "Young Miguel gets some of the credit. He has some innovative ideas. He used to hack video games for his friends, now he is investing in crypto for them and helping me devise ways to disguise things."

"I'd heard that," Boone said. "And here is an important question… could you do without him?"

"Why?"

"From the sound of things, with the right training, he has a bright future."

"He has a larcenous heart."

"All the better. I have a job for him. It's here in Medellin."

"Is it dangerous?"

"No more than what he's doing now. If he does it well, he'd have fun, make some money, and do some good."

"And wait, if you order now, you'll get —"

"Okay," Boone laughed. "I am making a pitch, but I'm serious."

Over at the pool, Miguel and the girls climbed out. He laughed with them, then grabbed a towel and headed toward where Boone and Joshua were sitting. "Let's talk about it when he gets here," Joshua said.

When Miguel arrived and took a seat, he looked happy. "I'm starving," he said.

Boone signaled for a menu and nodded toward the girls. "They are abandoning you?"

"They are going to the mall for a time," he said.

"But you got their phone numbers?"

He smiled. "Oh, si. Their phone and room number." He winked. "They are German, I think. Inga and Gertie."

Boone chuckled. "Is that good?"

"I think it might be very good," he said. "I've never seen such blonde hair."

"Boone has a job for you," Joshua said. "If you are interested."

"If it involves German girls and fancy hotels, I am very interested."

"That part is up to you. The job would involve being in Medellin for a time." She could see she had his attention.

"Doing what?"

"There is a small software company that is developing a payment system… part of one."

"Like Visa?"

"Exactly, only using blockchain. And it's for a special application. A single city, for the moment. A universal token system that is scalable to a global level. They need to test the code, find out how robust it is. To do that they are hiring gamers to try to beat it, find its flaws."

"Oh, like finding the undocumented instructions and…."

"Something like that."

"Why kids?" Joshua asked.

"Because it's guaranteed they won't follow the rules. They won't assume anything about the system. They'll try to break down any walls or obstacles they encounter. That's what AT&T did back when kids were hacking phones. They hired the most aggressive ones, like Captain Crunch, to show them where the weaknesses were."

"So, hire a thief to test security?"

"Exactly. See, Miguel, I can get you hired on as one of the testers if you are interested. It is a good-paying job."

"But you would wish me to do more than test this software?" he asked grinning.

"Ah, you see right through me. Yes, I want you to document all the 'undocumented instructions' you can find. I want to know about any holes in the security, any possible ways it can be breached."

"So not just bugs," he said.

"No. You'll need to report the bugs to them to earn your keep and not be caught. Let them fix superficial things, but if you can, keep anything you think we can exploit to bring down the system to yourself."

"Who is this we?"

"I am the de facto head of a group called the Bitpats."

Miguel scowled. "Is that a religion?"

She laughed. "It's an informal group of volunteers, digital warriors, who don't like the way things are going in the world. We don't like bulletproof systems that collect our data."

"You want me to be part of this group?"

"Eventually. When you know enough about us to decide if you agree with what we are doing."

"You are going to bring the payment system down?"

She nodded. "With your help. In return, when you finish, I'll see that you get some training from some of the best programmers in the world. When you add that to what you are learning about the financial tools from Joshua, you'll be able to write your own ticket."

"If it's all as much fun as this sounds, I am ready," he said.

Then his burger and fries arrived, and that took his full attention.

"I think there might be a lot that we can do together," Joshua said, smiling.

"It's all a give and take arrangement."

"And in that vein, it seems that you are offering to provide some services to expand our business offerings nicely, then stealing away my able right hand… that averages out, I imagine."

"And when I return your right hand, he'll have a lot of new skills."

"I'm still thinking of your homegrown ransomware," Joshua said.

Miguel looked up expectantly. "Ransomware?"

"I'll tell you all about that too," Joshua said. Then he turned back to Boone. "I like it. The distancing, separate teams on various parts is good. The possibilities are endless."

"They are," Boone agreed. "We need to be flexible to survive whatever is coming."

"Sounds ominous."

She grinned. "It could be. Whether it is… that depends on us. And how flexible and smart we are."

Joshua looked out over the pool area, then back at her. "We can do that. Be flexible."

Boone looked at Carmen, who had returned and was now sunning herself in her bikini. She wondered idly how flexible Joshua might be about sharing her. But that was for later. She was throwing enough new things at the man already. Later, if they formed a relationship, she would see. Anything like that would be dessert.

Miguel was looking over at the German girls toweling off. "I was going to invite you all to dinner at a nice restaurant," Boone said, "but if you'd rather stay here…"

"It's nice here," he said.

She smiled. "Your room key will let you charge a meal when you get hungry. Or three meals."

"Three meals."

"You might find room service is most convenient if blonde German girls like to eat in bed."

Miguel beamed. "I think I like Medellin. This part at least."

CHAPTER 28

A SMALLER, QUIETER LIFE

"Every new beginning comes from some other beginning's end."

— Seneca

**San Antonio Palopó
Guatemala**

Mateo Chatzi looked around the little villa and was pleased. Situated in the highlands of the Sierra Madre mountain range, in a village on the eastern shore of Lake Atitlán, the house offered a lovely view of green hillsides and soft clouds rolling in over the lake.

It was a lovely villa, all neat and tidy, open and filled with light; it was nothing like any place he'd had since... well, he'd never lived in anything quite like it.

Like all the other changes he was making, this one refreshed him, but he had a way to go before he'd be entirely comfortable with it. Although he'd grown somewhat jaded about the lavish, overdone places he'd been living for so many years, adjusting to a different and entirely new existence still took time, even if it was attractive.

The places he'd lived before had been mini palaces, built to impress people—the government people, the businessmen, the ones who admired, even craved the trappings of success. They were ostentatious displays of power. He'd enjoyed that for a time, certainly, and still enjoyed flexing his power, but for now, for this life, to stay alive, all that would be far too visible, too high profile.

Taking a hard look at his new life, Mateo saw that everything was different now — including the country. A new man in a new place. He dressed in shorts and a tee-shirt. Again, this was not the attire that anyone who knew him would expect. And that was the point. He wasn't that person any longer.

In time he'd grow used to it, but for now, it felt odd. The entire life fit like some suit in one of those modern styles that he never would have chosen for himself. Even the tiny town of San Antonio Palopó wasn't the kind of place he would have selected if it weren't for the people looking for him.

But it would do. He would impress himself on this place. He would become an invisible force and shape things without being a known entity.

He had a new name, a new passport from Peru. Tricia Campbell had come through for him. He'd opted to be a little more patient and now he had an identity that he felt truly suited him, one he related to. He had become a man who'd immigrated from Greece to Ecuador as a teen and lived there contentedly. Recently, he had moved to Guatemala where he was investing money.

Coincidentally, a certain Mateo Chatzi had died in a car accident. How tragic.

Now the lawyer who sat in his living room had brought him even newer papers. Through her efforts, his Peruvian persona had been granted Guatemalan investor residency. That moved him one more step past the identity he'd purchased.

His old friend Jose Defamo stood watchfully in the doorway. Mateo noted the man's hands folded in front of him, at the ready, and how he shifted his weight. His obvious discomfort amused Mateo. The man didn't feel comfortable dressed in casual clothing; he was always on edge with strangers close to Mateo.

Yet, neither of them expected any trouble from the lawyer. After all, the woman didn't know anything about his past. She knew him to be a wealthy Ecuadorian who had hired her to get him an investor residency. To that end, he'd made a refundable purchase of $60,000 in government bonds.

"So, it's all done?" the man who was no longer Mateo asked.

The lawyer put his Ecuadorian passport on the coffee table with a dramatic flourish, then sat some forms next to it. "All done. Of course, you must maintain the investment for five years."

"That's no problem at all, Ms. Juarez. I might even increase my investment in this beautiful country."

"If you are interested in investing businesses, I can put you in touch with people," she said. "I know of some excellent ecotourism possibilities."

He grinned. The idea would never have occurred to him, but it was brilliant. No one would expect him to get involved in tree hugger shit. "I just might take you up on that. I'd have to do some research."

"Of course. And, if you wish, after nine months you can apply for Guatemalan citizenship."

He stared out through the open patio to the lush hillsides, then turned back to look into her lovely brown eyes. He liked lady lawyers, especially women like this one. Ms. Juarez was svelte, charming, and graceful. If he had to deal with mind-numbing legal crap, at least he could enjoy the presence of a competent, lithe woman. Fortunately, he could afford to hire whomever he wanted. "Why would I do that? Do I need citizenship?"

"If you wish to travel … right now you would lose your residency status if you spent more than a year outside of the country. Become a citizen and you need to spend only twenty-one days here during the first year and less after that."

Mateo shrugged. "I doubt I'll be doing much traveling in the near future." It wouldn't be all that safe. Even if the facial recognition software could be fooled, there were dangerous people out there who knew him.

"I just wanted you to know. If you change your mind.…"

"I might do that," he said. "Having a second passport isn't the worst idea in the world. Is it complicated to get one?"

"Not at all," she said happily. "Most of the paperwork will be already on file for your residencia. We update it, pay the fees … it's pretty straightforward."

"That sounds promising," he said. He'd worried that doing that might raise his profile, the profile of his new identity. He didn't want anything drawing attention to him, but this seemed rather innocuous. "The only thing is that I'm a private person. Sometimes, some places, when the local officials see you have money to invest, they get ideas."

She touched his hand with her long, delicate fingers, making him tingle. "Silly. A shell company handles the investments, the payments, the entire thing. That's our first step, and I've got a company in mind that we can use — you can own. The citizenship applications would go through the same, trusted, people I've been using."

"Trusted," he thought. In his experience, that meant she had them on her payroll. That was the proper way to do it. "I like you better all the time," he told her, and then basked in the brilliant smile she flashed at him.

As he escorted the woman out to her car, he considered inviting her to dinner. Company, lovely company was always nice, and a woman like this one, obviously a climber who would do what it took to make it to the top, wouldn't mind spreading her legs for him. Certainly, accommodating the lust of an old lecher wasn't a big deal if it got her money and power.

Then he stopped himself — he needed her in this role as his intermediary. Better to keep this one as a business associate, at least until his new identity was well established. He'd let her research investments for him and give her other tasks. The chump change that would cost him would keep her alert, watching out for him. She knew he wanted privacy; it was in her interest to help him keep it and establish herself as one of a handful of advisors in the rich man's circle. There was power in that.

She took his arm as they walked out on the gravel driveway to her BMW and the way she stayed close, he knew he was right. She was his for the asking, but he'd be patient. It would be delicious to pluck this fruit later. In the meantime, if he asked her, she'd send girls to his place for him to enjoy. She'd send him beautiful whores without a thought. And then, later, when he crooked his finger, she'd still be there. After all, she was a businesswoman—a different kind of whore.

It was something he'd seen, and experienced, before.

He watched her go, enjoying the idea that she would be waiting in the wings for his future pleasures.

As he walked back in, he nodded at Jose. "I think we are in good shape, Carlos."

Jose was still getting used to the idea that he had a new name too. The man was rather set in his ways, but you couldn't buy the kind of loyalty Jose showed.

"I hope so," he grunted. He was never happy with Mateo's security, always looking for holes. He could be annoying, but that was how they'd survived this long. "I worry."

"About what?" He sat on the couch and motioned for Jose to take a chair. When the man did, he poured them each a drink from the decanter on the table. "Tell me about your concerns."

Jose grunted again. "Too many people know about this new identity."

Mateo smiled. Jose was telling him what he expected to hear. It bothered him as well. "And you'd like to clean up the loose ends?"

"We don't even know how many know." He nodded toward the door. "This woman will keep her mouth shut."

"But you worry about the one who got us this new identity? You worry about this Tricia Campbell?" Jose nodded. "Perhaps, if you had a private chat with her, you might convince her to give you the names of everyone she works with."

Jose cocked his head. "That would take some serious leverage."

"You mean pain."

Jose nodded. "I'd need to make her feel pain and then expect worse."

"You'd enjoy that."

Jose allowed himself a flicker of a smile. "Then, of course, she would have to be eliminated, so that she didn't warn the others I was going to visit."

Mateo knew Jose's sadistic streak well. He only restrained himself if Mateo insisted. He could interrogate someone effectively but preferred torture. When Mateo didn't object, Jose delighted in stretching things out over a lengthy period. He'd take his time and enjoy the process. "Well, amigo, I don't think we have further need of Ms. Campbell's services," Mateo said. "Just ensure that you bring me her computer so we can learn what records she might have kept. And I prefer her body isn't found."

"That should be easily done," Jose said.

Jose's face told Mateo that he was anticipating the time he'd spend with Tricia Campbell. The man never had enough opportunities to satisfy his lust or cruelty. "And I'm sure that you will be happy to be away from this boring village for a time and on a mission."

"I'll have my best people keeping an eye on you while I'm gone."

"I know you will, my old friend." They sipped their drinks. "And I know you enjoy your work. Take as much time as you like."

Jose drained his glass. "Then, I should check the flights to Quito."

"You think she's gone back there?"

"She has. I've had her watched," Jose said.

"For you or me?"

"Both. I knew that eventually we would need to do something concerning her. I wanted to be prepared when you gave the order."

This was why Jose was his right-hand man. "Excellent. Have a good trip to Ecuador. Let me know if there are any problems."

"I always do, sir."

As Jose left, Mateo's own libido made him think of the realtor who had sold him this villa. Ellena, that was her name. Ms. Juarez had found her for him. She was a leggy, elegant woman who bleached her waist-length hair a brilliant silver. Like Ms. Juarez, she was an ambitious and aggressive woman—two qualities that he found exciting and useful in women. Together, they could provide lots of entertainment.

Now that he'd bought this house, Ellena was far more replaceable from a business perspective and less useful to him as an ally. She'd flirted enough to make it clear that he could have her; he expected that she would be quite a tigress in the bedroom. That appealed to him.

While Jose's hobby of inflicting pain didn't appeal to him directly, imagining what Jose would do to the delicious and helpless Tricia Campbell once he got her alone, had him excited. He was in no mood to spend the night alone, especially when Ellena might be happy to join him in his bed.

She sounded delighted to hear from him, and of course, she'd love to have dinner with him. "An early dinner would make the evening longer," she said. The coquettish edge he heard in her voice pleased him.

"Early then." He hung up and summoned Tina, his cook. She was a local woman his realtor had recommended as being efficient, a good cook, with passable English, and discreet. A stout woman in her forties with sparkling eyes, Tina seemed to love cooking and her new job.

"I'm expecting company for dinner," he told her. The delight in her face was amusing. "One person will be joining me. We'd prefer something light… or at least nothing too heavy."

Tina raised a finger. "I'm sure she would enjoy a fresh fish and steamed vegetables. I purchased a pargo rojo this morning that would be perfect."

"Yes," he said. "I love the way you prepare it." Pargo rojo was the Spanish for red snapper; now he found his mouth watering. If it was as good as before, he'd see that Jose sweetened her paycheck. "That sounds excellent, Tina. We wish to eat early." He motioned toward the spectacular view. "Please serve the food on the terrace, along with an extra bottle of wine, and then you are free to retire for the evening.

"Once I serve the meal, I will be gone," she said cheerfully. She understood that he wanted her to mind her own business. She refilled his drink and set the bottle back down. "I will wash the dishes early in the morning."

As she headed toward the kitchen, her kitchen, Mateo sat back and sipped the fine Scotch. Every time he examined his new life, he found it developing satisfactorily indeed. Under other circumstances he would have invited the lovely Tricia to visit his new home, perhaps to celebrate. She had a luscious body that a man could plunder happily. Unfortunately, the way things were, it was important she be eliminated.

He sighed at the thought that Jose would have to kill her. The loss of a beautiful woman always struck him as tragic, but at times, it was unavoidable.

CHAPTER 29

UNDER TEMPORARY MANAGEMENT

"I'm not interested in preserving the status quo;
I want to overthrow it."

— Niccolò Machiavelli

Soho House Berlin
Torstraße 1
Berlin, 10119
Germany

By design, his own rather careful design, the green-eyed man was the last one to enter the dark recesses of the plush private dining room of the Soho House Berlin. As he walked in the doorway, he could see the others, the members of the Oculistica, sitting around a white-linen-covered table, drinking wine and waiting.

He wanted them waiting.

The man liked this place. Years ago, when he'd first tasted affluence, he'd become a member of this private club, although he seldom brought anyone here. It was a pleasure to have some secrets, especially an innocuous one like being a member.

He hadn't called this meeting, but he felt certain he knew what it was about. If he was right, then it was an ideal choice. Perfect for an important gathering, one that needed to be kept secret.

The staff made discretion into a religion. On-site personnel swept the building for bugs by several times a day; the building had multiple entrances and exits, with well-dressed, hidden guards at each and cameras pointing out that would let someone leaving spot anyone lurking and waiting for them.

And people did lurk. In addition to the club's guards today, men of his own stood near each door as well, each of them armed and alert. The green-eyed man took precautions. He had informed the club of those precautions to prevent any confusion. For a long-term, established member, they were delighted to accommodate him.

The green-eyed man had been looking forward to this meeting. He'd made his first move in the game, and now he needed to see what the response was. It could go a number of ways.

Climbing up from where he'd started, getting to the top of the heap had meant doing some nasty work, both for himself and for others. Surviving at the top of this particular heap, when you didn't have the leverage of some influential organization, required that you maintain your edge, remain willing to be ruthless.

Nikolaj had earned his position in the Oculistica by doing the dirty work of the Old Man and others like him. He'd done tasks they were willing to order but didn't have the skills or the stomach to do themselves. Well, the Old Man had the stomach for it. He lacked the training, the conditioning. His weapon of choice was money, and it had worked for him for a long time.

Nikolaj knew the others, regardless of their power and influence, were afraid of him. They lived in a world of leverage, but he grew up in a world where there was no mystery in snapping a man's neck — it was simple mechanics. That he'd broken more than one gave him the first-hand knowledge that instilled confidence. Knowing not only how to do it but that he was capable of it, gave him an aura of danger. In its own way, that proved to be beautiful leverage.

As a result, even though he now had men like Franz and Enrique working for him, to the extent possible, he preferred doing the dirty work himself. He confronted fewer unpleasant surprises that way and, in general, he found the results more satisfying, even if the task was not always easy or pleasant to do.

Even Franz couldn't be expected to always think and act the way Nikolaj did when he faced unusual situations. Using Franz was convenient but relying on him entirely was the kind of mistake that drug lords and crime bosses made... just before their downfall.

Having your hands on things was the best approach.

Now he looked at his strong hands, reminding himself, then he adjusted his cuffs and strode into the room. A short, nearly bald, overweight, but well-groomed man looked up from his wine glass. "Glad you could make it," he said.

"I'm still early," the green-eyed man said. He'd expected the rebuke. "Your impatience doesn't grant you the right to be rude."

As the green-eyed man took his seat, the chubby man ran his fingers nervously through his absurd comb-over and stood up. "Now that you are all here, I'll introduce myself. My name is Douglas Downes," he said. "The bank association sent me here to fill in for the Old Man."

"What do you mean?" Dione asked. "Is he sick?"

"No, but he seems to have been kidnapped."

"Kidnapped?" Park said. He glanced around nervously. "Is this something to do with us, with the group? Or is it just about him?"

"He has enemies and many people would see him as a target for ransom," the green-eyed man said, stirring the pot.

The chubby man shook his head. "We don't really know. We don't think it's about us." He glanced over at Osk and she nodded.

"From the evidence we've gathered, it appears that Somali pirates took him," she said.

"Evidence?" Park asked.

She nodded. "A sailor found his boat floating dead in the water. The crew were all shot dead. It looked as if there had been a firefight. The Old Man is missing. We checked his place in Seychelles, and he isn't there. Given where it happened, and the fact that the bullets came from the type of automatic weapons the pirates use, we've assumed they took him."

Downes' phone beeped, and he glanced at it. "And now we have confirmation."

"A ransom demand?" Anna asked.

Downes nodded. "Yes. A preliminary demand was sent to three of his banks. There is a video clip of him tied up and a demand for cash. A million dollars."

Park rubbed his face. "So, will they pay it?"

Downes made a stern face. "We don't cave in to ransom demands. It's against our policy. That would be the beginning of attacks on all of us."

"Indeed, it would," Osk said. "That's why refusing to pay ransoms is the official Interpol line. We always recommend against paying."

"And unofficially?" the green-eyed man asked.

Osk shrugged. "Depends on the person's value to the ones with the money, I suppose. It isn't illegal to pay a ransom; it just sets a bad precedent."

"Letting him die just sets a different precedent," Nikolaj said, "not necessarily a better one."

"Does Interpol have any useful information on the current situation?" Downes demanded. "Anything beyond the obvious?"

Osk smiled. "Not really. We know a few things about the attack itself. For instance, our ballistics tests confirm that the killers used AK-47s that they most likely bought from gun runners operating in Yemen. I can tell you that there were at least four shooters. We suspect, given the similarity to other attacks in that area, that the attackers swept in with high-speed Zodiacs that came in under the yacht's radar. And, if you like, I can entertain you with a host of other less than helpful information."

Anna Rasburn refilled her wine glass. "There isn't anything there that might be any real use in getting him back."

Osk's phone beeped. "Neither is this... my people tracked the ransom demand. It came by text message after being bounced off a number of satellites."

"Sounds sophisticated," Dione said.

"Which is not unusual for pirates in this age," Osk said, sounding matter of fact. "The major point is that we have no solid leads. Even saying they are Somalis is an assumption."

The green-eyed man gave the banker a thin smile. "So, Mr. Downes, as the representative of bankers and the banking industry everywhere, what do you propose?"

"That we go on with business as usual."

"Of course," Anna said. "But with everything compromised, you might want to consider making certain you know who took him. What if it is the KGB wanting leverage over us?"

"We..." Downes was trying to think through the ramifications.

Nikolaj looked at her and smiled. She was enjoying this. "One solution might be if I were to attempt a rescue."

Downes sat down and took a long sip of wine. "Rescue? Is that even possible?"

"Of course, it is possible."

"You could bring him back alive?"

"I can't say how probable that is. They might kill him, or maybe they have already killed him. But I could determine for certain who has him and get an idea of what information they were after."

"Who do you use?"

"Use?"

"Do you hire mercenaries? How do you find where he is?"

"Mr. Downes, having deniability can be taken to outrageous lengths. You aren't an elected official. You know my own people are specialists who do precisely that sort of work. I'm asking you, on behalf of the banks, to authorize an operation. How we find him is not something you should concern yourself with."

"What if he is alive?"

The man was trembling. It was subtle, but the green-eyed man had trained himself to spot such things. He smiled at the man. "If you want me to ensure we arrive slightly too late, then I can arrange that."

The room was quiet as Downes fidgeted.

"You said you are filling in," Anna said. "If the Old Man served any purpose at all any more, it was to make the hard decisions. Now that is your job."

"Look," the banker said, "If you want to try to rescue the Old Man, go ahead. If you locate him that will resolve a certain amount of unpleasant uncertainty."

Nikolaj lifted a glass of wine and tasted it. It was disappointingly mediocre. "Such as the uncertainty over whether the decisions you make during his absence will stand?"

"No, no. The association is frustrated by his reactionary positions on things."

"What does that mean?" Park asked.

"I've been asked to see that all our operations proceed as close to normal as possible."

Park looked at him. "Yes, but we had arrived at a few crossroads. The Old Man opposed several projects. I need some direction that will stand."

Downes looked puzzled. "What do you mean?"

"The Old Man was expressing reservations about some of our plans for the smart city."

Downes perked up. "Are you referring to the issues he raised in the dossier? I read that on the way here. I wasn't sure if that was the most recent information."

"Basically, it is," Park said. "We've made minor tweaks here and there to improve things. His major complaint was about using blockchain technology — he opposed our digital Phoenix."

"Look, the Old Man was brilliant in his time," Downes said. "But he is a fucking dinosaur. We, the younger bankers, are eager to get on board with the technology. We have to, if we are to survive. Implementing blockchain is overdue. Do you agree?"

Park nodded. "Both Dione and I think that too."

Downes looked around the table, then waved a hand at the head waiter. "Okay, if that's the only major problem, then the banking sector of this group supports your efforts. Go full steam ahead."

"And what if I rescue the Old Man?" Nikolaj asked. "The way things are going, that might complicate things for everyone."

Park nodded furiously. "It will be impossible to backtrack if he reverses your decisions."

Downes mopped his face with a napkin. "I'll explain to the association that the decisions have been made and must be final. They've urged me to be decisive."

"Then give me a decision," Nikolaj said.

"What decision?"

"I guarantee I can find the Old Man. I might be able to get him out. If there is an option, I need you to decide the outcome. Tell me if I should bring him back alive or dead."

Downes swallowed hard. "He has become an impediment."

"Say it," Nikolaj said calmly. "Tell me what you mean."

"Don't rescue him."

"Be clear, sir. Do you want me to kill him?"

"I … yes."

Nikolaj raised his glass. "To our temporary and future management. We have an actual decision."

"There are other issues," Dione said. "Some might need rethinking… in conjunction with your new information on what the association wants. A lot of financial details, planning …."

"Then let's order a meal and review it all," Downes said. "I think better with good food."

"I'm sure you do," the green-eyed man said. He stood up, smiling. He was pleased. "But if you'll excuse me, I should organize my intentionally abortive rescue mission and see if I can provide that resolution you would like to have."

"Fine, fine," Downes said sounding unconcerned. Clearly, he wanted to spend time with the financial people talking about money.

The green-eyed man smiled at Osk and she nodded, letting him know that she was recording everything — as he'd asked. If anything important or questionable came up, he'd be able to hear it later.

Nikolaj left happy. He'd learned what he came to discover. The stupid bankers didn't have a clue what was going on. Despite their claims to forward thinking, they thought linearly. They were predictable adversaries when they were strong enough to be adversarial.

This man Downes already proved far more acceptable as a member of the group than the Old Man had ever been. He was more ambitious and had a lot to prove... to the group and to his peers. That made him willing to take a few chances. A man who was just starting to build his power base had to be flexible, whereas the Old Man had an agenda set in granite.

It was good to be rid of him. Now his job was to tidy things up and take care of any loose ends.

Outside of the building, he sent a text message that would let his men slip away from their posts. They hadn't been necessary, but the insurance was well worth the price.

A black SUV pulled up, and a door opened. Nikolaj got in the back, next to a blonde man. "Hello, Franz. Any news?"

The German shook his head. "That fucker Mateo is still invisible. Somehow he managed to drop off everyone's radar entirely."

"How?"

He frowned. "I don't know yet."

"Damn. What about his money?"

"It's gone too. My financial tech tells me that he liquidated all his assets and converted the cash into cryptocurrency — Monero. We know it went to a wallet, but that's empty now. Where the fuck it is, how to get at it, or who has access to the money now are all unknowns."

"That's not good."

"Is he such a threat?"

The green-eyed man laughed. "He's no threat at all, except to the Old Man's pride, and that isn't going to matter for long. I'm more concerned about this new superpower of his, this ability to go dark that quickly ... and take it all with him. I want to know how he did it. I want to understand. Mateo isn't that bright about such things. He would've had someone doing it for him."

"Exactly. I've been following that idea."

"And?"

"We heard that Mateo had been in Panama and Ecuador a few times recently. With the money trail a dead end, I went to Quito to see if I could find any breadcrumbs. Per your instructions, Osk's people fed me some chatter about new players in the bogus identity game and that they worked in that area. No one disappears without a trace, and none of the forgers I know had heard a peep from Mateo or his people."

"He didn't contact any of the top ones in Europe, either."

"Osk had intel concerning an American woman who was operating out of Quito helping people get new identities. She's a US lawyer and a lot of this is legit relocation work, but Interpol found out that she had traveled in and out of Panama and Mexico using different identities. She was working pretty openly in Quito."

"So, we interrogate her."

He sighed. "There was an incident. It spooked her and she disappeared herself."

"Explain."

"I found her easy enough, working in Quito. When I shadowed her, I found she already had a tail. I decided to find out who else was interested in the woman."

"Mateo's people?"

He nodded. "A guy named Jose Defamo."

"Mateo's muscle."

"That was what I guessed at the time."

Nikolaj stared out the window, seeing people walking the sidewalks as if the world was a calm place. "Once she got him a new identity, Mateo sent him to kill her. Tie off loose ends. He knew we'd track her, squeeze her."

"I imagine so. That would leave any trail to his door stone cold. Anyway, I saw Defamo break into her apartment while she was out. I was torn. I knew you wanted to learn how she was getting identities and wasn't sure the best way to learn that. I was pretty sure he was waiting for her to return so he could kill her. That apartment seemed like a convenient place to question him, so I let myself in. He was more alert than I expected." He shook his head. "He pulled out a gun. I tried to wound him, but he was a moving target and my shot killed him."

"Sloppy."

"In my defense, this was all on the fly. I was looking for the woman, not expecting to deal with a professional assassin. It just went sideways."

"All right." Nikolaj suppressed his disappointment. This was a perfect example of why contracting work out could be a mistake. "So, did you stay and grab the woman?"

He shook his head. "Defamo's gun didn't have a silencer, so I got out of there. I watched from across the street as the cops went in. When she came home and found the cops with the body, she kept her head. They questioned her and sent her away. She grabbed a cab and went straight to the airport."

"You followed the woman, I hope?"

He nodded. "I sat behind her on a flight to Panama but lost sight of her going through immigration. I got stuck with some immigration official who was having a bad day and needed to take it out on someone. By the time I sorted it out, and they let me through, she had disappeared. I had my people check, and no one bought a ticket to anywhere else under the name she was using. Either she switched identities, or she is still in Panama."

"She has to have left a trail. Put as many people on it as you need to. I want to know how she does this. That's more important than finding Mateo."

"I already did. Osk's people are reviewing all the biometric data of women leaving the airport — CCTV footage, passport scans, all of it. They are talking to cabbies, bus drivers, anyone who might have taken her into the city."

"Good. And when you find her, don't accidentally kill the bitch. I want to know how she gets such good IDs and where Mateo is." Franz nodded. "In the meantime, I need help getting in touch with someone who can have an intimate and revealing conversation with another acquaintance."

"I'd be glad to help." His eyes brightened.

"No. I want you focused on finding that woman. We need to know what magic she uses. I want it. While you do that … I need to get in touch with those Mossad girls you told me about," he said.

"The sisters?" Franz smiled, thinking about them, and the green-eyed man wondered if he knew them better than he'd let on. "They definitely get results."

"Are they available now?"

"For the right job, always," Franz said.

"I'd need them coordinating with an assault squad. They'd have to go into a combat situation."

"That's nothing to them."

"They would have to do their work quickly and in the field. They'll have to be damn good."

"If the target is expendable, they are the best," Franz said, turning to stare out the window. "These ladies are incredibly efficient, more than a little insane, and quite dangerous. They also enjoy their work as much as anyone I've ever seen."

The green-eyed man sat back and studied the man's face. He had seldom heard Franz speak of anyone with such obvious high regard in his voice, and that was significant. The man had contempt for most of his fellow humans and reserved his respect for competence and money. "They sound perfect for this task. Send me their contact information."

Franz scowled. "I don't have it."

The green-eyed man tensed. "Why not?"

"Because they initiate all contact," he said. "When they are available, they let me know they are on the market, then they check in periodically to see if I've heard of anything interesting."

"This won't wait."

Franz looked at his watch. "I expect to hear from them tomorrow; I'll let them know that the job is urgent and have them contact you," he said.

Nikolaj was uneasy. The idea of being contacted, not being the one to make contact, didn't sit well with him, but he understood. With people like these, that wasn't negotiable. All the top pros got to dictate the terms they worked under, just as he did with his clients.

It was odd being on the client side of the situation, though. Normally, when he didn't rely on his own people, he turned to Franz. "That will be excellent," he said. "Give them the satellite number in case I'm not in cell range. I'm going to be setting up the mission and running it."

Franz nodded and the green-eyed man sat back. Overall, other than the minor frustration of not having Mateo in his pocket, he was happy with the way things were going. Soon enough, the smart city project would be online. The Oculistica would see how well that worked and relax.

It was great to have the bankers think that the Smart City project and the introduction of a Phoenix crypto were going to solve their problems. The premise the Oculistica worked under was that controlling finance would give them the world.

The truth was that the net result of the project would be to hand him the reins of power. Then they'd see what a stupid little social club this nefarious global organization really was.

All this world domination crap, the struggle to control the financial world with digital money, of tracking business transactions globally ... that all sounded great, but Nikolaj, who cared little for the technology, saw that all he really needed was data.

But that meant more than collecting financial information — much more than that. True power would come with total digital surveillance. Technology existed, or could be developed, that would make it possible to know who was where at all times, and even what they thought. The supercomputers that he had his team assembling in Eastern Europe would process it all, let him know who was working with whom. He'd know attitudes and agendas.

There would be new organizations, new ways the world worked, but the value of a constant stream of data would continue to increase. Once he had access to that, well... he'd have everything. Absolutely everything. All a person had to do was ask the right questions. With the answers his new system would give him, for all practical purposes, he'd own the world. And the down payment was little more than an investment in hardware and the software link to the Smart City systems that his people had installed.

Franz sat back, staring at him, evaluating him.

"What is it?"

"You are going to run this mission? A combat situation, you said."

"Right."

"You live a pretty soft life these days. Do you spend as much time training Systema these days?"

The question surprised him. Not that Franz knew he studied the Russian combat art; no, Franz also practiced it and they had trained together a few times, exchanging ideas and techniques. What surprised him was the impertinence of his questions. Well, he was stinging from his recent failure and wanting to bring Nikolaj down a peg.

"What's your concern? Are you afraid I'm getting soft?"

Franz made a face, then refilled his own glass. "Curious, is all. Old soldiers don't age well. I wouldn't want you holding up your men in the field."

"Old? Okay, I haven't been training hard lately," he said.

He could see that Franz found that a feeble excuse. "You can lose your edge easily. Too easily. That puts your people at risk."

He wanted to say something, put Franz in his place, but the man was right. "Maybe it's more a matter of having people like you doing too much of the work for me."

"Perhaps that's it," Franz said. "Or perhaps fine living and excellent booze makes it too easy to forget the delectable taste of blood. If you like, I could head up the team in the field for you."

The green-eyed man watched Franz warily. Having the younger man tease him was new. He seemed to lack the proper respect, and that was dangerous. If he got it into his head that killing the man who ran enforcement for the Oculistica would raise his price, well… that might get sticky.

"I'll be tasting the blood of my enemies soon. You just find Mateo Chatzi," he said. "And find that woman."

"I'll find them both," Franz said. "And when I corner Mateo, after he tells me everything I want to know, I will bring you his balls in a jar."

The green-eyed man grinned, knowing that, for Franz, that was not a figure of speech. "Call me if airport security stops you and wants to know what you have in the jar. I'd be glad to explain."

"They won't find them," Franz said.

The green-eyed man started to explain that he was making a joke, then stopped himself. That wouldn't mean anything to Franz. Not a damn thing.

CHAPTER 30

A FLUID SITUATION

"The privacy and dignity of our citizens [are] being whittled away by sometimes imperceptible steps. Taken individually, each step may be of little consequence. But when viewed as a whole, there begins to emerge a society quite unlike any we have seen—a society in which government may intrude into the secret regions of a [person's] life."

— *William O. Douglas, Supreme Court Justice*

Privilege Aluxes Isla Mujeres Hotel
Isla Mujeres, Mexico

If she hadn't been thinking so intently about the sudden and rapid changes that her intel suggested were taking place, Boone would've noticed Anchara's sour attitude sooner. Not that noticing would have done anything, but it bothered her that she'd missed seeing that her girlfriend was sulking even more than she usually did whenever Boone spent time on business other than their travel videos.

And it had happened before, but it was different this time. Before, when she came out of her haze of work to realize Anchara was angry, all she had to do was pay the woman a little more attention for a time. That would fix things. Spending some time alone with her and letting her know she was important would soothe those ruffled feathers.

This time, she wasn't so sure.

She understood part of the reason for Anchara's anger. This trip was supposed to be a getaway... a work trip, to be sure, but a SindiLux work trip. Unfortunately, her other world, her other life was intruding. She'd had to take breaks to deal with emergencies, and the repercussions of those actions required other actions.

Which meant Anchara was neglected.

"At least let me show you the place," Anchara said. Grabbing her hand, Anchara led Boone up the stairs in their suite and out onto a balcony.

As they stepped into the bright tropical sun, Anchara waved her hand delicately and pointed past the swimming pool sitting in front of them, out to the pristine white sand beach. "It's as lovely as the pictures," she said, her voice almost a sigh. She pointed down to the courtyard. "It's a watery delight. There's a crystal-clear pool right there, we have this private pool right on our balcony, and then that gorgeous beach leads into the ocean."

"It's the Caribbean Sea, actually," Boone said as she walked out on the balcony and slipped an arm around Anchara's slim waist. She pointed to the southeast. "Somewhere in that direction are the Cayman Islands."

"Picky," Anchara said.

"You know I like to be accurate, love. But I agree the view is gorgeous."

"It's a paradise."

Boone winced a bit at the overused, terribly abused term, then she took a breath and gave herself a moment to take it all in, absorb everything that was wonderful about the place. She needed to get her head straight.

While she loved staying at these high-end places, she wasn't as much in love with beaches as Anchara. The girl assumed everyone liked the beach. They'd started with beach resorts and, as Sindi, she gushed over them. Anchara assumed her enthusiasm was real (and sometimes it was).

Boone had never set her straight.

And now, in an attempt to move Boone and herself back into the center of Sindi's world, Anchara had arranged what she thought was a special treat — time together at a what was to her a special place.

Boone had no intention of destroying that idea. If Anchara was going to try so hard to please her, she would be pleased.

And things were lovely. She let out a sigh of contentment.

She took Anchara's arm and kissed her. "Of course, now we have to make several videos to pay for all this fun in the sun," she laughed. "I'm sure you made management some ambitious promises when you arranged all this."

Anchara laughed. "Work, work, work. Ah, yes, you poor exploited woman. You are doomed to live out your days vacationing in grand places and making videos about them. We are obligated to spend time here relaxing. Whatever is the world coming to?"

Sindi winked. "I can only imagine. Perhaps the horror of slow room service?"

"I tremble at the thought." Anchara pointed out past the larger pool in the courtyard below and to the thatched-roof structures called palapas built on the sand. "The hotel's beach bar would be the perfect spot for the opening video."

"You think so? I was thinking about down by the pool."

Anchara shook her head. "There would be too much glare this time of day. But out under one of the palapas, with the sun this high, the light should be good. Besides, there are some sexy ladies out there in bikinis, which always works for the audience… and it is getting to be lunchtime."

Sindi nodded. Not only was Anchara's judgment always impeccable in such matters, but she was also getting hungry.

Anchara had developed a good eye for setting up the videos. And she'd learned by doing. Sindi thought back to the early days, a time when she'd shot her videos herself, using only the webcam built into a laptop computer. It was amazing that she'd ever gotten anything even watchable.

Now she relied on Anchara, not to mention a high-quality video camera and sophisticated editing software to make professional videos that the resorts and hotels liked.

Fortunately, video editing was another area in which Anchara shined. They made a perfect team, collaborating on the theme of each video, and then Sindi performing, improvising, and Anchara producing the final product. If she was honest, she had to think that Anchara did most of the hard work.

"Okay, slave driver. The beach bar it is. But Tricia will be here this evening."

Anchara scowled. "Fine. We'll shoot something now."

As they went back inside so Sindi could change into the colorful bikini Anchara had picked out for her to wear, Anchara sat on the bed and Boone sighed at her tense expression. "Go ahead, tell me what I'm supposed to do, Anchara. I can't ignore the rest of the world just because you want me to."

"Why not?" she asked glumly.

There was no point in getting into it. Anchara shut out everything but this fantasy world. She didn't want to know what was going on.

Unfortunately, whatever was happening was significant. At first, she'd thought there was a split taking place, a welcome fracture of the globalists. The ancient banker who ran the Oculistica had disappeared, but the details were sketchy. The official word was he'd been taken by Somali pirates.

Boone doubted that pirates would go after someone with connections like his, at least not without the backing of other powerful forces. Yet, it was possible. If the Old Man was dead, which seemed likely, that had ramifications. A vacuum in the power structure would be filled quickly.

On a more personal level, there was the fact that someone was after Tricia, and possibly Kenny and Joshua, maybe even Miguel. To keep them safe, both Tricia and Miguel were on their way, separately, to the hotel — much to Anchara's disgust.

Boone had given Tricia a heads up, and when she arrived, Tricia made a tremendous effort to be nice to Anchara. "Anchara, I understand you pick the hotels. This is certainly a delightful resort," she said. "It's gorgeous and located in such a beautiful spot."

That was true. The resort sat on a beach on Isla Mujeres, an island that was a short ferry ride from Cancun, Mexico.

The momentary flicker of pleasure crossing Anchara's face struck Boone as a hopeful sign. "It is, isn't it?" she said.

Then Tricia unknowingly sealed Anchara's less generous opinion of her. "I want to thank you both for bringing me here. Boone, it's been ages since I was on a beach."

Boone winced. Anchara hated being reminded that most people knew her as Boone. "We had to get you out of Panama. Anchara made the arrangements."

"Temporary arrangements," Anchara said. "She…" she nodded at Boone, unsure how to refer to her in front of this person, "thinks you need to get even further away from Ecuador."

"I agree," Tricia said. "And Panama and Guatemala. I have tracks there." Then she sighed. "But it looks like I won't be doing business as usual no matter where I am."

"Not visibly," Boone said. "But with the turmoil going on, I'm afraid that we will need your ability to transform people into crypto citizens more than ever. Governments are doubling down on surveillance, and we need to move freely. It used to be that we could manage that well enough, but now they are tracking how often a specific person goes to a place and even what they do there. When they establish smart cities, it will get even harder."

"Sounds like we need to become stainless steel rats," Tricia laughed.

"What?" Anchara looked puzzled.

"Science fiction books by Harry Harrison. He wrote about a future where things were so controlled that it was like living in a stainless-steel world. The stainless-steel rat was a person who didn't want to stay in the maze."

"Stainless steel or not, we will set you up in a safe place."

She shook her head. "So much of the work requires personal contacts, bribing the right people, for instance."

"We will get you helpers for that. I need you coordinating everything and improving the system constantly. Keeping it invisible will keep getting harder."

"You think so?"

"I know it. Now tell me exactly what happened in Ecuador."

"I don't entirely know. A week ago, I decided to rent a furnished apartment in Quito to do business in. I wanted to keep business away from my private life and that made more sense than an office. I gave that as my new address. I was getting to know everyone who had any influence on visas. That night, I went out to dinner with the minister of immigration. He invited me out so we could chat about the inducements the government might offer to get more rich people to relocate to Ecuador — a favorite topic of mine, as you will appreciate. We had a nice dinner, but when he dropped me off at my apartment, the cops were there. He came in with me and we saw that the place had been trashed. There was a dead man lying on the floor. He'd been shot several times."

"That must've been a shock. What did you do?"

"I stood there looking like an idiot. Then cops asked who he was. I told them I didn't know. They asked what he might've been looking for, and I told them I didn't know. The minister showed his ID and told them I'd been at dinner with him. He made the point that he couldn't be involved, but suggested they consider the possibility that whatever happened was related to a previous tenant, as I had just rented the place. Given that I had juice, the cops told me to get a hotel room, and we'd talk later. With the minister insisting, they let me stuff a few things in a bag. I caught a taxi to the airport and called you."

"Do you have any idea who the dead guy is… or was?"

She snorted. "I know exactly who he was. He called himself Jose Defamo. He was the right-hand man for one of my recent clients. Jose worked as his intermediary. I saw far too much of him. He is a cold bastard."

"And you got the client a new identity?"

"Hell yes. Kenny and I gave the man a brand-new, bullet-proof identity and then relocated him to Guatemala. Until now I thought he was a satisfied customer."

Boone scowled. "Maybe he wanted to stay that way."

"What do you mean?"

"If he was that concerned about disappearing… possibly it wasn't the authorities who were after him. And, if that's the case, and you did such a good job, then you became the only connection to his old identity."

"Shit." Tricia let out a long breath. "You might be right. Color me naïve. I hadn't thought of that angle."

"That would explain his muscle showing up on your doorstep to go through your stuff. He was going to find anything tying you to either of them. When you came home, then he could kill you."

"Fuck. But magically someone else arrived and killed him first? Why?"

"My guess is that whoever was after the client somehow learned about you and was following you. If that's right, then he wouldn't want Defamo killing you before he got you to tell him where and who your client was. Unless, of course, it was lucky timing that had them drop by the same evening."

"I'm not that kind of lucky, which means we have no idea who is after me."

"Although your client still will be. And there are other hired guns."

"Shit!"

"It doesn't matter who it is at the moment. Right now, the important thing is to get you to a safe place. Your route here was more direct than I would have liked, but we had to work fast."

"I'm putting you in danger!" she gasped.

Anchara snorted. "I have us booked on a flight to Amsterdam in the morning," she said. "When I knew Tricia was coming, I decided none of us could stay around."

"What about Miguel?"

"He is being rerouted. I sent him an encrypted text." She looked at Tricia and handed her a passkey. "I booked you a room here for the night, but you are booked out on a flight to New York tomorrow afternoon under another name from the list you sent me. Margo Evans from Duluth."

Tricia moaned. "New York? Do you hate me that much, lovely Anchara?"

Boone laughed. "You are going to be picky now?"

"This might be my last chance to be," she said. "And I didn't bring a coat."

Boone found Tricia's black humor was reassuring — her brain was still functioning clearly.

Anchara managed a grin. "You won't freeze. In New York, you'll change IDs and fly to Singapore, via Dubai. Then take the railroad to Bangkok. If I were you, I'd change clothes. Get a wig if you have time."

Boone shook her head in amazement. For all that Anchara didn't like Boone's world, she had a knack for logistics, especially sneaky logistics. "You see, fortunately, we've gotten good at hiding people. Well, Anchara has."

"I've had to," she said, not bothering to disguise a certain bitterness.

Tricia caught the undercurrent. "You are both fantastic. But now, if you don't mind, I'd like to go to my room, order a meal and some whiskey, and take a hot bath while I contemplate my future."

"Enjoy," Boone said.

When Tricia was gone, Boone watched Anchara close up her laptop. "Are we done with that now?" she asked, sounding snarky. When she heard herself, Boone added: "You did a good job."

"Yes, I have all the arrangements made."

Boone was relieved that, as upset as Anchara had been, she'd jumped in when it counted.

Anchara smiled and picked up her camera. "Well, we have time to make another video before dinner."

Suddenly, she decided that Anchara was right. Sitting around waiting would be painful and gain them nothing. Shooting the video would provide a distraction. She picked up the tiny bikini and smiled. "To the beach bar, then," she said.

"When they see you in that, your fans will be groaning with desire," Anchara said. Then she sighed. "And, since we will be in the bar, maybe before we start the video, you might want to order a double Scotch."

Boone wondered if she was teasing her. Anchara didn't drink much at all and preferred that Boone didn't either. "Seriously?"

Anchara grinned. "You look tense. If you need it to get your shit together, it's good. We can't have our video girl looking stressed out at a tropical resort."

Even with her off and on concerns about the relationship, Boone had to admit that sometimes the girl read her mind. And when it came to the videos, she was a pro.

At the same time, other things were out of control. For a long time, their trips had been all about making the videos. That had suited Boone. It kept her off the radar while others acted as her eyes and ears. The various Bitpats did their jobs, monitoring, hacking, creating systems...

But Anchara had gotten spoiled. She wasn't interested in the Bitpats, or what they did. She preferred to keep the outside world outside and live in the high-end travel cocoon she and Sindi had created.

Now, that was a problem. Even if things weren't moving so fast, increasingly Boone had started to feel trapped in Sindi's artificial persona. It was superficial. It could be fun, but to Boone, Sindi was nothing more than a mask to hide her real work.

In a way, that was a betrayal of Anchara. There was no way around that.

"Why do you bring them to us?" Anchara asked in bed that night.

"Tricia? Because I needed to hear her tell the story. There could be clues about what is going on that she isn't aware of."

"And Miguel?"

"Again, I want to hear details from him about the Colombian project. He was on the inside. Also, I want to evaluate him. He is maturing fast. I need to decide how best to use him."

"Wyatt and Rebecca could do that."

Boone studied Anchara's intense expression. This was the girl being possessive, and it was an unwelcome shift in her attitude.

It was one thing for Anchara to prefer Boone in her role as Sindi, but if she was going to be jealous of her spending time with anyone from that other world, that wouldn't do. On top of that, it irritated her. Even though it was flattering, Anchara was rejecting who she really was.

"The world is changing fast, Anchara. I've dedicated myself to making sure that those changes don't put people in a stranglehold — no more than they are already, at least."

"You don't have to do that. The others can do it."

"I do have to do it, or at least help make it happen."

"I don't like it. It puts everything at risk."

Boone scowled. "Maybe you'd better start learning to adapt, Anchara," she said.

"To you, not being you?"

"To the real world intruding on your fantasy."

"Sindi and that world isn't a fantasy," she said. "We are well known and travel the world... living wonderfully. You have thousands, hundreds of thousands of followers. That's unreal, Sindi. It's a wonderful accomplishment. But these other people come and take that away from us, from me."

"Other people?"

"Wyatt, Miguel, Kenny...."

"The men."

She scowled again. "Mostly."

"I know you don't like men much. And I know you have some reason to feel that way. You hate it that I do like to enjoy myself with them from time to time, but that's who I am. And yes, I think Miguel is a cute young guy, but my reasons for wanting to see him have to do with him become an asset to us."

Anchara's pout told Boone her argument hadn't made a difference. Again, Boone felt a small flare of irritation at the girl's narrow perspective. The reality was that she could do nothing about it for the moment.

Boone got up and paced the room.

"I didn't mean to upset you," Anchara said meekly.

"I need to think," she said. Everything was spinning. Wyatt and Rashmi had managed to elude the Oculistica, but who knew how hard they really looked for them? Now Tricia, Joshua, and Miguel were on the run. There wasn't as obvious a link to Kenny, so he would probably be okay. But they were all her responsibility now.

She shook her head. The idea that her friends were in danger made her stomach knot up. This was the life they had chosen, but the battlefield they fought on was so damn vague. They didn't even know all the players in the game.

The situation was beyond confusing. Were they dealing with a single enemy, or had they suddenly popped up on the radar of several entities? And were all Bitpats targeted? Or was it just that Tricia's operation got too high profile?

Boone shook herself to get rid of the unfamiliar and rather sickening feeling of helplessness that her thinking was bringing on.

"Come back to bed and I'll make you feel good," Anchara said softly.

"That sounds nice," she said. Then she'd need to rest. The coming days would be stressful.

CHAPTER 31

A RESCUE OF SORTS

"Consider the definition of a racketeer as someone who creates a threat, then charges for its reduction. Governments' provision of protection, by this standard, often qualifies as racketeering."

— *Charles Tilly, American historian, sociologist*

W. Kaxda Jaziira
Mogadishu, Somalia

It was midnight when the squad approached the port town, coming in from the desert. There were eight of them, all moving silently under a pale quarter moon with the stealth and grace of trained and experienced professionals. They were spread out in a broad row, staying just within sight of each other where they could observe hand signals.

The silent progression continued through the darkness until, still well outside of the town, they came within sight of a small compound surrounded by a low wall, topped with concertina wire. The squad leader, a muscular man named Enrique, raised his fist, and the squad closed ranks and lay down on the hot sand, their weapons trained ahead.

Enrique looked through night-vision binoculars and then turned to the man beside him. "There are two concrete block buildings with barred windows."

Then he handed the glasses to the man, who put them to his piercing green eyes and scanned the compound that lay across the sand.

The compound was about 10 km from the port and somewhat isolated, sitting in bleak terrain populated only by some sort of scrub trees, more bushes than trees, that dotted the landscape and the compound itself.

As the green-eyed man took in the situation, Enrique reviewed his troops and was pleased. They lay face down in the sand, unmoving, waiting for orders. Each carried a Chinese-made AK-47 equipped with a silencer; this was not his weapon of choice, but adequate for the mission. More importantly, they could be abandoned if necessary. They'd give no clue to the identity of his squad — it was an untraceable, ubiquitous weapon that implicated no particular government or organization. The explosives one of the men carried in his backpack were unmarked, and unexceptional — just enough power to do the job. The detonators were crude and could've been put together by any garden-variety terrorist.

None of the soldiers knew the source of the information that had provided the nature of the target or its coordinates. None of them cared. They were at work. Places like this were their offices, and they were well paid for their work.

Now they lay patiently on the still-hot sand, watching two scruffy armed men emerge from behind one of the buildings. The two men looked around and then walked out of the compound and split up.

"Posting guards," Enrique said.

"And that's the building we want, Enrique," the green-eyed man said.

They watched one of the guards light a cigarette. The glow illuminated his face.

Enrique snorted softly, then silently moved to stand beside one of the mercenaries and tapped him on his shoulder. "Creed, I want you to let that asshole know that smoking is harmful to his health," the leader said.

The soldier smiled. "My pleasure," he said. He was already sighted in on the man; now he exhaled and squeezed the trigger. The weapon pressed back into his shoulder with a satisfying recoil, but the silenced weapon made only a soft pop. The shot struck the guard in the face, snapping his head back and spinning him around like a rag doll.

He slammed into the wall and slithered to the ground, lifeless.

The other guard stood stock still, frozen in shock, unable to determine where the shot had come from. Then, looking around him frantically, he rushed toward the door. Enrique patted his sniper's shoulder again. The man fired and his second shot struck the fleeing man squarely in the back. His arms flew out and his rifle smashed into the ground seconds before he tumbled down on the sand.

Enrique turned to the green-eyed man who had watched in silence beside him. "Shall we ask the ones inside if they care to dance?"

Nikolaj nodded. "Send two men to secure the other building. When they are in place, you can send out the invitations."

Enrique raised a hand and showed two fingers in the dim moonlight. Then he pointed to the building and two of the men got up and flowed soundlessly toward the building. In front of the building's only door, they flopped down on the sand again, their weapons covering the opening.

Enrique gave a hand signal, then got up, heading for the other building with the remaining four soldiers following. The green-eyed man moved with them.

This building had two windows. At each, a soldier took up a position, standing just to the side to cover it without being seen. Enrique and the other two soldiers approached the front door. With a nod from the green-eyed man, Enrique kicked the door down and burst through, firing his weapon. The green-eyed man and the last two soldiers were right behind him, spreading out and firing as they went through the door.

Other bursts of gunfire from the windows raked the room. In seconds, the squad had cut down the three men sitting in the room. One knocked over a table as he fell.

The only person left alive in the room was the Old Man. He was naked, tied to a chair. The men had been torturing him.

Nikolaj smiled. "Well, Mr. Forte, I see these horrid people haven't been treating you well at all."

"Pigs," the Old Man spat. Blood was mixed with his spittle.

"Did they get what they wanted?"

"You think these amateurs could do that, Nikolaj?" the Old Man asked.

Nikolaj had to admire the man's bravado. "I have no idea, Mr. Forte. I would assume that you have a high threshold of pain, but one never knows until it is tested."

He walked closer, poking his toe at the remains of what had been an expensive Brioni suit and a few things that had obviously been taken from its pockets — two Gurkha Black Dragon cigars, a gold pen, a pair of glasses, and a calfskin Bottega Veneta wallet.

Enrique circled around the room, checking the men they'd shot. "All dead," he said, sounding satisfied.

The green-eyed man smiled, then picked up the cigars, the pen, and the wallet, putting them in his pocket. At his nod, Enrique turned and left the room. The soldiers at the windows disappeared silently, leaving the two other soldiers, both women.

"I apologize for annoying you by letting amateurs harass you," the green-eyed man said. "I hope you know that I didn't ask these people to attempt to get information from you. I doubt they had a clear idea of what you might be able to tell them."

"Idiots!" he said.

"Yes, I'm afraid so. These men were simply enjoying themselves." He nodded to the soldiers behind him. "I have too much respect for the legendary Charles Forte for that. For you, sir, I brought specialists. You deserve that much."

At his signal, the two soldiers put down their weapons and stepped forward. Opening her backpack, one brought out a small digital recorder, and a collection of knives that she held reverently as the other pulled off her helmet and shook her yellow hair free. "We prefer to work in privacy," she said.

Her companion held up a knife and admired it. "As you agreed," she said. "We have our little trade secrets to protect, after all."

Nikolaj saw the fire in her eyes and turned toward the Old Man. "These two are professionals. I firmly believe they will live up to your expectations. And it might amuse you to know that when I have access to your accounts, the money will go to a worthwhile cause. You wanted to change the world, to control it, and your money will make that change happen. I have some ambitious plans. Unfortunately, I know you would not approve of my strategy — you wouldn't consider a contemporary solution. That made this… and these friends of mine, my colleagues, necessary." He smiled. "They are twins. You might have heard rumors about them."

When he saw the look in the Old Man's eyes shift from rage to fear, Nikolaj smiled. "Good."

The second woman took off her helmet. Her head was shaved, and she smiled an evil grin as she took a knife from her sister. "Most of the rumors you've heard are true, I assure you. Especially the uglier ones."

"They did wonderful work for the Mossad for years but fell afoul of politics. Their superiors were unable to keep them on a leash short enough to satisfy the politicians who felt that there is such a thing as enjoying your work too much."

"We got very, very good at it," the woman said. "And found it incredibly… exciting."

"As with most soldiers, we got bored between assignments," the other woman said. "We were never good at simply waiting."

The other nodded. "We decided to give ourselves assignments to fill the time." She smiled. "That frightened our superiors. They wanted to stop us. So, we carved a few up, as examples, and left."

"Girls need their pleasures, after all," the one with hair said.

"That is fortunate for me," Nikolaj said. He turned to the women, who had begun taking off their uniforms. "I will leave you to your... pleasures."

The woman with the hair had already stripped naked, seemingly oblivious to the presence of anyone else. She picked up her knife and turned it to reflect the light. "We will have the information in an hour, perhaps less. At that point, he will still be somewhat alive."

"Fine."

"And then, we can ...."

"As we agreed. He is yours once I get the information."

"Then we start."

The green-eyed man left the room, aware of the terror in the face of the Old Man as the two naked women approached. One reached out, and he started to scream, but then seemed to choke on his own fear.

Outside, Enrique and the rest of the men waited by the other building. "No one has come out," Enrique said. "They seem to have heard nothing. Not even that scream."

"Then I'll go in first," he said.

The green-eyed man walked to the front door and opened it. Four men were sitting at a table, eating. They jumped up as he walked in. "What?"

Then a slow smile crossed the face of a tall, thin man. "Nik, I didn't expect you yet. What's going on?"

"Hello Massam," he said. Enrique and two other men stepped in behind him, their weapons pointed at the four. "I hope I didn't interrupt your meal, but we need to talk."

"So... talk," he said.

"I thought we had a deal about this adventure."

"You promised to pay us to take this man prisoner. This fucking banker."

"And I told you not to demand a ransom for him."

The man looked ready to deny the claim, then thought better of it. "I thought he might be worth more than you offered to pay."

"We had a deal," Nikolaj repeated firmly. "You fucked it up. I told you to wait for me to contact you. Instead of that, you hide him from me and tried to collect a ransom. If we were talking about an oil tanker, fine, but this is an important person."

"You see? You didn't tell us he was important."

"So, you decided that you'd torture him and get his bank account information and whatever other secrets you could extract from him."

The man fidgeted, wanting to reach for a weapon, evaluating his chances, but smart enough to glance toward the windows where more weapons were pointed at him. "I lost men capturing him. What you were paying was too little."

"Then you underbid the job. Losing men is a cost of doing business," Nikolaj said. He went to the table and sat down. He toyed with the untouched food on the plate, then tasted it. "This is such garbage food, Massam. All the money you get from your piracy business and you live like a peasant."

"This is how my people live."

"You could've invested wisely over the years. Although you do love to talk about the future, you are caught up in the world's fascination with the superficial and useless. And that makes you useless."

"I share with my people," he said, glaring hatred.

"The people who are your sycophants, at least. And you pretend to be strong and independent, but you give much of that money to the army for protection. I know that much. After all, the powerful people in your country's army are on my payroll too."

"You know nothing."

"Speaking of business matters, you really should think about upgrading your requirements for employment. Your people were slowly killing the prisoner. He is a tough bastard and if your goal was to get information, they hadn't even made a good start." A scream reached their ears. The green-eyed man put a hand to his ear. "I believe that is the sound of him explaining to my colleagues, true professionals, the things you wanted to know as well as everything I want to know."

At a nod from the green-eyed man, Enrique came around and took the weapons from the three pirates, then moved them to stand against the wall.

"Sit down," the green-eyed man told Massam. "We need to have a nice talk, and I need to kill some time. My people tell me it could take an hour or so." Massam glared at Enrique, then nervously pulled back a chair and sat facing the green-eyed man. Nikolaj nodded. "Now tell me, old friend, was this change in strategy your own idea or did someone suggest it to you?"

"Someone? Who would I be talking to that I'd tell about capturing this Old Man? Who would suggest this?"

"Perhaps the people you demanded a ransom from?"

"They said nothing. They never even replied. They wouldn't offer a penny for his skinny ancient ass. You told me he was worth money."

"In the right hands, he is worth several fortunes. Yours, unfortunately, are not the right hands at all. And I'm concerned. There is a great deal of meddling going on these days. People see things happening and try to change the outcome. Perhaps your old CIA contacts convinced you to handle this yourself."

"They are all gone," Massam said. "Retired or dead, all gone."

That sounded true. "I'm sure that was a blow to your cash flow. And when I tried to remedy that, to get you some income, you betrayed me. It's a shame — we've worked together so well before."

"You always came out best."

He pointed to one of the pirates standing at the wall. "Isn't that your younger brother? Ahmad, as I recall."

"Yes, that is Ahmad."

"Do you know anything, Ahmad? Should I have you join this conversation?"

"Infidel," Ahmad growled.

"Bad attitude," the green-eyed man said. He nodded at Enrique. "He is being unpleasant and not answering my questions."

Moving with lightning speed, Enrique spun toward Ahmad, pulling a KA-BAR 1217 combat knife from his belt and plunging it into the man. Ahmad shrieked, grabbing his belly. With blood spurting out, he fell to the floor. Blood pooled around him rapidly.

"Ahmad!" Massam screamed, jumping up, but Enrique was there to force him back into his chair.

"I suspect your brother needs medical attention," the green-eyed man said. "The blade didn't strike any vital organs, but I imagine he will bleed out rapidly. If I just knew who convinced you to change the plan, if I heard a believable story ...."

"It was the Old Man himself," Massam said.

"What?"

"Right after we captured him, he guessed that you were behind the attack, the kidnapping. He suggested we ransom him and said that he would match whatever they paid. When the bastards wouldn't pay ... well, if the man did have access to that kind of money, we thought it was smart to convince him to give it to us, anyway. You never said we couldn't torture him."

The irony made him smile. "Thank you," he said. "That story makes some sense. The Old Man conned you into playing his game but wasn't thinking clearly about what he was letting you know. Of course, he thinks banks are safe places for money, and that he was still in control. That didn't work out for him in the end."

"My brother..." Massam said.

"Yes, your brother. Your arrogant prick of a brother who helped you double-cross me." He pulled out an H&K 9mm and fired past Massam. Ahmad's head exploded as the bullet struck.

He fired again, this time catching Massam in the shoulder. The impact shattered the shoulder. The man screamed in pain and toppled over backward.

Enrique pointed his pistol at Massam. "Should I gut him or just finish him off?"

The green-eyed man shook his head. "Break his kneecaps." Enrique fired twice, with Massam's screams verifying his marksmanship.

As Enrique walked toward the door, he waved a hand; the soldiers at the windows shot the last two men.

They waited outside in the warm dark until the door to the building that the Old Man was in swung open. The green-eyed man went in alone and found the two women covered in blood. Their pupils were dilated, making them look like they were on some powerful narcotic.

"We have what you wanted," one said, handing him the digital recorder. It was sticky with blood. "Come see our work."

It wasn't a request. He stepped closer. They'd untied the Old Man and spread him out on the floor. Nikolaj saw a bloody living thing that might have once been a man. Next to him were his eyeballs, his penis and testicles, and sheets of his skin. Blood still throbbed in exposed blood vessels.

"If you have no more need of him, we intend to have some fun," one said.

"Eliminating what little life remains in him," the other said, wiping blood from her lips. "It won't be that great."

"Well, I've arranged a bonus for you. There is another one in the other building."

"What do you need from him?"

"Nothing at all," he said. "He's strictly for your pleasure. When you are done, leave the bodies to be found and call me. I've transferred your payment to your account."

One of the women looked at what was left of the Old Man. "Is he dying, this other one?"

"Wounded. Kneecapped and shot in the shoulder. He is younger too."

She picked up a hammer and raised it over the Old Man, then brought it down, smashing his skull. "A few more hours and this one would be useless."

The other woman wiped blood from her hands on her breasts. "We would like a few days with this other one."

"Take as much time as you like. Just call me so that I know when to send in troops to 'discover' the atrocities."

They nodded and one of them headed, calmly, serenely toward the other building.

"Who the hell are those crazy bitches?" a soldier asked Enrique as they moved back into the desert to rendezvous with a Blackhawk helicopter. "They are crazier than your run-of-the-mill serial killer."

Enrique grinned. "Ever read classical literature?"

"Hell, no,"

"You should. The boss calls them the Furies. Aeschylus wrote: 'Nothing forces us to know what we do not want to know, except pain.' Seems appropriate."

"We should get paid more for working with them," the man grumbled.

"So, you tell him that," the other one said. "I'd love to know how he takes it."

The first soldier grimaced, and then they went silently into the night.

CHAPTER 32

THE NEW ORDER

"Power is not only what you have
but what the enemy thinks you have."

— *Saul Alinsky, Tactics: Rules for Radicals*

Boa Vista Eco Hotel
Boa Vista, Roraima, Brazil

The modern-looking Boa Vista Eco Hotel rises up in the heart of the capital of Brazil's Roraima state. Charlie Turner found the city of Boa Vista, sitting on the western bank of the Branco River, slightly puzzling.

This modern city, unlike most South American cities, was planned — its streets radiated out from the center. It was a planned city, modeled after Paris by the architect Darci Aleixo Derenusson. It was efficient and modern, and all that, but Charlie found it lacking in character. Staring out the window of the hotel's most lavish suite, looking across the city to the north, he decided he didn't like the look of it much. Like Washington, DC, it was too clever by far.

He sighed at the thought that it was here, in this regular, small and boring city (of less than a million people) where finally, he was going to accomplish something important.

Well, that wasn't fair… he'd headed up important missions before, but this one was important to him — and very irregular. You could almost taste the irony. His government was paying good money to him and he was going to make his own country, at least in its present form, obsolete.

He turned and looked at the man sitting on the couch, veiled in a sullen funk. He knew what bothered the man. Carlos Herrera wasn't pleased that he was about to realize his dream of kicking the bastards out and taking over, for the simple reason that the CIA was involved.

It figured that he'd care about how it happened almost as much as whether it happened at all. Over the years, Charlie had worked with dozens of men like this one — men who wanted people to view their ascension to power as noble, people who thought they could merge their idealism with the pragmatism needed to take control of a country. Probably fucking Lenin was like that.

Trotsky had been, for sure. He was too idealistic, though, and that cost him power and then his life. Stalin had him chopped up with an ice axe in Mexico City by Ramón Mercader.

And that was weird and yet eerily appropriate. Where the hell did you even find an ice axe in Mexico City?

The reality was that idealism was usually the first casualty of any political upheaval — collateral damage of exerting the power it took to seize the reins of power, whether they were bad guys or saints. He was sure that people like Herrera understood that at some level, which was probably why he was nervous and anxious. He hated the idea that he needed help to do it and was well aware that the guns that put you in power could take it away.

Charlie Turner knew that Herrera had hoped for a bloodless coup, and it made him laugh. What a dreamer! What a fucking wet dream that was in this world; the entire idea that politics could be an honorable profession was nothing but fantasy.

Charlie chuckled, remembering himself when he was young. Once, back when he joined the CIA, he'd had such a fantasy. He thought that he could help make democracy great. And they put him to work doing the dirty work democracies are supposed to loathe — assassinations, corrupting politicians, running drugs.

When he woke to that, after a short time of self-loathing, he realized that it was just a goddamn joke — a joke on all of them.

He'd wanted to make the world safe for democracy — another joke. Now he was making the world safe for Charlie Turner. The only part of that he didn't like was that the mercenary Nikolaj was funding it. It was curious that the man honestly seemed to have no interest in the politics of it all. All he gave a damn about was making this new kind of government happen. He was paying for it all, too, as well as paying Charlie to throw his weight behind the project.

That had been easy. There were lots of people in the agency who'd gotten sick of politicians tying their hands and still expecting results. The assholes liked to pretend they didn't know how the world worked.

Romijn sure as hell knew that. He'd funded this operation and promised Charlie that he and his associates would have a free hand here — he could sell protection and information to the global players who came to Venezuela. And he didn't even have to quit the agency to do it. These days half his time was spent on operations that were off the books anyway, and this was just one more. But this time, when the smoke cleared, he would be set up to run his own operations.

It was fucking crazy, but then the world was crazy. Too bad his wife had to die before he began to see straight.

He turned to the window again and peered into the distance, wishing he could see the goal, the entry point. He'd memorized that map and knew it was a mere 220km away. There lay the tiny border town of Santa Elena de Uairén, Venezuela. They would stage their troops here, then move them to Santa Elena where they would set up their headquarters.

This city was well chosen. The location was convenient, and yet was off the radar. He just couldn't bring himself to like it. "Boa Vista... snake view," he laughed. "Not exactly the kind of name you pick to attract developers, is it?"

Across the room, Anna Rasburn laughed at him, giving him that superior bitch look. "Who gives a shit? No one will remember Boa Vista when this is done. We will put Santa Elena on the map, though."

"You think no one will notice military supplies coming in here?" Carlos Herrera asked.

"I doubt anyone will pay much attention," the green-eyed man said. "This is a business center after all; the city does a lot of commerce with Santa Elena. If they do look, well, the boats are going to be carrying aid… food for your starving people. At least that's what the labels and manifests say. And a lot of it is exactly that."

"The world will assume that the US is stockpiling supplies for the inevitable collapse of the socialist idiots in power," Turner said. "My presence would be noted, making it look like a normal operation to buy political favor." He grinned. "To gain leverage with your new government. It wouldn't be the first time."

Herrera let out a sullen laugh. "And instead of providing support, you are going to topple the government," Herrera said.

Turner laughed and slapped his leg. "Don't be an asshole, Herrera. Our democratic republic wouldn't dream of interfering in the affairs of a sovereign nation! That's your job. I'm just here to advise. You, backed by the amazing people of your country, are going rise up and overthrow the goddamn sonsofbitches while I cheer you on, on behalf of my own democratic and peace-loving government, of course."

Herrera glared at him. "I think you are slightly over trained in these matters to be just a cheerleader. Your government could send a minor functionary."

"Then it's a good thing my government doesn't know I'm here. We won't mention it until it's an accomplished fact. And then I will swoop in to consult with the victorious insurrection on the proper way to set up security."

"Yet now you will supply weapons, troops, and other materials."

Turner shook his head. "Not me, son. Congress has authorized some essential aid, and that is exactly what my boys and girls are providing. Nothing more. Whatever items Nikolaj and his people might add to the cargo is none of my business. And my people won't even take any of this shit across the border." He looked at Romijn, who nodded. "Someone else might, but the current government has refused any help, so until you are in a position to officially ask for aid, as far as I'm concerned, the cargo sits right here."

Anna said it plainly. "As we told you, the military assistance you are getting is funded through private sources."

"Private," Herrera said. "You mean corporate."

"We can't disclose identities," she said. "But you can assume they are primarily anti-communist groups plus people who are eager to do business in your country once you've established your new government."

Turner watched Herrera grapple with himself, balancing his desire to help his people with the reality that he needed help to do it and that the help came at a price. "Forming an official government means creating a consensus, negotiating with people,"

Anna shook her head. "We don't see it that way. Once it is discovered that you are still alive and returning with a potent revolutionary army, the people will rally behind you. It's a populist uprising and you are the face of it. And their enthusiasm will grow stronger when they find your army is distributing the food and medical supplies that the socialists refused. When their bellies are full again, and you are swiftly restoring power and the internet, they will adore you and respect your ability to bring about real change. You will have the leverage and a window of opportunity. By appointing people who back you, you'll set up the new government."

"You mean the people you pick?"

Turner chuckled. "None of us want any part of running your damn country, Herrera. We have plenty to do ourselves. You pick who you want and set it up however you want. Long as you provide the things we talked about, we don't give a shit who helps you or, within reason, what they do."

"Sooner or later, the people will expect us to hold elections."

"When they discover they have food and medical care and that they are free to speak their minds, even to complain about there not being elections, their bitching won't have any teeth. The people need to recover and what you'll provide will keep them content for quite some time," Anna said.

Turner nodded. "And when people do start asking for elections or representation, distract them by putting any surviving members of the government on trial for their treasonous crimes. No one will demand elections while that sideshow is going on."

Dione Bellamy chuckled. Herrera looked at her as if seeing her for the first time. In fact, he hadn't been aware of her being there. "You find this all funny?"

"Sorry, I was doing a little background work for your new government and I was thinking about what I learned. Just now it popped into my head and I double checked to amuse myself."

"What are you talking about?"

"Although your friends… us… will be providing help, you are going to have a lot to work with when it comes to rebuilding." She held up her cell phone. "This is a list of bank accounts of current government officials that my people have identified so far. I just froze all the accounts. When you give us the signal, they will be hacked by Venezuelan loyalists who will transfer the money back to the government."

Herrera's eyes grew wide. "That is amazing. Excellent!"

"That money puts a rebirth of prosperity within your reach. And, speaking to the point you were discussing, with all the international organizations, including the IMF and World Bank, celebrating your victory for the people, no one will be thinking about the silly matter that the government is not actually elected. Your people will be applying for the new jobs you've created and sending their kids to the schools you build."

Anna came over and sat next to Herrera. "Under the plan we've developed, you'll be redefining what it means to be a government. You'll eliminate taxes and establish a simple flat fee for living and working inside your sovereignty. I can guarantee that major corporations will be clamoring to open offices and hire people. It will herald a new age of prosperity. Once the people taste it, they won't mind having lost the vote at all. And the global corporations will ensure that other governments don't try to move in. All they'll be able to do is copy your model."

Herrera shook his head, then stared at Turner. "And the US government will let me just establish this new thing? The UN won't brand this a tyranny?"

Turner bared his teeth in his best imitation of a smile. "The CIA will be whispering in the politicians' ears about how great it is to have a new pro-free market government in Latin America — one with close ties to the US. Even when the idiots in charge realize that companies are leaving the US to set up operations here, making this their research and headquarters base, there won't be any public sentiment against you. By the time they figure out that your new arrangement is the economic doomsday bomb the political establishment has always feared... shit, we will have started five or six more."

Herrera's eyes teared. "So, you are betraying your country too?"

"Not me. Shit, the politicians did that years ago. Once they decided on the primacy of the bureaucracy over the principles of freedom, they put the whole country on the wrong goddamn track. It's sad, but nothing in the US had much to do with real capitalism or freedom anymore."

"Then you justify doing this and abandoning democracy?"

Turner shook his head. "Look, good things don't stay good things for long under any circumstances. Thomas Jefferson was one of the few who knew that. The democratic republic I believed in became a bunch of idiots fighting for power and wealth — leeching the blood out of the real Americans." Memories of his own idealistic beginning with the CIA flooded over Turner, angering him. Back then, he'd had faith. God had blessed America. His wife taught him that. Doing bad things for a good end seemed necessary.

Even as his government trained him to be an assassin, a corrupter of men, he'd trusted in God (via his wife), and in the mysterious workings of things.

Now he saw that the laugh was on him. Faith was a treasonous bitch. God might've been there once. Flawed men had managed to write the Constitution. Against all odds the greatest country the world had ever seen emerged from a petty dispute about representation. That was something. But God had turned his back on the country, just as he'd turned his back on Turner's wife. A God that left her to suffer agonies before dying was no friend of Charlie Turner.

His wife had put her faith in the preachers, and they had lied. His own faith had been misplaced. It had taken time to sort that out, that in the world as it was, a man needed to get back to trusting principles and not divine intervention. God didn't give a rat's ass about any of them. He'd been a fool not to see that, and now he would correct his mistake.

Turner nodded at the others. "They spent a lot of time and effort going the wrong way too. Their grandiose vision of a global, benevolent government was spinning a small mistake into a bigger one. A global government might seem like a noble thing, but it quickly becomes a heavy-handed blunt instrument. And, at the end of the day, run by a handful of people. If you aren't part of the elite, you are fucked. Bigger isn't better, or even as good. Regulation just expands, all the while driving out the good and innovative. Eventually it collapses under its own weight."

Herrera sneered. "And that makes it fine for you to join with your enemies?"

Charlie laughed. "They are not the enemies of my ideas, my principles. And my government calling them enemies isn't gospel truth. I've seen the truth, and it tells me to throw my lot in with reasonable people wherever I find them," Turner said.

The green-eyed man poured a drink and handed it to Herrera. "Take a breath," he said. "Throw away the political rhetoric for a moment. Then think about how much good you can do for your people with our people."

"At what price?"

"That's the question," Anna said, smiling. "You have a chance to define what the price is. For once, no one has to be oppressed. Not having a say in politics is not the same thing as being oppressed. If people have what they want, what they need, that is real freedom."

"And what if some group rises up?"

"Then, like any criminals, they would be stopped."

Herrera sat back. "And what is your involvement?"

Anna patted his arm. "If you aren't interfering with the companies who come here, if you are offering them passports and the right to do business, then none."

"Even the CIA will be opening an office in your new capital," Turner said. "The company wants freedom, just as your citizens do. We need a place to operate where governments don't insist on examining what we do."

"Our new capital? What new capital?"

"It's time to move forward into the future, Carlos," Anna said. "Caracas is a diseased dung heap. It's a crowded mess that hasn't been maintained. It needs new infrastructure. Rather than fix it, my clients are going to build you a new capital city — a smart city that will attract finance and business. We will build it to become a center of commerce."

"And what do they get out of it?"

"They will own their buildings; they will be free to ensure they have the infrastructure they need, because they can simply create it, and they will have a pleasant and tax-free place to live and do business. This will be the new Paris, the new London."

"A corporate paradise?" Herrera asked, his voice dripping with cynicism.

Anna shook her head. "The entire idea of a corporation is a product of the political system. It's as dead as the democratic system. You let companies operate here, free of taxes and political constraints, and you will open the door to an entirely new world."

"It could be a Pandora's box," he said.

She smiled. "We won't know until you open that door."

Turner pointed out the window. "And now, as we speak, your loyal troops are gathering in Santa Elena. They are being armed and fed. Medical facilities are being set up. We will fly you there by helicopter to take command from the headquarters you will establish. The mayor is a loyal friend, is he not?"

"Arturo," Herrera said. "We went to school together."

"We've already helped him win the hearts of the people, and now, with the help of major corporations, you will begin retaking your homeland, restoring prosperity and ending the feudal rule of the communists. Isn't that the dream?"

"It is a version of it," he said. "I wish I felt that it was an uprising of the people and not something imposed."

Anna squeezed his arm. "Make it one, Carlos. We offer help because we have a vision for Venezuela. It is completely compatible with yours. Accept the help, then you, in turn, can offer it to your people."

"Men and women will die," he said.

"They always do, Carlos. We cannot change that. But we can make life better for those who live. That is the reason the Oculistica was founded, to make the world better."

Herrera looked at the people around him and sighed. "I accept your help because I see no other way. *Es la voluntad de Dios.*"

"The will of God," Turner chuckled. "Well, at least the will of everyone here." He raised a glass. "To a new world, created, like this one, from chaos. It might not be a brave one, but it will certainly be one that heralds change."

"The Old Man will be spinning in his grave," Anna said, clinking glasses with Nikolaj.

He smiled. "Are you entirely sure he's dead?"

Her laugh chilled Turner for a moment. "A person has to believe in some things, Nikolaj. I can't imagine you would risk leaving him alive."

He looked at her levelly. "Some things aren't up to me."

CHAPTER 33

SHIFTING ALLEGIANCES

*"We hang the petty thieves and appoint the great ones
to public office."*

— Aesop

Bob & Edith's Diner
539 S 23rd St
Crystal City, Arlington, VA

"I hope that your fondness for this place isn't based on the quality of the food," Turner said, looking up at Claude Hoenig.

Claude cocked his head and grinned at his old friend. "You don't like the food here? I think it's pretty damn good."

Turner poked at his potatoes. "It's okay. There's nothing actually wrong with it, but it isn't what I think of for a business lunch."

"Why not?"

"If I'm eating out on someone's tab, or even just going for a genuine, completely legal, tax-deductible meal, I prefer fine French cuisine. Maybe a fancy Italian meal." He snorted. "This place doesn't even have a beer and wine license, much less a real liquor license. What kind of business meal can you have in a place like this? A three soft-drink lunch?"

Claude noted unhappily that Turner had continued to change since his wife's death. He was getting sour and cynical. He could understand why the man had turned his back on the church. His wife had been a true believer and, from Turner's perspective, when she died, painfully, it would seem that her faith had been little but false hope. It had failed them both. Saying that God worked in mysterious ways didn't make it better.

"This meal isn't on anyone's tab, Charlie. I invited you for the company… to chat. I doubt this meeting would qualify for any tax deduction."

Charlie raised his head, looking around the diner, clearly not impressed with what he saw. "Fine," he said. "I thought you wanted to talk business."

It was past the normal lunch hour, and the place was nearly empty. "Naw, think of this as just two old friends having a burger. A delicious burger, mind you. Still, some talk about work might come up in the course of things."

After his many years working in the CIA, his old friend wasn't easily surprised, but the lifting of an eyebrow told Hoenig that he had the man's attention. "Is the shit from working with your new associates finally hitting the fan?"

Hoenig grinned. "There is a lot going on. The work is good and has led me into uncharted territory. That's always a good thing. Well, usually a good thing."

The eyebrow wiggled again. Turner was unaware, and Claude had never told him about the way it betrayed him. It made it easier to play poker with the man. "How so?"

"You've heard the chatter about the background on the Mumbai smart city project."

"I heard the World Bank had some problems over there. Some companies got cold feet about getting involved. Of course, things changed when Old Man Forte disappeared."

"What do you know about that? I don't have any first-hand information other than he disappeared."

Charlie smiled. "According to Interpol, some Somali pirates made a ransom demand. Seems like the banks decided to ignore it. In his absence, a guy named Downes has been filling in for Forte and he encouraged the corporations to rejoin your little project. He isn't the force the Old Man was, but he fills the gap."

"And the project is expanding. Big time."

The eyebrow wiggled again. "In what way?"

"We are going to be using the tech in other cities. I think Venezuela… and soon."

"World Bank is getting pushy?"

"Not them. It's Nikolaj Romijn."

Charlie laughed. "Don't tell me that our friendly neighborhood assassin is getting involved in smart cities."

Claude nodded. "In a big way."

"Why are you telling me?"

"Because it involves US interests on a couple of fronts. I'm sure that freak Nikolaj Romijn is involved in a regime change there. I doubt it's on behalf of our government either. He does things for himself."

"Doesn't everyone?" Turner asked.

Claude wondered if he was serious. "I'm concerned that what he is doing will affect US policy there."

"The US government would be happy to see the good old boys they have down there out on their asses," Turner said. "But I get your point. If you were involved in the overthrow of a sovereign nation, even as a contractor, it could put you on the back foot for future government contracts."

"It's more than that. I don't want to work for enemies of the US. I might have left the agency, I might be putting my work ahead of other things, but you know I'm a patriot."

Turner sighed. "Too much so, at times. That's why you clashed with the agency. You don't understand that there is always a bigger picture and you only see a piece of it. You jump to conclusions and label things right and wrong."

"Sometimes that bigger picture is wrong."

That earned him a shrug. "Maybe. But you need to get on board with this change."

"Then you already know what they are doing, Charlie?"

"Hell yes, I know. The CIA is all in on what is going on in Venezuela. I've met the guy who will be taking charge — Carlos Herrera."

Claude rubbed his chin. "Herrera? I thought he was killed."

"Don't feel lonely. Lots of people did. But he isn't. He and I had a little chat. I think he'll do real well. Your buddies are rallying some serious international groups behind him. The country is seriously fucked, and they want corporations involved as well. The big tech companies will play, but they want that smart city idea set up down there as soon as possible. And so do your pals. Nothing wrong with any of that from the administration's point of view."

"Why in the world do you want to bring smart cities to Venezuela?"

"They can use the boost to the economy."

"Well, Charlie, if that's the real reason, shouldn't we do them in the US first? I'd think salvaging Detroit would be better for America."

Turner laughed, but his smile was sour, tinged with cynicism. "What? And catch all the blowback about government-controlled cities and the government stealing the personal data of its citizens for surveillance? Look at the crap China is getting. In the good old USA, the freedom of information folks would be raking in the overtime. Besides, we want to see that it works in the context of a real city before we bring it home. If it fails, it will fail spectacularly, and personally, I'd rather we messed up in Venezuela than on our own turf."

Claude knew that was true. "That's short-sighted and selfish. But it makes some sense, I suppose."

"It works out well that you called this little meeting because there is more going on with the Venezuela deal than you know. I will need some good people working there. We want to contract with you directly."

"To do what? Do you want your own smart city?"

Turner laughed. "I hadn't even thought of that. Not bad, Claude. No, the immediate need is right up your alley. The agency is going to set up an office there that specializes in Fintech."

"Why would you need that? Congress gives you funding."

Turner smiled. "I need it because backchannel funds need love too. You know the game, Claude. There are always payments being made that Congress is better off not knowing about. The government needs plausible deniability. There's nothing new in that, but there are news ways to do it."

"True. I never liked that."

"But you did it. And now you have some of the best programmers for setting up payment systems that won't come back to haunt us." He grinned. "Put in a good core group to run it and you'll have an operation that is independent of the Oculistica and protected by the CIA."

"I'd need to know more about what you are looking for. And I'd need to hire some more people. We are pretty stretched."

"Are you still in touch with Rashmi Patel or Wyatt Osgood?"

"No. Why?"

Turner gave a casual shrug, but the eyebrow said there was more to his question than he wanted to admit. "Their names came up. I was reviewing recent history and they seem to have been influential in writing the pieces that came close to making the Tanzania crypto work. That experience could be useful."

Claude shook his head. "I haven't heard from either of them since they disappeared."

"Really? Totally? I thought you were good buds with Osgood."

"I was. But even his sister hasn't heard from him recently."

"Right. And where is she again?"

"Ellen? She lives in rural Colorado. Why?"

"No reason. I just hate it when I can't remember something."

Claude tried to recall if he'd ever mentioned Ellen to Turner before. He was pretty sure that Wyatt and Turner had never met. It was time to get the conversation onto other matters.

"I'm still curious about why you are investing in Venezuela. It's a mess."

"A mess we are fixing."

"With the Oculistica."

"With other interested parties. In return, the new government will let us do things, run financial ops, we can't in other countries."

"So, it's not just a payment system you want?"

"It's never just one thing. You know how it goes… we do a few off the books operations and the conspiracy theorists get wind of it. Next thing you know we've got civil rights types bombarding us with requests for details of what we are doing. We can't always get away with claiming national security. This way, the main HQ can't even produce the documents."

"But you already have offices around the world. Why not use one of those? What's so special about Venezuela?"

Turner rubbed his hands together. "Upheaval. That's what's special. The new regime there will be trying a fascinating new experiment that will attract all sorts of new, information-age business, most of which didn't exist before. Being in on the ground floor lets the CIA create some new units, create an entirely new branch that is designed to work with the new sovereignty there."

"Congress won't fund that. Or like it."

Turned sat back and pushed away his plate. "That's why we won't tell them about it."

"How can that work?"

"How did Ollie north get away with his shit for so long? How do we get away with running drugs? You lie and file bogus paperwork."

"I hated that."

"But you know it's necessary."

"But the drugs…"

"We do what we have to, Claude. And it works. The only real challenge we've had is dealing with the cash, making it invisible."

"The same money-laundering problem that the cartels have."

"Right. And your financial tech solves that. We are starting to use cryptocurrency instead of cash."

"And the underworld accepts that?"

He smiled. "We just ran a little operation that helped convince a major Mexican cartel to decide to start using crypto."

"You helped a cartel?"

"We gave them a nudge in the right direction. It was an inevitable change."

"But a cartel?"

Turner shook his head. "Claude, we partner with all sorts from time to time. Have you forgotten already?"

"Well, you make it sound like you're doing everything you want to already. Why do you need me or Venezuela?"

"Setting up what we want in Venezuela is a giant step toward freeing us, Claude. A CIA fintech office in a place that is isolated, one that isn't even known about, much less accessible to the do-gooders who want to interfere with what we do, will let allow us to do the things that have to be done. I need to know I can count on you. Can I?"

Claude shook his head. "That wanders into a big, messy gray area, Charlie."

"No, it isn't. There is nothing gray about it at all. It's black — clearly fucking illegal. But it's necessary. And you are already involved. You are up to your armpits in all the fintech the Oculistica is involved in and in developing tech for them that they can use to spread their control via the creation of smart cities. Now we have a chance to deal the CIA into that. A patriot should understand the importance, the opportunity, and a businessman should see that this is the wave of the future."

"You're already painting me as one of the bad guys. Jumping in with both feet will make my position untenable, Charlie. I've been in contact with you, feeding you intel, to make sure it's on record that I'm not going behind my country's back. If you are working with them, going outside the rules even more, then increasing my involvement, even indirectly, seems like a bad, probably stupid move."

Charlie sighed. "In for a penny, they say. You might as well use this opportunity to do what you left the CIA to do ... get rich. Everyone with any power will be jumping on this bandwagon as fast as they can."

"Have you heard of the Bitpats?"

Turner laughed. "Of course. Have you checked out their cheesy website? Have you read their fucking manifesto? If not, let me save you some precious time. It's the drivel of true believers who want to return the world to a more pristine era."

"I've read it and I think they make valid points. I've grown increasingly worried about things. The more I found out how deep the Oculistica worked, the more concerned I got. That's why I contacted you, Charlie. I know first-hand that, besides having infiltrated the IMF and World Bank, they've got people in Interpol."

"Old news, of you mean this Osk Barstad woman. Sooner or later I'll figure a way to put that to good use. She's a seriously senior intelligence officer, but I can't point to anything she's done that I can use for leverage."

"When the Tanzanian project started to unravel, she put out red flags on Wyatt and Rashmi ... you know that."

"At the request of the Tanzanian government, one assumes. Rashmi did break him out of jail, and they were pissed. They also wanted to know how those two managed to pull off their escape. That's why your friends in the Oculistica told her to do it — that's her job."

Being associated closely with that group, having Turner use the word 'friends' even as a taunt, bothered Claude more than he wanted to admit. "My friends? You are working with them now, apparently."

"No, I'm using what they are doing."

"Look, from where I sit, a bit down on the food chain, it looks like things are spinning out of control. You say you are aware of what's going on, but you don't act as if it's important. You don't seem interested in doing anything about it."

Turner smiled. "Oh, I'm doing things, just not the things you want. I'm seeing the world in a new light."

"What does that even mean?"

"What is it you believe in, Claude? Is it capitalism and free markets and personal freedom, or is it the US government as it exists, hypocritical and corrupt?"

"The government isn't perfect, but...."

"Shit, it's beyond imperfect. Think, man. The government created us and trained us to do things that a democracy should never have done. Now there is something else emerging. Just as the US emerged after its revolt against the Brits, something entirely new is emerging. That smells of opportunity, so we've decided to use this new revolution to our advantage. This time the transition will be long and painful. The interconnectedness of things will force it to take time."

"I don't know what you are talking about."

"I won't pretend to be a believer, but the shit is about to hit the fan, Claude. Globally. We are in for a hell of a ride. In Venezuela, we are going to give ourselves a place to stand while it sorts itself out. And we will make money doing it. Nation-States are going to fall like the house of cards they are, and I want to stand on the side of history."

"Where does that leave me? I don't want to work with enemies of my country, but you are telling me that my country, the CIA at least, seems to want to work with those people even if it brings down the country. What the fuck am I supposed to make of that?"

"What do you want to do?"

"Bring down the Oculistica. Protect America from this upheaval."

Turner shrugged. "Show me a way. As you pointed out, the Oculistica is entrenched in the institutions. We are talking big guns, people with political clout, not just muscle."

Claude took a long breath. "That's exactly my point. They are threatening democracy."

"Or they are redefining it."

That set Claude back. "What does that mean?"

"You know the agency is a political tool. Always has been. These people are the real power behind the politics. Democracies can elect whoever they want, but that simply changes the face of the government, not its reality."

"There is a window of opportunity," Claude said. "With the Old Man gone there is a chance to act. The group isn't united and if we act now, maybe we can stop them."

Turner raised an eyebrow. "Really? Do you have a plan to save the free world? Have you developed some superpowers I should know about?"

"No. Not even close. I need your help."

"Me? I'm just a mild-mannered spook from the DC suburbs."

"We can work together. I think we have the resources we need if you will just convince the agency to start seeing them as a serious threat."

"They already do."

"You aren't acting like it."

Turner picked up the dispenser and squeezed ketchup on his French fries. "Here is a newsflash for you. The wise heads think the threat is a useful tool, and they want to keep that tool pointed away from us."

"What does that mean?"

"As it happens, I'm told by my superiors that even if these people are part of some coherent globalist power group, as the conspiracy theory folks say, the things they are doing right now suit them just fine."

Claude almost choked. That was spook-speak for admitting the government acknowledged the existence of the Oculistica.

"I passed along the fact that some of those people, bad people you've told us about, are behind a pending coup in Venezuela. That made them very happy, especially as there won't be any CIA-funded troops involved."

"Why would it be a good thing?"

"The same reason that our government sent you and me to sponsor one or two other revolutions in our day. America the beautiful conquers evil dictatorship however we can and replaced them with docile America-loving brutal dictatorships. In this case, the guy who will head up the new government is even more of a free market guy than they want."

"You could've backed him yourself. Then you'd nail the alliance."

"These days it's so much nicer and more politically correct to have it done for us. We have caught far too much shit from our allies and enemies alike for interfering in the internal affairs of other countries. No, if these pals of yours want to spend the money and effort to make it happen, we prefer to let them do that for us. Plus, because of their connections, the IMF, UN, World Bank, and all those folk are delighted to see it go this way."

Claude sighed. "Basically, the board of the Oculistica."

"If you say so, good buddy. I'm just a facilitator. I wouldn't know about fancy organizations."

"Your sarcasm makes you sound bitter, Charlie."

"The point is, the folks I report to just don't see that there is an issue, Claude. They don't get why trying to promote global prosperity is a bad thing."

"If the Oculistica can pull off regime change in Venezuela, it won't stop there."

"So what? Lots of places could use a face lift. Besides, you know damn well that that the domino theory that the great pompous asshole Kissinger came up with is the theoretical argument used for every intervention since the Vietnam war. The fucking thing never seems to pan out in the real world, but it never goes away either. It's an old chestnut."

As the waiter came to take their plates, he presented them with the bill. With a glance at the bill, Claude took out his wallet and handed him cash. "Keep the change," he said. Then he turned to Charlie and laughed. "After all I've told you, you really don't get it, do you?"

"What?"

"You still have that archaic 'us versus them' mentality."

"That's how it is."

"Except that, in this information age, those divisions aren't so clear. A lot of the folks you are calling 'us' are also 'them.' The major corporations supporting the coup and the new kind of government are name brand American companies. If you oppose them, isn't that un-American? Many of the politicians you would run to with the news of this scheme to conquer the world are in on it too. You can't draw lines in the sand. Actually, you can, but no one looks at the sand, they are streaming videos in cyberspace. You can fight if you want, but I'm not sure you know who you should hit. My bosses and their bosses are complicit, if not directly involved."

"You don't think cutting off the head of the snake will stop it?"

Turner shook his head. "It's not a snake, Claude. It's a fucking hydra, and it grows its heads back faster than you can cut them off. Last week I sat in a room with your green-eyed assassin. I could've killed him. I might even have gotten out alive. But what's the point? Instead we shared chitchat and some damn good Scotch."

"Chitchat?"

"He thinks he is making this revolutionary shit happen, but he's really a surfer riding a big wave. A wave of technology. It's sad that it's him. You could do so much more than him because you understand the tech and the people who make it happen."

"You think so?"

"I know it. If you would think about bringing that Wyatt Osgood and Rashmi Patel to Venezuela, to work with me, we would all get rich."

"Riding the wave?"

"Exactly." Claude sighed. It was pointless to argue with Charlie. There wasn't even any percentage in giving him more information in the hope that might change his mind. And Charlie was his only avenue, the only way he could think of that he could get his government to fight back.

There had to be another way to approach it, but apparently, Turner and the intelligence agencies had bought into the story the Oculistica projected.

"Look, I really don't know where those two are."

"That's too bad. Maybe your pals in the Bitpats know."

Claude gritted his teeth. "I don't know who they are. Besides, Charlie, this is all wrong."

"Wrong? What does that even mean in this context?"

"You are helping undermine the country. I can't and won't help you do that. If you are going to wade into deep water and you'll have to sink or swim on your own."

"Cute metaphor," Turner said. "Look, Claude, I wanted to tell you enough … I wanted you to have the chance to get on board with this while there is time."

"I'm not interested in being on board," Claude said. His head spun. Right away, he'd need to take steps to disengage from Park and his project. That was his only official connection. He had a few contracts with the World Bank for his companies. They could be broken.

And then what? He'd need time to think it through. Who else could he contact?

They got up and walked past the register. Turner grabbed a toothpick as they walked out the door outside into the bright sunshine. "Beautiful day," Hoenig said.

"It ought to be," Turner said. "But one last thing … for old time's sake, tell me, is there any way I can talk you down from that jousting stallion you've climbed up on?"

"What do you mean?"

"You are Don Quixote, riding into battle on your heroic patriot act."

"It isn't an act, Charlie. That's what you don't get. And you can't see that they are using you."

Turner smiled. "You always did think you were the one with the answers, Claude."

"Sometimes I'm right. This time, for instance."

Turner let out a long breath and raised his hand. "Not about everything, old buddy. And this time, smart money is on the windmills. But I am truly sorry about this."

As Hoenig turned to ask what Turner meant, two black SUVs and a black van with darkened windows pulled up. Men wearing ski masks hopped out of the cars, grabbed Claude Hoenig and thrust him into the van. Two men piled in after him, then the vehicles pulled away.

Turner stood, picking his teeth and staring after the vehicles. Even if his old pal Claude was on target with his assessment, and Turner's instincts told him he might be, fighting the changes was going to be like pushing a big goddamn rock uphill. That wasn't high on Turner's list of things he wanted to do.

It was sad for Claude, but after all the years in the agency, he should've known the consequences of trying to change the course of events. Officially, he would be held as a terrorist and be interrogated in a black site — they'd get every last bit of information he had out of him. He'd be convinced to sell his companies to a company that Turner owned.

Then he'd disappear.

Turner's stomach was tight. Fucking cheap-assed diner meals didn't sit well. Neither did walking Claude's high road. Making politics into a fucking crusade was for rebels and suckers. Mostly, Turner thought, for those who were both in large parts. Idealists who thought faith itself was something good — people like his late wife.

He stood in the warm sun for a bit, playing the "how things might have been" game with himself before writing it off as being as much of a losing proposition as going off on a crusade with Claude. The real high road was the one that was smooth and paved with the asphalt of current events.

Turner smiled. "Go with the flow, motherfucker."

CHAPTER 34

POLITICAL AWARENESS

*"Yes, our regulatory agencies are incompetent.
But they are incompetent by design."*

— *David Goldstein*
American blogger and former talk radio host

**Bellagio Shanghai Hotel
No. 1 Zhapu RD
Hongkou Dist
Shanghai, China**

Anna Rasburn glided into the suite where Park sat waiting to find out why she'd summoned him. And it was a summons. There was no doubt about that. It irritated him that she had such a high-handed way of doing things.

Yet he came. He always would answer her call — the elegant bitch terrified him.

He was never certain what the base of her power was... not really. Sure, she influenced major players. She had the ear of the green-eyed man, too. That made her a big deal, but there was something else. You heard rumors, but rumors weren't reality. Still, they often held a grain of truth and her strength, the base of her power, was something he didn't want to learn any more about than he had to.

Because of his fear and curiosity, he had flown to Shanghai to meet her at her hotel without asking why. It angered him to be so weak, to be doing what he was told, showing up at her hotel. The whole thing made him feel like a child called to the Dean's office.

He had a powerful position in the world, but things were seriously jumbled now. The lines of power within the Oculistica were blurred. The Old Man was dead, and Downes had taken his place. Yet, Downes was taking his marching orders from the green-eyed man. It seemed they all were.

Even though Park was out of the loop for much of what was going on, he knew that Dione Bellamy was working with the revolutionary government in Venezuela to create some sort of new financial structure. Why, what that was all about, he didn't know.

Even at home, things were different. His niece was back with her parents unharmed, but her father was both scarred and scared. Aditya, the haughty businessman was humbled. He'd never realized how vulnerable he was. It had made Park feel vulnerable too, in ways he never had before.

Until the kidnapping, the violence in his world was distant from him, easily made abstract. Even Mitch Childer's terrible death after the Tanzanian debacle wasn't real — it was something you saw on the news. That he had known the man, that he knew the truth about his death, made it worse, but not truly real. One day he was there, and the next, gone. The death itself was just something that happened.

But the kidnapping of his niece had touched his soul. They'd taken an innocent girl from a fucking high-end resort with no effort at all. Aditya, her father, still didn't know how it happened.

And that was just some drug cartel. Or was it? The green-eyed man had kidnapped an opposition leader of a government and turned him to his own purposes. Perhaps taking his niece had been a warning.

Besides his fear of violence, Park was troubled by not knowing his role in what was happening. What did they expect from him? He hadn't been told much of anything. Even worse, what if they didn't want anything from him at all? What if being out of the loop in Venezuela was a signal that he was redundant?

He hadn't done the things he'd done for the group to be cut out now. That wasn't fair.

The elegant hotel was exactly what he expected. It was the kind of place he sometimes saw in the videos he indulged himself in with that sexy black girl, SindiLux. She was a hot one and he could picture her at this hotel, sitting at the pool on the roof talking about the place and Shanghai. He wondered if she had. He decided that on the long flight back to the US, he'd search to see if she'd done one here.

A powerfully built man in an expensive suit stood at the door to the elevator that went to the penthouse. Park didn't know him, but when he approached, the man immediately swiped a passkey and opened the door. "Mr. Park," he said. He was addressing Park, but he was also announcing his arrival into a microphone.

The elevator swept him up, and the door opened into a plush living room.

Anna Rasburn stood at the wet bar fixing drinks with her back to him. Standing there, his eyes were drawn to her fine ass, encased in a tight sheath dress. She always dressed exotically, provocatively, making him wonder if he was supposed to acknowledge her sexual appeal openly. He'd watched her using her sexuality to advantage in meetings. Even the Old Man hadn't been immune. Every time Park thought he understood the nuances of power, someone like Anna demonstrated that they were more elusive and vaguer than he ever imagined. It was a lesson in humility.

"My dear Park," she said, turning to face him, bringing him a drink he didn't ask for, putting it in his hand. He smelled the alcohol and wrinkled his nose. "I'm afraid I don't drink," he said.

Her hand stroked his as she reclaimed the glass. "Of course, how foolish of me not to remember. Would you like iced tea?"

"Nothing, thank you," he said. He was sure she knew he was a teetotaler, and the gesture had been intimate, yet he was sure, insincere. She was putting him on the backfoot. She put the drink on the coffee table. "Please have a seat."

"What's going on?" he asked.

"So many things that it's hard to know where to start."

Without intending to, he spit out his favorite quote: "'Begin at the beginning,' the King said, very gravely, 'and go on till you come to the end: then stop.'"

Anna laughed, throwing back her head. "Alice in Wonderland. One of my favorites and a perfect way of seeing things, especially as we all seem to have gone down the rabbit hole now. As the Chinese proverb said, 'we live in interesting times.'"

"And so...."

Sitting, she put down her drink and grabbed a tissue to dab her eyes. "The beginning, I'm afraid, is rather unclear. Would you mind terribly if I started in what I think is the middle?"

"A lovely lady does what she wishes."

"Gallant as well as evasive. I am impressed, Park. I'm sure you know that there is now a new government in Venezuela."

"I heard there was a coup attempt, and it was likely to succeed." That was all he officially knew.

Anna smiled and glanced at her watch. "If I have the time zones right, and I am terrible at such things, there will be a declaration to that effect in three hours. They won't make the announcement until they capture the current president, which is happening now, Nikolaj says."

Park automatically pictured a map of that part of the world and placed Venezuela near Colombia. It surprised him how easily he accepted the news as true, how little it surprised him. How was it that the world had come to a point that it seemed reasonable that this corporate advisor could predict the success of a coup to the nearest hour?

One answer was Nikolaj Romijn. He had to be involved.

More concerning was that she was telling him about it. That meant she wanted him involved. "What do you want me to do?"

She smiled. "Nothing more than the normal things you do under such circumstances. Issue a formal statement that the World Bank supports stability in the region and is prepared to help an emerging government."

"I can't really offer them much assistance without knowing the new government is stable. The fiscal controls are pretty strict when it comes to that sort of thing."

"Don't worry. A bullshit public statement will be more than enough for the moment. It won't mean anything anyway, as the new government will reject your offer, along with any outside assistance. They will denounce all of you, including the IMF and the UN as globalist pirates."

"I see," he said, although he didn't see at all. "Won't the US government interfere?"

"They are going be delighted with the regime change, at least for the moment. Their intelligence agencies are singing the praises of Carlos Herrera."

Who was supposed to be dead? Park wondered. "And he is the new President?"

"Actually, they are going to declare a new form of government. But that's local politics. What's relevant to you is that they intend to break with many traditions. They'll have no interest in joining the OAS, or UN, or any other group. They are going to cut off most of their existing arrangements with other countries."

"Trade deals? Everything?"

She smiled. "Isn't that darling? They are going to demand a clean slate for everything, including loans from the IMF and the World Bank."

"Surely the group won't let them isolate themselves politically and economically. The resources of that country are amazing."

"That's certainly true, but there are many ways to exploit resources."

"Your companies...." It was dawning on him. Her clients were often frustrated in working with the corrupt national governments the group supported. "They've always helped the Oculistica in the interest of global stability."

"That's exactly right. But many of them have begun to think that perhaps the Oculistica has become an anachronism."

"The Old Man held back change, but…"

"Increasingly, he was against most of what my clients offer. Fortunately, he isn't an issue any longer. The younger bankers are more willing to embrace commerce and technology as it's evolving, yet even they remain stuck in the past."

"So, you and Nikolaj are turning your back on the group?"

"The group is being … reorganized. We need to acknowledge that it's reached the end of its usefulness in its present form. It has proven unable to cope with the changes."

"But we have all these grand projects we've designed to solve those problems."

"Look around you, Park. Nation-states are fracturing and struggling to survive despite having us behind them. They are grasping, fighting among themselves. Internal polarization is the norm in almost every country, and the larger, more developed they are, the more serious that is. Dysfunctionality in the new normal."

"We expected that. We encouraged it as the precursor to imposing global order."

"That's old thinking. And before we get to global order, we face a long transition period. The Nation-states are not powerless, merely in decline. In their death throes, they are capable of causing an immense amount of collateral damage."

Now Park understood. "Weakened sovereign governments leave your corporate clients vulnerable."

"That's one motivation to change."

"And the change is to what?"

"There are countries that, for various reasons, have an opportunity to redefine their roles. In that vein, Venezuela has decided to embrace the role of being friendly to capitalism and blockchain applications."

"That didn't work so well in Tanzania."

Anna laughed. "That... that was an abortion. It wasn't a matter of embracing tech and free markets — it was a cluster fuck. We saw the combined effort of a corrupt government and greedy vendors trying to co-opt the implementation of a viable digital currency."

"How will this be different?"

"There won't be any government involvement as it's been understood in the past. We envision individuals and companies making it happen for themselves with the blessing of this sovereign jurisdiction. For instance, there won't be any nonsense about creating a fiat currency at all. People will use whatever currency they choose. We rather expect it will be Bitcoin or Monero, but who knows? We are happy to be surprised. We don't care, although some of my clients might do what they can to influence their decisions."

"And if it is prosperous, what keeps other countries from invading Venezuela?"

"Self interest. Do you think the most powerful corporations in the world are going to put up with other countries stepping in? If Colombia wants to invade, they will be told that that would be the end of foreign investment in their country. And it would be bad PR. What country can afford to invade if the largest companies fund the defense? What country is going to be willing to look like a colonial power, especially when they'd need to rebuild its infrastructure before they could pillage it?"

"And you honestly think this will work?"

"I believe it enough to be heavily invested in the outcome."

"And the Oculistica is behind this?"

She patted his hand. "You being here is part of the process of seeing that we are all on the same page. We expect resistance from certain members, naturally. Douglas Downes will be sorely disappointed, although Nikolaj and Dione are having a chat with him this week. Dione is solidly behind it. She finds Carlos Herrera an attractive and amiable person to work with."

Park was suddenly glad he was being briefed by Anna. A visit from Nikolaj was never pleasant. He was being charmed instead of threatened. That was always good.

"Our plan is for our new vision of Venezuela to surpass the City of London and Singapore as the world's financial hub in a matter of years. Of course, that's a crap comparison. The new center won't be so much a physical location as a distributed city. Still, people with the skills and ambition will want to be here, where it is centered. It will have the attraction of a newer, unregulated Silicon Valley."

"Who deals with the infrastructure? Who provides police and courts?"

She waved a hand, elegant long fingers tracing invisible lines. "I have no idea, but it will get worked out. Those are just logistical details. The president, if supported, can create a community where law and order prevail. That's enough to start the influx."

"When will elections be held? What if the people reject the new government?"

She laughed again. "Park, you are so cute and wonderfully naïve. The reality is that such a system cannot tolerate democracy — in fact, the entire concept of politics is dead. It no longer has any place in this world. Actually, it hasn't been relevant for a long time."

"But...."

"In the west, we've told the people what they want and what they think for some time now, but we've been subtle about it. We used psychology and advertising and social media to create the world we wanted. Going down a different path, Singapore independently demonstrated that democracy isn't necessary for capitalism to thrive. Now we are going to dispense with any pretense. People will come to Venezuela because it will be functional, and safe, and modern, and offer incredible opportunities."

"But there will be no freedom?"

"All the freedom in the world to make things happen. What use is a vote? If you aren't taxed and have all those things, what the hell would you vote for? Why would you want to risk the possibility that your people could get voted out? No, the government will be run according to some defined principles that it simply administrates. It will charge a fee for citizenship and for services. There will be no taxes, no silly matters of patriotism."

Park tried to imagine it — and failed. "That sounds utopian, not like a serious plan."

Anna made a face, then turned her head, looking into the distance. "We've decided that this is the sound of the present — it is the arrival of a thwarted future. That birth will require some assistance for the present to emerge cleanly, but it will emerge. I suggest you go prepare for it."

"Prepare?"

"Some of my clients will be approaching you about the smart city technology you are developing. Some will want to join in the development, some will be willing to pay to see that anything that is functional, suitable for their needs, is available for Venezuela."

Park sat upright. "I haven't been able to reach Hoenig lately. His people are working, but he dropped out of sight."

"Nikolaj and I own those companies now, Park. Hoenig chose to retire."

"He never said anything."

"It was a sudden decision."

Her thin smile said it all, and Park shuddered. "What happens?"

"You will take operational control of his companies. Put in people who will make the magic happen and we will give you ten percent ownership in all three companies... the US fintech company, the Colombian software group, and the facial-recognition company in Mumbai."

"The one owned by Ritesh's friend?"

"It used to be owned by him. But he sold out to Hoenig. Unfortunately, he was in a terrible car crash a few weeks later."

Park let out a long breath. Her calculated tone defined things clearly — this was the stick; potential ownership in those companies, the ones who would dominate, a tasty carrot. He was being shown what could be his if he joined them and told about the things that could happen if he refused.

Park knew he was weak, but he was no idiot. The truth was that he had compromised himself and the World Bank long ago. This was just a matter of renegotiating his contract with a changing regime — a more important regime change than the one in Venezuela.

He looked at Anna. "I'd hope that while I am busy running these new companies and working with your clients on this new present, you might ensure that my niece is all right."

"Oh, I heard she had some trouble," Anna said, not even bothering to sound sincere.

"I'd like to think my family could take vacations and not have to worry about being bothered by cartels."

"Oh, Park, of course they can. We wouldn't want any harm to come to your family or friends. We will be looking out for your happiness."

Park resigned himself to the reality that he had no choice. Whether or not this plan succeeded, only a fool would oppose these people. "Then, I suppose I should get to work. I'll need to find managers for those companies and find out where they are in their projects."

"Of course. But we don't want all the pieces to come together too quickly. That might make it look… arranged."

"Delay the World Bank announcement about the coup?"

"Exactly. You are traveling on business, after all. Staying current with world events is difficult and analyzing the situation in Venezuela takes time to think through properly."

"True."

"I understand that your wife doesn't travel with you, is that right?"

"Never," he said. "We don't do much together at all these days."

"That's such a shame. Well, I've arranged a lovely suite for you in this hotel for two days so you can contact people, write your statement, and so on. If you require any help from me, I will be here as well. Feel free to charge food and booze to your room." Then she smiled. "Even if booze isn't your vice, you might have guests."

"Guests?"

She sighed. "I can only imagine that your wife's absence must make it difficult for you."

Park smiled. He was being watched, tested.

She smiled, then picked up a phone from the table. "Please have Chen bring the documents to us and the passkey for Park's suite."

After a moment, a door opened and a svelte, petite Chinese woman came into the room. She wore a black silk cheongsam that accented her tiny firm breasts and slim hips and she moved by him, giving him a whiff of some heady perfume and a sensual smile, as she passed to hand Anna a leather folder.

Anna took the folder and opened it. After a quick glance, she handed it to Park. "This is all the information on the companies, including passwords and URLs so you can access much more. We've also included written authorizations for you to assume operating and financial control of them. We are counting on you to get them on track, Park."

"Yes," he said, still entranced by this lovely young woman standing in front of him. She seemed to like the fact that he was staring at her.

"Chen will show you to your room," she said.

Knowing he'd been dismissed, but unsure what was truly expected of him, Park nodded and stood. "I'll get this done."

Anna nodded. "I've asked Chen to assist you during your stay," she said.

Park looked at the girl. She tipped her eyes down and smiled. "I'll be happy to do anything that will make your stay more pleasant. You need only tell me what you wish."

Park glanced at Anna, who grinned and nodded. "She will do absolutely anything at all, Park."

"I..."

"We treat our own well."

Then Anna stood slowly, walked to the window, and looked out over the smoggy cityscape.

Chen wiggled a finger and led him out. Following the girl, walking behind her flowing motion, took him into a lavish suite. Anna had style.

Looking around, seeing the girl moving through his room and knowing she was his to use, Park felt a bittersweet tang — a combination of sadness and joy. This beautiful lady was payment — he was being bought and paid for. That made him disappointed in himself. And yet, he relished what he was offered, and the woman he was about to take to his bed.

He paused, giving himself a moment to think. It would be easy to curse himself for being so shallow, for being corrupt, for being weak. Yet, as Chen slipped off her cheongsam and turned in front of him, facing him and showing him her flawless body, Park decided nobility was for fools. Under the circumstances, it was so much easier and rewarding to just be a man.

CHAPTER 35

DARK CLOUDS FORMING

"Tyranny, like hell, is not easily conquered;
yet we have this consolation with us, that the harder
the conflict, the more glorious the triumph."

— *Thomas Paine, The American Crisis*

Koh Chang, Thailand

Boone settled into her room at the resort on Koh Chang's Elephant Bay thinking that, under other circumstances, this was a place she could enjoy. Of course, Anchara wouldn't like this place much at all. It was basic, with simple amenities, but it was comfortable, the beach faced west, and the sunset was glorious.

All those things would have made staying here delightful if she weren't here on a mission.

Dressing in comfortable clothing, just shorts, tee-shirt, and sandals, she grabbed a flashlight and a small bottle of citronella bug repellant and put them in a cloth bag that she wore crossbody. The next step was to get a meal. What needed doing would require a full stomach.

The resort's restaurant, situated in the main building that housed the front desk and a lounge with a pool table, was little more than a few tables and chairs stationed on the porch. What else did a person need? She went to the front desk and ordered a simple meal of fried rice with pork and a Chang beer.

The two girls behind the front desk were chatting with each other, and Boone was sure they were speaking Khmer, Cambodian, not Thai. That didn't surprise her as Koh Chang wasn't far at all from the border… take the ferry from Koh Chang to Trat, turn right, and it was a matter of a couple of hours by car to Hat Lek — the border crossing.

Now, she took a seat at an outdoor table facing the water and let out a sigh. She tried to picture Anchara sitting with her, planning camera angles. Then she laughed. That was a total nonstarter. There was no way this place, as nice as it was, fit the SindiLux brand. Sometimes, times like this, she thought that was a shame. If she had it to do over, if she were starting out now… but the truth was, things weren't just starting. It seemed that some were ending.

A giggle stirred her from her reverie. One of the girls was putting a steaming plate and a can of beer and a mug in front of Boone, but still talking to the other girl — something funny.

The girl poured the beer and Boone gratefully took a sip, relishing it before digging into her meal.

Fried rice was simple, nourishing, and in this case, tasty. Eating simply was a method she'd learned to keep her body sane while jumping around the globe; it also let her think about what she had to do and not the food.

"Wyatt took a few days off and went to Koh Chang," Rebecca had told her when she called. Rebecca and Wyatt had been working out of a small hotel in Trat. The city was large enough to provide decent resources, yet off the main track for tourists. People passed through but didn't stay, which meant they were less likely to be stumbled across there.

"Why Koh Chang?"

"He got stuck on his project, so he took his laptop to see if a change of scenery would give him new ideas. I think the influx of pretty Russian tourists of the female persuasion might've influenced his thinking as well, assuming that counts as thinking."

"A change of location often can get you out of a rut."

"I can give him a call...."

"I'd rather pop in on him. Did he say where he'd be staying?"

"Elephant Bay Resort." Then she laughed. "If you have trouble finding him, check out the Muay Thai clubs."

"Muay Thai?"

"Kickboxing. Wyatt somehow became quite a fan. He even did a little training here in Trat. But Koh Chang has regular regional fights there for the tourists. It seems that he finds the combination of beautiful vistas, Russian girls, and people hitting each other to be a compelling attraction."

Other than that, Rebecca knew little. "He needed some space and time. I didn't even ask when he's coming back. With Miguel here, I'm kept busy. He's doing great, by the way. He's got a room near us and hooked up with a Swedish girl... maybe two. They look alike."

The next day, Boone had caught an early flight from Bangkok to Trat. At the airport, she had hired a driver to take her to the hotel. It wasn't far, but it involved catching the car ferry to the island and then taking the twisty roads to the southern end of Koh Chang.

When she checked in, she found that the girls behind the desk and the owner of the place all knew Wyatt. "I not see him this afternoon," the tiny girl who registered her said.

"Maybe he gets a massage now," the other girl suggested. She waved toward the road. "Many places for good massage."

"He ask about the fights," the other one said. Then she made a face. "I don't know about fights."

"Is this Thursday already?" a squarely built Brit sitting at a table drinking a beer asked.

"It is."

"If you are looking for the American guy who was working out at the training camp that Michael runs just up the road..." he nodded back toward the main road. "I saw him this morning, and he said he was planning to go tonight."

"I'm trying to catch up with him," Boone said.

The man ran his eyes over her and gave her a pleasant smile. "Are you sure you wouldn't rather hang around this lovely place? We could have a few drinks and get to know each other."

The come-on was nice... and rather flattering. "It's a lovely offer, but I'm afraid I need to find him as soon as possible."

He shrugged. "Another time then?"

"Perhaps. In the meantime, can you help me find him?"

A long sigh told her he didn't think she was serious. "Well then, if he goes to the fights it will be easy enough to find him there. It's not a big place or a huge crowd. The promotion puts them on at White Sand Beach; the first one starts at eight-thirty."

"They fight on a beach?"

He laughed. "No, that's just a section of the island. The fights are there. They have a regular ring and everything." He pointed to the road. "If you walk out to the main road and hop in one of the taxis which are really pickup trucks, you can be there in a few minutes. Before you get in, tell the driver to drop you at White Sand. It's about 100 baht. He'll probably drop you right in front of the place. But, when you get there, if someone isn't already stuffing a flyer for the fights in your hand, ask anyone for directions to the Muay Thai."

And so, that evening, Boone went to eat her fried rice dinner and get ready to go see some Muay Thai fights.

Everything was as straightforward as the Brit had said. After telling the driver she wanted to get off at White Sand Beach, she got in the back of the pickup where a well-dressed young couple sat giving each other moony eyes. Honeymooners, she thought.

The girl glanced around and sighed. "мне нравится это место," she said.

Boone amended her assessment — Russian honeymooners. She knew a little of the language, from some time spent on an ill-fated mission there long ago. Her shaky memory told her that the girl was just saying she liked this place. She was having a good time.

The man looked at Boone. "American?"

"African," she said.

That set him back slightly. "But what is your country?"

"Togo," she said. Lying to someone she didn't know about her origin was a reflex, a way to stay less visible. Togo wasn't a place most people would know or care about.

As she'd hoped, the young man lost interest. He'd probably wanted to show off his English while talking politics with a black American woman. It was doubtful he knew anything about the politics of Togo. Anyway, that kind of talk bored Boone. She hadn't been in the US for years now, couldn't relate to the people well anyway.

All three passengers got off in front of a hotel on White Sand Beach. It was a hub of activity. Some Westerners were setting up on a bandstand out in the restaurant, which flowed out onto the sandy beach. White sand, of course.

She was still early, so she bought a can of Chang from a vendor, took off her shoes and walked along the beach. Down the beach from her, she spotted a troupe that was putting on a show for the diners that involved torches — twirling them, juggling them...

But no Wyatt. She wasn't surprised. This wasn't his kind of scene. He wasn't in the bar either.

As the time for the match approached, she saw they were opening the doors. She bought a ticket and looked at the crowd, watching for Wyatt, needing to find him but not really ready to see him yet.

Taking a spin down the street in front of the hotel, she saw a night market that had fresh fruit and cooked food. She wished she'd known this would be here. The meal at the hotel had been fine, but what she saw looked far more interesting and tastier.

The time for round one approached, so she went back to the hotel and up into the small arena. There was a ring in the center and the seats rose up on two sides. One side of the ring was for trainers. At the back was a stage. Fight announcers sat in a booth high above the seats and rock music blared out of giant speakers.

The promoters were trying to create a party atmosphere — build the excitement. Some women in Muay Thai shorts and tee-shirts were carrying trays with various beers.

Just then, a ring announcer came in, the lights dimmed, and the show began, in a mixture of Thai and near English, sometimes at the same time. The fighters wore shiny capes of red or blue, and the promoters provided the pageantry to make it a true extravaganza.

Glancing up into the seats, she spotted Wyatt, his eyes fixed on the ring. She turned to one of the girls and bought two beers. As she took them, they seemed rather warm, but hey, they were at a sporting event.

Wyatt sat near the stairs and she went up and sat next to him and held out a can. "Come here often?"

As the fighters (mostly young men who couldn't be over 16, she noted) paraded around the ring and then filed out, his head snapped around. "Boone?"

She grinned. "In the flesh."

He took the beer. "You came all this way… I hope the fights are good."

The announcer introduced the first two fighters. They were both 16 years old, and each weighed 100 lbs. she heard. "So, you are a geek and a fight fan."

"As Walt Whitman wrote: 'I am large, I contain multitudes.' Working in Trat, I started to realize that I sorely needed to get into shape. Then, one day when I was on my way to our neighborhood massage place, I stumbled across a training camp. I watched for a while and damn if they didn't make working out seem like more fun than it has any right to be. I tried it, and took to it, sort of, unless you think being a marvelous fighter is the goal. Then I decided to watch some fights, see how it worked in a real situation. When I came here, of course, I had to sample the local stuff." He pointed at a young fighter in red trunks who was dancing toward his opponent in blue. "The way he moves looks good, but he's got no base control. If the other guy catches him coming in… Ouch!"

Just as he said it, the boy in blue (Boone couldn't think of them as men) executed a round kick that caught the dancer in red in the side of the head. His body went rigid, then limp, and fell like a stone.

As the warrior in blue jumped up and down in early celebration, the referee and a man who acted like he was a doctor attended the fallen boy, looking at his eyes, patting his face. In a few minutes, he was getting to his feet with help. The victor came over, put his hands together and bowed to the conquered.

"Showing respect," Wyatt said.

Then the winner slipped an arm under the loser's arm, holding him upright, on still wobbly legs and, as the announcer stated the obvious — that the fight had ended in a knockout in the first round — the two made a circuit of the ring.

Boone sipped her beer. "Somehow the fights make the beer taste better," she said.

Wyatt grinned. "Careful. This shit is addictive."

The next fight was two young women. Like the boys before them, they entered the ring wearing capes and a headdress that looked something like a lacrosse racket. "What's on their heads?"

Wyatt chuckled. "It's called a Mongkol. The coach puts it on them and takes it off them just before the fight. The fighter isn't supposed to touch it. Along with the ribbons on their arms, it's supposed to be a talisman. And the bowing and walking around they do before the fight are the sacred rituals of Wai Kru and Ram Muay." He laughed. "I read that. What that means, I have no idea. I'm still learning to kick properly."

This one was a short fight as well, ending when a kick to the stomach started the recipient projectile vomiting. As she lay on the ground, two boys ran out with rags to clean up the mess.

"Pretty violent," Boones said.

"That's why it's called combat," Wyatt said. "But there is beauty in it too, and although the object is to defeat your opponent, the fighters have no incentive to harm their opponents, at least in regional matches like this."

Boone raised a hand to summon the girl who was selling beer. When she smiled and made her way toward them, Boone laughed. "That might be, but it's new for me and definitely requires more warm beer."

At the end of the match, Boone had to admit it was all making a bit more sense. There were aspects of the pageantry she didn't understand, and they looked as if they came from the Buddhist culture. She made a mental note to look them up later.

As they filed out, Wyatt stopped. "What's wrong, Boone? You've never come to see me before, and since you aren't a fan of Muay Thai, I know it wasn't a chance meeting at the arena."

"No," she said sadly. "Let's get away from here," she said.

"We can walk along the beach," Wyatt suggested. "That's why they put it there."

"I knew there had to be a reason besides holding the ocean back."

"And now you know. Glad to be of service."

She could see that Wyatt was unsettled, and she wanted to tell him everything all at once. But she knew blurting it out wouldn't be helpful. She had to explain what she knew.

The remnants of the fire show had been left scattered on spits of sand that went out into the shallow Gulf water. Several of the beachfront restaurants were closing and the chairs and tables being moved to higher ground.

Wyatt grew impatient. "What is it?" he asked. "Or is this a walk of silent meditation?"

Boone turned her head and looked up at him. "No. There is something I needed to tell you in person … Wyatt, I just got word that Ellen and Harold have been arrested."

Wyatt stopped dead. "My sister and her husband were arrested? For what?"

"We don't know. The charges haven't been made public. The whole thing is shrouded in finger pointing. No one has the authority to speak on that subject."

"What the fuck?"

"What I do know is that a couple of days ago Homeland Security raided their pot farm. There was some unusual coordination between Homeland, the DEA, the IRS, and local police, and all three are using the Patriot Act as a smokescreen to avoid telling anyone anything specific."

"Damn."

"The thing is ... my sources claim the CIA instigated it."

"The CIA?"

She shrugged. "The people who tell me about the CIA's work are bright and connected. Unfortunately, they also see conspiracies everywhere. Sometimes they are right, unfortunately. In this case, they say that known CIA operatives were on site and directing traffic. If that's true, then I have a conspiracy theory of my own."

Wyatt sat down on the sand. "What do you think it is?"

"It's you." She said it softly, but the words hit Wyatt hard.

"Me? Why would the CIA want to hurt me, strike at me?"

"I don't think they are trying to hurt you."

"Then they screwed that up pretty badly."

"I think they want to find you."

He looked at her. "Is this because of Tanzania? If so, why now?"

"I suspect it's related to the work you did there, not the bogus charges against you. For some reason, they want to find you, get you out of hiding."

"Shit."

She sat next to him and touched his arm. "I'm monitoring the situation closely — I have people on it twenty-four hours a day. At this point, no one has been charged with a crime. They confiscated the servers and her crop, and the local police made some public noise about your servers being used to launder money. That stopped abruptly and I think that connected too closely to you and the real issue, so the monologue shifted to questions about the legality of the pot plants. It's just talking heads right now and no substance. I've had lawyers checking, but Homeland has the warrant sealed, so we don't know the provocation they came up with."

"She's a licensed grower. They did it all by the book."

"I know. I've contacted the lawyer they used. I put her on retainer for any prosecution there. She's proactively gone to the sheriff, whom she knows, with all the paperwork they filed and the documents showing the operation is legal. He doesn't seem to know what's going on. Neither does the local DEA office." She sighed, then touched his arm again. "Be prepared for it to go on for a time. Rashmi picked up some chatter that this raid was part of something bigger."

"Bigger?"

"She isn't the only one targeted. There have been multiple raids around the US, and some coordinated with the Mexican authorities. They hit the place you where were staying in Progresso too."

Wyatt ran his fingers through his hair. "Okay. If it isn't some kind of Oculistica payback, then who is it and what would they want from me?"

"I don't know. This is a blunt force operation. I can't see the Oculistica overtly working with the US government. If they wanted to get to you through your sister or interrogate her to find you, your sister would just disappear. They'd find a way to put out the word of what they want from you."

"I can't imagine why the CIA would be interested in me."

"I'm sure we will find out soon enough. Does Ellen know where you are?"

"No. I told her it wouldn't be safe for her to know. And I told her that before we came to Trat, so even that communication wouldn't give us away."

"Good."

Boone sighed. "Truth is, I was holding my breath all the way here. Then I decided that it wasn't the Oculistica. At the time of your escape, when they tried to set you up for the disaster that implementing Tanzania's crypto turned out to be, they knew exactly who you were. That's why we gave you new identities."

"And a ticket out of Dodge, for which I am eternally grateful."

"We have to expect that since then, they could've found you. But they didn't bother."

"The last moves we made have been as newly minted crypto citizens," he said. "The IDs Tricia got us are golden."

"We know that they called off Interpol."

"But they don't forget."

"Forget, no, but the damage you could do was done. Thugs kill people to show what happens when they are crossed, but in this case, even if they caught you, who do they demonstrate their wrath to? Regardless, we put in some tripwires in news and police channels to alert us to searches. Interpol did put your names and the old identities on their red flag list again recently. But that doesn't seem to be connected to this new full-court press."

"Then who? And why?"

She shrugged. "As far as we can tell, there has been a fracturing in the Oculistica, which means there will be new global alliances the UN doesn't know about. This could be tied to their power struggle. And I'm sure one faction is connected to the bizarre coup in Venezuela. We aren't sure what is going on, but some all-too familiar faces are talking up the noble opposition and the rebel troops sweeping toward Caracas."

Wyatt shook his head. "And how does my apolitical sister, Ellen, come into all this?"

She shrugged. "Is there any possibility, even a long shot, that the raid has nothing to do with you? Could Ellen or Harold have done or said something that got them targeted?"

He shook his head. "Doubtful. They keep a low profile. She doesn't even lobby to end the war on drugs or engage in any political activity. Partly for that reason." He smiled. "Also, Harold isn't too big on people in general. He likes for them to stay invisible and that suits her."

"Then we scratch that off the list. We scanned news reports and found nothing that might have made the US government see them as some kind of menace. Neither of them has even had a parking ticket."

"I think that requires driving a car into town," Wyatt said with a grin.

"The other possibility is that it's because of your servers."

"They are just ordinary computers that sit there mining crypto. They aren't doing anything hostile or dangerous."

"But the US government has been remiss in figuring out what crypto is all about. Factions within the government have been desperate to tie crypto miners to money laundering."

"If so... shit. Then it is on me. I should've paid more attention to the changes they were making in regulations, the concerns they had. I could've pulled the plug on them long ago, moved them to Iceland or something, but I assumed it was low profile enough, especially since she was running them on solar power."

Boone raised a finger. "There's one other thing we need to factor in. Another coincidence that can't be coincidental."

"And that is?"

"Claude Hoenig has disappeared."

"Disappeared?"

"One moment he was in Virginia and the next his wife reported him missing. We weren't monitoring him and have no idea whether he was killed or grabbed."

"And he was working with a faction of the Oculistica."

"So, there is a possibility that his disappearance might be related to a renewed or new interest in you and yours. You used to work for him and were privy to a lot of his projects. Maybe this raid has something to do with something you know and don't even know you know."

Wyatt started to speak, but she held up her hand.

"I know. But it doesn't have to make sense to us. Someone powerful out there is operating with whatever information they have. Some of those powerful groups have rather irrational leadership."

"Goddamnit. Ellen and Harold have nothing to do with us, or with Claude, for that matter. I kept them in the dark deliberately." Then he raised an eyebrow. "Charlie Turner," he said.

"Who?"

"Claude's old buddy from the CIA. The two of them go way back. They've stayed in touch and Claude made it clear to me, on the quiet, that whenever he felt it served American's interests, he'd feed the information to Turner directly."

"You think they might've bitten the hand that fed them the information."

"If the CIA thought a true patriot had more to give, they'd feel obligated to take it. And a disappearance in broad daylight is their style."

"How do you know he disappeared in daylight?"

"I don't. Maybe I've just seen too many movies. I assumed it."

"Wherever the links are, whoever is doing it, we are down to two realistic possibilities: These people are after either information they believe they can get from Ellen and Harold, or they see them as possible leverage. Or some combination of the two."

"Over me."

She leaned against him. "Take heart. At least they are in public. It's visible, unlike whatever happened to Claude. And I have people keeping eyes on the whole thing. We managed to get video proof of them being put into police cars and taken away. A news helicopter was on the scene until Homeland Security threatened to shoot it down. Now the farm is occupied by troops. I've got lawyers trying to get to Ellen and Harold, to talk to them, to represent them, but they are getting stonewalled by the Patriot Act zombies."

"You shouldn't denigrate zombies that way."

"Sorry. I failed political correctness. The point being, I don't have any good news yet. I don't have any hard news at all yet, but I wanted you to hear what I do know from my lips. I want you to know that I'm pulling out all the stops I can think of."

"Can we hack the jail?"

"To what end? Do you want Ellen and Harold to be on the run? The most we could do is spring them, but they'd still be suspects in whatever they are suspected of."

"But we could."

"Of course, we could. But we are holding off on that for a time. Until we know what they are intending, we don't know how far we need to go to spring them. Hacking the jail could make them look guilty and show that someone with that capability is interested in the case."

"That's Plan B."

"I hope we don't need to do anything but, just in case, I've got Tricia making up their new crypto identities."

Wyatt ran his fingers through his hair. "In case they need to go on the run." The sense of deja vu almost overwhelmed him. "Seems like we've been here before, you and I and Rashmi and Rebecca."

"Yes, we have. And Tricia. I doubt this will be the last time, either."

"I appreciate what you are doing. I appreciate you not sugar coating things." He stared out over the dark water of the Gulf of Thailand. Normally it was a restful sight, but not now. "You know, if this does have something to do with Claude, this raid on Ellen's might've happened no matter what I did. Even if I'd never gotten sidetracked with the whole Tanzanian thing, even if I was still working in a cubicle writing code for Claude…. If he crossed someone nasty, that could explain it. Claude certainly knows more than his fair share of nasty people."

"That's true. But we don't know what happened. We are totally in the dark."

"That sucks."

"It does, and I've assigned Kenny Lu and Rashmi the task of finding us some fucking light bulbs that we can turn on and shine into this darkness. Meantime, we need to sit tight. Don't travel, especially to the US. Don't even look at news from the US. You'll hear the real news as it comes in. From me."

"Waiting ... one of the hardest damn jobs in the world, when people you care about might need help."

"That it is."

"But those two are good people. And Kenny knows security."

"Better than most," she said.

"And Rashmi will be all over it." Wyatt took a long breath. "Given that we are walking and waiting, if not sitting tight and, to change the subject quite deliberately, I wanted to tell you that Miguel is working out well," Wyatt said. "He picks up everything faster than I ever did."

"Wonderful."

"Making me feel obsolete is wonderful now?"

"You'll never be obsolete. Rebecca said he's got a girlfriend."

"The little bugger always has a girl. Rebecca is, I suspect, a tad jealous. She's attracted to him. I think he'll notice that one day."

"Will that be a problem?"

"A problem? No. If something happens between them, it isn't my place to complain. We've never had anything but the most open of relationships. But it is slightly annoying when the guy is my ace student."

"I understand perfectly," Boone said. "I have a jealous friend whom I dearly love and who is supposed to have understood long ago that I'm not a one-woman woman, or even a person who is attracted more to one sex than the other. Since she has known that from the beginning, I find it annoying that any interest I show in someone else makes her pout. Without saying a word, she can cramp my style and that's a no-win situation."

With that, Wyatt nodded, and she saw his thoughts turn inward.

Boone turned her attention to what she'd done, what she hadn't done but should do, and began making a mental to-do list. Yet, all the time, she was aware of the man beside her. Some of that awareness, she thought, would piss Anchara off big time.

They sat in the dark, resting on the sand without speaking for a long time. Wyatt found himself looking at her, studying her face. It amazed him that she could look deadly serious, thoughtful, and sexy all at the same time. "Where are you staying?" he asked finally.

"At Elephant Bay… next door to you."

He laughed. "Of course. Then I can give you a ride back."

"A ride?"

"I rented a motorbike."

She smiled. "And do you know how to ride it?"

"Just enough to keep from falling over or hitting things, but that's okay because no one else on this island knows how either. Just watch them for ten minutes."

She stood and brushed the sand off her shorts. "With a recommendation like that, a ride through a Thailand night sounds impossible to refuse."

As they walked back up toward the road, Wyatt glanced back, again looking out in the direction of the Gulf of Thailand. He could see the dark shapes of the smaller islands that were destinations for day-trippers. He hadn't gotten around to seeing them yet. Now it was unlikely he ever would.

There were so many delightful things he wanted to do, places to see, but his tendency was to settle in, bury himself in work and ignore the outside world. Sometimes, he was too focused for his own good. I'm a lousy hedonist, he thought.

Far out to sea, past the dark shapes of the islands, he saw another blackness amassing, slowly and steadily building. "A storm," he said. "They typically come in from the west." He waved an arm. "It's going to sweep in from the Gulf, heading toward the Cardamom Mountains that separate Thailand from Cambodia."

"There are other storms too," she said.

"This looks to be a big one."

Boone took his hand and squeezed it. "That's the main reason I came," she said. "To point out the oncoming storm. Ellen is a victim of an early squall."

Wyatt gave her a thin, grim smile. It was all too easy to be angry at a messenger, but if Boone hadn't tracked him down, if they hadn't gone on this walk, he'd never have seen the storm coming. Either storm. Things might be falling apart, but Boone, like Rebecca, cared for him. It was in her every action.

That she cared for him as a person made him wonder how she thought of him as a man. Most of their interactions had been due to their common cause. Every time this woman was around, she made him aware of things he was ignoring. Some of them were just pointing out his blind spots, like the fact that leaving his servers at Ellen's made her an obvious target if someone wanted to get to him. Some went deeper and were unstated.

What a crazy sonofabitch I am! That was all he could think. Why did his brain go to a thought like that when Ellen was in trouble? There was a time and place for human reactions, like lust.

But then, how did you apply logic and common sense when everything had become surreal? The reality was that someone, a powerful someone, was after Wyatt Osgood. That was a curious if troubling thought. How odd to be someone that anyone cared enough about to pursue. For years he'd been the denizen of a cubicle. That was his life, and who he was. And yet... and yet, he'd been transformed. He'd gotten involved with a mad scheme and been framed for cybercrime in Tanzania. He'd been arrested and thrown in jail. Rashmi had broken him out with Boone's help — and when that had happened, neither of them had even known Boone at all. She'd emerged from nowhere to rescue them by remote control.

Now, Wyatt Osgood, docile DC fintech, was a wanted criminal. It was amusing and unsettling to think that he'd become a rebel in the eyes of the Powers That Be. Someone powerful considered him, Wyatt Osgood, some kind of serious threat. Must not know my own strength, he decided.

Actions had consequences. Ellen and her sweet husband Harold were paying for his actions, but that was because the enemy was ruthless and brutal. Appeasing them wouldn't do a fucking thing. He was a marked man. He, and Boone and the other Bitpats had done something unforgivable — they had stood up to them and successfully thwarted their agenda. Now they would have their pound of flesh, come what may.

It made him wonder about Boone's story. This wasn't the time to ask, but he wanted to know what horrific thing had put her on this path. What wrong was she hoping to right? What loss had she suffered? The woman could've been the head of a multinational corporation, or maybe president, and here she was, running a ragtag revolution of hackers, and coming to Koh Chang to take his hand and sympathize with his misfortune.

The world was a strange place.

And now, now that he had seen the clouds, he actually felt the cold front that preceded them as they came closer.

"The other big storm is the one to watch out for, Wyatt," Boone said, reading his mind. "There have already been casualties."

"I know," he said. "What can we do?"

"Be ready. Stand by. You all have your new identities and I'm leaving some backups, just in case. If you sense someone is closing in, I want you all to run. Don't give us a heads up. Trust that I will know soon enough. Split up and each of you go somewhere different, somewhere you can blend in or disappear, whatever works."

"Split up?" The idea, thrust out that way, was troubling. Leave Rebecca? Working with her, making love to her had become part of his settled routine. Then he sighed and shook his head. Boone wasn't talking about what they wanted, but about surviving. "Yeah, I get it. They'll be looking for us together."

She nodded. "It will be much easier for individuals to disappear."

The idea that this lovely, almost idyllic existence might have passed its shelf life was troubling. But he trusted Boone; she had brought him to Rebecca, brought him here. Perhaps that was going to end too soon. And life went on. He'd meet other people, have some other experiences.

"Living in the moment never had a more practical application," he said.

Boone smiled at him. "That's always true. Times like this make us see it more clearly."

Her smile, the sound of her soft voice in the night air as they got to his motorcycle were otherworldly. But she was right, and the idea that it could end at any moment made him feel his desire for Rebecca more acutely. It also made him unable to deny the acute desire he felt for Boone.

"If you do need to run, once you are safe, then contact me. Only me, Rashmi, or Anchara."

"I don't think Anchara likes me," he said, laughing.

"Not in the least. She tells me she is sure you have a thing for me." She laughed. "She's jealous of any men I spend time with, as I said."

And if that was true? He bit his tongue. "So, you have a struggle on yet another battleground?"

"That's a personal conflict that is my responsibility. I hope it is a manageable one, but I'm not going to even try to resolve it right now."

"Is there any indication that you are on the bad guys' radar yet?"

The smile she gave him told him that she heard the honest and personal concern in his voice. "I'm not at all sure. So far, Sindi seems to walk among them freely, but I'm not taking anything for granted. I flew from Bangkok using another identity."

"That's a relief."

"Don't let your guard down, Wyatt. They have the guns, the police, the governments, and the assassins. For the moment our identities, our crypto citizen IDs keep us off their radar but don't get cocky. By now they must know there is a resistance movement and they are working on finding us. I'm sure that whatever is going on, it is tied into the smart city project somehow. Using that technology puts their fingers around the people's throats. That raises the status of people like us, any high-tech resistance, from an annoyance to a serious threat." She paused. "That's yet another reason we need to find out what put them onto Ellen and Harold before we take action."

He nodded. It was a painful truth, but nonetheless true. "It's going to be a hell of a long struggle. We've got no easy way to stop them, and for them, rooting us out won't be easy."

Boone took his arm. "Promise that if something happens to me, you'll take over the fight… keep it going."

Wyatt grinned. "Me?"

"You."

He laughed. "I've never been in charge of very much of anything."

"I need you to do it, anyway."

"On-the-job training in leadership?"

"Promise me."

He shrugged. "If you trust me at the helm, then you are damn right I will."

The temperature dropped rapidly. Wyatt started up the motorbike and with Boone on back, her slender arms wrapping around his waist and making him tremble, he started the scooter and accelerated smoothly onto the road, turning onto the road that led back toward the resort.

All too soon they were there. They parked outside. As they scampered into the main building, large drops of rain began to fall. The skies opened as they ducked under the roof and went into the lounge.

"Want to make a run for it or wait and see if it stops?" he asked.

She pointed at two bungalows over by the swimming pool. "My place is nearer than yours, and if you need an incentive to make it worth making a mad dash through this downpour, I brought a bottle of Maker's Mark with me."

"Aren't you the wise traveler?"

"I wasn't ever a scout, but I try to be prepared."

"I'll race you," he said, lunging down the stairs and darting crossing the lawn with Boone right behind him. When they got to the porch, they were laughing. They were, he knew suddenly, living in the moment. He sank down, slumping in a plastic chair as Boone ran her fingers through her wet hair. She smiled at him, then unlocked the door and went inside. He saw her drying her head with a towel, then a moment later she came back onto the porch carrying the bottle of bourbon and two glasses. She left the door open and the porch light off.

She handed him a glass, then filled it. As she sat, filling her own, he raised his. "To Ellen," he said.

"To a successful rescue... once we know what we are rescuing them from," Boone said.

They drank then, and he made himself savor it, rolling it on his tongue while they listened to the heavy roar of the rain and watched as it formed puddles in front of them that grew as they watched.

Boone sighed and leaned her head against Wyatt's shoulder, almost startling him. "I'm tired," she said.

After a moment, he put his hand on her bare thigh and smiled down at her. "Soon this other terrible storm will rage around us as well. I'm fortunate to have good friends to weather it with."

"I like what Charles Bukowski wrote," she said. "'What matters most is how well you walk through the fire.' I think that says it all. And if you walk in a steadfast manner, your friends will all be inspired to do the same."

"We sure are not safe, and that seems odd. And oddly enough, it isn't as disturbing as I think it should be."

She laughed. "Wyatt, I haven't felt safe in years, and I'm pretty sure that feeling safe will be only an illusion for some time to come. But if I don't feel safe at least I do feel content."

Wyatt threw his head back, laughing and pulling Boone's warm body against his.

A clap of thunder exploded, echoing around them, bouncing off the buildings. The rain intensified. Wordlessly, Wyatt stood and held out a hand. Boone finished her drink, sat the glass on the floor and took the hand, getting to her feet. Then Wyatt stepped through the doorway and toward the bed.

For the moment they couldn't do much to fight the war, but for people who were truly alive, life went on.

THE END

ABOUT THE AUTHORS

J. LEE PORTER

J. Lee Porter is a former IT specialist, programmer, and data analyst for banking, security, and government agencies. He left the IT world behind on July 4, 2016, declaring it his personal Independence Day to travel the world full time in search of inspiration for his writing.

ED TEJA

Ed Teja is a writer, poet, musician, and boat bum. He writes about the places he knows and the people who live in the margins of the world. After being friends with tech giants, pirates, fishermen, and a coterie of strange people for many years, he finds the world an amazing place filled with intriguing, if sometimes crazed, characters.

BOOKS WE RECOMMEND

If the ideas in this book intrigue, horrify, or appeal to you, the authors recommend the following books. In no particular order, these and many others informed the themes and possibilities in our stories.

THE SOVEREIGN INDIVIDUAL
  by James Dale Davidson and Lord William Rees-Mogg
THE NEW CONFESSIONS OF AN ECONOMIC HIT MAN
  by John Perkins
THE INTERNET OF MONEY
  by Andreas M. Antonopoulos
THE AGE OF SURVEILLANCE CAPITALISM
  by Shoshana Zuboff
THE FEDERALIST PAPERS
  by Alexander Hamilton, James Madison, and John Jay
HOW TO LIVE — OR — A LIFE OF MONTAIGNE
  by Sarah Bakewell

And of course, everything by Ayn Rand, Aldous Huxley, and George Orwell.

Made in the USA
Middletown, DE
24 August 2022

72144540R10219